CW00855297

Knowing
Strangers

John & Norah,

with best wishes

Jo Howard

Knowing Strangers

Josephine Howard

HAMILTON & Co. (Publishers)
LONDON

Paperback ISBN 1 901668 05 3

Publisher

HAMILTON & Co. (Publishers)
10 Stratton Street
Mayfair
London

Chapter 1

Rachel sat, with Jenny in her arms, listening intently. As long as you could hear the engine, you were all right. Once that cut out, the 'doodle bug' could land anywhere. Jenny whimpered. 'Ssh, sweetheart, don't cry, you're a big girl now.'

She wondered how many other people in Redburn Street were huddled under the stairs, in the dark. Jenny sucked her fingers and clutched Benjy to her. As Rachel hummed quietly, the child slowly relaxed and slept. Rachel was reminded of the time when she was in labour with her. It had been during one of the worst raids of the Blitz. Three years ago now and the bombings had continued unabated. Even now she shuddered when she thought of that fearful night.

As she had lain on the hard, narrow bed, beads of perspiration covered her forehead. She had been absolutely terrified. The next contraction had started, almost before the previous one had finished. She felt the muscles in her back start to clench into hard knots, moving inexorably around her abdomen, pushing down until she felt her back would break.

She gasped for air then realised that the drumming in her ears heralded another wave of bombers. All night it had gone on; wave after wave of enemy aircraft. There would be nothing of London left. Could she be sure that she and her baby would survive the dreadful destruction?

Charles had been due home the following day. If only this baby had waited another twenty-four hours, Rachel thought. Although he would not have been allowed to stay with her, it would have been a comfort to know he was safe and close at hand. The bombing and the labour pains seemed to be going hand in hand, towards death. Rachel could feel the panic rising in her throat. This baby would never be born, she would be smashed to smithereens any second. She lay, limp with exhaustion. The world was tearing itself apart, she could not bear it any more. She thought of Charles, would he ever see his baby? She remembered his last leave so clearly. It was then that she had conceived this child that was trying to force its way out of the safety of the womb, into Bedlam. She saw a nurse walking past and called to her.

'Please help, I'm so frightened!' The nurse was very young and looked as frightened as Rachel felt. As she moved close to the bed, Rachel grabbed hold of her wrist. She held on with an iron grip and refused to let go.

'You are not leaving me until this baby is born. I've been on my own for hours. I can't stand any more.' Her voice rose with each word until she was nearly screaming. The nurse shouted to one of her colleagues. At this point, Sister arrived. She was not used to her mothers taking charge. Just who did Mrs. Warr think she was? There were other mothers in labour and they were not making such a fuss. There was a crash and a tinkle of glass as another window shattered.

'I'll examine you now,' said Sister, giving no indication that anything unusual was happening. 'and we will have no more of this nonsense!'

It is amazing how quickly panic diminishes once authority takes over. Meekly, Rachel let go of the young nurse's wrist and Sister's examination showed that the birth was imminent. Only half an hour later, Rachel produced - with surprisingly little difficulty - a healthy girl.

She lay exhausted her hair wet with sweat, numb with disappointment. The nurse had wrapped the baby and tried to hand her to her mother. Rachel turned her head away, rolled onto her side, and sobbed. The nurse put the baby into her crib ready to take her to the nursery

'You are very lucky to have such a bonny baby. My sister lost her little boy.'

Rachel did not reply.

Sister, brisk as usual, was certainly not going to stand any nonsense from a young woman who had created more than enough fuss already. The husband should visit today, she had heard he was due home on leave. She would have words with him. It was later that afternoon, when Sister Andrews was writing up patient's notes that Charles arrived. Eager to hear that all was well and that he had a son, he knocked tentatively on the office door.

'Come in.'

'I'm Lance Corporal Warr. I believe my wife was admitted last night.'

'Ah yes, she was and I am pleased to tell you that you have a healthy daughter.'

There was a pause. Sister Andrew studied his face. He certainly did not seem overjoyed by the news. Was this the reason Mrs. Warr was refusing to see her baby? Was it the father who had so wanted a son? Sister felt rising exasperation, men were the limit. Thank goodness she had never become entangled with one, give me my beloved cats any day. Still, it was not the first time she had faced this situation and she did not suppose it would be the last. Meanwhile that baby needed its mother. She could not be given just water indefinitely. She needed to be put to the breast within the next twenty-four hours. If Mrs. Warr was going to be any kind if mother, she needed to bond with her baby.

Sister Andrew would have been most surprised if anyone had told her that she used good psychology to sort out many of the problems she had to resolve with reluctant or disappointed patients. To her, it was just plain common sense! Her first responsibility was to the poor little soul in the nursery. She had two perfectly good parents who, now, seemed singularly reluctant to accept their responsibilities. After all baby Warr had not asked to be born. This was the first time that such a thought was given consideration. Sister Andrew might also have been surprised if she could have seen into the future and had known how often Baby Warr was to ponder this very same thought both during her childhood and also as an adult.

'Now then,' said Sister Andrew briskly, 'we have a problem.'

'There's nothing wrong with my wife is there?'

'No, not physically, but I hope you are going to be able to help us.' Charles looked surprised. This formidable looking woman, with her starched uniform, which crackled with every movement, seemed the last person in the world to require his or anyone else's help.

'Your wife was very badly frightened by the raid last night and I think this has affected her ability to accept that your baby is a girl and not the boy, I understand, she had hoped for. You know it is very common for young women to assume that they must give their husbands a son. To carry on the family name, I suppose.'

Charles shifted uncomfortably in his chair as he heard the echo of his own - so recent - thoughts.

'But you look a sensible and intelligent young man. I'm sure you are just relieved that everything has gone well and after all you are both young. Maybe the next baby will be the son she wants. What I would like you to do, is to encourage your wife to accept this baby and tell her how pleased you are.'

There was nothing Charles could say without appearing to be immature and selfish.

'Certainly, Sister, I'll do my best. I know it is not proper visiting time yet but may I see my wife?'

'Yes, under the circumstances, the more time you can spend with her, reassuring her, the better. Get one of my nurses to take you to the nursery. Have a look at your daughter. Tell your wife how lovely she is.'

3

Charles had never seen a very new baby and viewed the whole business with some apprehension. As he looked through the large window at the row of cribs, he wondered how on Earth anyone could tell one screaming infant from another. They all looked like Mussolini! He walked back towards the ward and pondered on the letter his mother had sent him, some months ago now. Did his mother really believe that Rachel had been unfaithful to him, the implication had been there. He did not know. He did not want to ask. Never ask questions you might not like the answer to - who had told him that? Perhaps the best thing was to have a word with his dad, man to man. That reminded him, he must call round to see them tonight, tell them the news. He supposed he had better tell his older sister, Caroline, too. She had always resented him for being the favourite child and taking up so much of their parents' time. Charles did wonder if his sister had married Jack just to get away from home. As far as he, Charles, could see, Jack had little to recommend him. A big heavily built man, he was slow moving both physically and mentally. Still family was family and at least he and Rachel had produced a child which was more than Jack and Caroline had managed.

When Charles walked into the ward, Rachel was asleep. He looked at her and realised how much she had changed. He had married a girl but this was quite definitely a woman. The neat perm had gone and her dark, fine hair was fanned around her face. The features of that face were fine and delicate. He hoped their daughter would be as good-looking as her mother. Rachel stirred and Charles put his arms around her and held her tight.

'Darling, I'm so pleased, I've seen the baby. She is beautiful, just what I wanted. You are a clever girl.'

Rachel looked at him quizzically; was he telling the truth? He had never stated a definite preference but she had always assumed that he would want a son. Perhaps everything would be all right after all.

It was feeding time and babies were being brought into the ward; most of them were crying. It was not usual for fathers to be allowed in the ward at this time since so many mothers breast- fed. Baby Warr was handed to her mother and screens were put round them. Charles perched himself on the edge of the bed; not sure what he was expected to do. Sister came in brisk and business like.

'Now come along, Mother, this little girl needs feeding.' She undid the front of Rachel's nightdress and quickly latched the baby on to her mother's breast. The sensation for Rachel was indescribable. She flinched with the first few sucks the baby took and then was

4

overwhelmed by a desire to give of herself to this tiny infant. Her whole body seemed to glow and she smiled with a huge contentment and satisfaction.

For Charles the experience was considerably less satisfactory. He could only be an observer. He had no control over the ultimate closeness between mother and child. There was something terribly animal about the whole performance. Had his mother breast-fed him? He did not know and would not ask. Rachel's engorged breast looked ugly, cow-like. He did not like it. Yet at the same time he felt a sexual response that was most alarming. At that moment, Rachel glanced up from her baby and saw an expression on Charles' face that she did not understand and which made her feel both uneasy and embarrassed.

'You know we must think of a name for the baby. Mother thought Christine would be nice, if it was a girl.'

Oh, she did, did she, thought Rachel. I wonder when Charles discussed names with her. Obviously when I wasn't around.

'Well, I like Helen. My best friend at school was called Helen.' This was not strictly true but of one thing, Rachel was certain. The child would most definitely not be called Christine.

Charles was pleased they had now reached the point when she was considering names. That suggested that the baby had been accepted. There was no point in causing friction by insisting on Christine, although he knew it would have delighted his mother. There would just have to be a compromise name.

'We don't have to decide today. Why don't you make a list of names you like and I'll make a list that I like and hopefully there will be a name or two that are on both lists.'

Therefore, it wasn't going to be Helen. He did not say so but his suggestion of lists said it all. She finished feeding the baby and suddenly felt very, very tired. She handed the baby to Charles and lay back on her pillows. He looked uneasy, maybe even a little frightened of this tiny scrap. Did he fear that he would drop her or that she would break? Maybe, for the first time in their relationship, Rachel felt that she had the upper hand. There was something she could do better than Charles. She smiled and closed her eyes. Perhaps being a mother was going to be a most satisfying experience.

Charles was not able to bring Rachel home from hospital as his leave had only been for four days. Mrs. Cardew came, in her car, to fetch daughter and grandchild. She found very small children and babies both trying and noisy. Although she had had three of her own, her social position had enabled her to employ nursemaids and nannies.

So her actual experience of bringing up children was very slight indeed. She scrutinised her daughter and was pleased to see that motherhood seemed to suit her. Rachel had always been an excessively difficult child and adolescent. Her antipathy towards Edgar, her stepfather, had created never ending emotional strife in the home. Whilst Charles Warr would not have been Mrs. Cardew's choice of a son-in-law, at least life had been considerably more pleasant since Rachel had married.

She glanced at the baby, peacefully asleep in her mother's arms. They had decided to call her Jennifer. It could have been worse, she thought. The three generations of women arrived at the Hendon home. It did not take long to get the baby settled and Mrs. Cardew soon left feeling she had done her duty.

She needed to get back home. It was only a few days to Edgar's meeting with his publishers. She had not yet finished the proof reading of his manuscript. She must not let him down. For a cool intellectual, Mrs. Cardew was an intensely passionate woman. She adored her husband, although she was somewhat in awe of him. Recently he had seemed rather distant and distinctly irritable. She had looked forward to being on her own with him. The problems caused by Rachel had been resolved by her marriage. Eleanor was doing important war work and Malcolm was in the Navy. Now was the time for Edgar and her to enjoy being together. Somehow, it was not how she had expected and hoped. If only they had had a child of their own. This had for so many years been an unspoken regret that came between them. She had her family, which suggested that, whatever the reason for them not producing a child, it was not likely to be her fault. Edgar was a proud man. He must have found his apparent shortcomings hard to live with. For many years, Mrs. Cardew had acted as his unpaid secretary, researcher, confidante, proof-reader, and adoring acolyte. Edgar Cardew did appreciate the usefulness of his wife's chosen role. However, Mary would have been dismayed to learn that being put on a pedestal by her, as he so unquestioningly was, could, and did cause him considerable irritation.

Rachel had quickly got into a routine with Jenny; she was a generally well behaved baby who rarely got her mother up in the night. She was not, however, facially like her mother as Charles had hoped. Other people had pretty babies, Rachel thought; Jenny most definitely was not pretty. Her ears stuck out and she had no hair at all for her first year. Rachel spent her days cleaning, washing and making broths and purees for her growing infant. She had been fascinated to see the

6

development of a personality with likes and dislikes. As her hair finally started to grow and her features became more defined, Rachel decided that perhaps her daughter was not the ugliest child in the world after all. Once Jenny was walking, Rachel found life, during the day even more hectic. She certainly had little time to relax. The child was highly inquisitive and into everything. Although Rachel loved Jenny, there were times, particularly in the evening when she longed for a conversation with another adult. She desperately wanted reassurance; to know that Charles and her brother, Malcolm, were safe. It's because I'm on my own so much that I feel so frightened. Mother wouldn't understand, she never shows her feelings. It's no good going to see Albert and Gladys, Albert would make her welcome, Gladys wouldn't. She got Charles' last letter out of the sideboard drawer. She had read it and reread it until the paper threatened to disintegrate. He had sounded so confident then. The 8th army and the rest of the Allied forces outnumbered the Germans 2:1. It had been later, when he came home, that she and his parents had realised what it had really been like.

Charles had arrived too late, by a month, for Jenny's first birthday. He had looked exhausted and despondent. Only relief that his immediate family had escaped the bombing seemed to lift the black cloud from him. On his first evening home, they had gone to see his parents. Gladys had clucked around him like a broody hen.

'Are you eating properly, son? You've lost weight.' Charles caught his father's eye, Albert winked. Having been in the trenches during the First World War and been gassed, he had no illusions.

'Mother, how on Earth can I eat properly? I eat what I can get! We live on Bully beef, tinned cheese, milk, and sometimes oranges. If you can get hold of some tea, you're lucky.' Gladys looked at her only surviving son in disbelief.

'I didn't see you through rheumatic fever and all the rest of it to see you die of malnutrition!'
'Well, if I do, so will plenty of others!' She tutted and disappeared into the kitchen.

'She doesn't understand son. You will always be her baby. Just like Jenny will always be your baby, Rachel.' He smiled. What a lovely man you are, she thought, you always include me in the conversation.

'How are things really going?'

Charles looked at his father, uncertain whether he should say too much. It could drive his mother to distraction.

'It's their bloody guns, Dad, we don't stand a chance. They go through our tanks like a knife through butter.'

Albert nodded, giving silent encouragement for Charles to continue. Rachel listened, wide eyed with horror as Charles continued with his account.

'We're tired all the time. Heaving the equipment about, digging always-bloody digging. Every time we move whether its backwards or forwards, its another trench.'

Jenny stirred in Rachel's arms. Thank God, you are too young to know what an awful world we live in. Gladys came in, from the kitchen, Charles stopped.

'Now come along, food's ready. This will build you up, son. I've been saving my coupons for weeks. Got a nice bit of stewing beef. Thought you'd really enjoy that.'

Charles put his arm around Gladys' shoulder, bent down to kiss her.

'Be careful, Mum. You'll spoil me.'

Rachel had been nursing Jenny; then of course, she'd been little more than a baby. Looking down now, what had changed? Jenny was older but the war went on. The All Clear sounded and Rachel carefully carried a still sleeping Jenny upstairs to bed

Gladys and Albert adored Jenny so agreed to look after her when Malcolm wanted to take Rachel out. Home on leave, now that the worst of the Battle of the Atlantic was over, he had a desperate air about him. It reminded Rachel of the young Battle of Britain pilots she had met. So often, only once of twice, before news came through that they had been shot down. Everywhere around us is death, she thought. Thank God, my family has not been touched by it yet.

Malcolm wanted to take Rachel out with him because the idea of getting involved with a girl when the future was so uncertain was more than he could bear. She had tried to explain to Gladys and Albert but only Albert seemed to understand. 'Bring that brother of yours over, my girl. He can tell us how things are going.' Gladys had pursed her lips at this suggestion.

'I'll bring some food with me, Mum. I don't want you to use up all your coupons.' Gladys had nodded her acknowledgement of the offer but made no comment.

Charles sat in the blistering heat. Sweat oozed from every pore. It drained the life out of you. He brushed the flies away. It was an unconscious movement, made a thousand times a day. Hordes of them, came from nowhere, trying to land on your face, in your eyes, ears nostrils. There were times when he thought they would drive him mad, not the guns. He sat on an empty ammunition box, trying to shave with a not very sharp razor. He only had a bit of mirror, perched precariously on another box. His skin was the colour of mahogany, with deep lines around the eyes, from constantly screwing them up in the glare of the desert light.

'How long 'til we can have a drink, Sarge?'

Charles looked at the young conscript.

'Five minutes less than the last time you asked! What did you do with your shaving water?'

'Threw it away.'

Well, next time, bloody drink it!' He swore silently as he nicked his chin. Christ Almighty! That will really give the flies something to go at! He thought again about the letter his mother had sent him. What had she meant, Rachel was always out, out where?

It was during Malcolm's leave at the end of October '42, that the massive victory at El Alamein was announced. Now they really had something to celebrate. He took Rachel and a group of his naval mates to a jazz club in the West End. It was there that Rachel met Alec. He was a drummer in a jazz band although he worked for an electrical company, during the day. Since he was in a protected industry, there had been no question of his joining the forces.

When he first saw Rachel, he was more moved than he cared to admit. He found her utterly captivating, an effect greatly heightened by her apparent unconsciousness of the effect she was having on the men in the club in general and on him in particular. They talked during a break in the music. He was pleased that it was her brother she was with. He was not surprised that she was married and greatly heartened to hear that her husband was in North Africa. This was not your run of the mill girl. Rachel was most definitely someone special. She and her brother came to the club several times, in the company of a group of other naval men and their girls. Alec decided he was going to get to know her better. He made a point of sitting next to her on the third visit.

'Do you like jazz?' he asked. It seemed such a feeble question. After all, if she did not, she would not be there. He was both infuriated and intrigued that she could make him feel like a gauche youth on his first date.

Rachel smiled, 'I don't know much about it, I have mostly listened to classic music.'

'Well we can soon remedy that, would you be able to come here next Thursday? We are having a special jam session.'

'That would be very difficult, you see my brother brought me here but he goes back to sea tomorrow. This is our last night out.'

'That doesn't matter, I'll pick you up if you like, bring a girl-friend if you want.'

'It isn't as easy as that, you see I have a little girl. My in-laws are looking after her. Can you imagine what they would say if you turned up on the doorstep? Particularly my mother-in-law who can't stand me anyway. I'm sure she wrote to my husband suggesting that I was not behaving myself. What a confounded cheek! I've never been unfaithful to her precious son and I don't intend to be.' There was no harm in making things absolutely clear. Then, thought Rachel, she could go to the jazz club, with Alec, with a clear conscience. In fact it was several weeks before they saw each other. Jenny went down with a bad attack of whooping cough. This meant that Rachel spent every minute, day and night, nursing the child. During this time Rachel had plenty of opportunity to think about Alec. She knew he found her attractive. After so long alone, it was a delicious feeling. Charles seemed to suck confidence out of her; Alec was a completely different kettle of fish. He had made her feel safe and special. I suppose I am just feeling lonely, she thought, I do love Charles. He is everything to me. Once the war is over, we will start again.

When she took, the now recovered, Jenny, to visit her grandparents, she still had not decided whether or not she would go to the jazz club. She had largely lost touch with the girls in the factory. So she knew that if she did go, she would go alone. No harm will come of it, she thought. I just want an evening out. I'm still a young woman, if I did not have Jenny, life would be so much easier. If Charles had not been so mean about buying new Durex, I would not have become pregnant in the first place. Children need both their parents. It wasn't fair of him to run the risk that I would have to bring up a baby on my own. Rachel knew that she loved Jenny but the experience of a little freedom, for the first time in her life, told her that she really was not ready to be a wife and mother. Once Charles was home for good, there would be no opportunity for going to jazz clubs or anywhere else much.

All he was interested in was chess and politics. So I must take the chance while I can, then I will be better able to settle down and be the good little wife. By the time she reached her in-laws, she was quite sure that she would be doing Charles a disservice if she did not make the most of her comparative freedom while she could.

Alec had given up expecting to see Rachel again. He did not of course know of Jenny's illness. So it was quite a surprise when she walked into the club. She was alone and obviously very nervous. The band was in the middle of a set so he could not go over to her to speak or buy her a drink. However, he caught her eye and gave her what he hoped was a reassuring grin. He just hoped no other man would approach her and frighten her away. As soon as he could, he strolled over to the table. He wished to appear casual and relaxed, this was a woman who would need careful handling. She had made her position abundantly clear on their last meeting. Although Alec did not believe she or any other woman, for that matter, was seduction-proof, he would have to take his time.

'It's good to see you, Rachel. How are you?'

'Oh, I'm fine, my little girl's been ill, she had whooping cough, but she's much better now.'

'What will you drink?'

'Umm, I don't know. I don't usually drink alcohol, could I have some lemonade?'

This would do his reputation no good, Alec thought, going to the bar to ask for lemonade! He offered her a cigarette.

'I don't smoke, thanks.'

He grinned at her. 'You must have some vices.' She smiled back. Of course, she knew what he was implying but she did not feel threatened. This was nice, she felt special, she felt safe. He was not criticising her. She relaxed, she was glad she had come.

He took her home at the end of the evening. Jenny was staying overnight with her grandparents so Rachel went back to Hendon. She and Alec walked arm in arm down the darkened streets. The night was warm with a cloudless sky and the stars were very clear and bright. They got to Rachel's house; it had been a delightful evening. I don't want anything to spoil this, she thought. Half of her hoped that Alec would kiss her on the cheek and go; the other half desperately wanted to be kissed passionately and taken to bed. Her mind was in a turmoil, would she be able to live with her conscience if she were disloyal to Charles? Would he ever know? How did she know what he was getting up to, so far away. He might never come back. They stopped at her front door.

'I hope you've enjoyed yourself, I have.'

'Oh, yes and thanks for seeing me home. You will have a long walk back.'

'Don't worry, its a nice night.' He smiled and waved as he walked away. Be patient my lad. Of one thing he was certain, he would be seeing Rachel again, often.

Rachel walked, thoughtfully, down the stairs. It had been a lovely evening; she remembered it so clearly. The first of many lovely evenings. She hadn't done anything wrong. Just enjoyed the company of a kind man. Albert had understood her need to go out. Although she had been suitably vague about where she went and with whom. She had assumed that he had persuaded Gladys to let Jenny stay. It didn't stop her always referring to Rachel's outings as 'gallivanting'. Rachel didn't care, you're only young once. I've been through enough, I'm entitled to a little fun.

Arranging the weekend away was just as difficult as Rachel had anticipated. Her mother-in-law's disapproval had now reached a point where the two women barely spoke. It was almost impossible to leave Jenny with the Warrs. Even Albert could not make Gladys relent. Jenny was not a baby any more, in fact she was a very active, talkative and demanding three-year-old. When Alec told Rachel about his friends in the country, the thought of going away for a few days was too good to be true. I've not had a day away since before Charles and I were married. How long ago that seemed now, How we have all changed.

The news swung from good to bad all the time. After the success at El Alamein, Charles had moved on. Rachel thought he was somewhere in Algiers - if he was still alive. The Blitz had finished not long after Jenny had been born. Now it was the 'Doodle bugs' that created havoc. When would it end? Just to get away for a weekend, would give her the strength to carry on.

'I'll have to bring Jenny with me.' Somehow that eased Rachel's conscience. She was taking her little girl for some fresh country air. Who could object to that?

'I don't expect John and Freda will mind, they have plenty of room.' Alec had not expected this. He had met Jenny once and not been particularly impressed. Still, he was not inclined to be impressed by children anyway. He only hoped that his friends would be understanding. Rachel's husband was bound to come home on leave soon; time was not on Alec's side. He realised this was no longer just a quick affair - in fact it was not an affair at all! Increasingly Alec found his emotions entangled with this intriguing woman. It was painful, pleasurable, as well as a totally new experience. He hoped that if he could get her down to his friends in Suffolk, he would be able to purge her from his heart. Once you had screwed a woman, even the most fascinating one, she lost that fascination and became just another conquest.

Alec borrowed a friend's car and he and Rachel, plus a sleeping Jenny, set off for Bury St. Edmonds late on Friday afternoon. Here I am, he thought, to the casual observer, a respectably married family man. Yet here is a woman I have never slept with and a child who is not mine. He had not been able to contact John and Freda to warn them about Jenny. Knowing what a freewheeling relationship they had, he expected to be teased about his newly acquired 'respectability'. In fact their reception was pleasant and welcoming. John and Freda had no children of their own and made a great fuss of Jenny who clearly enjoyed being the centre of attention.

Once the child was asleep, on a camp bed in the small spare room, Freda and Rachel went to prepare the evening meal. John eyed Alec speculatively.

'She looks a bit of alright! Where's the husband?'

'Serving King and Country somewhere in North Africa. Probably not for much longer.'

'Good in bed is she?'

'I don't know.' Alec could feel his colour rising, not so much with embarrassment as anger. He did not want Rachel talked about like this. Whatever his original intentions, she was not just a quick screw. She was special, he feared he was falling in love with her. This was a situation he had always shied away from in the past. Commitment equals heartache. Now here he was involved with a married woman. He must be going nuts.John watched him.

'You don't know! How long have you been seeing her? My God lad, you're losing your grip.'

Alec did not answer, he could not. He gazed into the fire but there was no satisfactory answer. All he knew was that he wanted to love Rachel, protect her and live with her always. He could not say why she was different or why she had such an effect on him. He was even prepared to take on Jenny, not because he liked her particularly but because she was part of Rachel. Of course all this was nonsense. Charles would come back and that would be that.

After the meal Freda said, 'John and I will wash up, you two can go for a stroll before it gets dark. You said you wanted some country air, now's your chance.'   Rachel checked that Jenny was still asleep then she and Alec left.

'We won't be long,' said Rachel who suddenly felt very anxious about the whole situation. Freda had asked her in the kitchen if it was O.K. for her and Alec to share the put-u-up settee in the living room. This was it, Rachel thought. I don't want it to be my decision, I don't want anyone to know. It should just happen. What would Jenny say when she woke up in the morning? What if she told her father that she had seen her Mummy in bed with another man? What if? What if? Her brain

was reeling. Never mind if Jenny told her father, what if she told her grandparents! She must put a stop to this at once. It was all a dreadful mistake.

They walked down the country lane, there was no-one about, Alec put his arm around Rachel's shoulders. He could feel her stiffen. Something had happened to frighten her. He stopped and put his arms tightly around her. She made a token gesture of trying to pull away. Then stood with tears streaming down her face.

'What on Earth's the matter? I wanted you to enjoy yourself this weekend. Have I upset you?'

She clung to him and sobbed. It was several minutes before she was able to speak.

'I'm frightened.'

'What of, me?'

'No, of what is going to happen here and when we get back to London.'

'O.K., what is the worse thing that could happen?'

'Charles will find out that I have been away with you. He would never believe that I have not been unfaithful.'

'But how would he find out?'

'Jenny is not a baby, she is bound to tell her grandparents about going away and my mother-in-law will delight in passing on the information.'

'So what can Jenny say? Mummy has a kind friend who took Mummy and me to stay in the country for a few days. What could be nicer?'

'Yes, but how does she explain that Mummy's kind friend shared Mummy's bed!'

So that was it, 'Who said we would be sharing a bed?'

'Freda, she said we would be on the settee in the living room.'

Dear Freda, always kindhearted she probably thought she was doing us a favour. 'Don't you dare give it another thought, my girl. If necessary I will sleep on the floor in the outhouse! Now come on you are going to enjoy yourself.'

They walked down the lane with their arms around each other. Alec started to whistle. They saw a pub and decided to call in.

'It's time you were introduced to demon drink, I can't be the only one with vices.'

After two glasses of cider, Rachel felt very strange indeed. Her head was swimming and everything seemed to be moving.

'I think it's time to get you home' Alec lifted her to her feet and steadied her. We will have to sort out the sleeping arrangements before John and Freda go to bed, he thought. They left the pub and walked down, the now dark, lanes. Rachel was giggling and tugging at Alec asking to be kissed. If I don't make the most of this situation, Alec thought, John will be right. In the light from the moon, they could see the outline of a partially demolished hayrick.

'Come on,' said Rachel. 'Let's climb into that rick. I used to play with my sister and brother on my uncle's farm in Shropshire when we were children.' She let go of his arm and started to pull herself up onto the top of the rick, where she collapsed in a giggling heap. This was all he could hope for. He lay beside her.

The fragrant smell of the hay mixed with the smell of her hair. The scent of apples on her breath was unbearably sweet. He kissed her and felt his body melt with overwhelming desire. She clung to him trembling.

'I love you, Rachel.' She did not answer. He gently undid the buttons of her dress and slipped his hand inside to cup her breast. She gasped and then wept. He could not stop, he must have her now or be haunted by her for ever. He kissed her again and slipped her dress down to reveal the creamy white skin of her shoulders. They felt like silk. He stroked and kissed her breasts. She moaned but made no attempt to stop him. Neither did she make any attempt to encourage him. He took her hand and placed it on his erect penis still encased in trousers and underpants.

'Undo my trousers, sweetheart, please, I want you so much.'

Rachel knew this was the point of no return. A woman can hardly claim rape if she helps with unclothing the offending organ. She did not care. The moonlight was magical, it bathed them with a silver glow. All of this had nothing to do with Charles, his mother, Jenny, London or anything else. Mankind was destroying itself. She would bring new life into the world. A son, by a man who had made her feel like a real woman - not a silly little girl.

She undid the buttons, taking her time. She wanted to savour every second of this night. She lay back, breathless and looked into Alec's eyes. He carefully lay on top of her and with infinite gentleness entered her body. This was indescribable. His body was on fire, he could scarcely breathe. Rachel started to move in rhythm with him. She gave little cries; she clung to him. The moon shone on her face, her lips were parted. He kissed her again and again. She sobbed and clung still tighter, pulling him further and further inside her. At last he felt the whole world explode. He lifted his head to the sky and cried out, like a wolf baying at the moon. Rachel's scream blended with his deeper notes like the mating cries heard in primordial forests before time began. She was his, at last.

Charles' letter, announcing his forthcoming leave arrived a month later. It was the same day that Rachel realised that she must be pregnant.

Chapter 2

Rachel did not know what to do. Her mood swung wildly from exaltation at her creation of a new life, to despair at her disloyalty to Charles. Her certain knowledge, that Charles would never forgive her, only added to her despair. She knew of many women who had been unfaithful to their husbands, during long separations. For most, there was no evidence of their extra-marital activity. For those who did have illegitimate children, some were adopted but some were accepted as their own, by husbands coming back from the fighting. Perhaps such men felt as she did, that in a world of destruction, they must rejoice in new life and cherish it.

Such speculation did nothing to help Rachel who knew, with absolute conviction, how Charles would see her betrayal, for which there could be no forgiveness. Wouldn't mother-in-law gloat; all her worse predictions made flesh! Rachel felt very much alone. Since the weekend with John and Freda, she had seen nothing of Alec. She had no telephone, she had no-one to leave Jenny with. She had told him he must not call at the house. The nosy neighbour, next-door, would be bound to notice a visitor. Then the whole street would know. She had written to him, care of the club, to tell him she was expecting his child. She had not had a reply and had no idea whether the letter had actually reached him.

In desperation, she decided to visit her mother. It was no good just arriving because Mary Cardew had a very busy life. When she was not helping Edgar with his manuscript, she was either at her club, playing bridge, or visiting friends. Rachel wrote a short note suggesting she visit the house in Wimbledon, one day the following week. Charles would be home the week after that. She must decide what she was going to do.

Mary Cardew opened the letter, whilst having breakfast with Edgar. It was usually a civilised start to the day. Little was said. They both spent the time reading their papers and opening mail. Mary had always felt that the silence was companionable, reinforcing the solid foundation of their relationship. It was a luxury, only indulged in, since her children had left home. Recently, however there had been a brittle note to their existence. Silence suggested distance rather than companionship. It made Mary feel uneasy and now this, a letter from Rachel.

Edgar had always disliked Rachel; he could not cope with her emotional outbursts and her general waywardness. She may have appeared quiet and shy to the outside world, but her resentment towards him created an atmosphere that he found wholly unacceptable. He was not sufficiently interested in Mary's children to speculate on how his replacement of their father must have seemed to them, all those years ago. Eleanor and Malcolm had accepted him readily enough but they had their mother's love and approval in abundance. Rachel did not.

Mary read the note, folded it carefully and put it in her dressing-gown pocket. Of course she would have to see the girl, it was her duty. However, she would not tell Edgar. It was easy enough for a visit to be arranged during the day; Edgar was never at home now. Better still, she would drive over to Hendon. That would ensure that Edgar did not find out; there was no need to upset him.

It was several weeks before Alec received Rachel's letter and then only by chance. The bar man had tucked it away on a shelf, meaning to pass it on but forgot all about it. Far from destroying Alec's feeling for Rachel, the weekend in Suffolk, had merely confirmed his worse fears. He loved her. It was only because he asked the barman if, by any chance, a woman had been looking for him, that the letter was remembered. Alec read it and found he was trembling so much he had to sit down.

'Bad news?'

'Yes and no, it would have helped if you had passed it on straight away.' Poor kid she must think he had run out on her. He looked at the date, three weeks ago. She must be going frantic.

'Sorry mate, I just forgot, you know how it is.' Yes, thought Alec, but do you know how it is? What on earth was going to happen? He knew what he wanted but what did Rachel want? Well, he was going to have to go to see her. He understood her fears about his being seen. There must be a way round it. He would write her a note and push it through the letter-box after the session at the club, tonight. He would call the next morning - he could wangle an hour or two off work. If he was wearing his office suit and carrying a brief case, any nosey neighbour would probably assume he was on official business.

Rachel heard the letter-box rattle. She glanced at the clock, by her bed, ten to twelve. Probably some drunken lout, she thought and soon fell asleep. Jenny woke her in the morning.

'The postman's been, Mummy'

It was much too early for the postman. Anyway, the 'letter' was a note, not even in an envelope. She did not recognise the writing.

'Who's it from, Mummy? Is it from Daddy?'

'No sweetheart, it's just a friend who wants to pop round. Do you remember Alec, he was the kind man who took us to see John and Freda.'

Jenny thought for a moment. Alec had been all right, as grown-ups went but she would much rather have seen Grandad and Grandma Warr. She missed them.

'When can we see Grandma and Grandpa? Can we go soon?'

'Yes, we will go soon.' It had better be soon, thought Rachel, before it becomes obvious that I am pregnant. Gladys Warr had eyes like a hawk.

'Guess what, your other Grandmother it coming to see us today. Won't that be nice.' Jenny was not too sure. She had not seen much of Grandmother Cardew and what she had seen had been distinctly frightening. Grandma Warr was tiny and fussed around her, cooking favourite meals and giving her things to play with. Grandmother Cardew, on the other hand, was very tall and thin; she had a deep gruff voice and she used lots of long words. All in all, it was not going to be at all nice to see Grandmother Cardew. Jenny screwed up her face and started to cry. It was at that moment that Rachel realised what Alec had put in his note. He was calling here today! Dear God, Alec was coming, her Mother was coming. Jenny's cries got louder. Suddenly Rachel leapt out of bed and ran to the bathroom. She was violently sick. She knelt beside the toilet as the waves of nausea swept over her. Tears streamed down her face. Was this just morning sickness, panic or a combination of the two?

Jenny had followed her mother into the bathroom. She stood quietly, sucking her fingers. After a moment she said,

'I'm sorry, Mummy. I didn't mean to make you sick. I'll be a good girl.' The child came and patted Rachel's back. Rachel turned and clutched the child to her. She stroked the fine, dark hair, just like her own.

'Oh, sweetheart, I'm so sorry.' Jenny was puzzled, what was Mummy sorry for? She felt a twinge of fear in the pit of her stomach but did not know why.

Alec felt ridiculously nervous as he approached Rachel's house. He tried to look businesslike, an insurance man, perhaps, making a routine call. He knocked and waited. He could hear running feet, the child's, he thought. Then a heavier firmer tread. The door opened. Rachel looked tense and white-faced.

'Hello, Alec, you had better come in.'

'My Grandmother Cardew is coming to see us today. I don't think I like her very much.' Jenny ran ahead of them, up the hallway. Alec gave Rachel a quizzical look. 'So I'm to meet your Mother, am I?'

'Good God no. I'm sorry it's worked out like this. I could not put her off. I must see her before Charles gets back.'

'What are you going to do?'

'I don't know. I just don't know.' Alec longed to put his arms around her, comfort her. Jenny came running back from the kitchen.

'What are you talking about? Come and see my new dolly, Alec. She's got lots of clothes my Grandma Warr knitted for her. My Grandma Warr's ever so nice. She's nicer than Grandmother Cardew.'

'Sssh, you mustn't say that. It isn't kind.'

'When do you expect your mother?'

Rachel glanced at her watch. She said she would be here in time for lunch, so I suppose it could be any time now.'

It was gone eleven, there seemed little point in trying to continue any kind of conversation with the child around. He could also see no point in running into the dreaded Mrs. Cardew at this point in the proceedings.

'Look I will go now but I have got to speak to you. Do you understand? We must meet and discuss properly what you want to do. Here is my address and telephone number. Can you get to a 'phone?'

'Well, there is a box down the road, I would have to pop out when Jenny is asleep. But you are at the club in the evenings aren't you.'

'Not on Tuesdays and Sundays.'

'I'll 'phone you next Sunday, I should know by then exactly when Charles is coming back.'

Alec turned to leave. When he opened the door, he found a tall imposing looking woman standing on the doorstep. He knew instinctively that this must be Mary Cardew.

'Excuse me,' he mumbled, 'I was just leaving.'

'Hello Grandmother,' Jenny said, suddenly on her best behaviour. She had upset Mummy once this morning, so she had better be a good girl now.

'This is Alec, he took me and Mummy to the country.'

'Mummy and me.' Mary Cardew corrected her only grandchild automatically. Jenny blushed, wrong as usual, Grandmother always made her feel uncomfortable. She would not say anything else.

'Yes, Mother. Alec knows Malcolm and because I have felt so tired and of course, Jenny has been so ill with whooping cough. It seemed a good idea to have a break. Alec was very kind.' She knew she was gabbling, she also knew that what she was saying did not, somehow, sound very convincing.

Mary Cardew said nothing. She eyed Alec up and down. He looked respectable enough but she did not think he was her social equal. There was an assurance about him that unnerved her slightly. People were either her equals - therefore of considerable social standing or they were her inferiors - servants, tradespeople and did as they were told. She suspected that it would not be easy to tell Alec what to do. Also how was he involved with her daughter?

'I must go,' Said Alec, 'don't forget, you know how to get in touch with me.'

Rachel smiled even though her face felt stiff with anxiety.

She closed the front door behind Alec and faced her mother.

'Come through to the kitchen. Would you like tea or coffee? I've made some soup for lunch and brought some bread from the local bakers. It's usually very good. We like it, don't we Jenny?' She was gabbling again. Jenny stood mute. Her fingers were in her mouth.

'If you do not stop that child from sucking her fingers, her teeth will stick out.'

'I do try, Mother, but it's difficult, she hasn't been well and she's missing Charles.'

'Really.' Mary Cardew doubted that. 'Surely she hardly knows him.' From her own, admittedly limited, observations it seemed unlikely that Charles was any more at home with small children than she was.

'When is he home again?' Clearly something was going on. Although Mary did not know what, the chances were that if Rachel were involved, it would be messy. Who was this Alec? She thought of her own life, so ordered and secure now. She had been foolish to worry about Edgar. Clearly he was immersed in his work, that must be why he had been so distracted recently. She would ask Cook to prepare something special for dinner this evening. She had so much to be thankful for.

'It will be some time next week Mother. I don't know exactly when.' Rachel was not sure her mother had heard. She thought of all the times in her childhood when her mother had not seemed to hear her. Had she ever heard? All of my life, I have been a disappointment, first my mother, then my step-father, then Charles, will Jenny be the next? I just want someone to love me for myself.

She prepared and served the lunch but felt so anxious that she hardly ate anything.

'What on Earth is the matter with you? Why are you not eating?'

Rachel could feel a lump in her throat, so large that she could not swallow. Tears filled her eyes; she blinked hard.

'For goodness sake, not in front of the child! Does she have a rest after lunch?' Although Mary had three children of her own, Nanny had always taken control of the daily routine in the nursery. Jenny sensing her mother's distress, put her spoon down. 'I've had enough,' she said firmly.

'Nonsense !' said her Grandmother, 'Eat up or you will never be a big strong girl.' Soup was spooned into her mouth and there seemed little chance of any protest being heeded. Immediately afterwards, she was taken upstairs put firmly into bed and told to stay there to have a sleep. She did not argue.

'Now then, what is the matter?' Mary was fairly sure she knew but just hoped she was wrong.

'I'm expecting a baby.' Mary sighed, she was not wrong.

'I suppose that young man, what's his name, is the father.' Rachel nodded.

'Does Charles know?'

'Not yet.'

'Will you tell him, when he comes home?'

'I don't know.'

'Well you can't keep it a secret for long.' What on Earth was the girl thinking of? What would she tell Edgar? What would Charles do? Mary could feel exasperation rising in her. This really was the limit. She had done everything she could to stop Rachel marrying Charles in the first place and now she had leapt into bed with the first man who caught her eye. And what of the poor child upstairs?

'I never wanted this to happen but Charles is so difficult. He is always criticising me and finding fault. I've done my best, honestly I have. I do love him really.'

'So how will you explain this baby, that is hardly evidence of undying devotion. How do you think I have managed with your step-father? He is not the easiest of men. Marriages have to be worked at you know.'

'So why did my father kill himself?'

Mary was not often discomforted but the circumstances of her first husband's death had been wrapped up cosily in vague hints of mental instability. Such a tragedy, you know, a talented man. She had certainly never discussed the dreadful truth of his suicide with his children or, for that matter, with anyone else. This was dangerous ground.

'That is hardly relevant to the present situation, which you have got yourself into. What we need to decide is do you want to stay married to Charles? Will you have the baby adopted? Might Charles accept the baby as his own?' She could not voice the obvious other choice; would she leave Charles and set up with this Alec - assuming of course that he would stick by her.

Rachel held her head in her hands. All these questions, how could she be expected to make a decision when her head ached so?

'I'm not going to do anything yet. I will wait until Charles comes home He has been away so much, in some ways, I feel I hardly know him.'

Alec walked from Rachel's house feeling positively elated. He was going to be a father. Of course there were problems but for the time being he was not going to think about them. Be positive, do what I can on my side and see what happens once Charles comes home. From what Rachel had told him, her husband seemed a pretty cold fish. How on earth would he ever cope with a woman as passionate and emotional as Rachel? No wonder the poor girl had been so unhappy. He, Alec, would make things right for her and that was all that mattered.

After work that day, he went back to his flat, in Hampstead. He shared it with Gwen. Theirs was a comfortable, open-ended relationship. They had known each other for years, started as lovers and ended as friends who, when the mood took them, went to bed together. Although Alec had talked to her about Rachel, Gwen saw little chance of anything coming of the relationship. Secretly, she thought Alec was most likely to make a fool of himself. Certainly he was behaving strangely out of character. Gwen's natural kindness and her affection for Alec made her hope he would not be hurt.

As Alec travelled home, he decided he must ask Gwen to find another flat. If Rachel decided to leave Charles, she must be able to come to him. That would not be possible if Gwen were in situ. It would be difficult because Gwen had been a good friend, more like an older sister than just a mistress. Even, on occasions, she had been like the mother he never had. No, this was not going to be easy.

When he arrived home, Gwen was preparing their evening meal. He had not told her of Rachel's letter or of his intention to visit her that morning. He poured them both a drink.

'I had to call to see Rachel, this morning.'

'Oh, I thought she told you not to go to the house.'

'Well, yes but Tony, you know, the barman at the club, gave me her letter. The stupid fool has had it for the best part of three weeks!'

Gwen said nothing. She could not remember ever seeing Alec so agitated.

'You see Rachel is pregnant and it is mine.'

'Oh! What's she going to do, does the husband know?'

'I doubt it, I didn't have a chance to talk to her, the kid was there and then the mother arrived. She says she is going to ring me on Sunday. I'm going to have to see her and find out what she wants to do.'

'You're really serious about all this, aren't you.' Alec did not answer. His expression said it all.

'Listen love, you are going to have to consider two possibilities. If she decides to stay with her husband and pass the child off as his, which she could do - just, if he comes home on leave soon; you will have to forget her. If on the other hand, she decides to leave, or the husband finds out, do you want to take her on? She'll certainly bring the little girl with her. You would be taking on a ready made family.'

This was the moment Alec had been dreading, but Gwen had given him the opening.

'Of course I'm willing to take her on. I love her, I've never felt like this before. We have nothing in common, our backgrounds could not be more different yet I would go through hell-fire for her. These weeks, when I've not known how she was or how she felt, have been purgatory. I don't know if she loves me but I don't care. I just want to take care of her and keep her safe.'

Gwen watched Alec. Well, love may be a many splendoured thing but it certainly did not seem to be making him very happy. She wondered if, when the red-hot flames of passion had abated, Alec and Rachel would have the same comfortable companionship that she shared with him now.

'If Rachel left Charles, she would have to come here.'

That is what all this was leading up to, she thought.

'So what you are really saying is, would I please find somewhere else to live.' Gwen smiled. 'Don't worry, I've never fancied being gooseberry. How long have I got?'

'Oh! love I'm so sorry, you've been so good to me. I hate it to be like this but I don't know what I'm doing, I'm in absolute turmoil.'

'Ummm, I rather gathered that. So one of us had better be practical. I'll sound out some of my girl-friends and see if they know of anyone who needs a flat-mate.'

Alec put his arms around her and held her tight.

'You don't deserve this, I'm so very sorry, we will still be friends won't we?'

'Of course we will, you daft sod, now come on I've not been slaving over a hot stove to see a good meal go to waste.'

Mary Cardew had not stayed with Rachel for long. She really had no patience with the girl. She had received all the benefits of wealth and position, an excellent private education and had been nothing but trouble. If the the worst came to the worst, she would just have to give Rachel an allowance from her own private income but beyond that she would not go. After all, if Rachel was old enough to marry, against parental wishes, she was old enough to resolve problems that she had brought upon herself.

Having done her duty, Mary considered, with satisfaction, the prospect of a civilised evening with Edgar. They would dine quite early then he could tell her how the manuscript was progressing. She would ask Cook to poach a salmon. She wondered if there would be any strawberries available, they would make an excellent pudding, served in champagne with fresh cream. Humming quietly to herself, Mary left the car on the drive, for Bert to put away. She had better have a word with Cook now. The kitchen was large and airy, Cook and Susan, the maid, were having a cup of tea, at the kitchen table. Why on earth did the girl always look guilty, whenever she sees me, Mary thought. Am I such an ogre? Susan bobbed her head and rushed into the scullery. Almost immediately Mary heard the clatter of crockery.

'I've decided we will have poached salmon tonight, Cook, then strawberries.'

'Yes Ma'am.' Cook smiled. She had been with the family a long time. She knew that Mrs. Cardew's bark was worse than her bite.

Mary walked up the hall; she glanced at the hall table. There was a note, a telephone message, it was from Edgar. He would not be home for dinner as he had to meet some researcher who was helping him with his book. Mary sighed; so much for a civilised evening, the delicious meal followed by stimulating conversation with her brilliant husband. She sat down by the window and looked out at the garden. It was glorious, Bert really did do a first class job. She thought about all the lovely things around her, genuine antiques many of them. Everything cared for, polished, gleaming. She was a very fortunate woman. She had everything money could buy. So why did she feel so lonely? She rang the bell for the maid. Susan appeared like a startled rabbit.

'Yes Ma'am?'

'Tell Cook to cancel the order for dinner. I shall be dining alone. Ask her to make up a tray, something light for 7 o/clock.'

'Yes Ma'am.'

Charles could not wait to get home; the trains had been slow and crowded. Never mind, he had ten days leave and had been promoted again, since he had seen Rachel. He was now a corporal and the way things were going would be a sergeant before long. He knew Rachel would be pleased for him but her pacifist tendencies would mute her enthusiasm. His parents, on the other hand, would be thrilled. He wondered what Jenny would be like. Of course, he had photographs but that told you nothing about temperament or character. He must really get to know her this time. He supposed he would also have to get to know Rachel again as well. After such long separations, they could easily feel like strangers.

He walked down the road towards his house. It was a great piece of luck getting the extra three days. He had not expected to be back before Wednesday. He took his front door key from his battledress pocket. He had carried it everywhere with him, a talisman, guaranteeing that he would be coming home. As he opened the door, there was a child running towards him. She stopped.

'Mummy, Mummy there's a soldier here.' She put her fingers in her mouth and stared. She was not a pretty child but she did have the greenest eyes he had ever seen. She continued to stare at him, unblinking.

Rachel came out of the kitchen. She felt weak and faint. She had not expected him today. Perhaps it was a blessing. She had had no time to get herself worked up. Also the decision to ring or not to ring Alec had been taken out of her hands. She could not now ring him and that was that. She walked towards Charles, slightly unsteadily, wiping her hands on her apron. He opened his arms wide and held her to him.

'Oh! darling I am so glad to be home.'

Rachel gave a sob. Poor kid, Charles thought, it must have been rough, on her own with a small child. Still, the war would not go on for ever. Everything was going to be all right.

'Come and give your Daddy a kiss.'

'Give her time to get used to you,' Rachel whispered under her breath.

'Let's go into the kitchen, Jenny, and I will show you the presents I have brought for you.' The solemn stare changed into a wavering smile and Jenny allowed this stranger, her father, to take her by the hand.

Alec stared out of the window. He had spent all day pacing up and down, smoking and drinking cups of tea. He knew such behaviour was going to achieve absolutely nothing but what else could he do? He certainly could not go out. The flat was spotless so there was no cleaning or tidying to do. He did not feel like
eating so there was no point in cooking a meal. Gwen had gone out with friends, onto the Heath. Under normal circumstances he would have gone too. A walk, a pint at 'Jack Straw's Castle' , a bit of a picnic, what better way to spend a sunny Sunday. But for Alec, the circumstances, at the moment, were anything but normal.

Gwen had been as good as her word; she had spent the previous few days contacting friends, making enquiries. She had the offer of at least temporary accommodation, whenever she wanted it. Alec felt a pang of regret. He had set the ball rolling. He thought about his life; settled, comfortable, he enjoyed his work, he enjoyed his music. He had good friends. What on earth was he doing? He was breaking a marriage, but wouldn't it have broken anyway? He would probably be taking a child away from her father, but she hardly knew him. He would soon have the responsibilities of a husband and father. Was it a good swap for the life he had now? He remembered the time he had spent with Rachel. So little to go by; all he knew was that she had bewitched him. He had only to close his eyes to see her face, abandoned, wild, touched with silver by the moonlight. This was his woman. There was no going back. He must just be patient and wait.

Rachel did not protest when Charles suggested - so soon after his arrival - that they visit his parents. In fact, she was glad to go when most of Gladys and Albert Warr's attention would be directed towards their son and grand-daughter. She could sit quietly in the background. After Charles' leave, she would not have to visit again for a few weeks, while she decided what to do. The visit went smoothly with cries of, delight and disbelief from Gladys as Charles recounted his exploits in the North African desert. Gladys even suggested keeping Jenny for the night so that Charles and Rachel could have some time on their own. Well, thought Rachel, this is it.

For different reasons, they both felt nervous. Charles had not been able to completely forget his mother's hints that Rachel had been less than faithful. Should there ever be even a hint that his mother was right, Charles knew he would never be able to touch Rachel again. He was, therefore, terrified that something in her behaviour or attitude would make him doubt her. He loved her, but to be worthy of that love, she must be beyond reproach.

For Rachel the problem was one of comparison. It was one thing to feel that your husband's love-making was uninspired when you had no experience of another man. Now, Rachel knew only too well what a truly fulfilling sexual encounter was like. She resented what Alec had done, not just the baby, although God knew that was a desperate problem. She and Charles would have grown together, once the war was over. It was Alec's fault she would be denied this. Always now, at the back of her mind, would be the memory of that night with him. It would undermine and ridicule the performance of the man she loved, really loved. For she did love Charles didn't she?

She felt strangely shy in the bedroom with Charles and hurriedly undressed putting on an all enveloping nightdress. Charles smiled broadly; she did not know how her action reassured him. With consideration for, what he felt, were her delicate feelings, he slipped into bed - fully clad in pyjamas. He kissed her and held her tightly to him

'My God, I've missed you.'

'It's been awful without you Charles.'

'I'm sure the war will soon be over and then we can get on with our lives and make a decent home for Jenny. We may even give her a brother or sister.'

'Oh! yes it's better to have more than one,'

He stroked her hair and then let his hand slide down her neck. He fumbled with the fastening of her nightdress. He slid his hand inside and fumbled again, this time for her breast. He felt such an upsurge of desire that it frightened him. He musn't lose control. He had scarcely seen a woman never mind been to bed with one, since his last leave. His hand slipped down to her thighs, he started to tug at her nightdress, pulling it higher until it was bunched around her waist. She lay mute, receiving his kisses, trying to push the anxiety away, willing her body to relax. She wanted to enjoy this physical reunion with the man she loved but her body seemed to have gone on strike.

He undid the drawstring of his pyjamas and rolled on top of her. He unceremoniously pushed inside her body. It hurt. She cried out.

'I've hurt you, my darling, what have I done, are you all right?'

She clung to him, he could not withdraw. Suddenly in that moment, she knew what she must do. The child she was carrying should have been his, would have been his if it had not been for Alec. It was all his fault. He had taken advantage of her; he had known she did not drink. He had deliberately got her drunk. So many men were like that. She had heard the girls at the munitions factory talk about it. It was Charles who really loved her; he wanted to protect her and her children - their children. She would give him a son this time. She had been overdue with Jenny. There would be no problem. If the baby seemed to come a little early no-one would suspect anything. Thank goodness she had not been able to 'phone Alec. She would not do so now. He would soon forget her. She must get rid of his address and 'phone number. It would not do to leave that lying about. As she drifted off to sleep, she could hear Charles gently snoring. She leant against his back, she would not say anything to her mother yet. That was one thing to be said in her favour. Mother would not bring the subject up nor would she talk to anyone else about it. As long as it did not bring scandal to the family name or upset Edgar, she would go along with whatever Rachel decided - however much she disapproved!

Had Mary known of Rachel's decision, she would have been able to concentrate her mind entirely on the problem of Edgar. It had been a thoroughly disagreeable day and now, at eleven thirty, he still was not home. She hoped he had not had an accident. She was loath to telephone his club. He did so dislike anything that smacked of interference. She got out of bed and glanced out of the window. She breathed a sigh of relief as she saw his car coming up the drive. I am being entirely stupid, behaving like a love-sick adolescent instead of a sensible, intelligent, mature woman. She hurriedly got back into bed. It would not do for Edgar to think she was checking up on him.

Edgar walked slowly and quietly into the bedroom

'I didn't expect you to still be awake, dear. Had a good day?'

'Oh yes, and you?'

'Busy, very busy, sorry I'm so late. Got into lengthy discussions with this researcher chap.'

'Well get into bed quickly and let me massage your shoulders; you look terribly tense.'

'Thanks all the same, my dear, you are so good to me. All I really want is to go to sleep.'

He got into bed, turned his back and within minutes, his deep breathing made it obvious, he was asleep. Poor man, Mary thought. He really does work too hard.

Gwen came bursting into the flat, followed by several of the friends with whom she had spent the day.

'Alec, where are you?'

She looked in his bedroom but he was not there. Jean shouted from the living room.

'He's here.'

Gwen looked closely at Alec as she walked into the room. His eyes were bleary with sleep. The room was thick with cigarette smoke, a half drunk, cold cup of tea was beside him.

'She didn't ring, did she?'

Alec slowly shook his head; he could not speak.

Chapter 3

Jenny now thought her father was the most wonderful man in the world; she cried bitterly when he went away. During his leave, they had been out every day.

They had visited Grandma and Grandad Warr. On one of these visits Uncle Jack and Aunt Caroline had been there. Grandma had been very excited and told Jenny that she would soon have a new little cousin. Jenny was not sure what that meant but felt happy that Grandma was pleased; it was bound to be something nice. Mummy had seemed happier while Daddy was at home. Jenny had only heard her being sick once, so she must be feeling better.

They went to visit Grandmother Cardew and had afternoon tea. It was too cool an autumn day to sit in the garden so they ate in the dining room. Silver ornaments gleamed and Jenny's plate seemed so thin that she felt sure she would be able to see through it if she held it up to the light. When she had finished eating the delicate wafer thin sandwiches and tiny fruit bejewelled cakes, Jenny asked if she could get down and play outside.

'Jenny, well brought up little girls do not leave the table until everyone has finished eating. Now listen to what your Daddy is telling me.'

Jenny looked at her mother, hoping for some support but Rachel gave her a nervous smile and looked away. Jenny sighed, resigned herself to being bored and started picking at the lace edge of the starched white tablecloth. At least Edgar Cardew was not there. She definitely did not like him. Eventually the grown-ups seemed to have finished.

'Would you like Bert to show you around the garden?'

'Yes please, Grandmother.' Escape at last.

'You must be careful not to trample on any of the plants. If you ask Bert politely, he may let you pick a few flowers to take home.'

Jenny grinned, perhaps Grandmother wasn't so bad after all.

'Go to the kitchen, ask Susan to find Bert. Tell him I wish to speak to him.

Jenny turned quickly and made for the door.

'Don't run!' said Grandmother.

Jenny felt very sleepy but contented as she went home that evening. She clutched a large bunch of flowers to her chest. They had been wrapped with wet paper around their stems, to stop them from wilting. This had made a damp patch on the front of her dress but she did not mind. Mummy said she could arrange them in the best vase when she got home. All in all it had been a nice afternoon; she liked Bert a lot. He reminded her of Grandad.

Gwen did not move out. There was no need. Alec was very subdued and drank rather more than usual. Gwen nursed him as she would have done if he had been recovering from a serious illness. He continued to play at the Jazz club but on his evenings off would sit with a glass in one hand and a cigarette in the other. On such evenings, all he wanted to do was talk. Gwen was a good listener and did her best to appear attentive, even when her mind wandered onto other things. After all, she had heard this story so many times. The sooner he could talk the wretched woman out of his system, the better. Then life could get back to normal.

'What I can't get over is, she is expecting my child. My child for God's sake!Surely I have some rights?'

'Can you prove it's yours?'

Alec thought for a moment, being realistic, no he could not, in any case would it make any difference if he could? Not really. It was up to the woman to decide, in a situation like this, whether the father had any chance to claim his child. Alec's one fear was that the child would end up in an orphanage. That would be history repeating itself. That was something he could not accept; it was not necessary.

'Should I go to see her again?'

'Look Alec, you gave her your address and 'phone number. She knows where she can find you, you must leave it to her now.'

Rachel felt at peace with herself. She had done the right thing. She was making everyone happy. Jenny was pleased that she was going to have a little brother or sister. Charles had written back immediately he received her letter telling him of the pregnancy. Rachel sighed with relief when she received that letter; he was obviously delighted. Her in-laws were thrilled; the baby would be born about a month after Jack and Caroline's. Three grandchildren to make a fuss of, what could be better.

Rachel had told her mother, in a letter, what she intended to do. She had not had a reply. This was Mary Cardew's way of saying - You must do as you please; do not involve me. Alec was the only small cloud on the horizon. How Rachel wished she had never told him she thought she was pregnant. She could write and say she had lost the baby and did not want to see him again. That would be an end to it.

Somehow she could not do that; it would be denying the existence of the child inside her. It would be tempting fate.

It was a very cold winter and Rachel kept Jenny in as much as possible. The child had a tendency to get bronchitis. Mr. and Mrs. Warr suggested that Rachel and Jenny spend Christmas with them. Jack said he would pick them up in his car. Rachel was not particularly close to her sister-in-law, Caroline and she actively disliked her brother-in-law, Jack. She remembered when she and Charles were newly engaged. They used to visit the couple quite often, for an evening of whist. Jack would rub his leg against hers and put his hand on her thigh, under cover of the card table. She had been too frightened to say anything then. It was much too late now to make objections to his collecting them, to spend a Christmas with the family.

Charles had written a very loving letter to Rachel and also enclosed a short note for Jenny. She was delighted. She took this, her first proper letter, to her grandparents; she could show it off. It was a very traditional Christmas.

Now that the anxieties of the previous months had been resolved, Rachel was more able to relax and enjoy herself. Needless to say, her mother-in-law, Gladys, was constantly on the move since she would not allow either of the pregnant women to lift a finger.

Gwen had arranged for all their available friends to come to the flat for a communal Christmas. She and Alec had become closer and whilst Gwen had little sympathy for Rachel, in a way the silly woman had done her a service. If Gwen thought of Rachel at all, it was rarely. When she did, she assumed that Rachel was a spoilt little rich girl who had wanted a fling without any consequences. If she were old enough to be a wife and mother, she was old enough to know how to protect herself. Her dismissive attitude was largely because she cared a lot for Alec. She did not like the way Rachel had picked him up and dropped him.

The party was going well, everyone brought some food or drink; there was plenty of music and space had been made for dancing. This was how Christmas should be spent, with people we like best. Never mind those turgid days with relatives you didn't like and only saw out of duty. In fact, Gwen got on well with her family but had not been able to afford the time or the money to travel back to Wales. This, she thought, was a pretty fair substitute.

She danced with Alec most of the evening. They had been drinking steadily but had reached that comfortable and pleasant plateau where the faculties are still intact, with the senses relaxed but heightened.

Alec looked carefully and intently at Gwen's face, he grinned at her and kissed her firmly on the lips.

'I've been a real pain in the arse recently, haven't I?'

'Well... I've known livelier flat-mates.'

She kissed him back. This was really nice.

'I don't know anyone who would have put up with me the way you have.'

'Why, have you looked?'

He slapped her bottom hard.

'Ouch! I always knew you were a bully!'

'Well promise you will let me go on bullying you for ever and ever.'

Things were moving too fast, too soon, thought Gwen. This is a combination of drink and the rebound and I'm not buying it.

'Oh, I don't know about that, for ever and ever is a long time.' She gave him a hug. 'Tell you what, lets see how it goes this year and reassess the situation next year.'

Alec opened his mouth and then closed it again. Since it was Christmas Day, she wasn't committing herself for too long.

'One day at a time, sweetheart; we've no need to rush.' She kissed him again. 'Now it is quite definitely time I sat down and took the weight off my feet.'

'I suppose you're right,' Alec said.

Since none of Mary's children was able to spend Christmas with her and Edgar, they dined alone. Whilst for most mothers, the ideal Christmas is one spent surrounded by their children and grandchildren, Mary's views were quite different. She had never known her mother who had died giving birth to her. Mary's father, with the typical logic of many Victorian men, had held Mary personally responsible for the tragedy. Even when he remarried and fathered another child by his new wife, he had little time for his youngest daughter. The new stepmother was far too bound up with her new baby son to give much time to Mary. If she had never quite learned how to deal with family life - small children in particular, it was hardly surprising. Since also, she had had servants throughout her marriage to George Rowland and now Edgar, she had never gained first hand experience of what motherhood involved.

After a beautifully presented meal, Mary suggested a stroll around the grounds before it got dark. Somehow she felt oppressed by the house and all the beautiful things within it. She could not shake off the feeling of foreboding. It was natural, she supposed, she had a son in the

Navy; God only knew where he was. Eleanor was doing some kind of war work that was all very hush hush and of course there was Rachel - anything could happen there.

'I'll ask Bert to make up the fire in the drawing room for when we get back - shall I?'

'Yes,' said Edgar, 'I'm sure a breath of fresh air will do us both good.' He smiled at her gently. Mary could feel a tightness in her chest and her heart thumped. I am a fool, she smiled to herself. After all these years, he only has to smile at me.

Officially Rachel's baby was due at the end of April. She knew, in reality, she would be full term at the end of March. Still, midwives allowed for two weeks either side of the due date. So with luck, if she could manage to take things easy at the end, she might be able to hang on past due date, as she had with Jenny. Just ten days overdue and everything would slot into place.

It had been a harsh winter with a lot of frost, giving icy roads and pavements. When Rachel ventured out, she walked with great care, in order not to slip. She stopped visiting her in-laws, by bus, on the grounds that she was getting very tired. Sometimes on a Sunday, Jack would come over to collect her and Jenny. He was usually in an expansive mood these days. Perhaps now his wife was pregnant too, he would direct his attentions towards caring for her, instead of groping other men's wives, Rachel thought.

It was on the 10th. March that the accident happened. Rachel and Jenny had walked to the bakers. It was an extremely cold day; there had been a very heavy frost. As they walked down the road, Rachel held tightly to Jenny's hand.

The child seemed particularly happy and was trying not very successfully to skip on the frosty pavements.

'Do be careful, darling, you'll have us both over.' The words were scarcely spoken before Jenny stumbled and sprawled on the pavement, dragging her mother down with her. Rachel gasped as the breath was knocked out of her body. She lay still then pressed her forehead against the cold pavement to try to stop the dizzy, sick feeling. People came rushing from all directions. She could hear a babble of conversation, above which was the sound of Jenny crying. Strong hands helped her to sit up. Someone had fetched a blanket to drape around her shoulders.

'Better not move her.'

'She can't stay here, in this weather.'

'She must be near her time.'

'Get her to the hospital.'

Rachel recognised the woman who lived two doors down.

'Please don't worry. I'm fine, really. I'm just winded. Could you help me up and if I could just get home to rest, I'll be fine, honestly I will.'

There was a great deal of muttering but when it was realised that nothing exciting was going to happen, the crowd drifted away. Only the baker, who had come out of his shop and Rachel's neighbour remained. Rachel turned to the woman,

'Are you going home now?'

'Well yes, I've got all I need for today.'

'If you would just give me your arm, I'm frightened I'll slip again.'

They started walking slowly back up the road. Jenny had stopped crying and was walking very quietly beside her mother. This was all her fault, she knew. She wanted to be as inconspicuous as possible; otherwise she faced a good telling-off. After a few yards, Rachel stopped.

'We've got no bread. That's what I came out for.'

'Wait here,' said her neighbour. After a few minutes, she returned.

'Mr. Brooks says, have these for now and he'll call round when he shuts the shop tonight. He'll bring you a loaf. I think he wants to check you are all right.'

Rachel clutched the brown paper bag with some bread rolls. The smell of the warm bread, combined with the feeling of shock she was experiencing after her fall, reduced her to tears.

'People are so kind.'

'Well it's a pretty rotten world if we can't help each other; there would be no hope for us, love.'

Jenny felt like crying too. No-one had spoken to her and the burden of guilt felt heavy on her shoulders.

'I'm sorry, Mummy, I really didn't mean to hurt you.'

'I know, but you must be careful, you see, particularly when this baby is born. We don't want any accidents then, do we?' With great clarity, Jenny realised that this baby was going to make a lot of difference to her life.

They got back home and the neighbour insisted that Rachel put her feet up while the kettle boiled.

'What you need is a good, hot cup of tea. Do you want me to look after your little girl for an hour or two so you can rest? My name's Betty, by the way.'

Rachel sighed,'That would be lovely, I really could do with some sleep. My name's Rachel and this is Jenny.'

'Right, come on, Jenny, give your mum a kiss. I'll give her some tea and bring her back in time for bed.'

'You are so kind, I can't thank you enough. 'Rachel pulled herself to her feet and winced as she felt a stabbing pain, low down in her back. I must have pulled a muscle when I fell, she thought.

After Betty and Jenny had left, Rachel climbed very carefully up the stairs. She tried to convince herself that she did not have any pain in her back. If I go to bed and rest, everything will be fine. I've just shaken myself up a bit. She lay down but could not get comfortable. The pain was moving around her abdomen, as though it were being squeezed. She tried to take some deep breaths. She rested her hands on her bulging stomach. Please baby, don't come yet; please baby, everything will go wrong. It's too early. Hot tears ran down her face. She dozed for a few minutes; the sounds from outside increased and diminished as she drifted in and out of sleep. She thought she heard Charles speaking to her. Surely he could not be home on leave yet? She dreamt that she was in labour; was it Alec or Charles sitting beside her? She woke with a start. She could hear whimpering, then realised that she was making the strange animal noises. Sweat ran down her forehead and stung her eyes. The pain crept with jagged claws, from her back, round her straining abdomen, meeting in an agonising knot under her ribs. She gasped. What am I going to do? she thought. Dear God, please help me. She looked at her watch, I'll time the contractions. I don't have to do anything until the pains are five minutes apart. It could be a false labour. If I just rest until Betty brings Rachel back, maybe it will stop.

She glanced at her watch again. It was 5 o/clock. Mr. Brooks would be round soon, with some bread. If I don't answer the door, he is bound to think something is wrong. If I go downstairs carefully now, when he does come, I will only have to walk a few paces. That's the best thing, she thought. While I'm upstairs, I can go to the toilet, that will save me having to come upstairs again. She stood up very carefully and walked to the bathroom. As she sat on the toilet, she glanced down and saw there was blood on her knickers. Dear God, please, please don't let this baby come yet. Why on Earth had Jenny been so stupid? She always had to do what she wanted. Just like her father. If she had done as I told her, this would never have happened. All I want is to be happy, to be a wife to Charles and mother to Jenny and this baby. I just want to show my mother that I can be a success; I do deserve her praise. Now it is all being snatched away, I will never convince anyone that this baby is seven weeks early. She cried but suddenly the pain gripped, squeezing, tearing at her. She looked at her watch; it was more than ten minutes since the last pain. That made her feel better; maybe it was just a false alarm. If I can just get downstairs, I'll put my feet up until Mr. Brooks arrives. Once Betty brings Jenny back, I'll put her to bed and go myself - straight afterwards. A good night's sleep will let everything calm down.

She sat on the top step. If I go down one at a time, on my bottom, it will be less of a strain. She was half-way down the stairs when she heard a knock at the front door. She stood and walked slowly down the rest of the flight. As she reached the bottom, she was gripped by another contraction. She tried to speak normally as she clung to the newel post.

'I'm coming.' Let me just have a moment to let the pain pass. She wiped the sweat from her forehead and upper lip. There was another knock at the door. It was no use, she would have to go. She could not stand upright and half-crouching, she stumbled to the door. She took a deep breath as the knocker went a third time. She opened the door and holding onto it with one hand and the frame with the other, made herself stand straight. Mr. Brooks looked at her, his smile quickly changed to concern.

'Are you all right, love?'
Rachel's face was grey; her skin had a thin sheen of sweat that made it look oily. Her hair was damp.

'I'm sorry I took so long. I was asleep upstairs.'

'Are you sure you should be on your own? Haven't you someone who could stop with you?'

'It's all right, Betty, two doors down is looking after Jenny. I'll get her to give me a hand, if I need it. The baby isn't due until the end of next month.'

At that moment Rachel felt a warm trickle of water down her legs. Slow at first, the trickle increased until, when she glanced down, she was standing in a small pool of water. Mr. Brooks followed her gaze. As a family man, with three children of his own, he knew immediately what had happened.

'Well, my dear, it looks like your time has come. Your waters have broken haven't they.'

Rachel nodded at him in panic, terror in her heart had struck her dumb.

'Now don't get upset, you've been through all this before. It's never as hard the second time. Let me help you upstairs. I'll get the midwife and tell Betty to hang onto your little girl for the time being.'

Going upstairs was even more difficult than coming down. With every step, the same thought went through Rachel's brain. What am I going to do? What am I going to do!? Mr. Brooks was talking to her but the sound of her thoughts reverberated in her brain. She could not hear him. At last, she half fell, was half dragged onto her bed.

'I won't be long, I'll just go to see Betty, then once the midwife arrives, you will be as right as rain.' Rachel tried to smile at him, he was such a kind man, if only he knew. This may be the beginning of a new life but it was an end to hers, of that she was certain.

'Your husband is in the army isn't he, surely we can contact him somehow. Maybe he could get compassionate leave. What about your mother, does she live near here?' Rachel shook her head.

'What about your in-laws?'

'No, no, don't tell them.'

Mr. Brooks was beginning to lose patience. His Jane had never carried on like this and she had three, like shelling peas, she had always said. I only wanted to do the woman a good turn and bring her some bread. At this rate, I'll be delivering the baby myself!

'Well, you definitely can't stay here like this. I am going to see Betty now,' he said briskly and left the room.

He went to Betty's house. He could hear running feet and Jenny opened the door.

'Is my Mummy all right? I want to see her.'

Betty stood behind Jenny, wiping her hands on her apron.

'What's the matter, Stan? Is Rachel not so good?'

'She's in labour, if you ask me. Her old man's in the army. She says her mother doesn't live locally and she nearly threw a fit when I suggested contacting her in-laws. But if you ask me, the first thing we need to do is get the midwife.'

'What's labour?' asked Jenny.

'Ssh love, your new baby might be on its way.'

'Well, she's just told me, it isn't due until the end of next month!'

Betty raised her eyebrows. 'Really, you do surprise me, still perhaps its a big baby.'

'Perhaps its why she doesn't want anyone told; it wouldn't be the first time a soldier has come back to find a cuckoo in the nest!' Stan sighed, once again, he was glad he had been declared unfit for active service.

'I'll send my girl, Janet, round to the midwife's, with a note. Then we can see what Rachel wants to do. I can't stay with her too long; I've got my own family to look after. I don't mind looking after Jenny here, overnight, but Rachel can't be left on her own.'

Jenny started to cry, she was frightened. She wanted to be with her mother.

'There's not much I can do, I'll be off now.'

'Thanks Stan, you're a good bloke.'

Jenny continued to cry, quietly. What was happening? Where was Mummy? Why can't I see her? Betty looked down at the child's tear-streaked face. She looked so forlorn and frightened. Betty bent down and hugged her.

'It's going to be O.K. love but we need to get hold of the lady who is going to help your new baby out of Mummy's tummy.' Betty took the child by the hand and led her into the kitchen, where the family was having tea.

'Now you sit down next to Bob, have something to eat. Janet take a note round to Sister Burns while I go to see if Jenny's mum is all right.' She wrote a note and Janet left, running. Jenny's crying had become gulping sobs.

' I want to see Grandma and Grandad Warr.'

That was the obvious solution, get the child to her grandparents.

'Where do they live, Jenny?'

'I don't know.' She started to cry louder.

'Look Bet, you can't go on like this. She's not your responsibility. Go and see her mother and find out where the grandparents live.' Bob loved his wife dearly and admired her willingness to be a good neighbour, but there were limits.

'Right, I'll go now. You stay here, Jenny; be a good girl and try to eat something.'

Rachel lay on the bed; the pains were very strong, coming every five minutes. In her heart, she knew that the labour would not stop. She must accept the inevitable. Perhaps I will die giving birth, some mothers do. Then I will not have to face anyone, not Charles or his parents or my mother. Their faces loomed before her; they were all mouthing their disapproval, their condemnation. She could not hear what they were saying. Why should I have to die, its not my fault. A pain gripped her and she cried out. If Jenny hadn't pulled me over, this would not have happened. No, that is terrible, Rachel thought, I should not blame the child. If Charles had been kinder and more understanding I would never have gone out with Alec. Alec got me drunk, he must have known what he was doing. He is responsible for all this. I hate him, he has destroyed my life. Another pain gripped her, she felt as though her back would break. She screamed and Betty, who had just arrived, came running up the stairs. At the same time, Sister Burns knocked on the door. Hearing Rachel's scream, she came straight upstairs too.

'Now then, Mrs. Warr, we can't have all this commotion; let's have a look at you.' A quick examination showed that labour was well advanced. Sister Burns sent Betty for clean towels, boiled water and cotton wool.

'Right, my dear, we need to make you a bit more comfortable.' Swiftly and firmly Rachel was undressed, put into a nightgown and propped up on pillows.

'May I have some water, please?'

'Just a sip. Where's the bathroom?' While Sister Burns was out of the room, Rachel was able to think. As with her previous labour, someone was in control now. It enabled her to collect her thoughts The feelings of panic and terror subsided. She must contact her mother. She could not just turn her back on her own daughter. That's it, she would ask Betty to go to the 'phone box and ring. Jenny could stay in Wimbledon, there were servants to look after her. It wasn't much to ask. As far as the in-laws were concerned, she would deal with that problem later. The first thing was to get this baby born. She sank back on her pillows but immediately the next contraction came. She stifled a scream, she must not make Sister Burns cross.

Betty came back into the bedroom, Rachel looked much better and inwardly Betty breathed a sigh of relief. I've done my bit. I'll find out where the grandparents live then I can go home. She had just started wondering how she would be able to make contact, if they were not on the 'phone, when Rachel spoke.

'Betty you have been so kind to me, can I ask just one more favour? Would you please 'phone my mother. She has a car and could come to collect Jenny. I should have thought of it before.'

Betty took the number and some money and went to the 'phone box on the corner. She quickly got through to Mrs. Cardew's house. There was a delay while the maid, who had answered the 'phone, found her mistress. Betty explained that Rachel was in labour and the birth was imminent. She said she was looking after Jenny but the child was rather upset and it would be better for her to be with her family. There was a lengthy pause.

'I see,' said Mrs. Cardew, 'I will be with you as soon as I can.' Mary's heart sank. This really could not have come at a worse time. Surely the baby was not due for several weeks yet. She and Edgar were going to Cambridge, in two days. He was giving a lecture to the History undergraduates and she desperately wanted to witness his academic triumph. It occurred to her that Mr. and Mrs. Warr should be the ones to care for Jenny. After all, from what Rachel had said, they really were doting grandparents. That was the best solution for everyone. Obviously Rachel could not be left alone after the baby was born. Susan, the maid, could be spared until Rachel was able to cope. Mary would have to tell Edgar what she had decided but felt sure he would be so pleased not to be personally involved, that she foresaw no difficulties.

Betty went back to Rachel and told her that her mother was on her way. There was nothing more to do. Since it seemed that the baby would arrive very soon, Betty went home.

'How's things?' said Bob.

Betty explained what was happening but failed to notice the look of alarm on Jenny's face, when she heard that she was going to be collected by Grandmother Cardew. Jenny did not want to go there; she wanted her mother or Grandma Warr. She slipped quietly out of the room and tiptoed along the hall. She could reach the doorknob as she had when Mr. Brooks called. She let herself out of the house. She was going to tell her mummy she didn't want to go with Grandmother Cardew; she certainly did not want to see Edgar who was much too frightening to call Grandpa.

Once out of the house, she ran the short distance to her own home. The door was shut and she could hear her mother screaming. What was happening? A lady was supposed to be helping mummy get the baby out of her tummy. Why was Mummy making such a terrible noise? That lady was hurting her Mummy; she wasn't helping at all. Jenny started to bang on the door with her fists.

'Let me in, let me in. I want my Mummy, you're hurting my Mummy.' She started kicking the door. Tears streamed down her face. Perhaps Mummy was screaming because she was frightened. Jenny was frightened. She started screaming too. She made so much noise that the next door neighbour came out to see what was happening. At that moment Betty, who had realised Jenny was missing, came running along the road.

'It's all right. I'll take care of her.'

As the neighbour's door shut, Mrs. Cardew's car drew up at the kerb. She sat, for a moment, in the car and looked at her grandchild with distaste. The child was hysterical, screaming, crying and kicking at the front door! All of her life, Mary had held her emotions in check. This had always been her survival tactic as a child, and now she was appalled by the scene before her. Rachel had always been over-emotional, clearly the child took after her mother.

Jenny stood sobbing and shaking. Her face was streaked with black and wet with tears. Her nose was running and she hadn't a handkerchief. As her shoulders shook and she tried to gulp back the tears she said, 'Someone is hurting my Mummy, up there.'

Mary walked from her car and glanced up at the bedroom window. She heard Rachel give a great cry of anguish and pain. Then there was silence. A silence, that was finally broken by the unique wailing cry of a new born baby, announcing its arrival in the world. Jenny clasped Betty's hand.

'Betty,' she sobbed, 'I've wet my knickers.'

Chapter 4

Rachel lay back on the pillows cradling her son in her arms. She examined his face and tried to remember what Jenny had looked like when she was born. What was it Charles had said, all babies look like Mussolini! Just the sort of dismissive comment he would make, she thought. Of course it was possible to pick out similarities with a baby's family, albeit in miniature. She stroked the baby's head, amply covered in fair down. Certainly the colouring was different and whilst Jenny had been virtually bald for the first year of her life, this baby already had a good head of hair. What of the features? He had not opened his eyes yet. All babies had button noses; his ears nestled closely to the sides of his head, unlike Jenny's, which stuck out. I will drive myself mad like this. A baby is a baby, this is my baby and Charles will be his father and that's an end to it.

Sister Burns had been bustling about. The afterbirth had come away with no problems; there was little more to do except weigh the baby. Then she would settle mother down and ensure that there was someone to stay with her until her own mother arrived.

'There we are, worth the effort, wasn't it. Let's get this young man weighed.'

Rachel handed the baby to Sister, he looked a good size, too good for comfort. Jenny had been just over seven pounds. If anything this baby was bigger.

'7lbs 9oz, well you are a fine young man. It's probably a good thing this baby was born now and not in two weeks, you might not have had such an easy time.'

Rachel shivered even though she was not cold. There were so many questions she wanted to ask but, in her heart, she knew the answers.

'Supposing he had been born two months early, instead of two weeks?'

'Of course, the big problem then is breathing. You see, their lungs are not able to cope very well at that stage.'

'But, what about weight?'

'Naturally that's a big problem too; babies fill out in those last two months. So you would have been a pathetic little scrap, wouldn't you.' Sister Burns tickled the baby under the chin and smiled at him, a warm, gentle smile. It was so unlike the brisk, efficient, po-faced woman who had taken charge so effortlessly. Rachel wondered if the midwife had children of her own but did not feel she could ask.

She had been vaguely aware of a commotion going on outside whilst she had been giving birth. It had sounded a bit like Jenny, but surely not. Betty was looking after her. Still it was time the child saw her new brother.

'Right , my dear, you and baby are settled. All I need to do now is to make sure there is someone to keep an eye on you.'   'My mother said she would come over. I expect she has gone to the neighbour's house.'

'I'll call in on my way home. Of course, I will pop back tonight, to see that everything is O.K. and be in again in the morning.'

'Thank you, Sister.'

It's a good thing that my mother will be accompanied by Jenny and probably Betty as well. It would limit the awkward questions. She lay back and wondered how long this euphoria would last. How long before the storm clouds gathered. Whilst Charles knew little about the mysteries of childbirth, his mother was only too well versed. I won't be able to keep her away for long.

Betty had suggested that Mary went to her house, to wait for news.

'There's no point in us waiting here and besides we need to get Jenny cleaned up.'

Mary had no option, she had told Edgar she would not be long but clearly it was going to take longer than she had anticipated. Still this woman, Betty, had obviously been very kind, both to Rachel and Jenny.

Bob had finished his tea and was sitting in his armchair, by the stove, in the kitchen. The top buttons of his trousers had been undone, his braces were off and his shirt open at the neck. The children had gone out to play and he felt at peace. The kitchen table was cluttered with the remains of their meal; Betty would clear that when she got back. He heard the front door go and hoped that everything was sorted out with Rachel. The kid seemed O.K., a scared little thing. He had had a lousy day at work and did not want any more bother. He realised that more than one person was coming up the hallway. So much for a bit of peace and quiet, he thought. Betty and Jenny walked in followed by a very tall, thin, austere looking woman. Suddenly, Bob felt uncomfortable and, more importantly, undressed! He hastily did up his trouser waistband, pulled his braces up and got to his feet.

'Bob, this is Rachel's mum, Mrs. Cardew. She's come to take Jenny back to her house.'

'Pleased to meet you,' Bob said. There was no attempt on either side to shake hands. Jenny looked close to tears again; she really did not want to go to Grandmother Cardew's house and the minute they let her see her Mummy, she would tell her so.

'Come on, love, let's get you cleaned up. I've got some clean knickers upstairs. We'll wash your face and hands, comb your hair and you'll be as pretty as a picture. You don't want your Mummy to know you have been crying, do you?'

Jenny meekly followed Betty upstairs, leaving Mary in the kitchen with Bob.

'Sit down, make yourself at home; would you like a cup of tea?'

'No thank you, I expect I shall be able to see my daughter soon, then I can get the child settled.'

There was an uneasy silence. These hoity-toity, stuck-up women were all the same, Bob thought. Frightened to get their hands dirty. They may look down their noses at people like us, but it's my Betty that's looking after this ones grandchild.

The salt of the earth - how often Mary had heard that phrase - but so were her servants. That doesn't mean I want to socialise with them!

'I expect you would like a grandson this time.' Bob asked, unable to cope with the silence any longer.

'Surely, the most important thing is for the child to be healthy.'

Well that's put me in my place, Bob decided. He picked up the newspaper, let her get on with it.

Jenny came into the kitchen. She looked clean and tidy.

'Can I see my Mummy now?'

'Hush child,' said Mary. 'Would you mind going to see if there is any news yet, Betty?'

You can tell she's got servants, Bob thought, giving her bloody orders. Betty walked up the road to Rachel's house. Sister Burns came to the door with her coat on.

'I've just finished, mother and baby are doing well, it's a boy. I'll be back tonight to settle them down.'

'Thanks, Sister, is it all right for Rachel's mum and little girl to come over?'

'Yes, then arrangements must be made for someone to stay with Mrs. Warr for the next few days.'

Betty nodded and ran back to her house. A little boy, how nice; all's well that ends well. She burst into the kitchen.

'You've got a little brother, Jenny, isn't that nice.'

'Can I see my Mummy now?'

Mary stood up, 'Thank you for all you have done, I appreciate your kindness. I am sure you have plenty to do, we will not take up any more of your time.' She smiled briefly, took Jenny by the hand and left.

'Well, she doesn't seem too pleased.'

'It takes all sorts,' Betty replied as she started to clear the table and tidy her comfortable and much loved, if somewhat shabby, kitchen.

Jenny positively hurled herself at her mother who had to raise her arm to protect both herself and the baby.

'Careful, love, you will knock us both over.'

'Mummy, Mummy, why were you making that noise? I could hear you outside. No-one would let me in. Who was hurting you? Mummy I was so frightened.'

'SSh, ' Rachel put an arm around the child, 'Look, here is your new brother.'

'What is his name?'

'We haven't decided yet, shall we ask Daddy?'

'Will Daddy be home soon?'

'I hope so.' Rachel smiled at Jenny and then glanced up at her mother standing in the doorway. Mary had watched quietly. Here were her flesh and blood, child, grandchildren. Why do I feel so detached? All I want is Edgar and peace and quiet. Why is life so messy? She walked towards the bed and looked at the sleeping infant.

'He looks a fine chap, well done, my dear. Now we must sort out some arrangements for the next few days.'

'Jenny could stay with you couldn't she?'

'Unfortunately that will not be possible. We will be away.' Jenny, who had been playing with her little brother's perfect toes, stopped and looked first at her grandmother and then at her mother. Hope rose in her heart.

'I suggest I take Jenny to Charles' parents.'

Jenny started bouncing on the bed.

'Oh! Yes please, yes please.'

For a moment, Mary was stung by the child's clear and enthusiastic preference for her other grandparents. Still it was not to be wondered at. No doubt Mr. and Mrs. Warr spoilt her dreadfully. Rachel lay back on the pillows. I cannot fight fate. She felt sure that Mrs. Warr would be over to see the baby immediately. What will be will be.

Mary had never been to Gladys and Albert's flat but it was easy enough to find. It was one of a large block with the unsavoury name of Peabody Buildings. She and Jenny climbed two flights of not very clean concrete steps. The sound of their feet echoed up and down the stair well. Jenny was chattering endlessly, something about a budgie called Joey which apparently belonged to the Warrs. They walked along a balcony. Jenny wriggled her hand free and ran ahead. She knocked loudly on the door and shouted through the letter box.

'Gran, Gran, I've got a new baby brother.'

The door opened as Mary reached it, Gladys looked shocked to see her there. The contrast between the two women was marked; could not have been greater, physically or socially. A fact that both women acknowledged. The only thing they had in common was their mutual disapproval of their respective children marrying each other. However, Mary was uncomfortably aware that Gladys - whether she knew it or not - now had the upper hand, morally. No matter how humble her origins, the woman was no fool. She had had, so Mary believed, five children even though only two had survived. It was clear to Mary that some awkward questions would be asked.

'Is that right? Has Rachel had the baby already?'

'Yes, earlier this afternoon, a boy.'

'You had better come in.' Jenny had already rushed in to tell Grandad the news.

Gladys took great pride in her home and Albert sometimes complained that she always had a duster in her hand. As Mary entered the living room she was struck first by the claustrophobically small size of the place, secondly by its extreme cleanliness and thirdly by Albert's welcoming smile. Whoever Charles got his rather stiff, imperious manner from, it clearly was not from his father.

'Shall I put the kettle on Mother? You will have a cup of tea won't you, Mrs. Cardew?'

'No thank you, Albert. I am already rather late, we have people coming tonight. I did tell Edgar I would not be long. We need to sort out arrangements for Jenny and, of course, Rachel and the baby.'

'But surely she must be in hospital; that baby has come much too early, poor little mite. We're not going to lose him, are we?' Gladys felt her heart being squeezed by fear. Surely history would not repeat itself yet again. Dear God, I lost three sons, not again dear Lord, she prayed silently.

Mary watched Gladys. This is going to be awkward.

'Oh, no. There is no fear of that. The baby seems perfectly healthy. I think the best thing would be for my maid, Susan, to come to stay with Rachel until she is strong enough to manage on her own.' Gladys said nothing. The two women looked at each other for several seconds.

There was nothing to say. Jenny seemed perfectly happy sitting on her Grandfather's knee, sucking her fingers. Mary felt too weary to make any comment about the probability of protruding teeth.

'I must go now. I will get Susan over to Rachel as soon as possible today. Unfortunately I did not have an opportunity to collect any of Jenny's clothes.' There was a pause. Obviously Gladys and Albert would want to see the baby. Somehow Mary could not think of the child as her grandchild yet. She had transport, the baby's other grandparents did not. The offer would have to be made.

'Would you like me to drive you over to Hendon now?'

Gladys smiled, a thin lipped smile that did not reach any other part of her face. Behind her steel-rimmed spectacles, her eyes were like pebbles. Of course, she wanted to see the baby but not with Mary Cardew around.

'That's very kind of you but no thanks. My son-in-law will take us over later. I want to get Jenny sorted out first. I've got a spare nightie here so she will be all right until tomorrow.'

Inwardly, Mary breathed a sigh of relief. Her duty was done. All she wanted was to get home. She would tell Bert to drive Susan to Hendon, once the girl had packed a case. Mary moved towards the door.

'Say goodbye to your grandmother, Jenny. Give her a kiss.' Albert stood up. Smiling, he walked towards Mary. She bent down, offered her cheek to the child and left.

Jack was not particularly pleased to be dragged half-way across London after a tiring day. He was a commissionaire at the Dorchester and had to be obsequious all the time, bowing and scraping to the toffs. At least ferrying his mother-in-law about kept him in her good books and he wouldn't have to listen to Caroline complaining about her varicose veins for a couple of hours. Gladys seemed very quiet. Jack would have expected her to be cock-a-hoop. Caroline had seemed surprised that the baby had arrived; he had thought it wasn't due until after theirs. Since he didn't take much notice of women's talk, he assumed he had misheard and that Caroline was put out because Rachel had stolen her thunder.

The door was on the latch when Gladys and Jack let themselves in. Rachel was asleep. Gladys looked at the baby in his crib. It was the one that she and Albert had bought for Jenny. She lifted the cover gently to see more of the sleeping infant. She was overwhelmed by such a mixture of emotions that she gasped. Rachel woke with a start. Gladys sat down on the edge of the bed. Her legs could no longer support her. Part of her was exultant. Everything she had ever suspected about

Rachel was true. It must be. Part of her was terrified, terrified of what Charles would say and do. Part of her ached with grief, a grandson to fill the aching void where her own sons should have been, was to be denied her. Jack called from downstairs,

'I'm making a pot of tea, do you both want one?'

The two women looked at each other. Gladys knew, with absolute certainty, that this baby was, as near as damn it, full term. It most definitely was not six or seven weeks early. So, the baby could not have been fathered by Charles.

'I think we have some talking to do, my girl, don't you?'

'Do you want tea or not?' Jack shouted.

'Well?'

'I'm too tired to talk Gladys, please. But I would like a cup of tea.'

'Just one cup, please, Jack.' Gladys called down.

'Isn't it good that the baby is such a good size, even though he came rather early.'

This was unexpected. Once Gladys had seen the baby and realised he could not be her grandson, it did not occur to her that Rachel would try to brazen it out. Jack came upstairs, puffing a bit. He knocked on the door and came in.

'How's the little mother, then?' He grinned at Rachel and glanced into the crib.

'He's a fine looking lad, just like his mum.' Again the grin, but it suggested something smutty, something unclean; humour or good nature had nothing to do with it.

While Jack was in the room, Gladys was thinking about what she should do.

Whatever her suspicions, she could prove nothing. Charles had been rather cool when she had suggested that Rachel was not all he thought she was. If she, Gladys, opened her mouth, she could make a lot of trouble for herself. Charles was due home in five weeks. Let's see what happens, I'll bide my time.

'I won't be much longer, Jack. I'll just get some clothes and toys for Jenny and than we can be off.'

Rachel sipped her tea; so there was not going to be a show down. She did not know whether to feel relieved or apprehensive. After all, Gladys was bound to say something sooner or later. Was she just waiting until Charles came home?

Gladys came out of Jenny's bedroom with a pile of clothes and the child's favourite stuffed animal, a red and black rabbit. Jenny always took Benjy to bed with her, Gladys had made him.

'Your mother's maid should be here soon, will you be all right?'

'Yes, thank you.'

Gladys gave one last look at the sleeping baby. 'I hope he lets you sleep tonight. I expect you will be glad when Charles gets home.' She walked past the bed, to go down stairs. She did not kiss Rachel.

Susan was a great help to Rachel and the two young women soon established a routine that suited them both. Jenny came home after two days and she brought Grandad to see the new baby. Although Gladys had said very little to Albert, he was well aware of the undercurrent of antagonism between her and Rachel. He was, by nature, a peacemaker, so tried to jolly things along and was suitably admiring of the baby.

'Have you and Charles decided on a name?' Rachel, realising that the baby would have to be registered, had written to Charles to tell him of the 'premature' birth, reassure him that all was well and to ask him to suggest some names. Susan had posted the letter yesterday.

'I'm waiting to hear from Charles. We had not definitely decided on a name.'

At times Rachel felt so happy, it hurt. Nothing could harm her. The episode with Alec was a dream. The future was with Charles, Jenny and the baby. However, at 2 a.m. as she sat up in bed giving her son his feed, the cold hand of fear ran an icy finger down her spine. She stroked her baby's head and rocked him. Did she really have a future? Something awful was going to happen. With the morning light, Jenny came into bed with her; the baby made mewing noises like a kitten. How silly she was, she had nothing to fear.

Gladys had always dreaded the Post Office messenger boy coming to her door. Telegrams meant bad news.

'I can't open it Albert. Something had happened to Charles, I just know it.'

Albert smiled as he opened the telegram. He wished Gladys did not worry so muchbut he would not change her after all these years.

'Nothing to worry about, my dear. It's from Charles. He has got compassionate leave. He will be home the day after tomorrow.'

Gladys sat down. So, when Charles came home, the baby would be less than a week old. If the truth were going to come out, it was more likely to do so sooner rather than later. Gladys had kept away from the baby. Not because she could not love him but because she was frightened she would love him too much. If Charles learned the truth, Rachel would still have the baby; it was she, Gladys, who would lose yet again. Best to say nothing, she decided, what will be, will be.

Charles strode up the road. He felt ten feet tall, a son, his son, Stephen, after his uncle and Albert after his father. He could hardly wait to see him. Rachel had said everything was all right, even though he had come early. She would not have said that if it weren't true. Still, the commanding officer seemed to think he should take his leave earlier than planned. Not many C.O's were so understanding. He opened the front door and whistled. A woman, he did not know, came out of the kitchen.

'You must be Mr. Charles,' she said, 'I'm Susan. I work for Mrs. Cardew. I've been staying with your wife until she can manage on her own.' Charles grinned at her.

'Where's my son and heir?'

'Upstairs, sir, with your wife, they are having a rest. Jenny is with your mum and dad. Her uncle Jack came over to fetch her.'

Charles put down his kit bag and bounded up the stairs two at a time.

He burst into the bedroom and stopped in his tracks. Rachel was lying, her body curved around a sleeping baby. He was encircled by her body and arms. Protected and safe, sleeping with his arms above his head; his fists curled and his head turned towards his mother's breast. He made little sucking movements with his lips but otherwise was still; the slight movement of his chest, the only indication that he was alive. Charles touched his cheek with a forefinger. The tiny head moved around, the mouth seeking hopefully. Rachel stirred. Charles sat on the bed. He wanted to sing and shout, my son, my son. Oh, what good times we will have together. I will teach you to play chess. We will go everywhere together. He touched the tiny clenched fist and immediately the fingers opened and clutched his. He felt tears in his eyes and realised that Rachel was watching him. He bent over and kissed her with great care and gentleness.

'What a clever girl you are.' Rachel smiled. The future starts here, she thought. Susan brought a tray with tea things for them.

'The midwife will be here soon.' said Susan.

'Does she come every day?' asked Charles. As Susan went downstairs, Rachel said, 'Send the midwife straight up when she comes. I expect you want to have a wash and change after all that travelling.' Charles just sat beaming, holding Rachel's hand and stroking the baby's head.

'Will you go to collect Jenny afterwards? She will be so pleased to see you.'

'Yes, but I want to see this young man properly first and make sure the midwife tells me all I need to know, so that I can look after you and Stephen. What do you think of the name? It was one of the ones you chose wasn't it?'

Rachel nodded, she could feel her heart thumping. She did not want Charles around when the midwife came.

'Mother will be pleased, she had a brother called Stephen. He was killed in the First World War. You know, you don't have to be around for the midwife. I know you will look after us and Jenny is desperate to see you.'

'Well all right, I'll get washed and changed and if she hasn't come, I'll set off for Mum's. If she comes every day, I can always see her tomorrow."

Jenny ran to the front door, she opened it and flung her arms around her father's legs. She clung to him so that he was totally unable to walk. Gladys and Albert came to the door; there was much hugging, kissing hand-shaking and slaps on the back. They eventually managed to get into the living room. Life was perfect, Charles thought. Loving parents, a loving wife, a loving daughter and now a son who would love and be loved by me. No-one could ask for more.

'And what do you think of your new brother?'

'He's very nice but what is his name? Mummy won't tell me, she said we had to wait until you came home.'

'Shall we call him Stephen?'
Jenny thought for a moment. 'What do you think Benjy?' She made the toy rabbit waggle its ears. 'Benjy thinks it's a good idea.'

'She has had her tea, son. Are you going to take her home tonight?'

'Yes, Mum. I want all my family under one roof.' He smiled and put his arms around her. 'Thanks for all you have done and you Dad. We could not have managed without you. The sooner I am out of the army the better. Then we can be a real family.'

Gladys and Albert watched from the balcony as Charles and Jenny walked hand in hand down the road. Albert put his arm around Gladys. Once again, he was reminded of what a frail little woman she was. Life hadn't been easy for her but everything looked rosy now. Everyone knew that the war would soon be over then Charles would be home for good. Life would be perfect.

'Cooee, Mrs Warr, shall I come up?' Rachel never knew when the midwife would come but hopefully not for much longer. Jenny and Charles had gone to the shop, with luck, the midwife would be gone before they returned.

'Yes, Sister, come in.' Charles had insisted that Rachel stayed in bed and her breakfast tray was still on the end of the bed, even though it was gone 11 a.m.

'My, you're being spoilt!'

'Yes, my husband came home last night.'

'Well, that is good news, is he pleased with his son?'

'Absolutely delighted. He arranged for Susan to go back to my mother's immediately. He wants to be in charge and do everything himself.'

'Mmmm, well don't be surprised if that doesn't last. Men soon get tired of dirty nappies.'

'Well actually, I was wondering if you need to come after today. Everything is going so well. I could always come to the clinic if I have any worries.'

Sister picked up the sleeping infant and started to undress him.

'You know, it's only a week since you had him.' She weighed him.

'His weight is good; he has regained his birth weight and a bit besides.'

'So you will leave us to it then will you?'

Usually mothers were happy to see the midwife for the full ten days. Still, everything was going well and she had a lot of other mothers at the moment.

'All right, Mrs. Warr but you must promise to come to clinic in four or five days and if there are any problems before that, you must let me know.'

Rachel felt an overwhelming sense of relief. She smiled broadly as Sister left. Jenny and Charles were walking up the street as the midwife let herself out of the front door.

'That's the nurse who looks after Mummy and Stephen.'

'Here's the key, you run on ahead, I want to check with the nurse that everything is all right.'

'You must be Mr. Warr, your wife is so pleased you are home. In fact, I believe you want to do me out of a job.'

Charles looked puzzled.

'Your wife said she can do without me now.'

'Is that wise, Sister? Don't you have to keep a special eye on premature babies?'

'Whatever makes you think your baby is premature? Your wife went full-term and it was a normal delivery. The baby was a good weight and has gained since. I don't think you will have any problems at all. But I have made your wife promise that you will contact me if you are worried about anything.'

Charles stood in a daze; he felt as though he had been punched in the chest and could not breathe. Rachel had lied to him, why?

Jenny ran straight upstairs, 'Daddy is talking to the nurse, can I hold Stephen now?'

Rachel felt her heart lurch. This was it. Still, I must assume nothing has been said.

'Mummy, what's the matter? Can I hold Stephen?'

'No, not now, dear. Just go downstairs and ask Daddy if he will make me a cup of tea.'

Charles was sitting at the kitchen table. Why did she lie? There could only be one reason. She was trying to hide something, something to do with Stephen. There was only one thing a woman in Rachel's circumstances would want to hide from her husband. That was when the baby was conceived. He thought back to when he was on leave, the end of July. So the baby could not be due until about the end of April, nearly six weeks away. Charles put his head in his hands. He felt sick. He could hear Jenny clattering down stairs. She rushed into the kitchen.

'Mummy says, please can you make her a cup of tea.' Charles moved around the kitchen like a robot, not speaking. Grown-ups are funny, Jenny thought, one minute they are all happy and jolly and the next, they scarcely speak to you. Still I can always rely on Benjy, he's my best friend.

Rachel sat in bed, Stephen was lying beside her, he would need feeding soon. I will know by the expression on his face. But if he knows, what am I going to do? He can't make me give Stephen up; can he throw me out? If he did, where would I go? For the second time that week, Rachel thought about Alec. This is stupid, I don't know that there is a problem yet. She heard Charles coming up stairs. She tried to take some deep breaths but her chest felt as though it were in a vice. She glanced up and smiled as he came in but her face felt stiff. He knew; his face was white and his eyes seemed to bore straight into her brain.

'Done all the shopping, dear. You were very quick.'

He raised an eyebrow, 'Too quick?' He handed her the cup of tea.

'I'm going to take Jenny over to my mother's,' he said, 'she can stay the night. I'll see you later.'

He is going to get Jenny out of the way and it will give him a chance to check up on things with his bloody mother. Won't she enjoy putting the knife in. What am I going to do? She paced up and down the bedroom. Her mouth felt dry. She could hardly swallow. Her brain was like a gramophone needle stuck in the same groove. What am I going to do? She could not settle, she could not rest. I can't face him, he is so cold when he is angry. She thought of the time, early in their marriage, when she had bought a pretty casserole dish and he had ranted and raved at her. They could not afford such extravagance. She wasn't at home with her wealthy family now. What was the matter with her? What was she thinking of? On and on he went. He would not listen to her explanations. It would be useful, she could make stews with it, in the oven. At this, he had screamed, why couldn't she make stews on the stove, in a saucepan, like his mother? Then came the silence. For two whole days he would not speak to her. Going to bed was the worst time. He was rigid with disapproval and anger. He flinched if she touched him.

She thought about the casserole dish which had caused so much trouble. She had never used it. She did not dare; frightened that if Charles saw it, it would remind him of her stupidity. She went to her wardrobe and felt at the back of the top shelf. It was there. She lifted it out and stroked the rounded sides and looked again at the decoration. It was a hand-made dish and whoever had made it had done so with love and artistry. It had beauty, she thought. Beauty is important - at least to me it is. If Charles could not see that, what else would he not see or understand?

He will never forgive me, that is certain. So if we stay together, life will be unbearable. If we don't stay together, I have nowhere to go. My mother would, as usual, put Edgar first and there was no-one else. She sobbed quietly. Alec has done this to me, he got me pregnant. I might have had a son by Charles one day and I would not be in this position now. Stephen stirred in his crib. It's time I fed him. He was a beautiful baby but what trouble his existence caused. What would she say if Charles wanted to know who the father was? I can't face it, she thought. Tears streamed down her face and onto Stephen's head as she held him to her breast. There was no way out of this, she thought, this is not the beginning of the happy life I dreamed of. It is the end of everything.

She fed and then placed the baby carefully back in his crib. He was soon asleep. She stroked his cheek. What future will you have, my baby? You would be better off without me. She glanced at her watch, it was three o/clock. What time would Charles be back, he had not said. She could prepare a meal, behave as though everything was normal.

She felt sick with fear. She sat down in the kitchen, put her head in her arms and wept.

She woke with a start as the front door slammed shut. Charles was back. She got up quickly and went to put water in the kettle. Behave as though everything is normal, she thought. Charles came into the kitchen. The expression on his face terrified her. His hazel eyes had always been his most noticeable feature, now they seemed to totally dominate his face. They stripped her mind bare. Once again she felt that he could see inside her head. He would listen to no excuses, he would have no compassion; he had been made a fool of, by her. There was no forgiveness, no future.

'How long did you think you would be able to deceive me?' The words were whispered but impregnated with an implacable hatred that made Rachel gasp. She wished he would hit her, that would discharge some of the tension that crackled between them.

'How long?' he repeated. She noticed that his hands were shaking.

'You are a trollop, a tart, a fornicator. You have used my parents to look after our child so that you can go out and open your legs for anything in a uniform!'

'No! No! It wasn't like that. Believe me.' she sobbed.

'Why should I believe anything you say. You let me believe that the bastard upstairs was mine. But he can't be, can he?' He gripped her by the shoulders and shook her, hard. She tried to put her arms around him but he pushed her away from him. His face was absolutely drained of colour and he seemed to have difficulty breathing.

'Mother tried to warn me but I didn't believe her. She told me you were out all the time. Can I be sure Jenny's mine?'

'Your mother never liked me, she always tried to come between us.'

'Don't you dare criticise my mother. Why should she like you? Who wants a prostitute for a daughter-in-law?'

'I was only unfaithful once and it wasn't my fault, I never intended it to happen.'

'Oh, really and that makes it all right does it?'

'He got me drunk, I didn't know what was happening. I only wanted to take Jenny away from the bombings for a weekend.'

'And who, pray, is he?'

'Alec, I can't remember his other name.'

Charles looked at her in total disbelief.

'Bloody clever of Mr. Alec. He doesn't mind screwing you but he doesn't leave his name. How very convenient for him.'

'What are we going to do, Charles? I do love you really. I'm sorry truly I am. Please forgive me, please let's try again. No-one need ever know.'

He looked at her. She had borne a child by another man. She had a son, he Charles did not. Every time he looked at that bastard child, he would be reminded of what she had done. He could not bear it.

'Please darling, it's because we have spent so much time apart. Come to me, let me put my arms around you. Let me comfort you.' He stared at her in disbelief. He thought back to his last leave. She had been so keen to make love then. Why? Because she already knew she was pregnant. She came towards him with her arms wide. 'Please, darling.' He had never felt such total loathing for anything or anybody. He wanted to take a knife and carve harlot, on her forehead.

He wanted to hurt her. He wanted to hear her scream in agony, as he was screaming now - inside. Her hands came to rest gently on his shoulders. She could not be sure what he would do. Fear prickled in her stomach. Suddenly he drew back his head and with a great rasping in his throat, he spat in her face. He turned abruptly and went out of the house, slamming the front door behind him.

Gladys and Albert tried to behave as though everything was normal. There was Jenny to think of. They all had tea together but it was a very subdued meal and afterwards, Jenny just wanted to sit on her grandfather's lap and be cuddled. Poor little scrap, he thought. God knows what is going to happen now. He thought of all that Gladys and Charles had talked about. Albert had suspected that all was not as it should be when Stephen was born but had kept his thoughts to himself. What was the old saying, it's a wise man who knows his own father. Of course, if Stephen were not Charles' son, then Rachel had done wrong. But these were difficult times. She was young and lonely and goodness only knows how many other women had done the same. They were not married to Charles, that was the difference. Albert loved his son and was very proud of him but knew that deep down, they had little in common. Charles was like his mother in many ways. He had her determination and her strong belief in right and wrong. Life for them both was very much a matter of black and white. Albert, on the whole, believed that life was mostly shades of grey. We will just have to wait and see, he sighed, gave Jenny a hug . 'Come on, little lady, time for bed.'

Rain was pouring down and strong winds lashed it into his face. Charles put his collar up as high as he could and bowed his head. He wished he had put on his army trench coat but when he left the house, rain was the last thing he had been thinking about. His hair was plastered to his head. Even though he was walking as fast as he could, his teeth were chattering with the cold. He had been walking for hours and it was dark. The streets were deserted. Anyone with any sense was safe at home in the warm, in front of a roaring fire.

Jenny would be in bed by now, at least she was safe and warm. I'll go to my parents' house, Charles decided. I've got to talk to someone. He realised that although he had not taken much notice of where he was going, he was not too far from Peabody Buildings. Perhaps it was instinct .in times like these, to return to the nest. He smiled grimly to himself. When did he come home, how long ago? Only two short days, then he had everything. Now his life was in tatters around him.

He walked into his parents' living room. Gladys jumped up, with a cry.

'Oh! son, you will catch your death of cold. Where have you been? Take that wet jacket off, come and sit by the fire. Put the kettle on, Dad. He needs something warm inside him.' Gladys bustled round clucking and giving little cries of dismay, as Charles peeled off wet socks and revealed that not only was his jacket wet, so was his shirt. She rushed out and came back with Albert's warm dressing - gown. Charles could feel himself relax. Here he was safe. No-one could hurt him here. Albert came in with a large mug of tea.

'I've put a shot of whisky in, son,' he winked, 'to keep the cold out.'

Charles clasped the mug with both hands. He could feel the circulation coming back into his fingers and pins and needles in his toes. His shoes were steaming on the fender. Gladys had taken his jacket, shirt and trousers away but Charles couldn't worry about that now. He felt drowsy with the warmth and the whisky. Why couldn't life always be like this?

Charles told his parents of the scene he had had with Rachel. Gladys had folded her arms and adopted an expression that had righteous indignation stamped through it. Albert, on the other hand, felt an overwhelming sadness. Sometimes being in the right did you no good at all.

'So what are you going to do?'

Gladys went to speak but Albert held up his hand to silence her.

'No, Mother, this is for Charles to decide. We must not interfere. You know we will do what we can, but it is your life. You have got to think of those children.'

'Dad, I've only got one child to think of and she's upstairs.' Gladys knew in that moment that her instinct to keep away from that baby had been correct. She knew with, absolute certainty, that she would never see the child again. She got up and went into the kitchen. She went to the sink and clung to it until her knuckles showed white. That baby is nothing to do with me; he is not my grandchild. My grandchild is upstairs. Perhaps, Caroline and Jack will give me a grandson. That's what I must concentrate on.

Albert regarded his son and was at a loss to know what to say. Had he been in the same position, at the end of the First World War, which he supposed he could have been, he knew what he would have done. That baby would have been his baby and he would have made sure that it soon had a brother or sister. Nothing like a house full of children to keep a woman faithful.

'You know you will have to go back to talk to her.'

'But Dad, what is there to say? This is the finish.'

'Well then, there are loose ends to be tied up. You can't just walk away.'

'I can't bear to go back to that house, now that I know.'

'So what will happen to Jenny, you can't just take her away from her mother, she's little more than a baby herself.'

'What sort of mother is she likely to be?'
Albert sighed. 'What are you going to do then?'

'I shall stay in the army and of course divorce Rachel, on the grounds of her adultery. I will apply for custody but as Jenny is so young, I don't suppose I shall get it '

'Charles, for God's sake don't do anything hasty. You two have had so little time together with the war and everything; give yourselves a chance.'

'It's not me that's done wrong, Dad. Anyone would think you were on her side.'

'It's not a question of taking sides; it's a question of making the best of a bad job. After all Jenny did not ask to be born, how is all this going to affect her?'

Charles stared into the fire. He knew in his heart that his father was doing his best but it wasn't good enough. Charles knew he could not live with the deceit and that was that. He supposed he owed it to Rachel to tell her so. The sooner he got it over with the better.

'Can I borrow some dry things, Dad? I'll go back, but I'm not making any promises. I will tell her straight, I will provide for Jenny but that is all. She has brought this on herself.'

I wonder if he will ever learn, thought Albert. Is this the arrogance of youth, or will he always be so sure that he is right.

Rachel stood with Charles' saliva running down her face, it mingled with her tears. She went to the sink and wiped it off her face but the tears would not stop. Her sorrow was so great that she was in physical pain. She knew now why poets always referred to the heart when talking about feelings. She could feel the knife that was Charles' words twist and turn in her heart till her flesh cried out in torment. There is nothing left now, there is no reason to go on living. Everyone will be better off without me. No-one will grieve, Jenny will soon forget me and Stephen will never have known me.

She felt suddenly calm. The worst had happened but she knew what she was going to do. Jenny was safe, Stephen was the problem. She did not know if or when Charles would come back and in any case she was frightened to think of what he might do, after his behaviour this afternoon. Who could she leave Stephen with and what could she give as a reason for leaving him? She suddenly remembered Betty. That was the answer. She would leave her front door open, push a note through Betty's door and then run as fast as she could. She looked in the kitchen drawer for a piece of paper but there was none. She scrabbled in her handbag and eventually found a crumpled piece right at the bottom. She quickly flattened it and wrote,

Betty,
 Please look after Stephen
    Thank you and God bless
        Rachel

She ran upstairs. Stephen was sound asleep. He would not be due for another feed for a couple of hours. Betty would know what to do. She kissed the baby on the head and could feel the tears starting. 'Goodbye, my darling.'

She crept out of the house carefully pulling the door to, but not closing it. It was quite dark, a miserable, wet night; what does it matter, thought Rachel, as she walked to Betty's front door. With great care, she pushed the note through the letter box. She waited. No-one came. Fortunately the kitchen was in the back of the house, so it was unlikely that anyone would hear the letter box rattle. She looked up and down the street. No-one was around. She gave two loud knocks and then ran as fast as she could until she could get round a corner and be out of sight. Her heart was beating so loudly, it sounded like a drumbeat in her ears. She waited until she felt calmer and then walked to the nearest bus-stop. She caught a bus to Charing Cross and then walked down to the Embankment.

She looked at the river, swollen with winter rain. The surface of the water looked sluggish and viscous, by the light of the moon. She walked along for a while until she was sure no-one was around. I came into the world naked and naked I shall leave it. Carefully, she removed her clothes and folded them into a pile. The wind tugged at her hair and made her shiver. She stood looking up at the moon and remembered the night, only nine months ago, when that same moon had witnessed the act that led to her being here now. She pulled herself up onto the river bank wall. The wind and rain beat against her but she knew this was nothing compared to the cold arms of the river waiting below. She jumped. The shock as her body hit the water knocked the breath from her. She felt herself dragged down, down. Her lungs ached, why could she not breathe in the rank-smelling, freezing water? One deep breath, to fill her lungs, while she was below the surface and that would be the end. Then her head broke the surface. Too late. She was buffeted and dragged along by the under tow. She used her arms to protect her face from bits of wood and other detritus. She could feel her body becoming numb with the cold. She welcomed it. Soon my mind will be numb too.

Suddenly she felt a violent pain in her head. As she was carried down the river, she had crashed into some kind of mooring pole. She could feel herself losing consciousness. Thank God, she thought, this is the end, at last. She was slipping away from life, she started to feel warm. She imagined she was like the picture of Ophelia, in the National Gallery; she was floating down a river in that. What a pity that I have not got flowers in my hair, like Ophelia, Rachel smiled to herself in the dark. She spread her arms wide. There was a sickening jolt which made her scream in agony. It felt as though someone was trying to pull her hair from her scalp. She felt her head and realised that somehow her long hair had become wrapped around some wooden planking. As she looked up, she could see that the planking had become wedged in metal steps which led from the Embankment, down to the river. She was stuck. Short of wrenching her hair out completely, she could not free herself.

The young policeman shone his torch down by the steps. There was no traffic and no-one about, on this miserable evening. Just his luck to be on duty tonight. He thought he had heard something but it was difficult to tell. No-one would last long in that, he thought, as he looked at the dark surface of the water. Suddenly there was a glimmer of something white. He walked towards the steps. He climbed over the gate and leaned on the rail.

'Anyone there?' he shouted. There was something, he was sure. His boots rang against the wrought iron steps. Then he saw her, when he was halfway down. It was a woman. He leaned forward and grabbed her arm

'Leave me! Leave me!' she screamed, 'I want to die.'

'Don't be so bloody silly, woman.' He managed to drag her round to the bottom of the steps. The wooden plank, entangled in her hair, made it very difficult to manoeuvre her up onto the steps. The fact that she was naked and fighting him, made it worse. In desperation, he slapped her face. She lay still and then started sobbing. At least she wasn't fighting him any more. He half dragged, half lifted her onto the second step. He needed to get her out of the freezing water.. He managed to drape his macintosh cape over her and then started to untangle her hair so he could free her from the plank. All the time he worked to free her, she sobbed.

'Now then, love, it can't be as bad as that. We'll soon get you warm and dry.'

'Why couldn't you leave me. Don't you understand, I want to die. Please leave me, I beg you.'

The policeman took no notice, he made sure he stood between Rachel and the water as he dragged her to her feet. He wrapped the cape even tighter around her and half walked, half carried her up the steps. At the top he lifted her over the gate and still hanging on to her, climbed over himself. He held her tightly in his arms, hoping that some of the warmth from his body would stop her shaking and shivering. He half carried her to the kerb and fumbling in his pocket, he got out his whistle. After a few minutes, he saw a taxi. He whistled and waved with his free hand. When the taxi stopped, he said,

'Here mate, take us to Charing Cross Hospital. I've just fished this one out of the river.'

Once inside the hospital, Rachel was quickly put into a hospital gown. She was examined for injuries and told the doctor that she had recently had a baby. The doctor and nurse exchanged glances. Emotional disturbance after the birth of a baby was not uncommon.

'We had better notify your husband, he will be worried about you.' the doctor said. Rachel started screaming; she tried to get out of the bed. The nurse grabbed her but Rachel fought and lashed out. Her screams got louder. Other medical staff came to assist. Rachel was quickly restrained and it was decided to give her something to quieten her down.

They had not managed to get her name or address. The policeman was waiting to take details because, obviously if the woman had tried to commit suicide, there would have to be criminal proceedings against her.

'Good evening, Constable. I don't think we will get much out of our patient tonight, we have had to sedate her. Quite frankly, I think it would be better if she were transferred to a psychiatric hospital. I am going to arrange for her to be taken to Friern Barnet.'

'Right, well I had better get back to my beat. I will make a report and see what happens tomorrow.' That's my good deed for the day, he decided. Still remembering the woman's sobs and entreaties, he wondered how much of a good deed she thought he had done her!

Charles walked slowly up the street. This was not going to be easy. He was surprised to find the front door not shut properly. He went inside, closing it behind him. The house was in darkness. He walked from room to room and then went upstairs. Rachel and the baby were not there.

Chapter 5

It was Janet who heard the knock at the door. She skipped down the hallway and opened it. No-one was there. As she closed the door, a scrap of paper caught her eye. She picked it up, There was a name and address on it, the address of someone called Alec. She walked back to the kitchen and showed the paper to her mother.

'There was no-one at the door, but I found this.'

Betty looked puzzled. 'I don't know anyone called Alec.' She turned the paper over and read Rachel's message. Silently she handed it to Bob.

'For Christ's sake, Betty, whatever next. Haven't you done enough?'

'Something serious must have happened. I'll have to go along to see if that baby is all right.'

'You're just an unpaid, bloody babysitter. It's not right. Where's the husband then? It's his responsibility.'

'I know love, but I can't do nothing. I'll just pop up and check what's happening.'

Betty was surprised to find the front door open and the house in darkness. She called out and wandered from kitchen to living room. No sign of life. She walked upstairs and called again. No reply. She went into the main bedroom and found Stephen in his crib, asleep. She sat on the bed. What do I do now? Bob would hit the roof if she took the baby back. But he can't be left here. Where on Earth were his parents? Rachel should not be going out and about yet. Where was Jenny? Well, this would teach her not to get involved.

She took a deep breath, picked Stephen up and marched back to the house. Bob looked up from his paper, his jaw dropped, but before he could say a word, Betty started.

'It's an absolute disgrace, Bob, this poor little scrap was alone in an empty house. I think its a matter for the police.' Bob closed his mouth and then grinned.

'First sensible thing you've said all evening.'

Stephen started to whimper. Betty felt his nappy, he was soaked. The next problem would be feeding him. Betty thought Rachel was breastfeeding. Surely she would be back soon, what if she wasn't? Bob stood up.

'I'll walk round to the police station and tell them what has happened.'

'Had you better pop into Sister Burns and tell her too? Unless Rachel comes back soon, we have nothing to feed Stephen with.'

'Right, it strikes me that this kid's mother is totally irresponsible.' He walked down the hall feeling thoroughly disgruntled. To add insult to injury, when he reached the front door, he realised it was raining, hard.

The station sergeant said he would send someone round as soon as he could. Sister Burns said she would bring a bottle etc. in case it was needed. When Bob got back home, his eldest, Janet was holding the baby and John and Martin were standing close by, obviously fascinated.

'You two lads,' Bob said, 'just run up to 52 and see if anyone is there yet.'

As the boys ran up the hall, Betty shouted.

'Don't shut the front door of 52, Rachel may not have taken her key.'

Sister Burns arrived first, no more pleased than Bob had been at being dragged out on such a miserable, wet evening. By now Stephen was showing clear signs of hunger.   'Can I use your stove to sterilise this bottle, please? I'm going to have to make him a feed.'

'I don't think he has ever had a bottle, Sister.'

'Well, unless his mother comes back soon, we have no choice. How long has she been gone?'

'It must be the best part of a couple hours. She put a note through the door.'

Sister tutted. Young women, these days, had no idea.

The policeman arrived just as Sister tried to persuade Stephen to take a bottle. He pushed the teat out of his mouth. He pulled faces. He kept nuzzling Sister's bosom. He wailed plaintively. The three children stood in a semi-circle silently watching. The policeman tried to ask Betty some questions while Bob leaned back in his chair, with his eyes closed. I don't know what I've done to deserve this, he thought. Eventually, Stephen gave up his resistance and accepted his feed.

After getting as much information as he could, the policeman said he would check to see if either Mr. or Mrs. Warr had come home.

'I'll come with you,' said Betty. 'I need to get some clean things for the baby.' 52 was still in darkness. Betty quickly got what she needed.

'Had I better take the crib too?' she asked the policeman.

'I suppose you'd better, if you are looking after him until the parents return.'

'Mmm, I suppose so.' She could not imaging what Bob would say.

66

'It's a criminal offence to abandon a baby, you know. When Mr. and Mrs. Warr get back, they're going to be in hot water.'

After some discussion between the policeman, Sister Burns, Bob and Betty, it was decided that Stephen would stay where he was until tomorrow. If there were still no signs of the parents then, a more permanent arrangement would have to be made. Bob looked at the children's faces, they were obviously delighted. He wondered if they would feel the same should Stephen wake them up in the middle of the night

Charles sat on the bed. The house was empty; not only was the baby gone, so was his crib. Charles did not know if Rachel had made any friends nearby. He could only assume that she had gone to her mother's. He put on his trench coat, shut the front door and walked to the 'phone-box.

'Hello, Mr. and Mrs. Cardew's house.' Charles pressed button A and heard the money clatter into the box.

'Hello, Susan, it's Charles Warr, would you ask Mrs. Cardew if I could have a word with her.'

'She's giving a dinner party, Sir. I don't think I can interrupt.'

'Well, it is very important. You see, Rachel is not at home and wherever she's gone, she's taken the baby with her.'

'Oh dear, I'll see if I can have a word with Madam, but Rachel and the baby are not here.'

Charles waited, for what seemed like hours He did not know what he was going to say to his mother-in-law now. If Rachel was not there, it was not likely that her mother would know where she was. How much did she know? Had Rachel confided in Mary; knowing both women, it did not seem likely.

'Hello, Mary Cardew, speaking.'

'I'm so sorry to have to 'phone you like this, Mrs. Cardew, but Rachel has gone missing with the baby. Has she been in touch with you this evening?'

Mary sighed, the storm clouds were gathering.

'No, Charles, I have heard nothing. Are you sure she hasn't just gone to her neighbour. Betty I think she's called. She helped Rachel a lot, you know.'

'Where does she live?'

'Number 50, I think, it's two doors further down.'

'Thanks, thanks a lot. I'm sure that's the explanation. I am sorry to bother you like this. Bye.'

'Goodbye, Charles.' Mary put the 'phone down. She stood for a few moments. She looked at her reflection in the large hall mirror. She could never have been called beautiful, certainly not pretty but she was still a handsome woman. Let's just hope it's a storm in a teacup, still there was a knot of anxiety in the pit of her stomach. Beneath the apparently coherent conversation, she had had with Charles, she had picked up a very high level of agitation. Something had happened. No doubt I shall find out what soon enough. She patted her hair into place and assumed a gracious smile as she glided, apparently serenely, into the dining room, to her guests.

Charles called at number 50 on his way back from the telephone box. Bob opened the door. Although he vaguely recognised the young man, he did not know who he was.

'Good evening, I'm Charles Warr, we live at 52.'

'You'd better come in.' Bob walked heavily up the hall and into the kitchen.

'We've found Stephen's father, Betty. He's looking for Rachel, I expect.'

'Oh! I am glad to see you, we have your son upstairs. What an evening we've had. What on earth has happened? We got this note through the door.' Betty scrabbled in her apron pocket and pulled out a scrap of paper. She handed it to Charles. He read the message and then turned the piece of paper over. His hands shook slightly as he folded the paper and put it in his pocket.

'Rachel seemed very upset today, so I took Jenny over to my parents. I have no idea where she could have gone. I couldn't believe it, when I got back and found the house empty.' He had no intention of letting Bob and Betty know any more about the events of the day or that Stephen was not his son.

Bob rubbed his hands together, with relief.

'You will want to take Stephen home, won't you. I expect Rachel will be back soon. You know what women are like, up one minute down the next.'

He winked, one man of the world to another. Charles paused, he had not considered that. He most certainly did not want the baby in the house. Supposing Rachel did not come back, he would have to look after him and feed him. What with? Betty watched and eventually said. 'We had to call the police out because we did not know what had happened. There could have been an accident. Perhaps you had better go round to the station.'

'Yes, I'm sure you're right. I had better report that Rachel's missing.'

'Then, it's better if Stephen stays here tonight, isn't it, Bob?' Bob nodded, 'I suppose so.'

Rachel had refused to give her name either at Charing Cross Hospital or at Friern Barnet. She felt groggy and strangely detached from reality. All she wanted was to be left alone. Why couldn't I just die, then I would find peace. She was taken to a side ward and a doctor came to examine her. He kept on asking questions. Where did she live? What was her husband's name? She had recently had a baby, was it a boy or girl? What was it called? Where did her parents live? On and on and on. Interspersed between all these questions she was asked again and again, what is your name? Rachel clamped her hands over her ears and started to scream. Her screams reverberated up and down the ward. The other psychiatric patients started to moan and cry out. They were frightened by the sudden noise. Night nurses moved quickly around the ward, soothing and calming the occupants. Rachel continued to scream.

'Leave me alone, for Christ's sake, leave me alone.' The doctor tried to put his hand on her shoulder, in a comforting, reassuring way. Rachel snarled and grabbed his arm. She sank her teeth into the back of his hand. The doctor cried out and hit her, hard on the side of her face, with the flat of his other hand.

'Nurse!' he shouted. He took his handkerchief from his pocket and wrapped it tightly around his left hand which was bleeding badly.

'This patient needs to be restrained.' The nurse hurried out and quickly returned with two colleagues, one of whom carried a heavy canvas garment. Rachel continued to scream and lash out, kicking and punching anything within reach. By now she and the doctor were locked in a writhing embrace on the floor. Rachel lay on her back. The doctor sat astride her chest. There were smears of blood on her face and arms from the doctor's hand. She was heaving and gasping for breath and crying great gulping sobs.

With quiet efficiency, the staff got her into the strait-jacket. She made no protest. She had expended the last of her energy and was as limp and unresisting as a rag doll. They gently helped her to her feet.

'Is she all right here, or do you want her in side ward 4? ' Staff Nurse Smith asked.

'I doubt that you will have any trouble tonight but for her own safety, we'll move her,' the doctor replied.

Rachel allowed herself to be half led, half carried to the new side ward. She was losing blood after having Stephen and her legs were shaking.

None of this is real, none of it matters. She was placed gently on the floor. It was soft. She imagined she was at home in bed. She barely felt the prick of another injection of sedative. She dreamt she was flying. Her arms stretched wide, her hair streamed behind her. She looked up at the sun and felt herself drawn higher and higher, her skin was glowing, giving off the reflected heat and light from the sun. Peace at last, she smiled as she slept.

Charles walked into the police station. He felt edgy and strangely defensive. He had done nothing wrong.

'My name is Charles Warr, I wish to report my wife is missing.' The station sergeant told him to sit down for a minute and he would get someone to take details. Charles sat down on a hard wooden bench. Why is it, he thought, that the police always make you feel guilty. It was not long before another policeman came to Charles and directed him to an interview room.

'My name is Jackson, D.C. Jackson, Now I need to get some information.   'Name?'

'Charles Warr.'

'Address?'

'52. Redburn Street.'

'Wife's name?'

'Rachel'

'Age?'

'24.'

'Appearance?'

'5 feet 10 inches, shoulder length hair, brown and brown eyes.'

'Have you a photograph?'

'Not with me.'

'How long has your wife been missing?'

'Since 5 p.m. this afternoon.'

The policeman raised his eyebrows. 'It's only 10 p.m. now Sir. What makes you think she is missing. Maybe she has just popped out to see a friend and forgotten about the time.'

'My wife had a baby a week ago and when I got home this evening, not only was she missing, the baby was gone as well. Fortunately, I found that my neighbour was looking after him. You see, my wife had written a note and pushed it through the neighbour's door.'

'I see, do you have the note, Sir?'

Charles felt in his pocket and handed over the scrap of paper. The policeman read it and then turned the paper over.

'Who is this Alec?' Charles could feel his face flush.

'I don't know?'

'Could your wife be visiting him, could he be a friend?'

Charles could feel the tension inside him increase; with a great effort he spoke in, what he hoped was, a normal voice.

'I don't know, Officer.'

'There's a telephone number here, Sir. I think the best thing would be for me to give the gentleman a ring.' The policeman left the room. Charles sat, numb with disbelief that this could be happening to him.

'I've managed to get through to Mr. Davies. He could not help us much, he has not seen your wife for some time.' The officer looked searchingly at Charles.

'Are you able to think of any reason why your wife might have gone somewhere without telling you? What about her parents?'

'No, I've all ready checked there.'

'Did you have a disagreement about anything?'

Charles paused, fractionally too long, before he replied. 'No.'

'What time was it when you last saw your wife?'

'It was about 5 p.m.'

'How did she seem?'

'Well actually, she had seemed rather tired and tearful, so I took our daughter, Jenny, to my parents. So Rachel could have some peace.'

'I see, so you left the house with Jenny at about 5 p.m.'

'Oh, no. Actually, I took Jenny over earlier.'

'Then you came back. By the way, where do your parents live?'

'Camden Town.'

'So what time did you get back?'

'I suppose it was about 4.30 p.m. '

'And how was your wife then?'

Charles could feel sweat running down the middle of his back. His mouth was so dry, his tongue could hardly move.

'She seemed rather quiet.'

'And you went out again at 5 p.m., knowing that your wife was not quite herself?' The policeman's intense gaze made Charles squirm.

'I've not done anything wrong, as far as I knew, everything was all right when I went out again. She is the one who has gone off.' Charles could hear a shrill note creeping into his voice.

'Quite so, Sir, but abandonment of a child is a very serious matter. It is most fortunate that you have kind hearted neighbours who were willing to look after your son.'

My son! Charles thought, if only you bloody well knew.

'So where did you go, when you left the house at 5 p.m.?'

'I went for a walk.'

'Doesn't that seem a strange thing to do when your wife is' he flicked through his notes,' quiet and tearful. Wouldn't it have been better if you had stayed in and kept an eye on her?'

'I suppose so, but I didn't expect all this.'

'No, Sir, I am sure you didn't. Now while I was out 'phoning Mr. Davies, I asked the desk sergeant to check with local hospitals to see if your wife has been admitted. After all, she could have had an accident.' Charles nodded.

'The best thing you can do, is to go home and get some rest. Will you be able to care for the baby on your own or will your neighbours keep him?'

'They have said they will look after him.'

'So then if you go home, we will let you know when there is any news. Incidentally, if by any chance, we have not traced your wife by tomorrow morning, we could do with a recent photograph.'

'Right, thank you, Officer.' Charles got up and walked out; as he got to the door, he turned.

'Could I have the note my wife wrote, please?'

'I need to keep this as evidence, Sir. As I said abandonment is a very serious offence.'

'Could I just see the note for a minute?'

D.C.Jackson handed the note over and watched, without comment, as Charles scribbled Alec's name address and telephone number onto the back of an envelope.

'Good night, Officer.'

'Good night, Sir, try to get some rest.'

Charles stumbled as he walked down the steps and out into the street. At last, it had stopped raining. He turned up his collar and thrust his hands deep into his pockets. Although it was dry, it was still a raw night. A cold, bitter rage sat in Charles' stomach like a lump of lead. This Alec Davies had admitted knowing Rachel, how many other men did she know? Was Davies Stephen's father or was it some other unknown man? Rachel had been responsible for all that he had been through this evening. The humiliation was intolerable. Of one thing, Charles was now certain. He would not support or care in any way for some other man's bastard.

He let himself in and walked into the kitchen. It seemed like a lifetime since he and Rachel had stood there. He thought about what he had said, he did not regret a word. She had betrayed him. He did not want to sleep in their bed, he would be too forcefully reminded of her.

72

The smell of her skin would be on the sheets. He would never again share a bed with her, he must accept that. He got a spare blanket and made a makeshift bed on the settee, downstairs. He ached with exhaustion but when he lay down, he could not rest. He tossed and turned. Eventually, he must have drifted into an uneasy dream-filled sleep. He was at Alec Davies' house. He had forced his way in. He had a hammer in his hand and he was beating Davies on the head. No matter how hard or how frequently he smashed the hammer down, Davies still laughed. He sat up with a start. Sweat was pouring off him. The bang, bang, bang was not the sound of the hammer. Someone was at the front door. He staggered to his feet, walking like a drunk down the hall.

'Mr. Warr?'

'Yes.'

'We've managed to trace your wife, Sir. She has been admitted to Friern Barnet psychiatric Hospital. We thought you would be happier knowing where she is rather than leave it until the morning.'

'Thank you, Officer, is she all right?'

'I can't really say but I understand that the doctor, treating her, will speak to you in the morning. Are you O.K, Sir?' Charles had slumped against the door and for a moment it looked as though he would fall to the ground. He took a deep breath. 'Yes, I'm fine, it's been a very worrying time. 'The policeman smiled sympathetically. 'Yes, I'm sure it has. Still, I expect things will look better in the morning.'

When Rachel woke up, she was wholly unable to make out where she was. Nor could she understand why she could not move her arms. She seemed to be lying on the floor but it felt soft. It was too dark to see much. There seemed to be a window or was it a door? Whichever it was, a dim light shone through. She lay still and tried to remember what had happened but everything was confused. She felt bruised and her limbs ached. The top of her head felt very sore and her throat was parched. She tried to shout but the only sound she made was a pathetic croak. She tried to stand up but found it was impossible without her hands and arms to help her. She tried to roll over to get herself closer to the wall. She managed to struggle into a sitting position with her back leaning against the wall. That too felt soft. She pushed with her feet and legs and managed to slide her back up the wall, until she was standing. She felt very shaky indeed and feared that she might fall over. She took some deep breaths and continued leaning against the wall until she felt reasonably sure that her legs would not buckle beneath her.

She tried again to remember what had happened. She knew she had been in water but where and why? There was an oily, rank smell that she thought must be coming from her. She had splashed water in her face but that had been clean. She had been in her kitchen then. Why had she washed her face downstairs? She usually did that in the bathroom. She groaned, she felt so desperately tired but she must have something to drink.

Suddenly the light, from what she now decided was a window, was reduced. She stared hard and could just make out the outline of a head. Someone was looking in. Rachel tried to shout but her throat was parched.

'Help me!' she croaked.

It was enough. She heard a key turn in a lock and a nurse came in.

'Hello, my dear, are you feeling a bit better?' At this point, Rachel slid to the floor in a crumpled heap. She started to cry. The nurse knelt beside her and put an arm around her.

'Now then, my dear don't cry, you are safe here. We'll look after you.'

'But where am I? What's happened?'

'It seems you fell in the river and nearly drowned 'The events of the afternoon came rushing back. She cried out in despair.

'Let me die! Please, I beg you.'

The nurse stood up. 'Now that's just silly talk.You're a young woman with your whole life ahead of you. The police have made enquiries and let your husband know where you are. He must have been worried sick.'

'I won't see him, I won't see him, I won't see him.' Rachel started to rock and bang her head against the wall. We're going to have trouble with this one, Nurse Kershaw thought. I'd better let the doctor know she's awake. She soon returned with the doctor who was surprised that the sedative had worn off so quickly.

'Well, Mrs. Warr, I believe that is your name. We can't have this'. Rachel continued to mumble to herself and rocked backwards and forwards. Suddenly she turned to him.

'Why won't you let me die? There is nothing to live for.'

'Nonsense you have a husband and two children who need you.' Rachel sobbed as though her heart would break.

'Charles doesn't need me, he's never needed me and now after what I've done he just wants to get rid of me.'

'What have you done that's so terrible?'

'Committed adultery,' Rachel whispered.

'Well, you aren't the first and you won't be the last.'

'But the baby isn't my husband's. He found out today.'

'Oh! I see.'

'I won't see him, promise you won't make me see him.'

'We can't make you see him but wouldn't it help if you talked things over?'

'No! No! No!' Rachel's voice rose to a harsh croaking scream.

'All right, Mrs. Warr now calm down and let's see if we can make you more comfortable. Would you like a drink of water?'

'Yes, please.'

'Nurse, will you get a blanket and a pillow as well.'

'What is this place? Why am I in a strait jacket?'

'You were very distressed when you arrived and unfortunately, you attacked one of my colleagues. We had to put you in this padded cell because we were concerned you might hurt yourself'.

'Or someone else.' Rachel whispered.

'Yes, that's true.' The doctor looked at her, slumped, bedraggled, her hair in tatters, her face streaked with tears. She was still an extraordinarily fine looking woman. I do hope, the doctor thought, we will be able to help her to sort out her problems and help her to pick up the threads of her life.

Mary Warr sat at her dressing table. She carefully removed the pearl necklace and earrings then started to brush her hair. She could see Edgar in the mirror. He seemed preoccupied, distant.

'I think this evening went very well, my dear.'

Edgar made a non-committal grunt.

'As your lecture, at Cambridge, was such a success, don't you think it would be advisable to organise something similar at another university?'

Edgar looked at her sourly.

'Will you be able to cope with all your family commitments?'

Mary sighed, since Edgar had no children, he would never understand that you never really severed the umbilical cord. He certainly would never understand all the problems that Rachel could present. Mary wondered if she were abnormal because she could not summon up more active concern about Rachel's apparent disappearance. Obviously, she did not discuss the matter with Edgar, he would be appalled by such dramatic behaviour. She would drive over to Hendon in the morning and see if there was any news.

She got into bed and sat, almost self-consciously beside her husband, aware that she was nowhere in his thoughts.

'I think that lecture tour of the States will go ahead after all.' Edgar appeared to be thinking aloud.

'How wonderful, my dear, what could be better. We could have a holiday afterwards. You know I have been quite worried about you. You have worked so hard recently.' She smiled and tentatively placed her hand over his, on the bedspread. Edgar did not move his hand but neither did he give any indication that he was aware of her presence. Mary shivered, am I always fated to be alone?

Alec sat with Gwen, eating breakfast. As was their custom, they both read a newspaper.

'Some poor cow threw herself into the Thames last night.' said Gwen. 'A policeman fished her out.'

'Must have been desperate.'

'Ummm, I suppose there are easier ways than leaping into ice-cold, filthy water, on a dark and stormy night'.

'All in the name of love, I suppose.'

Alec thought back to the 'phone call he had received the previous evening. The policeman had only asked if he knew a Rachel Warr. It had taken him aback; damaged the veneer of calm that he had worked so hard to put in place to cover the hurt he felt about Rachel.

'Does it say who the woman is?'

Gwen scanned the article. 'No, just that she was fished out and taken to Charing Cross Hospital. Why?'

'Well, it just seems a bit odd, after that 'phone call I had last night.'

Gwen stared at him. The last six months had been very contented for both of them - or so she thought. She had never brought up the subject of Rachel and neither had Alec. They behaved like a happily married couple.

The 'phone rang. 'I'll go,' said Gwen, 'It's probably Jane to arrange where to meet for lunch.'

After a few moments, she came back.

'It's for you, some man, won't give his name, very abrupt.'

Alec went to the 'phone.

'Alec Davies speaking.' There was a heavy intake of breath.

'I believe you know my wife. In fact I'll be a bit more precise, I believe you seduced my wife. My name is Charles Warr.'

Alec leaned against the hall wall. He was annoyed that he should feel so shaky.

'I've met your wife, she came to the jazz club, where I play. A couple of times, I think it was. But I haven't seen her for a while.'

Gwen stood beside him. She rested her hand on his shoulder, comfortingly.

'Did you know she was pregnant?'

'Yes, I believe she did tell me.'

'Oh! so you aren't the father. I seemed to think you were. Why did you give her your name, address and telephone number? After all, you say you only met her a couple of times.'

'I only wanted to be helpful, it must be hard for a young woman to manage on her own when her husband is in the forces.'

'And how helpful were you, I wonder? Its interesting that you didn't deny seducing my wife. Am I to assume I hit the nail on the head?'

'You can assume what you like, Mr. Warr, but let's get one thing straight, I don't know you and I'm hardly likely to. Any problems you have with your wife are no concern of mine.'   There was a short pause.

'I see. So it is no concern of yours what happens to the child she gave birth to. I certainly do not intend to support another man's brat. So I shall take it to the Hospital and let them sort out what to do. It is unlikely that my wife will be able to look after it or herself. Still, as you say, it is no concern of yours. I will wish you a good morning.' The 'phone went dead.

Alec stared at Gwen. She had read about people aging overnight but she could see it happening before her eyes. Alec's face seemed to shrivel. The colour drained from it and she could visualise him as he would be in fifty years time.

'Come and sit down. I'll make you a cup of coffee.' She lit a cigarette and handed it to him.

'Rachel has had the baby.' Alec whispered.

'Boy or girl?'

Alec shook his head, in disbelief, 'I didn't ask!'

'I presume that was Rachel's husband.'

'Oh, yes. He asked me if I was the father, I denied it.'

'I wouldn't worry about that, he'll soon get over his outraged indignation.'

'Somehow, I don't think so. He is going to take the baby to the hospital and hand it over to them. He said Rachel was in no state to look after herself never mind a baby.'

'Well that's it then.' Gwen handed him a mug of coffee 'Look love, these things happen all the time. Yes O.K. it was wrong, certainly it was stupid not to take precautions but you didn't rape her so she is as responsible as you are. Anyway how many native women has the high and mighty Charles laid, on his travels? Or doesn't he have natural urges like the rest of us?'

For the first time, since the 'phone call, Alec looked her in the eye. He took hold of her hand. 'My dear, Gwen, don't you realise what's past is past. That is not the point. I have a child and if I am not careful, that child is going to disappear from my life without my even seeing .....I don't know if I have a son or a daughter. For God's sake, don't you see, I will not have my child go through what I went through. Have you any idea what it is like being brought up in an orphanage? Regimented; no family, no love, no close relationship with any one. Branded at school, called a bastard, after all, most of us were. Never wanted for ourselves, tolerated - just.'

'Hang on, what's the matter with Rachel? Is she just going to let all this happen? Doesn't she have some say?'

'According to Charles Warr, she isn't fit.'

'That doesn't mean she never will be, does it?'

'I don't know, something drastic had happened but I don't know what?'

'So what are you going to do?'

'I will have to go over to Rachel's house and see what's what.'

'I don't think you will be welcomed with open arms. Do you want me to come too? I'll ring into work that I'm sick.'

'I should go on my own; it's not fair to involve you.'

Gwen felt deeply hurt, how could she not be involved after the last six months. Was this an indication of how superficial Alec's feelings for her were? Was she just a stop-gap? Good old Gwen, always around when needed.

'Well, I am involved, I'll go and 'phone now. Then we can face the dragon together, in his lair. One thing is for sure, he is less likely to throw a tantrum if there is a witness around'.

Charles 'phoned Mary Cardew next. Unfortunately, she was not at home and he had to speak to Edgar. The two men had always been wary of each other. They secretly both thought the other pompous. Edgar did not know that Charles had 'phoned last night and therefore had no idea that Rachel had been missing until traced to a psychiatric hospital. Charles found Edgar's response to the news difficult to assess. It seemed as though Edgar wished only to distance himself from the whole business. In that respect, Charles and Edgar's feelings were remarkably similar even though their reasons were diametrically opposed. Charles asked Edgar to pass the news to Mary.

As Edgar put the 'phone down, he made up his mind about what he wanted to do. The human brain really is an extraordinary piece of equipment, he thought. For months he had agonised about his life and now, everything was crystal clear. The decision was made. He smiled to himself as he went to his study to write a letter. Mary would not be back for a while. He had plenty of time.

Charles walked back to his house, deep in thought. He must go over to his parents. They had no idea of the latest developments. There was Jenny to consider as well, what would happen to her? For the time being, she could stay where she was. He supposed he had better go to Friern Barnet to see Rachel and her doctor. Then of course there was the baby. Could he really just dump the child at the hospital? He somehow doubted it, despite what he had said to Alec Davies.

He was so deep in thought, he did not see Betty until he almost ran into her.

'Any news of your wife?'

'Oh, yes, she has been traced to Friern Barnet Hospital.'

'That's the mental hospital, isn't it?' Charles nodded.

'Will you be collecting Stephen now? He's been ever so good, only had me up once in the night, bless him.'

There is no escape, thought Charles. I cannot expect Betty to look after him any longer.

'If you come round and get him now, I'll show you how to make up his bottle. He's due for a feed in about an hour.'

Charles could feel the hair on the back of his neck stand on end, with horror. For Christ's sake, he was going to be left to feed and change this child; this child who was tangible proof that his mother was no better than a whore! Charles bit his lip to stop the stream of invective that rose in his throat. He walked in silence to Betty's house.

Stephen was lying asleep in his crib. As Charles looked at him, he thought of all that might have been. His life, always so ordered lay in tatters. With the end of the war, he had intended to return to his pre-war post in the Post Office and settle down to family life. That was never to be. What could he do now? He suddenly felt totally alone. Yes, he had parents, a daughter but he did not have a soulmate anymore. He did not have that one human being who would make him the centre of her world. He would never trust another woman as long as he lived.

Betty bustled about, collecting up all Stephen's possessions. Charles watched and wondered how such a small human being could need so much paraphernalia. He picked up the crib and the bags, Betty handed to him.

'Thank you for all you have done. I am sorry Rachel has caused so much trouble.'

'Don't worry love, that's what neighbours are for. If there are any problems, just come and knock. You know about the bottle, he's due in about 45 minutes.' She smiled encouragingly and led the way to the front door.

When Charles left Betty's, he noticed that a policeman and Mary Cardew were waiting for him. The policeman smiled and quickly reassured Charles that it was unlikely that any action would be taken, as far as abandonment of Stephen was concerned, since Rachel was now in a mental hospital. It seemed that she was suffering from severe depression and was not likely to be held responsible for her actions. The only problem now was whether she deliberately threw herself into the river or was it an accident. Of course, Sir did realise that it was a criminal offence to commit suicide. Charles nodded; he knew.

Throughout Charles' conversation with the policeman, Mary had sat, silent and unmoving. The sound of voices disturbed the baby who stirred and gave a thin plaintive wail. She looked at Charles who gave no indication that he intended to do anything about it. With some reluctance, Mary bent to pick up the baby. She felt awkward and uncertain. She had seldom held Jenny when she was this size and had had a nanny for her own children.

The policeman left, by which time Stephen was crying loudly. Charles and Mary looked at each other, uncertain what to do.

'I think he must be hungry. Betty has shown me how to make up his bottle. Shall I do it now?'

'Yes, that would be best.' Mary walked up and down trying, not very successfully, to sooth the baby.

There was a knock at the door. 'Please will you go.' Charles shouted. 'I'm in the middle of sorting this bottle.' Mary went to the door, with Stephen in her arms. The young man looked familiar, there was a woman with him who Mary did not think she had ever seen before. Alec was amazed to see Mary there but then acknowledged that, of course, she was the baby's grandmother; why shouldn't she be there?

'Good morning. I think we have met before, you must be Rachel's mother.' Mary remembered than that this was the young man who who was here when she called to see Rachel months ago. Nearly nine months ago, in fact. She assumed that he was probably Stephen's father. So who was the woman with him? Alec noticed the questioning glance towards Gwen.

'This is a friend of mine, Gwen Owens. May we come in please?'

'Yes, I think perhaps you had better do so.'

Charles came out of the kitchen, holding a baby's bottle. Mary walked back into the living room.

'I'm Alec Davies, and this is a friend of mine. I had a 'phone call from the police last night, about Rachel, so I thought I had better come over to see what had happened.' He could not meet the gaze of the man facing him. Never had he seen such implacable hatred on the face of another human being. He felt helpless, like a rabbit caught in the gaze of a venomous snake. He could do nothing, in case the slightest movement snapped whatever control Charles was exerting on, what were clearly, overwhelmingly strong feelings.

Stephen howled and it was Gwen who broke the stalemate.

'If you would give me that bottle, I will go and feed the baby.' She smiled reassuringly to both men and taking the bottle went into the living room.

'You are the father of that bastard in there, aren't you?' Charles pointed, with trembling finger at the living room door. He was leaning forward and hissed the words, inches from Alec's face.

'You've had your fun, now face your responsibilities . I want you and your bloody friend - whoever she is - and your fucking son out of my house. Once he's fed, that's it, out! Do I make myself clear?' Alec nodded. Charles turned and walked back into the kitchen, closing the door behind him. Alec was not sure what to do but felt that any conversation with Charles was pointless and possibly dangerous. He walked into the living room. Gwen was feeding the baby as though she had done it all her life.

'Am I to assume, from the conversation I have just overheard, that you are Stephen's father?' Mary said.

'Yes, I am,' and, thought Alec, proud of it . That is my son. I will make sure he has a better time than I did. 'Please would you tell me what has happened to Rachel. I had a 'phone call from the police last night.'

'It would seem that she tried to kill herself, by drowning, in the Thames. She is now in Friern Barnet Mental Hospital. It is unlikely that she will be able to look after the baby or her daughter, Jenny. I assume you know she has a daughter.'

Alec nodded, he felt like a small boy being told off by a teacher. Still Mary was bound to be worried.

'The important, immediate problem is the infant. Clearly Charles has no intention of having anything to do with him. Since you accept fatherhood, what do you intend to do?'

One thing was clear, thought Alec, Rachel's mother doesn't expect to have an active part in all this. He glanced at Gwen, if he was going to have the baby and that was definitely what he wanted, he needed her cooperation and support. Before he could speak, Gwen turned to Mary.

'I'm sorry I don't know your name, but we will look after the baby. Still, as he is your grandson, we had better leave our address and 'phone number; you will want to know how he is getting on, won't you.' She gave Mary a dazzling smile.

With an overwhelming sense of relief, Mary smiled back. What had seemed an insurmountable difficulty was resolved, thanks to this plump, motherly woman.

'If you have finished feeding him. I think it would be best for you two to leave, don't you? Charles and I had better go to the hospital to see Rachel.'

Gwen handed Stephen to his father. So full of milk that a little was dribbling from the corner of his mouth. He was like a rag doll. Alec gazed in amazement at this perfect child with the merest hint of a smile on his lips. Alec could not move. He would remember this moment for the rest of his life. He thought his heart would explode with joy. He wondered, once again - but this time with total lack of comprehension- how his mother had been able to put him in an orphanage.

Gwen came back from the kitchen.

'I've rinsed the bottle and had a word with Charles. We can take what Stephen is wearing and stuff for feeding him but nothing else. No crib, no change of clothes, nappies, nothing. I think we had better go now. We have a lot of shopping to do for this young man.'

Mary stood up. 'Let me give you some money for Stephen.' She pulled two large white five pound notes out of her wallet.

'You should be able to get quite a lot with this.'

'Thank you, here's our address and 'phone number. Can we have yours, in case we need to contact you?'

'I think it would be better, if I contacted you.' Mary said stiffly. Edgar was going to find the whole business difficult enough, without more people ringing up with problems.

'Please, will you let me know how Rachel is. If the doctors think it's all right, I'll take Stephen to see her. It might help her to get better quicker if she sees how much her baby needs her.'

Gwen had allowed her imagination to run away with her ever since they had arrived at the house. A family of Alec, Gwen and Stephen and perhaps another baby later. Clearly it wasn't going to be that simple.

When Charles and Mary arrived at the hospital, it was mid day. Neither of them was hungry, but the patients were being fed. The doctor was on his lunch break and so they were left to kick their heels in a deserted, desolate corridor. They were both deep in thought and the all pervading smells of stale bodies and overcooked cabbage did nothing to raise the air of melancholy that they shared.

Eventually, a doctor with a brisk and overly jolly manner took them to his office. He told them about all that had happened and that clearly Rachel was very ill. She would need to be hospitalised for some considerable time.

'May I see my daughter?' Mary asked.

'I do not think that would be advisable, for either of you.'

'Why not?' Charles asked. He had always viewed mental illness as just a get out clause for weak people who could not face up to life as he did. He had no reason to change his opinion. After all, Rachel had behaved disgracefully and now in his opinion, she was hiding her sins behind a make believe illness.

'It would be very distressing for you both and, more importantly, for her. My consultant wants to talk to you.' The doctor glanced at his watch. 'He should be here in about ten minutes.'

Charles gazed out of the window. It was all a bloody conspiracy. It would be upsetting for Rachel! What about him? He wasn't exactly happy about the situation which, most definitely, was not his fault. He was the injured party, not her. By the time the consultant psychiatrist arrived, Charles' sense of grievance had reached monumental proportions. Mary, however, had sunk into a brooding silent apathy. Rachel's long dead father seemed to be standing behind her, she could almost feel his hand on her shoulder. She remembered the erratic behaviour, the depressions, the sudden lifting of his spirits to dizzy heights, when he was capable of doing anything. Manic-depression, the doctors had called it. For Mary, with her horror of emotion expressed, it had been a nightmare. A nightmare from which she had only escaped when George had killed himself. It was only then that her love for Edgar could be made public. Now had George come to haunt her? Was his instability now manifesting itself in Rachel? She realised that the consultant, whose name she had not heard, was talking to her and Charles.

Charles was sitting forward. The veins on his neck and forehead were standing out and Mary could see the throbbing of his blood. She felt weary and strangely detached. As she watched Charles, she thought, not for the for the first time, what a pompous young ass he was. For a split second, she felt sorry for Rachel. He cannot be easy to live with, but then neither was Rachel. Her hopes that somehow marriage to Charles would stop Rachel making so much trouble, at home, were dashed. This young man, her son-in-law, so full of his own importance, had not been able to keep Rachel under control any better than anyone else. Charles suddenly stood up and leaned against the consultant's desk.

'For God's sake, what do you mean, I must leave my wife alone?'

'Mr. Warr, you have caused your wife very great distress.'

Mary thought Charles was going to explode. He clenched his fists until the knuckles gleamed white. There was not a vestige of colour in his face. From the expression in his eyes, Mary thought, the ordinary man in the street could be forgiven for assuming that Charles too was a patient.

'What are you suggesting I do? Leave the country so that my wife can carry on her illicit affairs untroubled!'

'Mr. Warr, I am not here to sit in judgment or to comment on the private lives of my patients or their relatives. My job is to do the best I can for my patients. I repeat, for whatever reason, you have caused your wife very great distress. I must ask you in the strongest possible terms to absent yourself from her life, certainly for the foreseeable future. I would add that your wife is so very ill that it had been necessary to draw up the papers to have her declared insane.'

Mary gave a gasp and Charles staggered as he sat down again. The consultant continued.

'This was deemed a necessary measure for your wife's protection. You must not see it as irreversible. He glanced first at Charles and then at Mary.

'We will need your signature, Mr. Warr.'

'What am I supposed to do? What about my daughter?'

'You must assume that your wife will not be fit to care for anyone - not even herself for some considerable time. I suggest you make whatever arrangements you can that do not, in any way rely, on your wife. Perhaps this is something you should discuss with Rachel's mother, here. Grandparents have a very important part to play in situations like this.'

Charles and Mary looked at each other. No word was spoken but they both knew that whatever Mary's role, it would be unlikely to include active involvement with Jenny's upbringing. For different reasons, they both felt a sense of relief. Charles knew that when he left the hospital, he would be going straight to his parents.

Alec and Gwen settled Stephen down on Gwen's bed, as soon as they got home. They wedged him with pillows to stop him from rolling.

'Right, I must go out and get some basic equipment, just to get us through the next couple of days. Then I will go to the welfare clinic and ask around my friends for castoffs, pram etc. '

Alec watched Gwen as she bustled about, writing out a list, thinking aloud about all she had to do. Life was very unfair. Gwen was the best friend he had ever had or was ever likely to have. She was more than a friend, more like a mother or older sister, something he had never known. He felt comfortable with her, safe. He enjoyed the times they spent in bed which could be passionate or soothing, tempestuous or gentle. Gwen understood him and he thought she probably loved him. If only I loved her, he thought. Gwen has been so much to me, has been such an important part of my life, for so long. Yet, his thoughts went back to Rachel, so short a time, so long ago. Now lying next door, asleep, was a perfect human being, evidence of what? Lust, madness brought on by moonlight and the extraordinary circumstances of war, or love? Alec feared it was love, feared because he could see that he was going to embark on a relationship that would bring easily as much pain as happiness. He sighed. Gwen stood behind him and put her arms around his waist.

'Don't worry love, we'll sort this out.' She kissed him on the cheek. 'I'm off now, can I have the ten pounds Rachel's mum gave you?'

After she had gone, Alec sat at the kitchen table. He was being totally unfair to Gwen. She was going to get herself deeper and deeper involved in this. She was going to take Stephen to her heart, that was obvious. The longer this situation went on, the more Gwen was going to be hurt. He would have to tell her, as soon as possible; once Rachel came out of hospital, he was going to get her to live with him, as his wife. He had no illusions about Charles, he would get rid of Rachel as soon as he could. He felt fairly certain that Mary Cardew would be only too pleased to have Rachel taken care of by someone else. He was that someone. He would look after her, she was like a delicate, fragile butterfly. He would make sure that no-one crushed her.

Mary did not offer to give Charles a lift, when they left the hospital. After perfunctory goodbyes, Charles caught a bus to Camden Town, to his parents whilst Mary drove to Wimbledon. She drove automatically and desperately thought of how she would explain the events of the day to Edgar. Whatever she said, he would be angry and unsympathetic. Still, they would be going to America soon. A long holiday would do them both good.

The house was quiet, as usual. Mary took a deep breath as she stood in the hall. It was so good to be home. She could hear very faint noises coming from the kitchen. She would go to Edgar's study to see if he was ready for afternoon tea. She certainly was. Edgar was not at home but there was an envelope for her, in his handwriting. He will probably be back soon, she thought, as she picked up the letter. I will order tea, he can always join me later.

She walked to the kitchen, had a word with Cook and then went to the drawing room. She tore open the envelope and started to read. After the first few sentences she stopped. Her hands were shaking, she put the letter down and gazed helplessly out of the window. She could just make out what must be Bert pottering in the far beds, getting things ready for a colourful Spring. It didn't make sense. Spring would never come. There would be no colour, no life, no anything.

Mary picked up the letter and started to read it again. There must be some mistake.

Dear Mary,

As I am sure you are aware, our relationship has changed, most particularly over the last few years. When two people marry, they hope to stay together for the rest of their days. Certainly we both hoped for that when we married so many years ago. Unfortunately people alter and not always in the same way. . . Mary put the letter down. I have not altered, it's you, Edgar, you have altered, not me. I still love you as much as I did on our wedding day. She picked up the letter again.

. . . .we have grown apart. We are not able to make each other happy any more. There is so much about you that I admire, Mary, you have a fine mind and have given me so much help and support with my work. You are a superb hostess and I have revelled in the immaculately organised social functions that have played such an important part in our lives together.

Even though it is not always considered appropriate for women to enjoy the physical pleasures of marriage, I have found you to be a passionate and generous lover.

In the past, we have brought much to each other but that is the past. I fear, that for both our sakes, our futures lie apart rather than together. I am confident that you will understand and will soon feel able to agree that my decision to leave you is the best one, for both our sakes. With that in mind, I have decided to stay at my club, for the next two weeks. After which, I shall be sailing to America, for the lecture tour. I will of course ensure that my solicitor keeps you informed of all decisions made, that might affect you. It is my intention to sell the house which, as you are aware, is my property. I will of course give you as much time as possible to find a home of your own. With your own private income, I am confident that you will be able to purchase a property, suited to your usual life-style, with no difficulty.

I wish you well and feel sure that we will both be able to look back on our marriage with few regrets.

Edgar

The letter slipped through Mary's fingers and fluttered to the floor. She leaned back in the arm chair. She could hear the ticking of the clock on the mantelpiece; it competed with the thudding of her heart. Her chest felt as though there was a band around it, squeezing. She was gasping for breath. Her eyes brimmed with tears. It felt as though pins were being stuck into them. She blinked and suddenly, for the first time since she was a tiny child, scalding tears streamed, unchecked, down her face. Her limbs had lost all their strength. She was incapable of lifting a handkerchief to her eyes. Tears continued to stream down her face; they dropped onto her silk blouse. She did not care. Nothing mattered any more. So it was that Susan found her, when she brought the tea tray in.

'Good afternoon, Madam shall I put the tray on the little table?' When she got no reply, she stood in front of Mary, thinking maybe she had not heard.

'Oh! Madam, whatever is the matter?' When there was still no reply, Susan put the tray down and ran back to the kitchen.

'Quick, quick, Cook, come quick. I think the mistress is taken bad. Looks like she's had a stroke or something.'

Chapter 6

Jenny lay in her Grandmother's bed. It was one of the special things about staying with Grandma and Grandpa. The mattress was made of feathers and you had to climb into it. Jenny wriggled and felt the feathers settle inside their casing. She was enveloped with softness and warmth. The final touch being the feather eiderdown on top. Here she was safe. She put her head under the covers and hugged Benjy tightly. She could shut out the world, she could forget all the tense conversations, from which she had been excluded. Here she was special; she could close her eyes and imagine she was a princess living in a castle with her mummy and daddy there all the time.

Jenny loved her Grandma and Grandpa very much, particularly Grandpa but she felt sometimes that she was in the way. No-one ever explained things to her. Where were Mummy and Stephen? When she asked, Grandma had told her to Ssh. Why was Daddy so angry? He seemed to be angry with her but she had not done anything wrong, had she?

She heard footsteps on the stairs, it sounded like Grandpa. She popped her head out from under the covers but kept her eyes closed, just in case it was Daddy. She knew she was supposed to be asleep. It must be Grandpa because she could hear puffing breaths and Daddy never puffed. She opened one eye and in the gloom, could see Grandpa leaning over her.

'You are supposed to be asleep, little chick.'

'I can't sleep, Grandad. Where's my mummy?'

Albert hesitated and then sat on the edge of the bed. He stroked Jenny's hair and tried to organise his thoughts and feelings so he could somehow explain the inexplicable to this dear child.

'Mummy isn't very well at the moment. She has had to go into hospital for a while but you are going to stay with us.'

'Is it because she's had a baby that she isn't well?'

'In a way, but you mustn't worry about anything because Grandma and I will look after you.'

'But what about Daddy, why can't he look after me too?'

Albert thought about the heated conversation he had had with Charles and Gladys.

He, always the peacemaker, had tried to persuade Charles that reconciliation should at least be tried. Even if Rachel wanted nothing to do with Charles at the moment, that was because she was ill. Give her time. Charles' reaction had been volcanic and Albert had been forced to accept that there was no chance of his son ever forgiving Rachel and therefore no chance that Jenny would ever be part of a happy, united family. His heart ached for the child but he realised he was a lone voice in the wilderness. Gladys had sided with Charles and that had seemed to be the end of the matter. Charles intended to sign on for nine years and Jenny would stay where she was. Charles was going to divorce Rachel and apply for custody of Jenny. Albert suspected that Jenny was not likely to see much of her mother, if Charles had anything to do with it. As for Stephen, God alone knew if he would ever be seen by them again. Perhaps it was as well that Caroline and Jack's baby was due soon. Albert hoped such a happy event might help to take Jenny's mind off Stephen.

Charles realised that his leave was nearly over; there was still so much to do. He would never come back to this house in Hendon again. He had seen the landlord and explained that he wished to terminate the tenancy. He had cleared all his possessions. There seemed little point in worrying about furniture. He was a career soldier from now on. If that blasted psychiatrist could tell him to keep away from Rachel, he would make sure he did. He would stay abroad, travel light. The army would look after him. He thought briefly of Jenny, his feelings were hopelessly mixed. Of course, he loved her but she was so like her mother; her expression, the way she sat with her hands in her lap, Rachel in miniature. As long as Jenny was alive, he would never be free of Rachel. He must get the divorce proceedings started before he went back to Austria.

He looked round the house and wondered what should be done with Rachel's clothes etc. They could not be left there but he saw no reason why he should clear them out. He decided to ring Mary Cardew, after all, she was Rachel's mother. When he 'phoned, Susan told him that Madam was not well but the message would be passed on as soon as possible. There was nothing more to be done here. He had told Susan that a key would be left at number 50, so that Mary could gain access to 52. As Charles walked towards Betty's house, he rehearsed what he would say. He wanted to give as little information as possible. Betty had been very kind but he shrank from her knowing what had happened between Rachel and himself. Betty wasn't in, which was a blessing. Bob took the key and seemed as relieved to know that his 'troublesome' neighbours were leaving as Charles was to be going. As Charles walked down the street for the last time, he thought about the saying, 'As one door closes, another door opens.' I wish I could believe that,he thought.

In twenty four hours, Alec and Gwen's life had changed dramatically. Gwen had managed to obtain by a variety of methods and contacts, all that Stephen needed and he had settled down well. The immediate problem now was that Gwen was going to have to decide what would happen about her job. Officially, she was ill but that would only provide a short breathing space. She was all for giving up her job and becoming a full time 'mother'. She could not understand why Alec was so reluctant for her to do so. He had not yet told her of his plan to live with Rachel and eventually marry her. Clearly, he knew he would have to say something soon. All of his life , he had taken the line of least resistance and managed, thereby, to side step a lot of trouble. However, this was one occasion where he would have to face up to and actively tackle a situation that was not just going to go away.

Clearly, Gwen must not give up her job. That meant Alec would have to make alternative arrangements for Stephen until Rachel was well enough to leave hospital. He decided to go to the local baby clinic and enquire about a creche. He must also visit Rachel. On impulse, he decided to do that first; maybe the doctors at Friern Barnet could make some suggestions or offer some advice. He would take Stephen, to the hospital,with him. It was bound to do Rachel good to see her son fit and well and with his Dad!

When he arrived at the hospital, it took an age to find which ward Rachel was in. Then there were the complications that he was not a relative, not her husband. After considerable insistence, Alec managed to speak to the Ward Sister. He explained who Stephen was and at last sensed that he had made a dent in officialdom's armour.

'You had better speak to Mrs. Warr's doctor.'
Sister bustled off, starched apron crackling. After a while she returned with a young man, probably younger than me, Alec thought. Together they went to a small office.

'As you are not a relative of my patient, I am not really able to discuss her condition with you.'

'I appreciate that, but I am left with her son, our son and I want her to see him. I thought it might help her to get better.'
The doctor gazed at Alec speculatively. 'How do you see the future for Mrs. Warr and her baby? I believe she also has another child.'

'I want to look after her, I want her to be my wife, eventually. I'm sure you realise there are complications.'

The doctor nodded, he had not met Charles but he had heard about him and Rachel's vehement refusal to see him. Alec continued 'Surely, the first thing is to get Rachel better. I don't know where Jenny is - that's Rachel's daughter - probably with her grandparents. But at least I can make sure she sees one of her children.' Stephen squirmed and gave a whimper. Alec realised that he had been gripping the child so tightly that it had woken him up. Alec comforted Stephen and when he looked up, realised that the doctor had been watching him closely.

'It would be good for Mrs. Warr to see this young man, but not this afternoon; she is having her treatment. Could you come back tomorrow?' Alec thought for a moment, tomorrow was Thursday. He too had 'phoned in sick but would have to go back to work on Monday. Perhaps he could make some sort of long term arrangement for Stephen tomorrow and then come back to the hospital on Friday.

'I need to find a creche for the baby, what would be the best way to go about it?'

'Who is looking after him at the moment?'

'A friend of mine, she has taken some time off work.'

'Where do you live?'

'Highgate.'

'I would try to get him into the local council run nursery there. Explain that his mother is in hospital. If I were you, I would keep it quiet that you and Mrs. Warr are not married.'

'Can I come back on Friday? I hope to have something sorted by then.'

The doctor watched Alec walk up the corridor with Stephen in his arms. He wondered why it was that men never seemed to be able to hold a baby without looking awkward. Still, he smiled to himself, it seemed that the chances of Rachel getting herself sorted out had improved a little.

Rachel walked down the corridor with a nurse. She had been told that she was to have some treatment but she did not know what. Life seemed so totally without hope that she did not care what happened to her. She had wanted death, she wanted it still. She had lost everything, everyone. She could not fight; her head hung down. Her hair was still dirty and ragged, from the wood that had been entangled in it; it hung over her face. It helped to shut out her surroundings a little. The nurse held her firmly and almost dragged her along. Rachel was aware of the drone of a one sided, inconsequential conversation but had neither the energy nor inclination to reply. Her legs felt leaden. She shuffled along like an old, old woman.

They arrived at a large room, with many wooden beds. Some were occupied by patients who appeared to be asleep but their stillness and uniform position, on their backs, sent a shrill note of alarm through Rachel.

'What's happening?' She clutched the nurse's arm and stopped dead. Towards the end of the room, doctors and nurses were gathered around one bed. The patient was strapped down, something was being held on either side of his head, by a doctor, Rachel assumed. Suddenly everyone stepped back and the body on the bed arched upwards, straining against the straps. Rachel could see the man's face. It was blue. There was something between his teeth. Rachel stood transfixed. She could feel the perspiration break on her forehead and upper lip. This was hell, she had died and this was her punishment for all eternity. She tried to break free from the nurse, to escape, anywhere. The nurse clutched Rachel tightly and shouted for help. Rachel started to scream and kick out with her slippered feet. She fell heavily onto the cold tiled floor and was held down by two nurses. 'What are you going to do to me?'

'This will make you feel better, Mrs. Warr. You must not be frightened. We know it doesn't look very nice, but you won't feel a thing.' The fall had knocked all further resistance out of Rachel. She allowed herself to be lifted and half carried to a vacant bed. 'But what are you going to do?' she whispered.

A nurse held her hand and stroked it gently.

'It's E.C.T., that is electro-convulsive therapy. It will stop you feeling so miserable.'

'Why are people strapped down? I can't bear it.'

'Sometimes patients throw their arms and legs about while they are having treatment and they can hurt themselves. We put something between your teeth so that you don't bite your tongue.' Rachel had never been so frightened in all her life. Even when Jenny was being born, during an air-raid. Childbirth was natural, this E.C.T. was not, it was barbaric.

She started to shake and could not stop. It was her turn now. The nurses and doctors quickly surrounded the bed. She was helpless, trapped. Is this how men felt when they went to the electric chair? She was told to open her mouth and a hard piece of rubber was jammed between her teeth.

'Right, Sister?' The doctor held two pads, with handles, on either side of her temples. Everyone stepped back. She opened her mouth to scream but felt a terrific blow to her head and everything went black.

Rachel had no idea where she was or how long she had been lying on the bed. The bright lights hurt her eyes. Her wrists felt sore. She tried to look at them but the effort of lifting her arms was too great. Her body was totally limp and lifeless. She moved her head, very slowly, but all she could see was more beds with people lying on them. A nurse was walking past and when she noticed that Rachel was watching her, came over.

'Wide awake now, are we? You see, it wasn't so bad was it?' Rachel looked closely at the nurse but did not recognise her.

'Where am I?'

'You are in the treatment room, you will be going back to the ward soon.' The nurse patted her arm. 'You lie still for a while and rest.'

Mary Cardew lay on her bed. The curtains were drawn shut to keep out the spring sunshine. She could not bear to see the stirrings of new life in the garden. The sleeping earth was gathering strength each day, preparing for growth, blossoming, rebirth, after a long cold winter. For Mary the pain of loss filled every moment and she grieved for Edgar, as though she had been widowed. Her doctor had been called, by Cook, after Susan had found her in a state of collapse. He could find nothing physically wrong and had no cure for a broken heart, only time.

Since his visit, Mary had spent most of her time in the bedroom. She supposed it was her bedroom now. By staying there, she was surrounded by the trappings of married life and married love. She somehow felt that time had been stopped; if she waited long enough, Edgar would come back.

Susan knocked timidly on the bedroom door.

'Excuse me, Madam, Mr. Warr's been on the 'phone again. He says will you collect Miss Rachel's things from the house in Hendon? You see, ma'am, he's let the house go and he says he is going back abroad and he's taken his stuff.' .Mary did not seem to have heard anything Susan had said, so she crept out, closing the door noiselessly behind her.

Mary lay still, she really could not think about Rachel and her problems. She was not surprised to hear that Charles was running away. But, where do I run to? Still, Eleanor will be home soon, she can take charge of everything. Mary closed her eyes and realised - no longer with surprise - that she was crying again, soundlessly. After a life-time of restraint and control it seemed that she was wholly unable to keep her feelings in check. I am behaving just like Rachel would. She gasped, the thought had hit her like cold water, thrown in her face. What on Earth would Eleanor think, if she found her mother like this?

She would feel the same contempt, at such weakness, as I feel for myself, now. She sat up and swung her legs off the bed in a decisive movement. She thought about Edgar's letter once again. This time she remembered how many positive comments it had contained. He may have left, but surely, if he thought as highly of her as the letter suggested, then it was reasonable to suppose that the separation was bound to be temporary. This highly intellectual, creative man, had to be humoured. She had thought he had been working too hard. A trip abroad would do him so much good. He would come back refreshed and they could start again. That being the case, I had better get Rachel sorted out. Edgar would not want to be involved in her problems. I will go to the house and get everything out tomorrow and I had better 'phone that young man, Alec - whatever his name is. I need to know what his intentions are.

Alec told Gwen of his decision to place Stephen in a council nursery. Although he did not tell her of his ultimate intentions, he felt sure she was aware that he was not telling her everything. There had been many awkward silences that evening and what conversation they had was stilted and stuck very closely to safe topics. When Alec told Gwen that he did not want her to spoil her chances at work, by having too much time off, he found he was unable to look her in the eye. When they went to bed, there was an awkwardness that neither of them had experienced before. An awkwardness that was only broken when Gwen put her arms around him and held him tightly as though she were comforting him. We are just brother and sister again, she thought.

Alec had far less difficulty getting a nursery place than he had expected. When he explained his circumstances, the person in charge, Mrs Wilson, seemed only too wiling to take Stephen as soon as possible. Taking the doctor's advice, he referred to Rachel as his wife and came away from the nursery glowing with the sympathy and approval lavished upon him by Mrs. Wilson and her staff. I cannot avoid telling Gwen what I hope for now, he thought. However, after due consideration, he decided to wait until he had seen Rachel. Supposing she did not want to be with him. Supposing she wanted to take Stephen with her and disappear. Could he stop her? He wondered if Stephen's birth had been registered. He, Alec needed to get his name on the birth certificate that would give him some rights, he hoped. He would see what state Rachel was in tomorrow, find out about registering the birth and if necessary do it himself.

Gwen had dressed Stephen in his nicest clothes, after she fed him.

'You are going to see your real Mum today, my lovely. Be a good boy now.'

'I'll never forget what you have done for me, Gwen.'

'You know me, the tart with the heart of gold.' She gave a harsh laugh. There was nothing Alec could say. He picked Stephen up, patted Gwen's arm and left. She watched them from the window; her heart felt like lead.

By the time he arrived at the hospital, Stephen was deeply asleep. Alec went straight to the ward Sister's office. He wanted Rachel to see Stephen at his best, before he needed his next feed or a clean nappy. He hadn't thought to bring anything like that with him. Sister welcomed him warmly enough but warned him that Rachel was likely to be tearful because of the treatment she had had on Wednesday. It seemed to have done her some good. He was taken to a small room, used by visitors, and told to wait.

When Rachel walked in, he could scarcely believe his eyes. She seemed to have aged forty years. She did not seem to know where she was or what was happening. Holding Stephen in one arm, he led her to a small settee and helped her to sit down. She gazed at him; her eyes were dull and devoid of expression. She glanced at the baby then back at Alec.

'Hello, Rachel, it is so good to see you. You know who this is don't you? Why don't you hold him?' Alec held Stephen out to her. Hesitatingly, she took him and sat gazing at him intently, without speaking. When Stephen stirred, Rachel quickly looked up, panic in her eyes.

'It's all right, he's just getting comfortable.' Alec said softly. Rachel continued to look at Stephen, as though she wanted to make sure she had imprinted every detail of his face in her mind.

'He may be a bit warm in here, why don't you loosen his blanket?' Slowly Rachel eased the blanket free so that he lay, uncovered in her lap. Alec noticed that Rachel's hand was shaking as she held Stephen's tiny hand in hers. She looked up and smiled. Alec found it hard to breathe, the pain of love in his chest threatened to choke him. He smiled back. Rachel did not seem to want to talk so Alec told her about the nursery place that Stephen would go to the following Monday. Although she did not give a reaction, she did not seem upset. He then talked very carefully about the future, a future they would share. Again, there was little reaction but at least she did not seem to find his plan unacceptable. Throughout Alec's one-sided conversation, Rachel gazed at her son and examined him minutely. After an hour, a nurse came in and suggested that Rachel needed a rest. She handed Stephen back to Alec and stood up. Alec stood beside her and gently put an arm around her.

'Thank you for bringing my baby, where's Jenny?'
This was the question Alec had dreaded. 'She's all right, you must not worry, she's being well looked after. Charles has seen to that.'

Rachel thought for a moment, obviously digesting the information Alec had given her.

'I want to see Jenny.' There were tears in her eyes.

'Don't cry, my love. Please don't cry. I'll try to arrange for Jenny to visit you soon.' God alone knows how, Alec thought. He held Stephen up towards her.

'Say goodbye to your mum.' He hoped that Rachel would kiss the baby so that he would have a chance to say his goodbye with a kiss too. Rachel put one arm around the baby and Alec was suddenly aware of the pressure of her other arm on his waist. They stood for a moment, a tableau. Alec leaned towards Rachel and his lips brushed her cheek. 'I'll come again soon.' he whispered, 'Shall I bring Stephen?'

Tears coursed unchecked down Rachel's face, she nodded her agreement.

Jenny held Grandad's hand as they walked up Kings Road. Grandma walked on the other side of Grandad. They were going to see Aunt Caroline and Uncle Jack. Grandma had told Jenny that her new cousin would soon be here. Jenny was too unhappy to think about new babies. She had a new baby but no-one would tell her where he was. She had cried bitterly before they came out because Charles' leave was over and he had left. Jenny had sat on his knee while he told her she must be a good girl for Grandma and Grandad. When she had said she wanted to see Mummy and Stephen, he had started to talk about something else. She felt angry and hurt and very, very frightened. Her whole life had changed and no-one would tell her anything. She felt more and more certain that it must be her fault.

She didn't much like visiting Aunt Caroline and Uncle Jack. There was nothing to do. She had to sit quietly and -as usual- be good. Jack was at work and Caroline wasn't feeling very well. She sat on the settee, with her feet up while Gladys made a cup of tea. All the talk was about the new baby. Jenny was bored.

She leant on the window sill looking down from this first floor flat and watched people walking past. After a while, she realised that a man was waving at her. She realised it was Uncle Jack. She waved back.

'Uncle Jack's here,' she said. Caroline adopted a pained expression and made a fruitless attempt to haul herself upright.

'I suppose he'll be wanting his tea.'

'Don't worry, dear. I'll get it ready, you rest.' Gladys was up and out of the chair and in the kitchen almost before she had finished speaking. Caroline looked at her father and raised her eyebrows. Albert shrugged.

'You know what she's like, never happy unless she's doing something.'

Jack came in, hearty and red in the face.

'Good to see you, Dad. Where's the little woman? In the kitchen I expect, the best place for women, well only one place better!' He rubbed his hands together and gave Caroline a knowing wink. She gave a warning look at Jack and then looked at Jenny.

'Hello, hello, who have we here. Well if it isn't my pretty little niece.' He walked over and picked her up. He tickled her under the chin and gave her a smacking kiss. It left a wet mark on her cheek and she smelt his breath, sour yet sickly. She grinned at him, she had never been called pretty before; it was nice to be made a fuss of.

'Now then Jack, don't swing her about, you'll get her over-excited then she'll never sleep tonight.' Gladys stood in the doorway, drying her hands.

'I'm getting a bit of tea for all of us but it isn't ready yet.'

'Let me give you a hand, love.' Albert stood up slowly, because he had been gassed slightly during the First World War, his lungs still played him up from time to time. Today was one of those days.

'And what about you, little lady?' said Jack. 'I bet you'd like to go on the swings.' Jenny nodded. 'I'll take her down to the gardens, how long will tea be?'

'About half an hour. Now you be careful with her, Jack, don't swing her too high and don't let her out of your sight.' Albert patted Gladys on the arm,

'Don't fuss, dear, Jack will look after her, won't you, son?' Jack smiled,

'Like she's my own.'

'Can I take Benjy?' Jenny held up the toy rabbit.

'Yes, now come on or we won't have time.'

Albert watched, from the window, as Jenny and Jack crossed the road. Jenny looked back and waved. Albert blew her a kiss.

The swing was in a private garden, in the centre of the square. It had thick railings all around it and dark laurel bushes shut out inquisitive eyes. In the middle of the garden area was grass and a couple of benches. Down a path was a solitary swing. The garden was used by the residents of the houses in the square. The gates was always kept locked and only residents had a key. In the centre of a bustling city, it was a small oasis where mothers and nannies could bring their children to play in safety. At this time of day, it was usually empty since most children were indoors, having their tea.

It was beginning to get dark and not very warm. Jenny shivered. Jack unlocked the gate which creaked as he shut and locked it. Suddenly, Jenny felt frightened. 'Are there any bogey men here?' she whispered. Jack laughed and picked her up.

'Of course there aren't.' He hugged her tightly, till she could hardly breathe. Again, she felt the sour, sickly breath, hot on her cheek.

'Are you cold? You were shivering just now.'

'A bit.' Jack walked over to the bench and sat down, with Jenny on his knees. He started to rub her hands with his.

'There that will soon warm you up.' He rubbed her back and then slipped his hand inside her coat and started to rub her chest. He tickled her neck again. She giggled. 'Where else are you ticklish, I wonder?' His hand moved down to her legs. 'Are these cold too?' Jenny nodded. Jack rubbed her legs. Her skirt had ridden up so her knickers were showing. She tried to pull her skirt down but his hands got in the way. Then he hugged her so that her face was pressed into his coat. She could hear something thumping in his chest, she supposed it must be his heart. She looked up at his face. He seemed to be sweating, even though it was not warm and he was breathing as though he had just run up a flight of stairs. Jenny could not understand it.

'Can we go on the swing now?' Jack did not seem to hear her at first.

'Uncle Jack, can we go on the swing?'

He looked down at her and smiled. He carefully smoothed her skirt down over her thighs stroking them as he did so.

Mary listened to Alec's number ringing, as she had several times already today. If he were at work, where was the baby? Perhaps that friend of his was looking after it. At last, someone answered. 'Hello, Alec Davies speaking.'

'Hello, Mary Cardew here, I thought you should know that my son-in-law has given up tenancy of 52, Redburn Street and removed all his effects. He has left me the job of removing anything that is Rachel's. However, my immediate concern is for Stephen. What, if any, arrangements have you made?' Alec smiled wryly to himself and wondered if he should be standing to attention. Since he had just returned from the hospital and had not yet had a chance to put Stephen down, he decided he could excuse himself such formality. He explained that Stephen would be going to a nursery from Monday. The matter of Stephen's birth being registered could not be cleared up because Mary did not know. Rachel had yet to be asked and Charles was heaven knew where. Mary suggested that Alec check with Somerset House. To his absolute amazement, he suggested that Mary should undertake the task since he, Alec, had to go back to work on Monday. There was a stunned silence as both Mary and Alec contemplated the sudden shift in their relationship. Mary was no more used to being told what to do than Alec was to doing the telling. It was finally decided that Mary did have more time for such an investigation.

'I visited Rachel, today. I took Stephen to see her. I think it helped although she was very quiet. She desperately wants to see Jenny. Is she with her other grandparents?'

'Do you think a mental hospital is a suitable place for a four year old?'

'Probably not, but we could try.' Mary noticed the word 'we'. I'm being sucked into this. Obviously, Alec could hardly go to see Mr. and Mrs. Warr and ask to have Jenny for a few hours so he could take her to the hospital.

'I think I had better write to Mr. and Mrs. Warr and see what instructions Charles has left. But I warn you, I think it highly unlikely that they will agree to her seeing her mother where she is.'

Alec could only agree, at least he had tried. He must do all he could to get Rachel well enough for the hospital to discharge her as soon as possible. Surely there would be no objection then.

'I do appreciate how much trouble you must have taken making arrangements for Stephen. What are your intentions for the future? Particularly as far as my daughter is concerned.'

'I love your daughter, Mrs. Cardew. I know that a lot of people will sit in judgment but that is their problem. What I want to do is look after Rachel and Stephen. If it turns out that Jenny comes to live with us, I'll do my best for her too.'

'I admire your determination, Mr. Davies and I wish you success. I shall visit Rachel tomorrow, hopefully I will be able to get more information from the doctor .'

Once Mary had finished talking to Alec, she sat down and allowed herself to relax. Maybe this young man was the one that Rachel needed. Despite the impression he gave, of being from a poor background, he certainly seemed to have Rachel's best interests at heart. Eleanor was coming home, from her job in the Midlands. She would be staying for the weekend, perhaps she will come to the hospital with me. Eleanor was so sensible she would know the best way to tackle the problems of both Edgar and Rachel. They could have a pleasant evening; they could discuss the man that Eleanor was seeing and catch up with all the other news. Mary went to the kitchen to arrange with Cook, what they would be having for dinner.

Alec replaced the receiver and turned round. He had not heard Gwen come into the flat. He realised that she must have overheard the conversation with Mary. They stood for a moment looking at each other. Alec could think of nothing to say that would not make matters worse.

'I wish you had told me what you planned.' Gwen spoke very quietly.

'I've been an absolute bastard, haven't I?'

Gwen shrugged, 'I don't suppose you wanted to hurt me, you just did what you thought would be best. Where do we go from here? I don't intend to be gooseberry.' Although it would have been best for Alec if Gwen had stayed until Rachel came out of hospital, he realised there was no way he could ask or expect her to do that. Gwen had to do whatever she wanted and if that was to leave tonight then Alec would do nothing to stand in her way.

'I've really mucked you about and I can't tell you how sorry I am. You think about yourself now. What about those friends you were going to share with, is that still a possibility?'

Gwen thought for a moment,' I think it would be best if I left this weekend. The longer it goes on the worse it will get.' She walked to her bedroom, a room she had used so little recently, and began packing. Stephen started crying and Alec went into the kitchen to make up his bottle.

Rachel lay on her bed and thought about Alec's visit. Slowly the confusion after the E.C.T. was clearing. There was a tiny seed of hope somewhere inside her. Perhaps things were not so black. She could not be sure if it was the treatment or the visit that had made her feel a little better. Certainly Stephen was a beautiful baby. She knew she would be having more treatment sessions and just the thought of it made her shake. There was no escape.

She thought Alec had said he would bring Jenny next time he visited, she did so hope so. Rachel was frightened that Charles and his mother would try to poison the child's mind against her. She tried to think about the future but could feel the panic rising in her throat. She did not think she would be on her own, Surely Alec must think a lot of her to visit her here. If he stayed with her, surely Charles would take Jenny away. He would never let Jenny live with her and another man. If she wanted to keep Jenny, she would have to live alone. The thought of trying to bring up two children single-handed was too fearful to contemplate. She could feel tears of fear and self-pity welling up. I must not even think of it.

Jenny was very quiet on the way home. It was dark and cold so they caught a bus. She felt she ought to tell Grandma that Uncle Jack had put his hand inside her coat and up her skirt. Grandma had told her that she must never let a man 'interfere' with her. Jenny had never been quite sure what that meant. She did not want to make Grandma cross because if she did perhaps she and Grandad would go away like Mummy, Daddy and Stephen had. Then she would have no-one. She clutched Benjy very tightly and leaned against Grandad. He would look after her.

Mary had written a letter to Mr. and Mrs. Warr, while she was waiting for Eleanor to arrive. It seemed probable that she would have to take the child to the hospital but surely not until Rachel was very much better. If we visit the hospital tomorrow, we can go to Redburn Street straight after and decide what to do with Rachel's possessions Then we can have the rest of the day to ourselves. Mary drank her dry sherry appreciatively and was glad she had pulled herself together. Self pity is so undignified and achieves nothing. By the time Eleanor arrived, Mary felt calm and, once more, in control.

She kissed her daughter and stood back to admire a striking young woman, so like herself. Eleanor was a good six feet tall with strong, very dark hair, pulled back into the nape of her neck. She had bright blue eyes and a strong chin. Although not slim, there was no surplus flesh on her long boned frame. She exuded confidence, intelligence and determination. In years to come she would be considered formidable. Mary smiled and rejoiced in the flesh of her womb, the daughter of her heart. Her pleasure was marred only by the expression on Eleanor's face. The two women embraced.

'It is so good to see you, my dear.' Mary smiled but felt a tremor of anxiety.

'You look worried, is anything troubling you?'

Eleanor led her mother into the drawing room, not sure where to begin. She had expected Mary to be, if not distraught, certainly deeply distressed. Eleanor's letter from Edgar had arrived the day before yesterday. He and Eleanor had had an understanding and a certain grudging admiration for each other over the years. Therefore their relationship had been relatively untroubled by disagreement. Clearly from the open nature of Edgar's letter he had intended to give Eleanor all the facts concerning his decision to leave her mother. This would help Eleanor to act as Mother's comforter.

'I have heard from Edgar.'

Mary looked surprised. Edgar was rather a secretive man and now, she had convinced herself that it was only a matter of time before he returned. She was surprised he had written to Eleanor. To her knowledge, he had never done so before.

'You know he has moved into his club, for a while. He needs to prepare himself for his lecture tour in the States.' There was a pause during which both women felt at a loss as to what to say next.

'But, Mother, I don't think you should regard the move as temporary.' Eleanor spoke very quietly. Clearly this was going to be more difficult than she imagined.

'Why not? Perhaps, my dear, you should read what he wrote to me. He has been under a terrible strain lately and all this dreadful upset with Rachel has not helped.'

'When has Rachel ever helped?' Eleanor had been mortified on so many occasions, during their childhood, by Rachel's sometimes bizarre behaviour. She felt that coping with Mother was going to be quite enough for the time being. Mary collected Edgar's letter from her bedroom and read most of it to Eleanor. She made no comment but took another letter from her own handbag and handed it to Mary.

Dear Eleanor,

Although we have enjoyed a harmonious relationship during the years I have spent as your step-father, I suspect this will be our last communication. The severing of our relationship is inevitable, in view of my decision to leave your mother. I would want and expect you to devote all your loyalty to her.

I have written, to explain, why I must leave. In an effort to spare her feelings as much as possible, I have not acquainted her with the most significant of those reasons. Essentially, I have fallen in love with another woman. Your mother believes that overwork has had an adverse effect upon our relationship. It is true that I have put in long hours on my current book. However, that is not the reason for the decision that has led to the present circumstances. I am sorry that I am leaving you to convince her of that fact.

I shall be leaving for the States very soon and will be accompanied by the woman I intend to end my days with. She has worked with me and helped me with my research. During the many hours we have spent in each others company, we have both come to realise that our relationship cannot remain purely professional.

It is my dearest wish that in time your mother will also find happiness, with someone else. Until that happens, I am confident you will provide the support she needs.

Edgar.

Mary felt a chill spread through her. This was utterly despicable. He could not tell her the truth, he hid behind his step-daughter. How long had he been deceiving her she wondered? Who else knew what was going on? She thought of the many people who had attended her dinner parties and wondered, had they been laughing behind her back or had they just felt sorry for her - poor old Mary.The recent heartache and despair shrivelled as she sat staring, unseeing into the fire. It was replaced by a deep loathing. He may wish to end his days with this unnamed woman, but as long as I live, he will not be able to marry her!

Eleanor watched her mother and, probably for the first time in her life, felt a great sorrow for this woman who had always seemed so strong and admirable. She knew that Mary had built her life around Edgar, to the point where her children might have justifiably felt neglected. What would she do now? Eleanor assumed her mother was in her mid-fifties - she had always refused to give her age - so much life left from the three score years and ten. Empty, bitter years, at that moment Eleanor promised herself that she would never let a man take over her life She was shaken out of her thoughts by her mother's voice. She had never heard such coldness and control.

'I believe Edgar has behaved contemptibly. He has deceived me and left you to do his dirty work. I will not have his name mentioned in my hearing again. I would be extremely grateful if you would write to Malcolm and explain what has happened. Life will go on. The most pressing problem at the moment, and not for the first time, is Rachel. We will dine and after our meal, I will tell you what we have to do tomorrow.'

When Eleanor got into bed that night, she was relieved that in forty eight hours she would be back in her own flat in Derby. It had been her intention to tell Mother about Robert but now was most definitely not the time.

103

Jack arrived at his in-laws unexpectedly that Saturday morning.

'Caroline isn't at all well, can you come round? I don't know whether to get the doctor or what.'

'Well, if you want to go straight back, I'll have to bring Jenny with me. Albert has gone to the cobblers, he could be ages.'

'I think you had better come now, if you don't mind.'

Gladys wrote a note for Albert then grabbed a coat for herself and one for Jenny. She pushed Jenny out of the door; the child only just had time to grab Benjy.

Nobody spoke in the car and Jenny wondered what all the fuss was about. After all that had happened recently, she decided it was best not to ask or to care about anything. Then no-one could hurt you. Even with Grandad, she knew old people died; she was frightened she might lose him too. She had often heard Grandma and Grandad talk about friends they had lost. When she looked at him, he seemed very, very old.

As they arrived at the flat, Caroline could be heard groaning. Gladys rushed in and after a quick inspection said, 'I think she's started, Jack, get an ambulance.' Jenny started to cry, the noises Caroline was making were dreadful.

'Keep the child with you when you have 'phoned until we can get Caroline in the ambulance.'

Jack took Jenny's hand, 'We'll go to the 'phone box on the corner, then we can go to the park. We will see or hear the ambulance when it arrives.' Jenny nodded.

Uncle Jack seemed very excited, as they rushed along the road. He used the 'phone box but then did not seem to know what to do. Jenny stood very quietly, with her fingers in her mouth. After a few minutes, he made up his mind.

'Come on, we'll go back to the flat and see how your Auntie is.' In the flat, the noises were louder. Jenny put her hands over her ears. She was very frightened. Gladys seemed cross with them for coming back.

'For goodness sake, Jack, what have you brought her back here for?'

'I just wanted you to know that the ambulance is on its way. What was I supposed to do?'

'Look at her! I expected you to use some common sense; take her to the park.'

'But what happens when the ambulance comes?'

'Don't worry, I'll go with her, you look after Jenny.' Jack looked as though he was going to protest but Gladys had already turned away, back to her duty of looking after her daughter.

'Looks like we're in the way here. Come on.' Jenny thought that perhaps people did not explain things to Uncle Jack either. Perhaps no-one liked him. She took his hand and walked with him to the garden.

Eleanor and Mary did not talk much at the breakfast table. The servants had been told nothing; conversation, in their hearing, had to be general. However, the post brought the first shock of the day. It was from Edgar's solicitors. Mary read it and then passed it to Eleanor, without comment. She could scarcely believe what she had read.

'How are you supposed to sort out your belongings in six weeks!'

'Clearly, Edgar does not think that an unreasonable expectation.'

'But you have nowhere else to go, even as a temporary measure.'

'Then clearly, I am going to have to start looking immediately. One thing is certain, my dear. I will not beg or plead with that man. He wants me out in six weeks, then I will be. May he rot.'

Eleanor had never heard her mother speak with such vehemence. On reflection, she decided it was probably better having to deal with an angry abandoned wife than a weeping, incoherent one. Her present attitude suggested that whatever Mother had to undertake would be done with a will.

'What is your plan for today?'

'We must go to the hospital and see if we can get any sense out of the doctors. Stephen's father wants to know if the birth has been registered. I suppose I shall have to tell our staff that I shall be leaving here. Once again, Edgar has left someone else to do the unpleasant jobs.' Mary spat the words out. It's her hatred that will keep her going, Eleanor thought. For beneath the brave exterior, she got a momentary glimpse of a crushed and broken woman.

'Who is Stephen?' Eleanor asked. For a moment Mary looked startled and then realised that, of course, Eleanor knew nothing of the most recent events.

'Oh, my dear, where do I begin?'

Jack unlocked the gate. Jenny hesitated before following him. She felt cold inside, her legs did not want to carry her but she had no choice. She squeezed Benjy tightly and stood while Jack locked the gate after them.

'We must celebrate tonight, Jenny. You are going to have a brand new cousin.' Jenny had never seen Uncle Jack quite like this before. He seemed to shimmer with excitement. He kept touching her. It was wonderful to be made a fuss of, to be noticed. She decided she would make the most of it while she could. The new baby will get all the attention once it arrives. They walked towards the swing and Uncle Jack pushed her until she was squealing with delight. He walked around to the front of the swing. Her skirt was billowing up and her knickers were showing but she didn't care. When the swing slowed down, he suggested they play hide and seek in the bushes. Jenny wasn't sure; the bushes were very dark.

'We can hide together,' Jack said.

'But who will find us, there's no-one here?'

'There might be, lets find a good hiding place. Then when someone comes along, we can jump out and say BOO!'

It seemed very strange to Jenny but she looked up at Uncle Jack and smiled She had learned, long ago, that grown-ups did inexplicable things. Uncle Jack smiled, with his mouth, but his eyes looked strange. Jenny felt a shiver go down her spine. I wish Grandad were here, she thought.

Jack soon found a large laurel bush just off the path. It was tall and there were few small branches or leaves near the ground. It was shielded from the path by younger and bushier plants and from the road, by railings and a hedge. Jack held her hand tightly and pulled her into the bush. A branch caught her leg and scratched it, she whimpered. Jack picked her up and held her tightly. She could hear his heavy breathing and feel his hot breath on her face. The same familiar smell made her feel sick. He tried to kiss her but she turned her face away. His full wet lips slid across her face, leaving a snail-like trail of saliva.

'Put me down, Uncle Jack, please, I want to go home,' she whispered. She could feel her heart thudding in her chest and there was a roaring sound in her ears.

Slowly Jack let her slide down towards the ground. Slowly down his chest and stomach. She was suddenly aware of something hard pressing against her. Jack held her there. Helpless, she could not reach the ground, she could not run away. She opened her mouth to cry out, in despair and terror. With her first cry, Jack had dropped her on her feet and grabbed her by the back of the neck, forcing her face into the material of his trousers. She could not breathe. Her cries died in her throat. The roaring in her ears got louder. She tried to hit him with her fist but he grabbed her wrist.

'Hold it! Hold it!' He hissed. She did not know what he meant. He let go of her hand and started fumbling in his trousers. She could not escape, he was still holding her by the neck. Her legs were buckling beneath her, she had not the strength to kick him. Then he grabbed her hand again.

'Hold it!' He pulled her hand against him. She could feel something hard sticking out of his trousers. 'Hold it!' He forced her hand to hold the thing. He was grunting. His grasp of her wrist was agonising. He started moving her hand back and forth, back and forth, faster and faster. He groaned. The grip on her neck relaxed. Her arm was aching, she felt sick and still he moved her hand back and forth. Suddenly he gave a cry that made the hair on the back of Jenny's bruised neck stand on end. He shuddered and was still. Jenny was paralysed with terror. She became aware that her aching hand and wrist were wet and sticky. She went to wipe her hand down her skirt but Jack stopped her.

'Don't do that.' He grabbed her hand and wiped it on his handkerchief.

Jenny felt totally numb. When Jack took her hand, she turned, without a word and picked her way carefully back to the path. Jack walked slowly and while he walked, he talked to Jenny. He told her that Grandma and Grandad would be very upset if they knew what she had done. If they found out what she had done, they would send her away. Uncle Jack did not want that to happen so it would be best if she did not say anything. He promised that he would not say anything either.

Jenny did not reply, his voice seemed to be coming from a long way away. She longed for her Mummy and Daddy; even though she did not know him very well, she longed for Stephen. She would have loved him and tried to be good to him. She longed for Grandma and Grandad. She longed for Benjy. With horror, she realised that she must have dropped him. With the resignation of the totally defeated, she did not tell her Uncle Jack. She had been so naughty, even Benjy did not want her anymore. I am all alone now. She thought of Benjy and felt as though her heart would break. She hoped a nice little girl would find him and love him.

It rained heavily that night and Benjy became saturated. A breeze rose shuffling last winter's leaves. Slowly, during the hours of darkness, his outline was blurred as more and more leaves settled under the branches of the old laurel tree.

Finally, he was completely covered.

That night, for the first time, Gladys and Albert were woken by the sound of Jenny, screaming in her sleep.

Chapter 7

He struggled out of a deep, dreamless sleep. At first, he could not place the noise: had a cat got into the flat? Then finally, wide awake, he realised it was Stephen. Alec wearily clambered out of bed and went to make a bottle. He would be very glad when Stephen slept through the night. Life had never been so hectic. Although he was in a routine and Stephen had settled well in the creche, there never seemed to be a moment to just relax. He thought about the evenings he used to spend at the jazz club. That seemed a lifetime ago.

Gwen had left the flat and was sharing with a girl friend. She occasionally popped round but there was a distance between them that neither knew how to overcome. She would always have a special place in his heart but after the way he had used her, he knew she must feel deeply hurt.

Weekends were taken up with washing, ironing and visiting Rachel. He felt he was slowly helping her out of the dark abyss she had fallen into. The E.C.T. was, according to the doctors, helping her to overcome her depression. It was still very distressing to see her after a session of treatment when she was so disorientated and tearful. She always asked to see Jenny but Mary Cardew had been unable to make any progress with the Warrs, particularly Gladys. Alec did not believe there was any realistic chance of getting Jenny into the hospital to visit her mother but he assumed that once better, Rachel would be able to demand access to her daughter.

Alec picked Stephen up. His face was scarlet with weeping and his arms thrashed about as he sought nourishment. As soon as he was in Alec's arms, his cries subsided into whimpers. These were immediately silenced as Alec put the bottle teat into his mouth. Alec glanced at the clock, 4 a.m. and a full day's work ahead. Not for the first time, he thought how much society undervalued the duties of young mothers. He was glad he had insisted on registering Stephen's birth. Now no-one could deny his right to parental involvement. He dozed intermittently, as Stephen took his feed and was asleep within seconds of placing the baby back into his cot.

Caroline was out of hospital, having survived a long and excruciating labour, the like of which, she believed had never before been endured by womankind. The baby, a girl, was called Pauline. She was a fat, fretful baby who already had the same whining note in her cry that was so often to be heard in her mother's voice.

Gladys fussed around her daughter and new grandchild; her knitting needles were never still. Jack viewed the interminable conversations about colic, nappies, teething, demand feeding etc. etc. with weary resignation. There were times when he felt like a barely tolerated lodger in his own home. Caroline had never been the most enthusiastic cook or housewife but now she claimed permanent exhaustion. So the only time he had a cooked meal was when Gladys came round or if he did it himself. None of their few friends had children so he could not compare notes with other new fathers. He suspected that Caroline was making a three act drama out of an event that other women took in their stride. He could not remember Rachel making so much fuss when Jenny was born. Of course, it was different with the second one, Gladys had drawn a veil of secrecy over that particular event. All he knew was that Rachel was in hospital with an unspecified illness. Jack assumed that the baby was with her. Jack knew that Caroline and Gladys had long and involved conversations about Rachel and Charles when he, Jack, was not around. However, these tete a tetes were more and more difficult to conduct as it was becoming difficult for the two women to have time alone.

The harsh winter, although now over, had taken its toll of Albert's health. He had had a couple of nasty, chesty coughs that had left him easily tired and often wheezy. Gladys had got into the habit of visiting Caroline on Saturdays. Then if Jack took Jenny out for an hour or two, Gladys could spend time with Caroline and baby Pauline. Meanwhile, Albert could have some peace and quiet on his own, with his feet up. Jack was quite happy with this arrangement.

Gladys took her responsibilities, for Jenny, very seriously. Looking after someone else's child was daunting, especially when that someone was Charles. For many months now, Jenny had seemed unnaturally quiet. She had no appetite and often succumbed to coughs and colds. She was having nightmares regularly and would wake up screaming with terror. No matter what Gladys and Albert did, Jenny seemed unable to explain what was frightening her. One night when Gladys went to check that she was asleep, she found the child standing in the corner of the bedroom with her nose pressed against the wall. Gladys tried to get her into bed but she refused to move. When Albert came upstairs, they decided she must be walking in her sleep. Albert put his arm around her. Her whole body felt chilled to the bone.

'What's the matter, my little chick?' he asked very gently. There was a long pause and then, as though she had given the matter considerable thought, she replied, in a voice devoid of inflection or feeling.

'I've been a naughty girl.'

'It's all right , my love, you've stood here long enough. You can get back into bed now.'

He very gently took her ice-cold hand. Her fingers curled around his and without protest, she let him lead her back to bed. She climbed in and, without a word, curled up on her side. Her fingers slid into her mouth, she gave a sigh and slept. Albert sat on the bed and stroked her forehead. Gradually he felt the warmth return to her and he tip-toed downstairs.

'What are we going to do, Bert?' Gladys sat on the edge of her chair her hands clasped tightly together. 'Supposing she had tried to come downstairs. She could have broken her neck. What would Charles think if she had an accident when we are supposed to be looking after her?'

'Poor little soul, she's only five and just think what's happened to her in her short life. She's lost her mum, her dad's miles away, she gets a brother and then he disappears. I don't suppose Charles is going to encourage any kind of contact between Rachel, Stephen and Jenny, do you? She's only got us and now with Pauline's arrival, she's bound to feel a bit left out, a bit jealous probably.'

'Do you think that is what it is?'

'Well the nightmares usually come after you've taken her over to Jack and Caroline's. Perhaps seeing the baby upsets her, reminds her of Stephen. I had hoped it would help to take her mind off her brother, perhaps I was wrong.'

'So, does that mean you don't think we should go so often?' Gladys bristled slightly. She had lost three sons, been deprived of the grandson she thought was hers and now Albert was suggesting she should see less of her grand daughter who, indisputably, was hers. Albert smiled at her; fiery as ever, age had not diminished the terrier like spirit in his diminutive wife. He patted her hand gently.

'Of course not, my dear, I know how much that baby means to you. All I'm suggesting is that Jenny could be involved more. Perhaps hold the baby a bit, help to give her her bottle. Make her feel useful, important.' Gladys raised her eyebrows. 'I think that's a pretty tall order. You know what Caroline's like , she will scarcely let Jack near the baby, never mind Jenny.'

Albert shrugged, his very bones ached with fatigue. He had forgotten what it was like to feel well; what it was like to have some

110

energy. I'm like an old clock, my spring has run down and I cannot rewind myself any more. He looked at Gladys and thought back over the years they had spent together. They had had their good times, but, oh, the sorrows and heartaches. He took her hand in his. It was gnarled, with swollen knuckles and veins like thick blue ropes, under the skin.The medals of work, the reward for struggling against all odds.

'We'll just have to do our best for her, won't we lass.'

Eleanor went back to Derby on the 6 p.m. train. It had been a harrowing weekend but at least she had been able to go to the hospital with Mother to visit Rachel and later discuss where Mother should look for property. I must write to Malcolm, she thought. At the end of the war, he had gone to America and was now working for an advertising organisation. Eleanor knew that Malcolm was the apple of his mother's eye. Although she did not resent that special feeling, she did think it merited a visit home.

There had been little opportunity to talk to Mother about Robert. As Eleanor relaxed in the empty carriage, she wondered if there was, in fact, anything to talk about. Robert was pleasant enough but rather too intense for Eleanor's liking. Another problem was that he was a devout Catholic. Eleanor thought about her mother's marriage. She had been six when her father, George, had died so had few memories of him. In many ways, it seemed to Eleanor that Mary's marriage to Edgar had been her only relationship. Eleanor knew instinctively that she could never hero-worship a man, as her mother had worshipped Edgar. She thought about Charles and Rachel. Charles was a prig and a bore, albeit a good looking one. Rachel was a complete nuisance and had always been. Clearly, after what the doctor had said yesterday, it was more serious than that. Schizophrenia was the official view, a polite word for insanity, Eleanor thought. The diagnosis had left her mother reeling. I will never put myself through all that. I will never marry. I will build my life around things, not people. People hurt you.

Jenny woke with a start, she had been dreaming. It had been one of her nice dreams and had included Benjy. It was with infinite sadness, that she realised, yet again, that he was gone and she would never see him again. She lay in bed and listened to the sounds of Grandma and Grandad in the kitchen. It was a school day and already, Jenny could feel the knot of anxiety tying her stomach into a tight, tense mass. Grandma made her eat breakfast even though she always felt sick in the mornings. Perhaps, Jenny thought, if I lie here and say I have a headache, they will let me stay at home.

She could hear Albert calling her. Telling her that her porridge was ready. Jenny felt her stomach clench and she retched at the thought of food. I had better go down, otherwise Grandad will have to climb up the stairs and it will make him puff. She often watched Albert, when his chest was wheezy. His face went a funny colour and it made a shiver of fear creep down her back. On these occasions she would sit very still and whisper in her head.

'If I am good, Grandad will not feel poorly.' She would say it over and over again. Then, she wanted more than anything to hug Benjy but he was gone. There was no-one to hug.

She walked down the stairs, counting them as she went...10, 11, 12. Gladys bustled out of the kitchen.

'Hurry up, Jenny, or Grandad will have to walk to school too fast.'

She slid into her chair and looked, with horror, at the steaming bowl. She blinked back the tears. She did not want any breakfast but if she did not eat it, Grandma would be cross. She did not want to make Grandad hurry because it would make him poorly. She did not want to go to school because she was frightened that maybe Grandma and Grandad would not be there when she got back. If she did not go to school, her teachers would be cross. She felt as though she was falling down, down, being smothered. Everything was closing in on her, she knew that even Grandad could not make things any better.

She picked up her spoon and scooped up some porridge, placing it gingerly in her mouth. She tried to swallow but it felt as though she had a pebble stuck in her throat. Albert watched her with deep concern.

'Have a little tea, to wash it down.' He smiled encouragingly.

'Then I'll have a spoonful and then you can have a spoonful.' A thin shaft of light, for a moment, pierced the despair which shadowed her every thought and deed. She smiled at him and swallowed.

'That's a good girl.' With help, the bowl was emptied before Gladys came out of the kitchen.

'There you are, that wasn't so bad.' She cleared, away the bowl. 'Now quickly, go and get washed and dressed. Grandad will wait for you down here.'

They walked along the balcony, Jenny in her school clothes looked a generation too old. Gladys was determined that the child would be a credit to her father and had dressed her in tunic, velour hat and gabardine mac., similar to the clothes Caroline would have worn, when she was at school. Albert talked softly and reassuringly but could feel the tension, in the child, like an electric charge. They reached the end of the balcony and started to go down the stairs. Better than yesterday, he thought. Suddenly, Jenny gave a whimper and letting go of his hand, leant against the wall. With a great gurgling and gushing, the porridge hit the concrete wall and stairs with such force that it splashed both Jenny and Albert's legs. He held her head as she heaved and retched until her stomach was empty.

She started to cry. 'I'm sorry, Grandad, I'm sorry.' She clung to him. The smell of bile clotted the air. He took her hand and led her back to the flat. When Gladys came to see what was the matter, Albert put his fingers to his lips. Jenny was quickly cleaned up and given a sip of water. Gladys put two plain biscuits in a bit of paper.

'Have these with your milk, dear. When you are feeling better.' She turned to Albert. 'Go down the other stairs, we don't want her being sick again. I'll get some disinfectant and clear up the mess.'

'Leave it until I get back.'

'I will not. What would people think? Besides walking the child to school will be quite enough.' She bustled off muttering to herself. It made Jenny feel bad. She knew she was in the way. Grandad and Grandma would not have all this extra work, if it were not for her.

They arrived at the school gates and Jenny's teachers were waiting to meet her. Jenny had run home so often that this seemed the only way to ensure she remained in school. Jenny's teacher, Miss Armstrong, was perplexed. It wasn't as though the child could not cope with the work. She was clearly bright and could read before she came to school. She seemed frightened of everything. Unfortunately, her appearance did not help. The poor child had had the most dreadful squint, caused by a bad attack of measles, she understood.

Of course, children could be very cruel. Before Jenny got her glasses, she was teased and called 'boss eyes'; now she had her glasses she was called 'four eyes'. The result was that she did not have any friends. At play and dinner times, she latched onto a teacher or dinner lady, in the playground, like a limpet. After several attempts to gain Jenny's confidence, Miss Armstrong had concluded that either the time was not right or else she was not the person Jenny felt she could open up to.

Rachel had been in hospital for ten weeks and was now desperate to get out. She felt increasingly disturbed by the behaviour of the other patients. I am not like them but when you are surrounded by lunatics, it is difficult to stop your behaviour becoming equally bizarre. She felt a dizzy new confidence in the future. The only problem was Jenny. Alec had not been able to bring the child, nor had Mary. I have got to get out of hospital soon, Rachel thought, before Jenny forgets me.

Mary had visited several times but they had been difficult occasions for both women. They had no natural empathy and secretly blamed each other for their respective unhappinesses. Mary's decision to marry Edgar had been an inexplicable act of disloyalty, as far as Rachel was concerned. Mary regarded Rachel's persistent bad behaviour, throughout childhood and adolescence - culminating in the present fiasco - as the root cause of Edgar's departure.

As Rachel's condition had improved, the diagnosis had been changed to manic depression. When Mary was told, she had mixed feelings. Anything was better than schizophrenia but manic depression killed - if a careful watch was not kept. George had succeeded. Would Rachel die by her own hand the next time she was engulfed by depression? The thought of watching or monitoring her daughter's behaviour for the rest of her life was a horrifying prospect. The only solution seemed to be Alec. This young man had shown a dogged persistence that Mary could only admire.

I have my future to think of, Mary thought. Her new home was a huge ten roomed flat, on the top floor of a magnificent mansion in Kensington. She had taken very considerable delight in removing eighty percent of the furniture from Edgar's house. The most difficult thing had been talking to the servants. She had said as little as possible and tried to give the impression that it was her decision to move, not Edgar's. She told the staff they could remain in the house until Edgar decided whether or not they were to remain in his employ. If they were going to be dismissed, he could do it himself. That is one job he will not palm on to me.

There was so much to be done to the flat. She wanted to have it decorated throughout. It was a luxury to be able to make all the decisions regarding colour schemes, curtains, carpets. Such freedom of choice drew attention to her loneliness. Although her income from her father's estate ensured that she would be able to live comfortably, she had decided not to have any servants either living in or daily. For the first time in her life, she had to fend for herself entirely. It helped to fill the days that now stretched before her, into oblivion, with only the hope that at least two of her children would bring some of their own lives to share with her.

She had written short notes to friends and the few relatives with whom she had contact, giving her new address. No reference was made to Edgar. It was with mixed feelings, that she read a letter from her second cousin Philip. In Mary's opinion, he was probably the most neurotic man she had ever met. He was an extremely creative and talented architect but his personal life had always been a maelstrom. His early marriage, to an Austrian 'countess' had produced one daughter and a level of anguish that beggared the imagination, during its stormy twenty nine month duration. The subsequent five years had seen the waging of a war of attrition between Philip and his ex-wife. This encompassed every mortal possession they had jointly shared as well as their daughter, Sarah, who was shunted back and forth between her parents until all those involved were reduced to a state of mental and physical exhaustion.

It appeared, from Philip's letter that matters had been concluded, if not satisfactorily, at least legally. He now found himself with a daughter, for whom he had custody - along with those possessions the divorce judge had decided he might keep. Included amongst which was a set of fish knives; the forks, Mary learned later from a highly indignant Philip, had been allocated -Mary guessed, by a wholly exasperated judge, - to the ex-wife! These were details not worthy of too much of Mary's time and consideration. However, what she could not ignore was the suggestion, from Philip, that he and Sarah should come to share Mary's flat. The cost and conditions of the divorce had left Philip homeless.

Mary sat in her favourite chair which, along with everything else, was covered in dust sheets. The decorators were coming in next week. She gazed out of the window. She was high up enough to see the tops of the trees in the street below and could watch pigeons flying past, at eye level. Certainly the flat was large enough for them each to have a bedroom. She would have her own sitting room. This would leave the large room at the back for Philip and the child to have for themselves. It was clearly possible but did she want a child underfoot? Mary had never found children's company agreeable and she suspected that Sarah would be a trying, precocious child. How could she be anything else when her parents had given her such a bad example? Mary contemplated the alternative. Did she really want to live alone? Whilst cherishing solitude, there was a difference between retreating to your own personal sanctuary from choice and being alone because there was no choice. On balance, Mary decided, with reservations, it would be better to invite Philip and Sarah to come to live with her and share expenses. After all, if it didn't work she could always ask Philip to leave. If she turned his suggestion down now, he would have to find somewhere else or someone else to live with; this opportunity would be lost.

Alec felt weak-kneed with delight as he led Rachel into his home, the home that would now be hers as well. He saw it, for the first time, as he supposed she must be seeing it. He had never been particularly bothered by his surroundings but looking at the solid but shabby furniture, he suddenly felt ashamed. This woman had come from a privileged and wealthy background. Surely she would scorn what he had to offer her. He watched her face anxiously for signs of disappointment.

She stood in the middle of the living room, taking in every detail of mud brown carpet, nondescript curtains. The armchairs that sagged and needed recovering but which Alec knew were comfortable. He could feel the panic rising in him, he had been a fool. When Rachel turned to face him, her eyes gleamed.

'I know its not much, Rachel, but we can do it up.' She moved towards him and placed a finger on his lips.

'Don't.' She said, as she put her arms tightly around his neck and hugged him. Alec felt his skin tingle with pleasure; all the struggling with Stephen had been worthwhile. He seemed to be glowing with joy. His heart felt as though it was bursting, so that he wanted to shout and dance. Can too much happiness kill you, he wondered. He loosened her grip and holding her by the shoulders looked at her, long and hard. 'I want to etch every detail, of how you look right now, into my memory. So when I am a doddering old codger, I will be able to recapture this moment.'

Rachel giggled. He wanted her now. All he wanted was to take her to his bed, no their bed and make gentle, passionate, endless love. This was his woman, for the rest of their lives. He took her hand.

'Come with me.' Just then, they heard a wailing from Stephen's bedroom.

She smiled at him, 'I'll go, he needs me now. You'll have to wait!' Alec watched her, by Christ my girl, you are worth waiting for.

'Jack's a long time.' Caroline glanced at her watch, 'it's going to get dark soon.'

Gladys had been sitting in her coat for half an hour. She tutted. She had to make Albert's tea when she got back. She stood up and went to the window.

'They're coming now.' She watched as Jack and Jenny walked up the road. There was something wrong. Jenny seemed to be limping. They stopped and Jack bent down and seemed to be speaking to the child. She looked, to Gladys, as though she were trying to pull away from Jack. There was definitely something wrong, Gladys could sense it. I'd better not say anything to Caroline, she'll only get herself into a state. Jack tugged at the child's hand, she seemed to be crying.

Once Jack and Jenny disappeared from Gladys' view, there was a delay before they arrived at the front door. As soon as the door opened, Jenny rushed in; she was crying. She ran to Gladys and sobbed into her lap.

'What's the matter, what's happened? I told you to be careful with her, Jack.'

'I have been careful, for goodness sake. It's not my fault if she decides to let go of the swing, is it?'

'Good God, where is she hurt?' Gladys started to examine arms and legs for evidence of Jack's laxity. 'Not her head! Did you bang your head, dear?' Gladys ran her hand gently over Jenny's head. There were no obvious bumps. Jenny shook her head, the tears continued to stream down her face.

'You know your trouble, Mum. You make too much fuss of that child. She's got to take a bump or two. She's all right, don't you think I checked myself. What kind of man do you think I am?' He patted Jenny on the head.

'You're all right, aren't you Jen. I look after you, don't I ?' Jenny looked at him but neither confirmed nor denied his statement. Jack cleared his throat and turned to Caroline. 'How are my two girls, then?'

Gladys put Jenny's coat and hat on. She felt deeply concerned but was not sure what it was that made her feel so uneasy. Was she molly-coddling the child? There was something about Jack that was not quite right but she could not be sure what it was.

'We'd better be off now.' She left, Jenny followed her meekly out of the flat. The tears had stopped but her eyes were puffy behind the wire framed National Health spectacles. Jenny still seemed to be limping, as she had when Gladys watched her walking up the road, with Jack.

'What's the matter, why are you walking like that?'

'My bottom's sore.' Jenny whispered.

Gladys leaned over, 'What did you say?'

'My bottom's sore.'

'Did you fall on your bottom, when you came off the swing?' Jenny shook her head.

'Well, you were all right before.'

Jenny made no comment, there seemed no point. Adults lived in a strange way that she did not understand. Uncle Jack had lied but she did not suppose that anyone would believe her if she said so. Besides if she told Grandma what had really happened, there would be trouble. She said nothing.

Albert looked quite worried when they got home.

'You're very late, I was beginning to think the worst.'

'It was Jack's fault, he was very late bringing Jenny back and what's more, he let her fall off the swing. She was in a terrible state when he got her back from the garden. I'm not sure we should let him take her out again, you know.'

Albert patted his knees, for Jenny to come to sit on his lap. He lifted her and as he sat her down, she winced. He looked at Gladys.

'She says her bottom's sore.'

'I think it would be a good idea if you had a nice warm bath, before you go to bed, don't you?' Jenny leant against Albert; she breathed in the familiar smell of tobacco and Brylcreem. He had a comfortable, safe smell. His woollen cardigan, that Grandma had knitted, was soft against her cheek. She felt her eyelids slide slowly down. She gave a sigh. Perhaps she would never have to go to the garden with Uncle Jack again. After today and the accident she was supposed to have had, perhaps Grandma and Grandad would stop it. She could feel herself being lifted carefully and gently placed in Grandad's chair. Everything seemed to be coming from a long way away.

'I'll get the tin bath out, Glad. She can have a bath in front of the fire and then a bit of supper. Poor little mite, she seems to be exhausted. Shall I have a word with Jack?'

'One of us will have to, I'm not happy about this. What will Charles say when he gets back?' She started to undress the child. She got down to vest and knickers before she noticed the blood. Her heart gave a lurch. She leaned her forehead on the arm of the chair. Even though she was kneeling down, she felt so faint, she was frightened she would fall.

'Albert!' she called in a harsh whisper. 'Look!'

Albert struggled in with a bowl of water, to be poured into the bath. They both looked with horror as Gladys eased the knickers off the still sleeping child. The crutch of the knickers was soaked with blood.

'No wonder she said her bottom was sore. She must have fallen on her bottom.' Gladys thought for a moment; she examined the knickers carefully.

'But surely if that had happened, there would be dirt or mud on them. But there is nothing, no dirt at all.'

'So what did happen? I'm going to see if there is a cut or graze or anything.'

'Try not to wake her.' Albert knelt by the chair and gently rolled Jenny on to her side. Gladys examined the child's bottom.

'There's nothing at all.' They looked at each other. Gladys' eyes were wide, her face white.

'Surely Jack would not have interfered with her, would he?'

'We had better check.' They carefully rolled Jenny on to her back again. She stirred than put her fingers in her mouth and slept on.

'I can't believe this, There must be another explanation, he's a married man. He's married to our daughter.' Gladys could hear the panic in her voice. This was a nightmare. Charles was coming home soon. Things like this simply did not happen in decent families. She carefully lifted Jenny's legs apart. Her hands were shaking. The skin between the child's legs looked bruised. She looked at Albert. He placed his hand over hers and squeezed it gently.

'You've got to do it, girl.' Gladys struggled to her feet and walked, with faltering steps, to the bathroom. She found a small piece of cotton wool. She knelt down by the chair dipped the cotton wool in the bath water, squeezed it out and gently wiped between the lips of the child's vulva. Jenny winced in her sleep. There was blood on the cotton wool.

Kneeling together, like a pair of mediaeval statues at prayer, Albert clutched Gladys to him. She shook silently, with grief, for Jenny, for Charles, for Caroline and for herself and Albert.

'The man must be a monster,' she whispered. Albert felt impotent with rage and frustration. Rage that his son-in-law was capable of this, the most despicable of all crimes; frustration that, as an old man, he could do nothing about it.

'What on Earth are we going to do?' Gladys whispered, her voice faint.

'First of all we must get Jenny sorted out. Then we can decide what to do next. Get those knickers out of the way, she must not see them.'

After Jenny had gone to bed, Albert poured out a small tot of brandy for each of them. 'For medicinal purposes, we both need this.'

'Do we say anything to Jenny?'

'I don't think we do,' replied Albert, 'least said, soonest mended. It won't happen again because she will never be left on her own with Jack.'

'What about Caroline?'

Albert rested his head in his hands and took a deep breath.

'God alone knows, my dear. It would destroy the marriage and would Caroline thank us for that?'

'What about Pauline?'

'Surely he wouldn't do anything to his own daughter.'
They gazed into the fire; they both felt totally out of their depth.

Mary sat and looked intently at her beloved son, Malcolm. He had filled out since she last saw him. She noticed, with disquiet, the hint of an American drawl, so unlike her own perfect enunciation. He was bubbling with enthusiasm for his work. America was the land of opportunity, he kept repeating. Clearly that was where he thought his future lay. She ached to tell him how much she missed him. In her new solitary state, all she wanted to hear was that he intended to return to England to live. She could not ask this of him; a refusal would have been more than she could have borne. It must come from him, be what he wanted.

He seemed to scarcely notice the surroundings and apart from a throw away remark about Edgar, when he arrived, had behaved as though everything was the same as when he left. Mary did not want sympathy but a little concern and understanding was surely not too much to ask. A niggling little thought kept burrowing into her consciousness, did he really care? She pushed the thought aside. I must not let self pity cloud my judgment.

'Shall we go out for a meal, my dear? As you can see, I am virtually camping out until the decorators finish.'

'Well actually, I will have to be off soon. Obviously I wanted to see you but this is really combining business with pleasure. I have to see the guy who heads our operations in the U.K.; we have arranged to meet for a meal at 8 p.m.' He smiled his dazzling smile and the warm brown eyes seemed to offer the world. No wonder all the girls fall for him, Mary mused. She smiled, although disappointment made her face feel stiff and cold.

'Perhaps you had better be off, you don't want to be late, do you?'

'Let me take you out for tea tomorrow, we could go somewhere grand. It will be my last free afternoon before I fly back home.'
The word home jarred on Mary. He was just a visitor, someone who flew in and flew out. He stood up and despite Mary's considerable height, she still had to look up to him. He kissed her lightly on the forehead and patted her shoulder.

'See you tomorrow, Ma.' He was out of the flat with almost indecent haste. She heard his footsteps running down the marble stairs. Was it her imagination or did she sense relief in his departure? Obviously she had made the right decision when she wrote to Philip, agreeing to his sharing the flat with her.

Now that Caroline had had several months to recover from the trauma of childbirth, she was quite anxious to be taken out and about, by Jack. It was nice to show Pauline off to anyone who would notice. Since they had a very limited social life, Caroline thought visits to Albert and Gladys would fill the afternoons quite satisfactorily. Mum is bound to offer some tea, Caroline thought, which will save me a job. She was very conscious of a chill in the atmosphere when they arrived. So she decided to make herself useful in the kitchen; help Gladys get the meal ready.

'Oh! tinned pineapple and evaporated milk, Jack's favourite.' Gladys made no comment. There didn't seem to be much conversation coming from the living room either. In a desperate attempt to break the silence, Caroline asked,

'How's Jenny after her fall?'

Gladys' face seemed to be set, like a mask.

'She's all right but she won't be going to the park with Jack again.'

Caroline looked at her mother, puzzled.

'That's a bit hard on the kid isn't it? She enjoys going on the swing. You can't protect her from every little bump all her life.'

Gladys had the bread knife in her hand and she turned, in fury, so that Caroline stepped back. Gladys pointed the knife at her.

'I'm telling you, she will not go out with Jack again and that's an end to it.'

She turned back and hacked at the bread with such force that Caroline feared she might do herself an injury. There seemed no point in continuing with that line of conversation so she walked through to the living room and started to set the table.

Albert had Jenny on his knee and was reading her a story. The child had not spoken since they had arrived. Pauline lay, asleep, in her crib. Caroline looked at Jack who was sitting on a dining chair. He looked uncomfortable. He was a big man and the chair looked too small for him. He glanced at Caroline, grimaced and shrugged his shoulders. Clearly something was wrong but goodness only knew what it was. Caroline was well aware that her mother could be difficult and snappy but Dad was a dear and was always relied on to smooth things over. She could hardly interrupt the story Dad was reading. Once the table was set, she returned to the kitchen. Gladys was banging the china around so heavily it was a wonder she hadn't broken something.

'What's the matter, Mum?' Gladys pursed her lips and eyed her daughter warily, almost about to speak, she obviously changed her mind about what she wanted to say.

'Your Dad's not at all well, it's his chest again. Dr. Costello says there is nothing more he can do.' Caroline felt a great sense of relief.

'I thought it was something I'd done.' Gladys looked up quickly.

'No, it's nothing you've done.'

The two women looked at each other. No-one seeing them together would have taken them for mother and daughter. Gladys was tiny, birdlike, quick of thought and action. Her sparse grey hair was fluffed up to hide the thinning crown and a net held every hair in place. She was more than capable of the sharp retort and had had the strength of character to reform her husband, occasionally wayward in his youth. Caroline was tall like her father. She had a heavy build which, combined with a natural laziness, made her slow moving and placid. Provided she was not expected to exert herself, she was amiable enough not to cause outright unpleasantness. Unlike her mother, Caroline disliked housework intensely and cooking not much less. This caused a running battle with Jack. He felt, not unreasonably, that if he was out at work all day, he should at least have a clean, tidy flat to come home to. He also expected some kind of meal. Since neither of them was good at communicating thoughts and feelings; they had spent much of their time, particularly since Pauline's birth, grumbling and complaining about each other.

Caroline paused and digested her mother's remark.

'So it's Jack then, isn't it?' Gladys made no reply. She picked up plates with bread and margarine and a home made cake and went through to the living room. Jack leapt to his feet.

'Give me those, Mum. Is there anything else to come through?'

'It's all right , I can manage.'

The meal was punctuated by the sound of knife against plate, spoon against dish. Gladys and Albert gave all their attention to Jenny, encouraging her to eat something. Caroline kept glancing at Jack. He was sweating heavily and seemed on edge. She hoped he wasn't sickening for something, not now she had Pauline to cope with. The baby stirred and Caroline picked her up.

'Do you want me to make her a bottle?' Gladys asked.

'Please, Mum.'

'Come and look at your little cousin, Jenny.' Jack said, holding out his arms. Jenny went white and shrank back in her seat.

'Leave the child alone.' Albert said quietly. Jack snorted with irritation.

'What the hell's going on? Is all this because she fell off a bloody swing and bumped herself? What the hell are you going to do if she has a really bad fall?' Gladys came out of the kitchen, her eyes were blazing. 'Don't dare use your foul language in this house, least of all in front of the child!'

Caroline looked from husband to mother, 'I do think you are making a fuss, Mum.' Gladys glanced at Albert, her mind was in turmoil. What would happen if she told Caroline what she and Albert suspected? Supposing they were wrong. What would it do to Caroline's relationship with Jack? What would it do to her relationship with her own mother? Gladys looked at Pauline lying in her mother's arms. She was beginning to get fretful, she wanted her bottle. If I upset Caroline, Gladys thought, I know what will happen. She will bear me a grudge for ever and she will punish me by stopping me from seeing Pauline. Very quietly, Gladys said,

'I'll go and get her bottle.'

Albert had been watching his son-in-law and had tried to imagine what had gone on when Jenny was on her own with him. The bile that burned its way into his throat threatened to choke him. He must say something.

'Jack, I don't care what you think of the way we are looking after Jenny. Charles gave us the job and I think you know perfectly well why she will not be going out with you again.'

Caroline was rocking Pauline who, at the sound of angry voices, had started to cry.

'What is going on, Dad?'

'I don't want to say any more.'

'Well, you can't leave it like that.'

'I've had enough of this,' said Jack. He pushed back his chair abruptly.

Jenny started crying.

'What have you been saying? Telling fairy stories, I wouldn't wonder.' He glared at her. Albert stood up, leaned on the table. His mouth was working with a greater rage than he had ever experienced in the whole of his life.

'She has said nothing, she didn't need to.'

Caroline looked from one to the other, totally bewildered. Gladys rushed into the room, bottle in hand. She stood beside Albert her face white, her breath coming in shallow gasps.

'I think you had better get out of our house.' Albert said.

'But I've got to feed Pauline.' Caroline wailed.

'You can do that when you get her home, it won't take long.' Albert stood up straight and looked Jack directly in the eye. 'Please go.'

Jack's face seemed to swell with a suffusion of blood. The thick veins in his neck stood out blue against his florid skin.

'You…..stupid….old…..man.'

Each word was followed by a measured and menacing pause. He raised his hand across his chest. Gladys gave a shrill cry and leapt in front of Albert, raising her hands to defend them both. The back-handed blow made contact with her left shoulder, knocking her half off her feet. She fell back against Albert and they both staggered, in a desperate attempt to retain their balance. Jenny started screaming and Pauline joined in.

Albert put his arms around Gladys who was crying quietly, her left arm hung limp at her side. Jenny had got down from her seat and cowered behind them, her screams diminished into sobs.

'Get out of my house.' Albert's voice was quiet but the authority it held was undeniable. Caroline quickly gathered hers and the baby's things; she too was crying. Jack stood as though rooted to the spot. He looked like a man, sleepwalking. When Caroline was ready, she tugged Jack's sleeve.

'Come on, Jack. We know when we are not wanted.'

The ensuing quiet in the Warr's flat was punctuated by the diminishing sounds of Pauline's cries, as her parents took her home and the gentle cries of Jenny, still clutching on to her grandparents.

Charles sat at his desk, in his office in Klagenfurt. He was now a commissioned officer in the Intelligence Corps. Although the war was over, his job of interrogating prisoners, charged with war crimes, was not. He read, with satisfaction, the latest letter from his solicitor. His divorce from Rachel was now absolute. He was legally free of her. His smile of satisfaction faded as he thought back to the days when he had courted her and, Joy of Joys, made her his wife. He gasped with the pain of bitterness, which seemed to turn a knife in his chest. His intense love had undergone the most dangerous metamorphosis of all, it was now an unrelenting hatred.

If he was free, so must she be. She could do what she wanted with whomsoever she wanted and there was nothing he could do to stop her. All I can do is control how and when she sees Jenny. He had, of course, been awarded custody. He knew he could not stop Jenny from seeing her mother entirely; it would put him in a bad light. However, he mused, I would be wholly justified in insisting that all contact be supervised. So Rachel would have to come to my parents' home and face my mother's wrath. It would hardly make visits protracted or comfortable. It may well be that, under such conditions, Rachel decides to keep contact to a minimum. Charles smiled to himself. That way, I get what I want but it will be Rachel who looks like the uncaring parent, I will just be the poor deserted father, doing his best.

He fed a clean sheet of paper into his typewriter and quickly typed a reply to his solicitor, suggesting a visit once a month, to the flat in Camden Town. He also asked about his furniture. His passionate feelings, on the night Rachel tried to kill herself, had subsided. He now saw no reason why furniture etc., that he had bought and paid for, should not be put in store. He presumed that Mary Cardew would have had everything moved to her home, in Wimbledon. There was certainly plenty of storage space. He knew he would eventually have to leave the army and he would need to set up home for Jenny and himself.

He quickly tidied his desk, it was getting late. There was some big 'do' in the officers' mess this evening. Officers, wives and girl-friends would be there. He had so far resisted all temptations to get involved with another woman. His good looks had led many young women both Austrians and W.A.C's to try their luck. He had maintained a cool distance and when asked if he were married, took great delight in declaring loudly, to any assembled throng, that he was an unmarried father. This did nothing to deter the keenest admirers. So Charles had all the benefits of endless flattery with none of the attendant risks of betrayal or deceit.

He paused for a moment and looked at the picture of himself with Jenny, that sat on his desk. He had spent so little time with her, she seemed a nice enough little thing but he could not in all honesty say that he missed her. Still, she would be all right with his Mum and Dad. They both thought the world of her. As he looked his vision blurred with unshed tears of anger and bitterness. The image of Jenny seemed to fade and was replace by that of Rachel. With a sick feeling in his heart, Charles acknowledged that he could not make a clean break; could not put the whole sordid business of Rachel behind him. Jenny's very existence made that impossible. She was living, breathing proof of his relationship with her mother.

The wound will never heal, every time I see the child, I will be reminded. The pain will never end. He sat with his head in his hands. He realised that the last thing he wanted to do, was go to the officers' mess and make polite, vacuous conversation with stupid, giggling women. What he wanted to do was get drunk.

Mary read Charles' letter with exasperation. She had enough to do organising the redecoration of the flat and installing Philip and Sarah. As far as she knew, Rachel had got all the furniture from the house in

Redburn Street Although it had been stored for a while in Wimbledon, once Mary had left, the furniture had had to be removed too. She did not see what all the fuss was about. It was paltry stuff, ugly, heavy and of little value. Having seen the style of furniture favoured by Gladys and Albert Warr, she could see where Charles got his taste from. She sighed. It was hardly feasible to reply to Charles' letter with the information that his furniture was now gracing his successor's flat. That would inevitably inflame an already acrimonious situation. She decided to pass the letter on to Rachel and Alec. It was their problem, let them sort it out.

Jenny had not seen Jack, Caroline or baby Pauline since the dreadful Saturday when Jack hit Gladys. Jenny knew that Grandma visited Caroline during the day, when Jack was at work and she, Jenny, was at school. There was never any mention of what had happened, even though Gladys still suffered considerable pain in her left shoulder. The movement in her arm was very restricted. Jenny was aware of a great sadness pervading the flat. Although neither Grandad nor Grandma treated her any differently, Jenny felt it must be her fault somehow. After all, wasn't she the cause of the dreadful argument?

She did everything she could to please her grandparents. Gladys did not like her to play outside with the other children on the council estate. She regarded them as common and therefore liable to teach Jenny rude words and bad habits that her father would not approve of. Jenny, in her efforts to please, stopped asking to go out. It was not so bad in the winter when it soon got dark but in the summer, she would spend hours looking out of the window, watching always watching. Sometimes she went up to her grandparents bedroom. There was a large dressing table with a row of tiny drawers beneath the mirror. These all contained items to fascinate a bored child. She would carefully remove the items one at a time and construct a story around them . She was particularly intrigued by the cards that commemorated the deaths of her infant uncles. She would have liked to ask Grandma about her dead sons, particularly little Bertie who had died when he was two and a half. However, instinct warned her that this would not be wise.

Another game, that kept her occupied for hours, was playing with the button box. It was a very large wicker work container with a lid like a Chinese coolie's hat. Jenny would try to match the buttons by colour or shape. She made patterns or told herself stories about the different garments the buttons may have come from. When tired of that, she would return to just gazing out of the window. High up, in the

126

bay window, she looked down at the lines of washing, strung around the square. She saw women talking on their doorsteps and children playing tig or careering around on their carts made from orange boxes and old pram wheels.

Her enforced isolation combined with her fear of being at school, led to Jenny becoming an extremely introspective child. She became increasingly uncomfortable in the company of children of her own age. Her world was peopled, almost exclusively, by adults most of whom were her grandparents' generation. Sunday afternoon was occupied with a walk to the War Memorial and back. Holidays were at Eastbourne where she and her grandparents stayed in a small, quiet, impeccably run, utterly respectable boarding house. She always took her bucket and spade and Grandad always helped her to make a complicated sandcastle. She hated to see their creation licked at and finally devoured by the voracious in coming tide. Funfairs and donkey rides were frowned on by Gladys as was contact with other children on the beach. This was particularly so for those children who ran around on the sand and in and out of the water in their knickers! Jenny of course had a new costume, in wool, hand knitted by Gladys every year. These costumes were stretchy and scratchy and took an age to dry but Jenny said nothing. She did not want to upset her grandmother.

Problems at school continued but in a more muted form. The rest of the class had sorted out who was going to be friends with whom and who would sit where. Jenny was always on the periphery of any activity and continued to seek out the company of any available adult, in time spent out of the classroom. She enjoyed the work she did at school and was usually top or near the top of the class in any tests. This isolated her still further from her classmates but led to her being selected to represent the school in a presentation of money, collected for Princess Marina's charity work. Jenny was amazed to receive this unexpected honour; Gladys was delighted to have something to boast to her friends about.

She fussed and fumed about what Jenny should wear. Finally she settled on a white dress with large red spots, white socks, black patent shoes and a big red ribbon in her hair.. Gladys was sure, that with Jenny's fine wispy hair, the ribbon would never stay in place until the moment came for Jenny to present the purse. So various arrangements of clips were tried along with plenty of practice of the required curtsy. After such extensive preparation, she could only hope for the best.

It was an extraordinary day for Jenny, beginning with the journey to the Albert Hall. She did wonder if it had been named after her

Grandad. That would have been nice but she knew it could not be so. He wasn't important enough. Still, he is to me. She glanced at him and Grandma. They looked happy and proud; it gave Jenny a warm feeling. They are really pleased with me. I will be able to tell Daddy all about it when I write to him next week. I will be able to tell Mummy when I see her. She gazed out of the window and wondered how long it was since Mummy came to Camden Town. It seemed like ages but she would not ask Grandma, it always made her cross if she mentioned Mummy. She had once made the mistake of mentioning Mummy in her weekly letter to Daddy. She had been amazed at Grandma's reaction, when she checked the letter for spelling mistakes. She had crumpled up the letter and thrown it on the fire.

'Don't ever mention your mother, in letters to your father, he does not want to hear about her.' At the time, Jenny had felt as though Grandma had slapped her. She could feel tears trickling down the side of her nose. She had brushed them away and got a clean piece of paper. She did not make that mistake again.

This time there would be plenty to say. As the children had come from schools all over the country, no-one knew anyone else. Jenny was not, therefore, at a disadvantage. The organisers had arranged for magicians and clowns to entertain the children during the morning. Jenny did not much like the clowns, they were noisy and silly but she was captivated by the magicians. She sat crosslegged on the floor, with all the other children and felt herself being sucked into a world where anything could happen. At lunch time the children were led into a large room with trestle tables, covered in sandwiches, sausage rolls, jelly, blancmange and little cakes.

She knew the presentation was going to be after they had eaten. She felt excited but also very nervous. She must not ' show herself up' by doing anything silly. Most of all, she must not be sick. There were now many mornings when Jenny managed to get to school with her breakfast still inside her. Occasionally, particularly after she had the nightmare, the terrible sickness would return. She checked her hair ribbon for the hundredth time. It was still there. She knew there were going to be photographs. She had to look her best for Grandma and Grandad, for Mummy and Daddy too. She hoped they would each be able to have a picture to mark this special occasion.

She heard the click of cameras and the flashes of light as she waited for her turn to walk across the stage. She clutched the blue velvet purse. It contained a cheque for the money collected in her area. She went through, again, what she had to do. It sounded so simple and she had practised it so often. The curtsy was the difficult bit. It was so easy to wobble or stick your bottom out. She bent her knees a few times, just to get the feel of it. Her legs felt very shaky, she was finding it difficult to breathe. Suddenly, she heard the name of her school and a firm hand pushed her from behind. She stepped in front of the curtain and walked unsteadily across to where the princess was waiting. Jenny looked up and saw a warm smile of encouragement. She handed the purse to the princess' aide and, holding her skirt in both hands, gave a curtsy. The cameras flashed. Jenny couldn't smile, she was concentrating too hard but at least, she thought, I did not fall over. She walked carefully across the stage to the other side. Her heart stopped pounding and she gave a great sigh, I've done it!

It was a cheerful ride home on the bus. Jenny sat on Grandad's knee and looked out of the window at the brightly lit shops, full of beautiful and expensive things. As they got nearer to Camden Town, the shops became fewer and those that she saw were small and ordinary; grocers, tobacconists, fish shops and fruiterers. There were barrows on street corners, piled high with gleaming fruit, glistening by the light of hurricane lamps. People were hurrying home, it was tea-time.

'I'm hungry.' said Jenny.

'Didn't you have anything at dinner time?' Albert asked.

'Oh, there was lots of food but I was too nervous to eat then.'

'Never mind, you were wonderful, Gran and I were really proud of our little girl.' Albert gave her a hug, 'What would you like for tea?'

'Could we.' Jenny paused, wondering if it was too much to ask. She knew Grandad and Grandma did not have much money.

'Could we have some fish and chips?'

Albert looked at Gladys, 'It would save you the job of getting tea. If you get Jenny ready for bed, I'll walk down to the fish shop.'

'Now don't overdo it, Bert. You know we can always have fish another time.'

Albert smiled and patted Gladys' hand, 'Don't you fret, I'm all right. We must give the kiddy her treat. It's been her big day.'

Jenny lay in bed, she was warm and sleepy. She felt her stomach which seemed to bulge a little more than usual. The fish and chips had been delicious. Grandad had let her pick up chips with her fingers when Grandma wasn't looking. She thought over the events of the day and smiled to herself. It was certainly a day to remember. Tomorrow she would tell the teacher and the rest of the class about it.

Although it was a cold morning, the sun was bright and the gap between the curtains let its light fall across Jenny's face. She had slept well, with no unpleasant dreams. She lay watching the pattern of the sun on the wall and ceiling shiver as the curtains moved slightly. She could hear the usual noises in the kitchen; Grandma was getting breakfast. It was so warm in bed, she decided to wait a few more minutes before she got up. She could not hear any talking from downstairs so perhaps Grandad was having a lie in too. She wondered whether to go for a cuddle, although that was usually a Sunday morning treat.

While she was deciding what to do, she heard strange noises from next door. It was as if Grandad was banging with something, then there was a crash. Jenny got out of bed and scuttled next door. On the floor by the bed was a broken glass. It was the glass Grandad kept his teeth in over night.

'Did you drop your glass, Grandad?' Jenny climbed on to the bed. There was no reply. Jenny felt uneasy. Grandad was not taking any notice. He was looking out of the window. Jenny lifted his hand off the eiderdown and held it in her own two. Still no response. 'Why won't you speak to me, Grandad?'

She knelt on the bed and leaned forward to give him a good morning kiss. As she leant against him, he seemed to slide sideways. Jenny could feel panic rising in her throat. Grandad was ill and it was her fault; she should never have asked him to get fish and chips. Grandma had told him not to overdo it. What would Grandma say now? A sob caught in Jenny's throat, she put her hand on Albert's shoulder and gave it a little shake.

'Please speak to me, Grandad. I'm sorry if I made you overdo it. I promise I won't ask for fish and chips again. Please speak to me.'

As she shook Albert's shoulder, his head suddenly slumped forwards and Jenny watched with wide-eyed horror as his false teeth slowly slid out of his mouth. With a stifled scream, Jenny scrambled off the bed and ran downstairs.

'Grandma come quickly, Grandad is ill. He won't speak to me.'

Gladys looked at the child's ashen face and fear gripped her heart. Wiping her hands on her apron, she pushed past Jenny and ran upstairs. Within seconds, Jenny heard the first scream. It made the hair on her neck stand on end.

'Go and get the neighbours, Jenny, quick!'

Jenny ran to the front door and stopped. Would Grandma shout if she went out without her slippers on? She decided that this time it would not matter. She could just reach Mr and Mrs Groves' door knocker, if she stretched. She was breathing in gasps and sobs. Something terrible had happened. She knocked again. Mrs Groves came to the door.

'Come quickly, please, Grandma says Grandad is very ill.'

Jenny ran back indoors, she stood in the hallway listening to her Grandma's sobs. Mr. and Mrs. Groves came in and went straight upstairs. Jenny walked slowly into the living room. She could hear frantic conversations and strange bumpings from upstairs. Then a piercing, keening cry; the cry of the bereaved, the desolate, the inconsolable. She put her hands over her ears and walked over to the big armchair. She climbed into it and sat with her knees up to her chin. Slowly, she rocked back and forth, tears streamed down her face. This was always Grandad's favourite chair, she thought. I hope he won't mind if I sit in it now.

Chapter 8

Jenny sat on the green painted tin trunk. It held all her possessions. On the lid were her father's name, rank and headquarters. As she sat waiting for the taxi that was to take her to Kensington and Mary Cardew, she thought about the previous two years, since Grandad had died. She had been seven then, on that terrible morning, which was branded into her brain, every detail as crystal clear now as when it happened. She had sat in her Grandad's chair, in her blue pyjamas, all morning. Mr. and Mrs. Groves had comforted her Grandma, until the doctor had come. He had not stayed long. Just long enough to pronounce Albert Warr dead, from a massive heart attack and to give Gladys some pills to calm her down. No-one seemed to notice Jenny, she neither moved nor spoke. She listened though, to the hurried and intense conversations between the Groves and the doctor, the Groves and the men who came to take Grandad away. At that point, there had been a renewed burst of uncontrolled weeping from Grandma, who was still upstairs. Other people came into the flat and whispered in corners with the Groves. Jenny was aware that she was being talked about, but what did it matter. She felt numb with grief and despair. It was a despair so great that she could not cry like Grandma. She wanted to disappear, to get smaller and smaller until there was nothing of her left.

Then Mrs. Groves had come and knelt beside her and put an arm around her shoulders. 'Don't worry, love, you'll be all right. Dan has gone to send for your Daddy. You can stay with your Auntie and Uncle until he gets home.' Susan Groves was startled by the vehemence of Jenny's reaction. The mute, stone-still child struggled out of her embrace, arms flailing, screaming at the top of her voice.

'No! no, no, please don't send me there.' She flung herself on the floor and resting her head in her hands, sobbed as though her heart would break. After that, there had been no further mention of Caroline and Jack. Susan had got Jenny dressed in the first things she could find. They weren't school clothes but Jenny thought no-one would mind if she did not go to school today.

Susan took her downstairs and made her a cheese sandwich but Jenny could not eat it. She sat at the table waiting for the nightmare to end. In a minute, Grandad would walk in and give her a whiskery kiss and everything would be all right. But it was not all right and as Jenny remembered that day, she forgot the coldness of the green tin trunk, pressing against her bare legs. She forgot her anxiety at moving yet again to a new home. She forgot her apprehensions about Mary Cardew who she scarcely knew. She remembered again the awesome grief and anguish, the overwhelming sense of loss that she had never been able to acknowledge because there had never been anyone with whom to share it.

Jean Williams came into the hall and watched Jenny for a moment. A strange child, she thought. Still, she's been through a lot, I suppose its not to be wondered at. Jenny had only been with Jean and her husband, Peter, for six months. It had been an emergency measure after the discovery that Jenny had been beaten by her foster father. It had been discovered by chance, at school, when the P.E. teacher had noticed bruises on Jenny's legs. She had been moved out at once and gone into care for a few days until Charles could be contacted. In desperation, he had asked Jean Williams to take the child. Charles had known Jean when she was in the army. For a while, she had had a crush on him and so 'for old times sake' had agreed to take her. However, as Jean and her husband were soon to move, to the North, where Peter was to take up a new job, the arrangement could only be temporary. Jean could sense the great tide of grief that was engulfing Jenny and sat down on the trunk beside her.

'It will be fine, you know. Everything will be just fine, you wait and see.'
Jenny looked at this pretty woman who had been so kind. There was no point in saying anything. Jean could never understand how she felt. I'm just a piece of lost property, that no-one wants to claim.

'Your Dad will be home on leave soon, that will be nice.'
Jenny nodded, her eyes brimmed with tears she dare not shed.

She had seen little of Charles since Grandad had died, she had not been taken to the funeral and Grandma was too ill to look after her. So when Charles came home, on compassionate leave, he stayed at the flat in Camden Town, nursing his mother. Jenny had been moved to stay with friends of the Groves, until something more permanent could be arranged.

The Bennett family had been a revelation to Jenny. They were loud and noisy and very friendly. Their enthusiasm for life and their desire to involve Jenny in everything they did unnerved the child. It was such a contrast to the structured, quiet, segregated life that Jenny had experienced with her grandparents. She retreated further and further into her shell as her only means of defence. After a while, the Bennett children gave up trying to persuade her to go out to play. She became a brooding presence in their home, no trouble, making no demands. Just there. Mr. and Mrs. Bennett felt increasingly uneasy. They must be doing something wrong but they did not know what. Jenny made them feel guilty; they were being paid to look after the child and clearly she was unhappy.

After eight months, Jenny learned she was going to live somewhere else. She was told it was rather too cramped for her to stay where she was. In her new home, she would be able to have a room to herself. Jenny listened and thought about the last eight months. She decided that the Bennetts did not really want her. It was nothing to do with being cramped. She wished she had been able to join in more but something had always stopped her. Now it was too late. I must try harder, she thought, with my next family. I must try to make them like me more.

Pat Clements had fostered children for five years. They were older children and usually only stayed for a short time, while more permanent arrangements were made. Pat had always wanted more than one child but she had had a very difficult pregnancy and nearly died giving birth to her daughter, Kay. Pat saw the children, she fostered, as a kind of company for Kay albeit both inferior and temporary. The money the fostering brought into the house was more than welcome since all her husband's grand ideas about promotion had come to nothing.

There was an uneasy atmosphere in the Clements' household, with Pat and Kay on one side and Douglas on the other side of an invisible divide. Douglas was given constant, if unspoken, reminders of his failings whilst Pat made it clear that all her time and attention was rightly devoted to Kay. This left only one role for Jenny, Kay's acolyte. Kay had more toys than Jenny had ever seen before. It soon became clear that whilst it was acceptable for her to sew clothes for Kay's dolls and to tidy up after Kay at bedtime, she must not expect the right to play with anything that was not hers.

By now Gladys was well enough to see Jenny, once a month. It was obvious though that she would never be well enough to have her back full-time. Douglas used to take Jenny to Camden Town in his car, on a Sunday. She was always made to feel that she was a nuisance, spoiling his chance of putting his feet up and having a rest. Although Jenny had never been as close to Gladys as she had to Albert, she was always pleased to see her Grandma, who was now the only member of her family with whom she had regular contact. Rachel wrote to Jenny regularly but despite Jenny's requests to visit, nothing was forthcoming.

Jenny tried very hard to get on with Kay and her parents but it was difficult to keep her feelings of resentment to herself. The final blow came at Christmas. Charles was home on leave and it had been arranged that Jenny spend the holiday with her Father and Grandma, at the flat, in Camden Town. She had been looking forward to this Christmas. She knew her Daddy would bring special and exotic presents from abroad and a present had come from Mummy, with a covering letter. The parcel had a French stamp and postmark. She could not imagine what her mother was doing in France and, from previous experience, realised there was no point in asking. She read the letter yet again. As always, it started...Dear Sugar Plum Fairy.... Mummy said she hoped the present would fit. So it must be clothes. She decided, whatever it was, she would wear it on Christmas Day.

It had been decided that Douglas would drive Jenny over to Camden Town on Christmas morning. On the face of it, he let it be known that he was making a great sacrifice; secretly he was pleased to be out of the house for a while. Christmas morning always reduced Pat to hysterics. I'm well out of that. Jenny only had two presents to open at the Clements' house, her mother's and a small gift from Pat, Douglas and Kay. That was a doll which looked what it was, cheap and nasty. Jenny started to open her other present, with trembling fingers. Under the wrapping paper was a layer of white tissue. She lifted it back and there it lay, the most glorious scarlet dress. It glowed like a ruby in the crisp white tissue. It had a froth of white lace at the collar. Jenny touched it gently. It was as soft as a baby's skin. She lifted it carefully out of its wrappings. The skirt was flared and full, the sleeves long. It was made of the finest wool. There was a pure white petticoat with a lacy trim attached to the inside of the waist. Jenny gasped in amazement. She ran with it to her bedroom and wrenched off her pyjamas, terrified that it might not fit. She slipped it over her head, it felt wonderful. She did up as many of the buttons, at the back, as she could reach. She rushed back into the living room to ask Pat to do the rest.

Kay was sitting on the floor, crying.

'It's not fair, why can't I have a dress like that instead of my stupid old green one?'

Jenny looked at her in disbelief. Kay had so much, surely she can't be jealous of me, for having this dress. She was going to offer to let Kay borrow it but then she clenched her lips shut. Why should I, she thought. She thanked Pat for doing up the rest of the buttons and went to finish getting ready. She collected the gifts she had made, a knitted tie for Daddy and a pin-cushion for Grandma. She had made another pin-cushion for Mummy and hoped Pat had posted it, as she had said she would.

She felt very grown up in her new dress and smiled all the way to Camden Town. Douglas said little, he could sense trouble brewing at home. He supposed he would be expected to pay out more money, so Kay could have a new party frock. Pat was ruining that child. Jenny thanked Douglas and ran up the stairs to Grandma's flat. She was staying several days and on the day after Boxing Day Daddy was taking her to a pantomime.

She knocked on the door. She was breathless and pink cheeked. The red of the dress gave a glow to her rather sallow complexion. She heard footsteps and with mounting excitement waited for the door to open. Charles stood in the doorway. He scarcely recognised Jenny. There was something different about her, a degree of confidence in her stance. Her eyes sparkled, she looked happy; she looked heart stoppingly like Rachel.

'Happy Christmas, Daddy,' she almost shouted.

'What on earth have you got on?'

'Do you like it? Mummy sent it from France.' She twirled round on one heel so that the skirt flared out, showing her thighs.

'You look like a tart,' Charles said. His lips compressed into a slit and his eyes were like stones. He turned on his heel and walked down the hall. Jenny stood, puzzled. What did he mean, a tart? She had heard people call women tarts but she was a little girl. Did he mean a strawberry tart, because the dress was red? She walked into the flat and the coldness of the atmosphere hit her in the face like a mailed fist.

Alec opened the door and, for a few moments, stood speechless. Rachel and Stephen were the last people he would have expected. Both looked tired and dishevelled. Rachel started to cry and flung herself into his arms, sobbing, talking incoherently into his ear. Alec looked down at Stephen who was white faced and looked very frightened. Alec smiled encouragingly but Stephen just blinked back tears of fatigue and relief to be home. He had not seen his father for eight months.

He put down the bag he had been carrying and waited for his mother to calm down.

'Dad, there's a taxi man waiting downstairs. Mummy did not have enough money to pay him.' Alec looked at Rachel who started to cry hysterically again.

'What was I to do? We had to get back to you in time for Christmas. You would not believe the trouble we have had getting here. Our place is with you. I realise that now. I'm so sorry, so very sorry. Please forgive me.' She clutched at him.

'How much does he want?' Alec asked.

'I don't know, I didn't ask. I just wanted to get back. Please say you forgive me.'

'We'll talk about it later. You take Stephen in while I settle up with the taxi bloke.'

As Alec walked upstairs again, he reflected on this utterly unexpected development. God alone knew where Rachel had picked up the taxi. The meter had clocked up a small fortune. There was no point in asking her, she was obviously as high as a kite. The last thing he wanted to do was trigger off a wild scene with Rachel ranting and raving in front of the boy. It certainly was not going to be the Christmas he had anticipated. Obviously he would have to ring Gwen and make his excuses. So what would he be able to do now about a Christmas for Stephen? He glanced at his watch. Bloody 4.00p.m. Christmas Eve. What the hell was Rachel thinking of? Still, he could not let the poor kid down, he looked as though he had had a fairly uncomfortable time. Alec sighed, there was no alternative, he would have to go out and see what he could get.

Rachel behaved as though she had been away for a weekend with friends, instead of disappearing for eight months. She had left a note, merely indicating that she had taken Stephen to France, for an extended holiday - to broaden his mind. At first Alec had assumed that lack of money would force her to return but within a month, he had received a postcard that told him she was teaching English privately. Since she was not his wife, he decided he could do little but wait; wait for her to want to come home. Now she was back, Alec realised how much more peaceful life was without her.

He was very successful with his last minute shopping and returned with a large chicken, Christmas tree - small but adequate and most of the other things, custom dictates, essential for a good Christmas. The bird and the tree had both been at knock down prices as shop-keepers frantically tried to off load items that would have little appeal in forty eight hours time. Alec decided he would not tell Rachel how cheaply their Christmas had been catered for. He felt intense irritation at her recklessness and certainly did not wish to encourage such behaviour or diminish her feelings of regret at her hurtful conduct.

By the time he had struggled upstairs with everything, Stephen was sitting at the kitchen table, stuffing a large cheese sandwich into his mouth.

'When did that child last eat?'

'Yesterday, Oh, don't be cross, we've had such a dreadful time. The crossing was so rough, we were both sick. Tell me you are glad we are back. You are aren't you?'

Alec looked at her and unwillingly admitted, to himself, that whatever the magic was, it still held him firmly in its clutches.

'I'm glad to have you back but your timing is lousy.' He looked at Stephen.

'Do you know your mother is a pain in the arse?'

Stephen grinned back. 'I know.'

'We are going to have a splendid Christmas, just you wait. Shall we show Daddy his presents?'

Presents I have paid for in taxi fare, Alec thought.

'No you will not show me anything. This boy is going to bed and we are going to do some serious talking!' Rachel pulled a face but decided not to argue.

They sat opposite each other at the kitchen table. Stephen had fallen asleep instantly and now, having eaten, they could contemplate the past and discuss the future. That was Alec's plan even though he knew from hard experience that when Rachel was manic, there was little chance of getting anything out of her. He poured himself a large gin. He was increasingly and uncomfortably aware of the large amounts of alcohol he consumed. It had started when he tried to cope with the violent mood swings. They alternately made Rachel so depressed she could not move, only to be succeeded by a wild, argumentative frame of mind when she was capable of absolutely anything. There had been times when he had been frightened to go to work and other times when he had been reluctant to return home - for fear of what he would find. He had written to Mary Cardew a couple times but had been left in no doubt that, as far as she was concerned, Rachel was his problem. He, the lover of peace and quiet, had found his emotions in a permanent state of turmoil. In everything he did, there was an underlying need to protect Stephen. Alcohol helped to deaden the senses. When Rachel left, he was plunged into an abyss of grief at his loss but now she was back, his mind prickled with apprehensions for all of them.

Rachel stood up and walked round the table, leant over the back of his chair, put her arms around his neck and kissed him.

'I've missed you. Have you missed me?'

Alec felt desire flood into his loins, he put his glass down and got to his feet. He put his arms around her and kissed her passionately. Eight months was a hell of a long time. She pulled away from him slightly, her eyes sparkled.

'You have missed me, haven't you?'

'My God, you are a hussy, get into that bedroom.' He slapped her bottom. So much for the serious talk. He gulped down the rest of the gin. To hell with it, drink and be merry, for tomorrow heaven alone knows what will happen.

It was a subdued Christmas for Jenny and Gladys. Their earnest desire to please Charles wilted under his disapproval. The more they tried, in their different ways, he more disapproving he became. Both the child and the old woman silently took full responsibility for the cool atmosphere and assumed that their respective undefined shortcomings were responsible for their beloved father/son not enjoying his Christmas. It was, therefore, with a sense of relief - hastily replaced by guilt - that Jenny returned to the Clements. She took with her the many presents that her father and Gladys had given her. Somehow she could take little joy in them. She had not worn the dress again, not even to the pantomime.

When she got back to her bedroom, she hung the beautiful dress in her wardrobe. She ran her fingers down the soft material and thought about her mother. Was she still in France? Unexpectedly her mind was suddenly filled with images of her baby brother. Except, she thought, he will not be a baby any more.

He won't know me and I don't know him. She was shaken by such strong feelings of isolation from everything and everybody that she felt quite faint. All I have, to prove that I have a mother and father, is what they give me. Daddy goes back into the army tomorrow and I don't know where Mummy is. I bet that Stephen is with her, wherever she is. It's because of Stephen that Mummy went away, it must be. It's his fault. She sat on her bed and clenched her fists, thrusting them into her mouth to stop cries of anguish escaping. It's wrong to hate a baby. Grandad had always told her it was wrong to hate anyone, but he was not here to remind her.

Pat called Jenny for her tea and carefully pushing the red dress back so it did not catch the wardrobe door, she went into the kitchen.

'Have you tidied up your room?' Pat asked

139

Jenny nodded and took no part in the conversation between Kay and her parents. Apparently Kay had been invited to a party, the next day. Pat explained that she had asked if Jenny could go too but that had not been possible. Jenny was not upset, it didn't seem important somehow. She only half listened to what Pat was saying. It seemed that Pat was going to take her out, some kind of compensation for not being invited to the party. Douglas would ferry Kay to and from the 'do'.

'We can have a nice afternoon shopping, just the two of us, can't we?' Jenny felt surprised but decided it would be nice not to have Kay around, always getting her own way.

Next day, they had a light mid-day snack since Kay would have a birthday tea and Pat was going to take Jenny to a tea-shop. It was a cold day with the threat of rain when Jenny and Pat left. As the sales were on, Pat had decided to go to the West End to see if she could pick up some bargains. They would visit the large department stores that Pat would not usually frequent.

The afternoon passed in a blur of people, lifts, crowds and sudden changes in temperature. They plunged out of one over-heated, over-crowded store into the cold wet streets before pushing their way into the next. Jenny was exhausted by her efforts not to get lost, in the seething, heaving mass of bodies. She tried to take an interest in the items that Pat inspected even though she knew there was not likely to be anything for her.

At last, Pat seemed to have burnt herself out and called a halt to the mad procession. They found tearooms and had toasted tea cakes, a pot of tea for Pat, milk shake for Jenny and some sticky cakes. Pat was obviously pleased with her purchases. Jenny wondered if she would ever be so effusive about shopping. Somehow, she doubted it. The best part of the afternoon, Jenny decided, was that Pat seemed so relaxed and chatty. Anyone looking at them would assume that she was Pat's little girl. She decided she would not mind if that was what people thought.

The journey home was jolly too. Everyone seemed cheerful despite the cold and the rain. Most of the passengers had parcels and bags. Jenny had to stand up, so an elderly woman could sit down. Pat put an arm around Jenny's waist.

'Lean against me,' she said. It felt good. Jenny helped Pat with her parcels and they half ran, half walked up the road; they did not get too wet. It was quite dark by now and the street lights reflecting off the puddles and off the rain drops on Jenny's glasses gave a sparkling world. Jenny breathed out hard and laughed at the clouds made by her breath. They got home to find the house in darkness. Pat seemed surprised. 'I expected Douglas and Kay to be back by now,' she paused,'I expect you would like a nice warm bath after being out in the rain, wouldn't you?' It seemed a good idea.

'Don't hang your coat in the wardrobe tonight, Jenny. It's wet. I'll put it on the back of the kitchen door, to dry off.'

Jenny went to her bedroom and was surprised to see the wardrobe door open. It had a funny lock and she sometimes had to press the door really hard, until the catch clicked. She went to shut it but something stopped her. She felt her heart give a lurch. She knew what she would find, or rather what she would not find, her beautiful red dress. She felt the colour drain from her face. I have been tricked, she thought. This whole afternoon has been one big trick. They must think I'm stupid. Her feelings of deep shock at the deceitfulness of grown-ups was replaced by a most terrible rage and sense of injustice. I have so little and Kay has so much but it still isn't enough. She has had to take, from me, what little I have.

In the past, Jenny had always done what she thought people had wanted her to do. She had bottled up years of hurt and loss, rage and despair. Standing, as she did now, looking at the empty hanger, she felt strength flow into her mind and body. She knew not how or from where it came. It was there because Douglas, Pat and Kay had done a terrible thing and they were not going to get away with it. I don't care anymore. Trying to be good has made no difference. They don't care about me, why should I care about them?

She had heard the front door open. She heard Kay being Ssshed by Douglas. They were supposed to get home before Pat and me, Jenny thought. Then I would never have known. She smiled grimly to herself but could not stop the remembrance of Pat's arms around her waist, on the bus. She clenched her fists and knew she must shut that out. Pat did not really care, that was plain to see now. She walked slowly down stairs. She was trembling so much, she had to hang on to the bannisters. It isn't because I'm frightened, its because I hate them. She pushed opened the kitchen door. All three people looked at her, Jenny almost laughed. They all had the same scared expression on their faces. Kay was standing by the stove, in Jenny's petticoat, the red dress was draped over a chair. For a moment, no-one spoke. Jenny felt as though she was expanding, growing with self-righteousness. I am in the right and they know it, there is nothing they can say or do that will alter that.

'Have you had your bath, dear?' Pat's voice sounded shaky and breathless.

'What is my dress doing down here?' She looked from one to another. Not one of them would look her in the eye. Kay started to snivel. Douglas stood up. As he did so, Jenny pushed past him and grabbed Kay by the arm and shook her. Pat let out a cry, 'Stop her, Doug!'

'You have to have everything,' Jenny shouted. 'You are never satisfied. I hate you. I'm not even allowed to play with your things. But you can do what you like, you're horrible!' By now, Jenny was screaming and crying. She had such a tight hold on Kay's arm, that Douglas could not pry her loose. Kay was screaming too. 'My arm, Mummy, she's hurting my arm. Stop her Mummy!' A kitchen chair was kicked out of the way by Douglas and there was a crashing of crockery, as it was swept from the table. The red dress lay crumpled on the floor, unnoticed as the struggle reached its climax. There was a sharp cracking sound and Jenny was sent reeling by the force of Douglas' hand connecting with her cheek. She stumbled and fell; in that moment, she gathered the dress to her and stayed crouched on the floor, like a wild animal waiting for the coup de grace. Kay was sobbing and showing Pat the finger and nail marks on her arms.

'She's drawn blood, Doug. I'm taking her to the doctor. You're a vicious little cat, that's what you are.' The last remark was aimed at Jenny as Douglas half-lifted, half-dragged the child to her feet. Her eyes blazed despite the tears that streamed down her face.

'You had no right,' she screamed, 'it's my dress, it's mine!'
Douglas shook her sharply, 'Stop making such a bloody row.' Jenny struggled to get free and successfully aimed a kick at his shins. He grunted with pain and letting go of one arm, gave her bottom a good walloping.

'You can't do that, I haven't done anything wrong. It's you, you let Kay have my dress.'

'For Christ's sake, shut up about the fucking dress.' There was a sharp intake of breath from Pat. 'Douglas, don't you dare swear in front of our daughter. I won't have it. I'm taking her to the doctor's.'

'For God's sake woman, she's got a few scratches. The doctor will laugh you out of the surgery.' Kay had been watching events and grabbed her opportunity. She groaned and inspected her arms, as though she were expecting a haemorrhage to start at any time.

'Look at you, what sort of father are you? You don't even care about your own child. Anything for a quiet life, that's you. No wonder you get passed over for promotion!'

142

By now Douglas was totally exasperated. Jenny continued to struggle and fight as though her life depended on it. He would be black and blue in the morning.

'Do what you bloody well like.' he shouted, as he manhandled Jenny out of the kitchen. 'You usually do!'

By the time they reached Jenny's bedroom, they were both panting. Although Jenny was quite small for her age, Douglas had been amazed by her strength. He flung her on to the bed but the springing in the mattress bounced her back, upright. She launched into him, fists flying. One side of her face wore the imprint of his hand, like a birth mark. He pushed her away.

'Calm down, Jenny. Enough is enough.' He tried to grab her and as he did so her fist caught him a stinging blow on the nose. Something inside him snapped and he grabbed her by the hair. He threw her across his knee and hit her again and again and again. And still he hit her, long after she had stopped struggling. She lay limp and motionless across his legs. At first he feared he had knocked her out. His hand felt as though it were on fire and his arm ached. He was gasping for breath. Jenny gave a shuddering sigh and slid to the floor. Shakily, Douglas got to his feet. He lifted Jenny on to her bed where she lay silently her eyes staring into a far distant place, to which he had no access.

'I'm sorry, Jenny but you really hurt me.'

'It's my dress,' was her only reply. He walked slowly downstairs, to face God knows what, he thought.

Jenny thought about that awful day and the days that followed, when she refused to come out of her room. She shifted uneasily on the green tin trunk, as though her flesh could still feel the pain of bruising. Once back at school, after the Christmas holidays, her teacher had noticed the marks even though a week had elapsed. Soon after that Jenny was moved, to stay with Jean and Peter Williams. It had been a happy time which made the upheaval even harder to bear.

'I wish you could take me with you.'

Jean hugged the child.

'I'll give you our new address. Promise you'll write.' Jenny nodded. Outside, she heard the hoot of the taxi.

Chapter 9

Stephen banged the kitchen door so loudly that the windows rattled. Alec looked at Rachel, with exasperation. Was she never going to stop talking about Jenny? No wonder the poor boy felt jealous. He did not know his sister and, if Charles had anything to do with it, never would. Alec poured himself another gin.   Considering what a rush it had been, with Rachel appearing out of the blue, they had had a reasonably successful Christmas. He thought about the situation with Jenny. The only way he would be able to stop Rachel driving everyone mad was to somehow arrange a visit. He decided that Mary was still the best person to approach, despite her previous reluctance to be involved. She was Jenny's grandmother, a woman of considerable presence, let her tackle Charles.

Alec was due back at work the next day and at the thought, felt a tremor of apprehension. He could not be sure that Rachel would not do something silly and rush over to Mrs. Warr's place. From what Mary had told him, old man Warr had died and Gladys had taken to her bed. According to Mary, Jenny was being fostered here, there and everywhere. He thought about his own miserable childhood, in the home, but at least I wasn't hoicked about from one place to another. Poor little cow, she must be having a pretty rough time of it. Perhaps Rachel was right to keep on about the kid. Maybe, if he could convince Rachel that he was doing something, she would leave well alone. Give her something else to concentrate on.

The next big task was to get Stephen into school. He would soon be five and was in urgent need of some structure to his life. The more Alec saw of the child's behaviour, the more he suspected that he had, while in Paris, been allowed to do what he liked. The best thing Rachel could do tomorrow was to go to the local primary school and get a place sorted out. He watched her as she moved around the kitchen. There was an agitation and a level of energy that both exhilarated and exhausted him. After four years of coping with the violent mood swings, the fascination had diminished, not one jot! I'm addicted, he thought, just a junkie.

'I'll contact your mother tomorrow and see if she can sort out a visit for Jenny.'

Rachel stopped what she was doing, her eyes lit up. 'Oh! please do, it means so much to me. I can't bear not to see her.'

'I know, but try to play it down a little, I think Stephen finds it a bit hard having her rammed down his throat all the time.'

Rachel bristled with indignation, 'Don't be so silly: he will love her just like I do. She is his sister after all.'

'Yes, I know, but he has never seen her, has he? He has always had us to himself.' Except, Alec thought, when you go rushing off to Paris, then he only has you. Rachel banged a saucepan down on the stove.

'Stop getting at me!' Her voice had the warning shrill note to it. Alec smiled, in what he hoped was a comforting manner. After more than four years, I should know it's a waste of time trying to reason with her. She is either so manic, she blows her top or else so depressed, I might as well talk to the wall.

'Nobody's getting at you.' He stood up and went to put his arms round her. 'I just want us to be a happy family and I know that won't happen until you see much more of Jenny.' Her body was stiff and unyielding and not for the first time, he thought, I am living with a creature from the wild, untamed and untamable.

As he held her to him, he felt the tension loose its grip. In a quiet voice, he suggested she call at the local school, the next day. Then he reassured her again that he would do what he could as far as Jenny was concerned. Rachel smiled and hugged him.

'You just don't know what it's like.'

Gladys sat in her arm chair, by the fire. She read Charles' letter again. It was the first letter since the end of his Christmas leave. It had not been a Christmas to remember. The aching void left by Albert's death seemed to get worse, not better. She still wore black and always would. It was not just her clothes that were black, life itself had lost all colour, all meaning. After the terrible row with Caroline and Jack, as she had predicted, visits had ceased. Jenny had been taken from her and Charles showed no signs of wishing to leave the army. I am just marking time, waiting to die. Waiting for letters from my son and letters from Jenny. There seemed little purpose in any of it and yet the spirit, that had seen her through so many troubles, would not allow her to slide into death and release from her anguish.

She tried to digest the contents of Charles' letter, somehow her brain was sluggish, unresponsive. Is this what happens when you live on your own? She had never lived on her own, until Albert died. Her present loneliness expanded each day into an endless wasteland. The tick of the clock a constant reminder of the hours still to be got through, to no purpose, towards no goal, save that of oblivion.

Charles had met someone called Jeanette. For Charles, it was quite a cheerful letter. Perhaps, he was getting over Rachel at last. Dear God, that woman had a lot to answer for. It seemed that this Jeanette was the daughter of the commanding officer and did some kind of civilian secretarial work, for Charles and the other officers. He wasn't going to say anything to Jenny yet, as he did not want to upset the child. He would not be home for another six months; it would be time enough to say something then.

Gladys sat, gazing into the fire; it would be nice to have a woman to talk to. Still, if this Jeanette was the commanding officer's daughter, she might think it beneath her to befriend a working-class nobody, like me. Gladys had often felt that Charles was ashamed of his parentage. He had done very well for himself but that was no excuse for forgetting all that Dad and I did for him. She knew though that she would never tell him so. The little boy, with the stutter, who had survived rheumatic fever three times, had an implacable certainty about everything he said and did that sapped Gladys' confidence. I must not upset him. He gets so cross and without him, I have nobody. She decided to reply to the letter straight away: that should please him. It would help to pass some time too, she thought. The home help can post it tomorrow.

Mary read Malcolm's letter with amazement. She sat down heavily and closed her eyes. Why did life have to play such tricks? She had been frightened of living in this great big flat on her own. Philip and Sarah were now firmly established, having brought a surprisingly large amount of furniture and other belongings with them. Life had settled into an acceptable pattern although Mary did not find Sarah a particularly appealing child. Now this, Malcolm was coming home, with a wife! Could they stay in Mary's flat?

Clearly it was impossible, there was one very small empty room which Mary had christened 'The Cabin'. It would be impossible for more than one person to use it. If only, she thought; how often people had annoyed her, in the past, with wistful 'if onlies'. Now with sickening realisation, she had lost the opportunity to have her beloved Malcolm living under the same roof. In all conscience, she could hardly ask Philip to leave.The unexpected blessing to her solitary state - stillborn. Her frustration and dismay temporarily blotted out the other bombshell - a wife! Why had Malcolm said nothing before? She could only assume he had thought she might object. The hurt, his secretive behaviour caused, rippled through her. Surely he did not think she wanted to interfere in his life, when she loved him so much. But then perhaps he did.

Maybe it was a blessing that she could not offer them accommodation. Maybe it would reassure him and his new wife that she would not be a nuisance. What she could do though was to sort out a rented flat or two that might be suitable. Of course, they need not be too far away from her flat need they?She would go to the local property agent tomorrow. She smiled, any problem could be solved Now it was time to prepare a meal for her tenants. Since she had always had servants, cooking was a new and surprisingly satisfying venture. The only drawback was Sarah's fussiness and her tendency to reject anything unfamiliar as 'disgusting'. Philip was singularly unwilling to check the child and Sarah was only too obviously aware of the fact. Mary had no such reservations and always told the child, briskly, to eat up her meal and stop fussing.

Sarah's parents seemed determined to outdo each other in how much money they spent on the child. A policy, Mary felt sure, they would come to regret. The child attended a private school which seemed to teach little, in favour of play and model-making. Mary, despite her privileged background, could see no purpose in private education. If a child is bright, she declared, she will do perfectly well in a state run school. Of course, Philip had always been an intellectual snob, so there was little point in discussing the matter with him.

She heard the front door slam and then the sound of voices. As she stirred the sauce for the evening's meal, she allowed herself, briefly, to daydream that it was Malcolm and his new wife - what was her name? Joanne, that's it. How wonderful if they had been living here. After dinner, they could have told me about their day, involved me in their discussions. I would have felt I belonged, instead of drifting in this great emotional void.

Sarah ran into the kitchen. Her cheeks were glowing and she was bubbling with excitement. 'We have made model villages today, mine was called Fogley and teacher said it was the best and I'm going to be an architect like my Dad.' All was said without pause for breath. 'What's for tea, Aunt Mary?'

'We are having cod with parsley sauce, creamed potatoes' Sarah pulled a face, 'I hate fish.'

'It's extremely good for you and if you are hungry enough, you will eat it.'

The tone of Mary's voice suggested that argument would be pointless. Sarah flicked her thick, long, brown hair - by far her best feature - over her shoulder and stalked out of the kitchen. Mary sighed, presumably she has gone to soften up her father. She gave the sauce a brisk stir, not a lump to be seen. She smiled, no spoilt nine year old was going to dictate diet in this home; neither would her father.

The meal was eaten in silence, Sarah sulked and pushed her food around the plate, Philip felt aggrieved that he could not remonstrate with Mary but he could ill afford to risk losing the home he had been offered, so fortuitously. Mary waited with breathless anticipation for Philip to give her an excuse to suggest that maybe their landlady/tenant relationship was a mistake. Then she could magnanimously suggest reasonable time for them to resettle before welcoming Malcolm and Joanne into her home.

Once the meal was over, however, Philip told Mary that he and Sarah would wash-up and tidy the kitchen. This was the final straw for the child who burst into floods of tears and declared that there was no point in living now that Mummy and Daddy hated each other. Mary walked out of the room, without comment. If Philip wished to be manipulated, that was his problem.

She sat in her sitting room and listened to the Third programme, allowing the serenity of Vaughan Williams' music to envelop her. Edgar was broadcasting later, a lecture on Communism. She always had such mixed feelings when he was on the radio. If she listened to his voice, she felt that there was still some contact, some common ground; she had done so much of the preparation for the lectures he gave. Afterwards, though, she felt drained of hope and filled instead with a bitterness that she could physically taste. If she did not listen, she was devastated by grief and guilt, that by denying his present existence, she was also denying the past, that he had shared with her. She stood and, with leaden feet, walked to the door and locked it. Whatever she decided, she would not be able to cope with any interruptions.

As she tuned the radio to the Home programme, ready for the start of the broadcast, the 'phone rang. It was Charles, ringing from Austria. It was a terrible line but eventually Mary was able to understand what he wanted. Jenny needed a home! He gave Mary the number of the people she was with and suggested that she 'phone them to discuss how, where and when the child would be moved. Mary put the 'phone down; a small brandy was essential. As she understood it, there was nowhere for the child to go. Charles would not consider letting her live with her mother and since he had custody, who could argue with that. Mary cupped the crystal brandy glass in her hands, savouring the rich aroma. All that is needed now is the smell of one of Edgar's cigars. Her heart seemed to turn over, she shivered violently. Glancing at her watch, she turned up the volume; immediately the room was filled with Edgar's voice. She closed her eyes and imagined that he was sitting opposite her. So close, she had only to stretch out her hand, to touch his sleeve.

Jenny stood in her new bedroom. 'The cabin' Grandmother had called it. She had explained that it was like the cabin of a ship. The bed was built in, with cupboards underneath and there was a small bedside table and lamp. Jenny did not have many clothes so the small wardrobe was amply big enough. She knelt on her bed and looked out of the windows. They were quite high up above her bed and when she lay down, all she could see was the sky. It did seem a bit like being at sea, she decided. Then you would only see sky and water, of course. She stood on the bed and leaned out of the window a little. Her room was at the back of the flat and looked out on the backs of the row of similar houses in the next street. As Jenny looked down, she felt quite dizzy. She had never lived so high up before. She turned round, leaning against the window sill and gave the room a close scrutiny. Pale blue walls, again conjuring images of the sea reflecting its colour. Pale grey carpet and curtains. The bed was firm but comfortable and had a dark blue cover. It was a plain room, no clutter or fuss. Nothing to suggest it was for a boy or a girl, Jenny suddenly felt safe. The sun was setting behind the house tops opposite and for a few minutes, the room was glowing with golden light; the coolness of the colour scheme was transformed into a warm and welcoming refuge. Jenny bounced off the bed and went into the kitchen for her tea. She watched Grandmother working quietly, preparing vegetables.

'Shall I lay the table?'

Mary looked round, surprised. Surprised by the child's quietness and willingness to help; a pleasant change from Sarah.

'That would be very kind, my dear. Although we do not lay tables, hens lay eggs. We set tables.' The correction was delivered gently and ended with a smile. I must remember that for next time, Jenny thought.

'Set the table for four. Knives, forks, spoons and forks. That's right, dessert forks pointing to the right, dessert spoons pointing to the left.' Mary watched the child, such a serious expression for a little girl. She was obviously clever, her school reports had been excellent. She must be settled into a new school as soon as possible. It would not do for her to miss too much time and spoil her chances of passing her eleven plus.

The front door banged and Jenny looked inquiringly at Mary.

'That will be Philip and Sarah, you remember I told you about them. They are a kind of distant cousin,'

149

Sarah rushed in but stopped dead when she saw Jenny.

'This is Jenny Warr, Sarah, my grand daughter. You remember I said she was coming to live with us. I am sure you will get on very well; you will be company for each other. Then each girl made a quick appraisal of the other. She is very pretty, Jenny thought, I wish I could grow my hair long like hers. Sarah eyed Jenny up and down with disdain, taking in the old fashioned school tunic, that Gladys Warr had bought, which refused to wear out.

'What school do you go to?' Jenny glanced at Mary. 'I'm not at school at the moment, Grandmother will sort that out soon.'

'Then why are you wearing school uniform? Haven't you got any others?'

Jenny felt her face go red and hot with embarrassment. Mary smiled at her.

'Go and wash your hands now, please girls'

'I'm at a private school.' Sarah said. Jenny made no comment. I don't think I am going to like you very much.

Mary arranged for Jenny to start at the local junior school on the following Monday. It allowed enough time for her to buy any items of clothing or other school equipment that Jenny needed. It was Jenny's fourth school in four years and although she hated being moved, she had become philosophical about it. After all, she had never been anywhere long enough to make very close friends, so at least there was no-one special to say goodbye to.

In the evenings, Philip and Sarah stayed in their sitting room while Jenny and Mary stayed in theirs. Mary was most favourably impressed by Jenny's knowledge and abilities. She was good at crosswords and quickly picked up the card games Mary taught her. She enjoyed sewing and embroidered a most acceptable bib for the new grandchild of one of Mary's friends. Mary took her to see Lawrence Olivier's film version of Henry Vth. The child had been enchanted. Mary realised how much she had missed of her own children's childhood. Having a nanny had been natural for a woman of her status and temperament. It had allowed her to continue her social life, as well as the work she had done for Edgar, without interruption. She wondered if her, sometimes distant, relationship with her children was the result of what always seemed, at the time, a most sensible arrangement. I must make the most of this opportunity to get to know Jenny. Perhaps I can undo some of the damage Rachel's irresponsible behaviour has done to this child. She realised that she had not yet informed Rachel of Jenny's latest move. At least now she will be able to see her mother more easily. I must invite her over for tea with Alec and Stephen. She emphasised the word must, in her own mind, knowing that such a visit would have to be arranged and, in her case, endured. I cannot escape my maternal duties entirely.

Rachel had always been such a difficult person to deal with - from birth. The task did not seem to be getting any easier. Mary 'phoned regularly and soon became attuned to the state of Rachel's mind by the nature of her response, to each call. Mary knew that Rachel was in a manic phase, at the moment. This was the most difficult and potentially dangerous aspect of her condition. One word out of place and Rachel could erupt like Vesuvius. Mary's greatest fear was that Alec would terminate the relationship, leaving Rachel to fend for herself and Stephen. The prospect of having to deal with such a situation, made Mary shudder. If Alec feels that he does have me in the background offering moral support, maybe he will stick it out, at least until the boy is older. Alec clearly loved Stephen a great deal. Perhaps he would be the cement that held the relationship together. Now there was another possible problem, Stephen; he had grown into a noisy, rowdy, boisterous disobedient little boy. Mary suspected that the frequent rows, Rachel talked about, were probably the result of Alec trying to curb the boy's often unacceptable behaviour.

Mary thought about Charles. What a clever man, to have escaped all this. He maintained that he had been forced to stay out of the country, on the instructions of Rachel's doctor. For heaven's sake, Mary had thought at the time and snorted with derision. Charles had remained in the army because that was where he wanted to be. He surely did not believe that anyone would be taken in by his feeble excuse. I had better write to inform him of my plan to have Rachel and family here, to visit Jenny. Whatever I think of him, he is her father and does have custody. It will be up to him then to tell me if he objects to the arrangement. Mary went to her desk and as she was writing, decided that she would enclose the bills for Jenny's school clothes. He will not escape his responsibilities for the child anymore than I can escape my responsibility for my daughter, his ex-wife.

Rachel put the 'phone down with a bang. She stormed into the kitchen. 'That was my bloody mother on the 'phone!'
Alec looked up from the paper and waited. He did not know how normal Rachel's relationship with Mary was, having no recollection of his own mother to use as a yardstick. It was certainly stormy.

'Jenny is living with her now! Would you believe it! An old woman. That bastard Charles would prefer her to be with an old woman than with her own mother. I won't have it, it's not natural.'

Alec watched, with alarm, as Rachel became increasingly agitated. He thought carefully, what could he say that would not inflame her already explosive mood. Secretly he thought it a good idea for Jenny to be with Mary. At least it would be easier for her to see her mother. That would put a stop to the constant carping on about not seeing her. He realised that it would not be wise to say so. Rachel most definitely would not appreciate his appearing to approve anything that Charles had arranged. He stood up slowly and tried to put his arms around her. Sometimes, just holding her brought her down a bit. I am acting as a human strait jacket, he thought. Perhaps, sub-consciously, it reminds her of being in Friern Barnet, when it was a strait jacket and not his arms that restrained her.

'Now come on, Ray,' he said, 'I know it's all wrong but let's be positive about it. Make the best of a bad job. You don't want Charles to think he has got the upper hand, do you?' Rachel looked at him sharply, her nostrils flared but she clearly appreciated the point he was making. He gave her a hug. This tall, slender woman with long legs and fine features, like a thoroughbred race horse, would his desire never diminish? I'm forty five, life should be taking on a more gentle tone. With a flash of insight that could not be denied, he realised that as long as Rachel was in his life, there would be no peace; without her there, it would be no life.

Charles read Mary's letter, screwed it up and tossed it into the bin. He looked at the bills she had sent and cursed. Surely, the money he had agreed to send, each month, should cover all expenses. He hadn't calculated for this. What a tight fisted old bat she was. Rachel had always claimed that her mother was mean. Since the divorce, he had dismissed everything that Rachel had said or done, in the same way that he had dismissed her from his life. Perhaps, in this case, she had been right. He thought about his finances. Even as an officer, he was not well off. There were his mess bills to pay. He sent money to England, for Jenny. Now his mother was virtually bed-ridden as well as house bound, he sent money home so she could have extra help. Now this. He was spending more money than he should on Jeanette. As a colonel's daughter and a wealthy one at that, he could not pinch and scrape. Austria was an expensive place to entertain; taking her to the officers' mess was hardly acceptable. He lit his pipe and sat, chin in hand, contemplating his life. If it were not for Jenny, I could make a fresh start. I could leave the army and go anywhere. His eyes caught the picture standing on the corner of his desk. It had been taken when Jenny was five. She was sitting on his knee and they were looking at a book together. Heads close, intent on what they were doing. She is the fruit of my loins, my flesh and blood, yet a ball and chain around my ankle. A sharp pang of guilt squeezed his heart as he realised what a dangerous track his thoughts had gone down. Poor kid, she had not asked to be born.

He started to clear the papers on his desk, he was taking Jeanette out for a meal later. He needed to get back to barracks, wash and change. He wondered again about staying in the army. He loved the life but he knew it could not last for ever. Jeanette had been talking about going home. Her father was due to retire next year and he and his wife would go back to Settle, in Yorkshire, where they still owned a cottage. Jeanette had decided that she too would go back to England and had already started looking for jobs. Maybe, now was the time for him to do the same. It might be worth while writing to his old boss in the Post Office. When he had been conscripted, he had been assured that after the war, there would be a job waiting for him. He left his office and as he did so, tucked Mary's bills inside his uniform pocket. The old skin-flint could wait. Tonight, he would do Jeanette proud.

She was seven years younger than Charles and had been swept off her feet by his gallantry and good looks. She had been recovering from an unhappy relationship when she first met him. His attentions did much to heal her emotional wounds. She knew her father approved of Charles, both as an officer and as a suitor. The only problem was religion. As a devout Catholic, a permanent relationship, with a divorced man was out of the question. This was one reason for her decision to return to England as soon as possible. She feared that since the relationship could not develop further, to continue at its present level would be too much of a strain for both of them. Besides, she wanted to be married and most definitely wanted a family. A friend of her mother's had a house in Earls Court. At the moment, it was occupied by the friend's son, Tom. There was ample room for Jeanette to move in. She would, in fact be able to have a self-contained flat at a nominal rent. It was an offer that she had decided to take up. She would get a job once she had settled in. She would tell Charles tonight.

They sat opposite each other at the small candle-lit table. Musicians were playing Viennese waltzes in the background. Charles looked at Jeanette and smiled. She was a pleasant companion, interesting and entertaining, in a restful way. She enjoyed the tales he told her of his exploits. She made him feel good. She was quite different from Rachel. If I were unkind, he thought, I would describe her as short and dumpy. In fact, it would only be because I am making an unfair comparison. Charles sighed, he slid his hand across the table and rested it on hers. It was like a child's hand, plump and rounded. She was like a ripe peach, even to the faintest hint of down on her cheek. Her features were unexceptional but when she smiled, she suddenly became very pretty. Like a milk-maid, bursting with health. Charles thought of the stunningly beautiful girls he had known when he was stationed in Cyprus. They were, he believed, the most beautiful girls in the world - until they were in their early twenties. Then almost overnight, they became fat and frumpish with small children clinging to their skirts, a babe in arms and a bulging belly. He looked intently at Jeanette. Was he seeing her at her best now? What would she be like in five, ten years time? Certainly her mother was a well upholstered woman. What had Oscar Wilde said, if you want to know what your wife will be like in twenty years, look at her mother. Suddenly the enormity of the thought hit him. Would Jenny turn out to be like her mother? Now that Mary was allowing, maybe encouraging contact between Jenny and her mother, it was Rachel and not he who would have the greatest influence on the child. He felt sweat break out on his forehead and mopped it with his napkin. He realised Jeanette had been talking and he had not heard a word he said. She looked at him. 'Are you all right?'

He smiled weakly, 'I'm sorry my sweet, I must seem very rude but I have the most fearful headache. I think perhaps I am sickening for something.'

'Shall we go then, have an early night?'

He paid the bill, wincing inwardly. Jeanette insisted on driving him back to the barracks. They sat in the car, holding hands.

'I'm sorry I've mucked up the evening.'

'It doesn't matter, but who is going to look after you when I've gone home?'

His look confirmed her hope that he had not heard what she had said in the restaurant. It was a relief really, his lack of response to her news had suggested he did not care. Clearly he was unwell and had not heard. She told him again of her plans. He smiled and squeezed her hand.

'Perhaps I will follow you to England.'

She felt a great upsurge of delight, maybe this was the answer, force the issue. The question of religion would have to be tackled later. Since he had divorced Rachel when she had been certified insane, surely that would allow for a special dispensation, an annulment. She leaned across to kiss him, he held her in his arms and rested his cheek against her hair.

'I had better not kiss you, my dear. I could have the plague! I hope to see you tomorrow.'

She watched him get out of the car and waited until he closed the door. She waved, as she drove off. There was a heavy feeling in her heart that she could not explain. He was going to leave the army. She had felt so delighted at the news but so soon the doubts. Why? Why does he never say he loves me?

Jenny sat on her bed and thought about the visit Mum would make tomorrow. When Grandmother told her, she had felt quite shaky. She had gone to her room to sit quietly. Mum was both exciting and alarming. Her moods were enough to make your skin tingle and the hair on the back of your neck stand on end. She always seemed to be full of wild and strange plans. She gave the impression that nothing was impossible. Despite this, Jenny was only too well aware that it was important to pick ones words carefully. On more than one occasion, lack of enthusiasm on Jenny's part had tipped Rachel's exuberance into demonic rage that left the child terrified and repentant. What she did not realise was that she had not seen the other extreme behaviour that manic depressives were prey to. Depression, black impenetrable despair that made the simplest task an insurmountable problem. Where to speak seemed pointless. Eating merely ensured that the body would continue functioning, any activity suggested that there was a purpose to existence though every nerve, in mind and body, denied it. At such times, death alone had and was the only purpose that could be justified, oblivion beckoned enticingly, irresistibly. At such times, Jenny did not see her Mother.

Mary also felt apprehensive about the visit. She had nothing in common with Alec, except Rachel. Stephen was a tiresome child who would probably rampage around her flat, leaving a trail of chaos behind him. Rachel was, of course, as unpredictable as ever. Mary knew Rachel was determined to have Jenny living with her. Even after such a short time, Mary realised she did not want that to happen. She surprised herself by acknowledging that she actively wanted Jenny to stay with her. Mary knew that she was not anyone's idea of an ideal grandmother. She was not a cuddly old lady, who dished out sweets and extra pocket money.

She knew she had a reputation for being aloof and undemonstrative. Since Edgar's departure, she had found it even more essential - for survival - to keep a very tight rein on her feelings. So why, she wondered this sudden desire for the companionship of a child? It occurred to her that maybe she was trying to make up to Rachel, through Jenny, for a childhood that was somehow lacking. Maybe it is my fault Rachel is like she is. No sooner had the thought presented itself than it was dismissed. There was nothing the matter with Eleanor or Malcolm. Rachel is her father's child. Mary walked to the kitchen. She could hear Sarah laughing at some game Philip had devised, with marbles and complicated runways. Jenny, on the other hand, was doing her homework. So much for private education. The child should have finished her work by now. She can help me make a cake for tomorrow, she'll enjoy that.

Stephen stood, with a mutinous expression on his face.

'I don't want to go. I want to stay here and play with Bobby.'

'Don't be silly and for goodness sake, stand still while I comb your hair.' Rachel tugged at the knots and tangles acquired since he was last given a thorough inspection.

'Ow! You're hurting me.' Rachel shook him roughly, she also felt strangely apprehensive. Alec glanced at his watch. They were going to be late, again. They were always late, for everything. He sighed under his breath. Rachel whipped round. 'What's the matter, now?'

'I think I had better 'phone your mother to let her know we are going to be a bit late.'

'For Christ's sake, will you stop making a fuss. We'll take a taxi.'

Alec blanched. He was in a well paid job now, with a large firm of electrical engineers but Rachel could get through money faster than he could earn it. He knew there was no point in arguing, he also realised, for the umpteenth time, that he should have kept his mouth shut. Bearing in mind, her upbringing, in such a privileged atmosphere, it was hardly surprising if she never gave money, or the lack of it, a second thought.

'Anyway, you will have to be especially nice to me now, I'm pregnant.'

Alec sat down, he felt his stomach lurch. He looked at her intently, as she struggled to bring some order to Stephen's wild, unruly mop. How long had she been home? Six weeks, seven. He thought back to Stephen's conception and a feeling of deja vu swept over him. Am I the biter bit? Rachel had been very vague about the time in France. Still, she could have conceived as soon as she came back, after all there had been enough occasions during the first week to conceive a football team! I must not become cynical and suspicious.

Rachel looked at him. 'So I've left you speechless for once. Aren't you glad?'

'Of course I am, of course but it has just come as a bit of a shock.'

'What's pregnant?' Stephen asked. Rachel took hold of his hand and placed it on her stomach. 'There's a baby growing inside there. It will be a new baby brother or sister, for you.'

'Well, I hope it's a brother. I don't like girls.'

Rachel laughed 'Well you will just have to wait and see won't you.'

Stephen looked thoughtful, 'If there's a baby in your tummy, how is it going to get out?'

Alec stood up briskly, ' We definitely do not have time to go in to all that now. Come along, if we hurry, we will catch the 3.00 p.m. bus. Then we will only be an hour late!'

Mary was exhausted. She sat by the fire with Jenny opposite her. The child was very quiet. The news of Rachel's pregnancy had been a bomb shell for them both. However, it had been clear that Stephen's jealousy had been the most difficult thing for Jenny to cope with. He had made it virtually impossible for her to make any contact, verbal or physical, with her mother. He had clung like a limpet and when he wasn't on her knee or draped around her, he was demanding her attention by interrupting everyone and being a thorough nuisance. Alec had tried, not very successfully, to distract Stephen and had also tried to talk to Jenny. She had seemed shy and embarrassed by his attentions.

'I don't think Stephen likes me.' Jenny whispered.

'Perhaps, it's because he doesn't know you very well.'

'I wish my Dad would come home.'

'It isn't very easy for you, is it?'

Jenny shook her head and looked close to tears. Why, Mary wondered, can I not just sweep the poor little scrap into my arms and love her? Why have I never been able to do that?   'Shall we see if we can finish the crossword?' Jenny nodded.

'Bring the footstool over and sit by me. Let's have some supper later. I think buttered crumpets would be nice.' Jenny smiled a wan smile and sat at Mary's feet. Mary placed her hand gently on the child's shoulder and felt her thin body lean, ever so slightly, against her leg.

'That would be nice, Grandmother.' she said.

Stephen did not like school. He made a scene every morning and Rachel often had to stay with him, in class, until he had become sufficiently occupied for her to slip away, unnoticed. Rachel told his teacher that he was a very sensitive child and that was why he was so difficult. Jean Smith's private view was that he was a naughty boy who was short of a smacked bottom.

With the bursting forth, into bloom, of all the Spring and early Summer flowers, Rachel too had started to show the presence of her third child. She seemed calmer than she had been for months. Both Alec and Stephen benefited from the comparative tranquillity of their home life. Rachel went to her mother's every two or three weeks, to see Jenny, while Alec took Stephen onto Hampstead Heath. This arrangement suited everyone and the disastrous visit, with Stephen, was not repeated. It did mean that if Mary wanted to see Stephen, she had to go to Hampstead, that seemed a small inconvenience. On such occasions, Jenny went too. Stephen largely ignored his step-sister's presence but now that Jenny was able to see her mother regularly, she seemed unperturbed by Stephen's attitude.

In fact Jenny felt very settled. The relationship with Mary was built on common interests. Jenny's desire to learn was equalled by Mary's desire to teach.

They went to museums and art galleries. In the warmer weather, as Summer brought a riot of colour to city window boxes and hanging baskets, visits to Kew gardens were a particular delight. On one blazing Sunday afternoon, Mary, Philip, Rachel and Alec took the children to Kew for a picnic. They found a secluded spot, uncultivated and far from the hot houses and pavilions. There was dappled shade under the trees and lush ferns growing in the long grass. The grown ups sat on rugs in the sun-shine while the children crept, barefoot, in the undergrowth. The drone of bees was heavy as the children picked fronds of fern to make head-dresses and capes suited to the elves and fairies they had become. At first, Stephen was scathing and reluctant to associate himself with silly games but since the grown-ups were talking about all manner of boring things, he had little choice.

The sunlight came in shafts through the trees, flickering and sending sparks of gold on all that it touched, as a slight breeze moved the foliage. Jenny felt as though she were bewitched and the others seemed to feel the same. They concocted wild and fanciful tales of mystery and magic and acted them out. Everything was beautiful, the real world did not matter, did not exist. All was magical.

When at last they were told to put on their shoes and tidy themselves for going home, the spell was broken. Stephen was tired and suddenly felt very silly standing with ferns in his hair. He snatched them out and muttering under his breath about 'stupid girls games' stomped off to Rachel. Sarah and Jenny gazed at each other but the magic faded and they saw only dull reality. Sarah ran to complain that Jenny always had to be the Fairy Queen and it wasn't fair. Jenny looked up and watched the branches moving slightly, changing the patterns of light and shade. She did not want to break the spell. The world of make believe beckoned to her. This had been the best afternoon she had ever had. I want to stay here for ever. Her bare feet felt cold and she shivered. She heard Mary calling. I'll write and tell Dad all about it, but I'd better not mention Mum and Alec.

Chapter 10

Mary checked her hair in the mirror and, having given herself a close scrutiny, decided she looked elegant enough to meet Royalty. Malcolm and his wife would be arriving any minute. She felt like a young woman, about to meet her lover. Her heart was pounding and her mouth felt dry. My relationship with Malcolm is going to be different now. I have to share him. He will be Joanne's husband first and my son second. She leant on the hall stand and gazed again at her reflection. It alarmed her that an acknowledgement of her, now secondary, role caused her so much pain. I must keep reminding myself that he is a married man. If I do not, I could lose him entirely. She stifled a thought that tried to inveigle its way into her consciousness.

'Of course he is not all that I have now. What nonsense.' She thought about Eleanor, so independent and apparently disinterested in family life. The cat who walks by itself, Kipling had said. And Rachel, there was always Rachel.

'Grandmother, what time are Uncle Malcolm and Aunt Joanne arriving?' Jenny stood quietly in the hall. She was neat and tidy. Mary wondered how long she had been standing there.

'Soon, child, have you done all your homework?'

'Yes, I've been reading. I've got a new Doctor Dolittle book.'

Mary smiled, the child was no trouble. She has brought much into my life.

Philip had taken Sarah to her mother's house. He always returned in a foul mood. Mary could not imagine what he did during the carefully timed visits. She knew he would not be invited in for a cosy chat.

When the doorbell rang, Mary jumped, even though she felt she had been waiting for hours for the moment to arrive. Malcolm stood, smiling. Standing next to him was a tall, dark-haired girl with eyes the colour of topaz which Mary immediately decided would miss very little. Mary was trembling with excitement at this, the sight of her darling boy.

'Come in, my dears, come in.' She put her arms tightly around Malcolm's neck and drew him to her, almost frightened to let go in case he was an apparition. After a moment, Malcolm eased himself out of his mother's embrace.

'I want you to meet, Joanne. I know you two must be dying to meet. Don't believe all she tells about me when I was a child, Jo, and certainly do not look at photographs of me on a bear-skin rug!'

'I'm very pleased to meet you, Malcolm has told me so much. Should I call you Mother?'

The two women touched cheeks and smiled.

'Of course, my dear, do come through to my sitting-room.'

'Now then, we have another young lady here who needs to be introduced. Why I do believe it is my little niece! The last time I saw you, you were in nappies. Come and give your uncle a kiss.' He knelt down as Jenny walked towards him. He was less alarming now he was not towering above her. He seemed to fill the place with noise and barely contained exuberance. She was not sure she liked it. It made her feel embarrassed. Grown-ups were supposed to be sensible. She kissed him and shook her new aunt's hand.

'You must be ready for tea, I've been very busy baking and Jenny has helped me. Come this way.'

'Oh! Honey, this is just beautiful.' Joanne breathed out heavily, deeply impressed by the dark rich glow of highly polished wood, rich upholstery, a Chinese carpet and cream silk walls. Sunlight warmed the room and made it glow. The view over treetops showed the panorama of London, to perfection. The tea trolley was set with snow white linen cloths, bone china and an extravagant array of home made scones and cakes. The silver teapot reflected light onto the walls and ceiling and light from the fire, on this cool early summer day, beckoned a welcome.

Once everyone was seated, tea had been poured and plates filled, Mary started to question her daughter-in-law. Malcolm had warned Joanne that his mother had a very direct manner. Still, she was less than prepared for what felt like an interrogation. Where had they met? How long had they known each other? When, exactly, did they get married? The pause, that spoke more clearly than any words, asking why am I, you mother not asked or even informed until after the event? Mary glanced at Malcolm, who cleared his throat nervously. He made no reply, offered no explanation. Certainly he had no intention of ever telling her that it had been his decision to exclude her from the wedding celebrations. Looking at her now, he felt a pang of guilt. His mother, the indomitable had an air of fragility, vulnerability that he had never been aware of before. He rapidly changed the subject to a discussion of where they were going to live. It seemed unlikely that they would take one of the flats Mary had suggested. Joanne insisted

161

that she did not want to live in a condo. Jenny who had been quietly observing the exchanges
asked, 'What's a condo?'

'That's what we call an apartment, or flat, is it? It's really condominium.'

'Oh.' Jenny glanced at Mary's face, there was little to suggest what she was thinking but Jenny sensed that her Grandmother felt hurt. Hurt that Malcolm and Joanne were already establishing their independence of her. She also sensed that Joanne had not been too favourably impressed by her new mother-in-law.

'Where will you live, then?' Jenny asked, feeling quite bold in defence of her grandmother's feelings.

'At the moment, we are renting a house in Wimbledon, Archie's, you know, Mother. He has been posted abroad so it was ideal while we had a look round. Basically, we want to buy, no point in renting if we can help it, is there. Only problem is a deposit.' Malcolm looked at Mary, obviously trying to gauge her response to his last remark.

'More tea, my dear?' Mary asked Joanne. Silently Joanne passed her cup.

Malcolm talked about his work. He was going to be given responsibility for designing advertisements for some of the company's most important customers.

'I've really landed on my feet,' he said, including both Mary and Joanne in his broad and charming smile.

'And you, my dear, do you intend to work?'

'Oh, sure but I want us to get settled before I start looking for a job. I don't want Malcolm's work upset by any moving house.' Joanne smiled back, an all American, broad, perfectly white, unblemished smile. It seemed to Mary to have Keep Off stamped across it. You ain't gonna run my life, lady.

'Of course, once we are settled, we're gonna start a family, aren't we honey?'

Joanne placed a perfectly manicured hand, bright with red varnished nails, lightly but proprietorially on Malcolm's arm. He smiled at her and flicked a glance at his mother whose face was devoid of expression.

'Since when did you want to be a mother, Jo? You always said you valued your independence and your figure too much!'

'I have you to thank. When I met you, the idea of a miniature Malcolm seemed awfully appealing. Besides my mom always said you can never have too many grandchildren. Don't you agree, Mother?'

Mary smiled but her mind was racing backwards to the time, five years ago when Malcolm had come home on leave, sick. It had taken visits to several doctors before syphilis was diagnosed. Malcolm had told her then that the doctors had been unable to say whether or not he would ever be able to father a child. Clearly, he had not talked to Joanne about it.

Charles opened the front door, instantly aware that the familiar smell of his mother's cooking was absent. That and the smell of wet washing, on a Monday, were always the triggers that sent his memories of his parents into action. Parents, who had lived here all of his life. He heard a soft whisper, it must be his mother.

'Is that you, son?' He walked down the hall and into the living room. Gladys sat, propped up in a bed. Her body hardly disturbed the flatness of the bed clothes. Her chest moved rapidly in and out with every shallow and wheezing breath. Her face was grey and the wrinkles with which Charles was so familiar were now deep grooves that could have been cut with a knife. Charles took her hand and as though physical contact sapped the last vestige of energy that Gladys had left, her head sank back onto her pillow. She clutched his hand, now with both of hers and with alarm, Charles watched as tears trickled down her face.

'It's good to see you, son. I've not been too good. It's my chest and we've had terrible fogs, I feel as though I am going to choke.' He patted her hand.

'Now don't upset yourself and don't try to talk. Could you manage a cup of tea?' Gladys nodded and dabbed at her eyes. She patted at her hair, as always, neatly corrugated in its net. He's home, my boy's home.

Charles went into the kitchen. Everything was neat and tidy. Surely his mother hadn't done the housework - not in her present state. He'd ask her later. As he stood waiting for the kettle to boil, he looked around him at the evidence of a frugal existence. There on the top shelf, was the cobbler's last that Dad had always used to mend the family's shoes. On principle, Mother would never get rid of it, too much sentimental value. Even though, it would never be used by her. The old boiler still stood, dominating the room, with its copper lid gleaming and the old wooden tongs looped through the handle. The ribbed glass wash board stood on the floor. He wondered if the geezer was still temperamental - the bane of his mother's life. Probably, he decided. Nothing changes.

He took two cups of tea through and perched carefully on the edge of the bed. Was it his imagination or did she look a little better? She's bound to be glad to see me. *I must make sure she sees plenty of Jenny, while I 'm home.* He had tentatively planned a few gentle outings but looking at the state of his mother, that was out of the question.

'Are the meals on wheels looking after you, Mum?'

'I can't eat it, son. I just can't face food, not when its been kept hot, for hours on end. I just put it in the bin. I don't want to hurt their feelings.'

Charles looked at her in disbelief. The thought of such wanton waste was wholly alien to him. He started to speak, but realised the rebuke that had sprung to his lips was best left unsaid. Sensing his annoyance, Gladys whispered,

'I don't want to be any trouble to you, son. I know you have enough to think about. I'm all right.'

'Well, while I'm home, I'll make meals for you. You need building up. I can't leave you like this.'

Gladys sipped her tea, 'The neighbours have been very good, dear. They do my bit of shopping and collect my pension. The home help comes in every day.'

Charles said nothing. *I should think the neighbours do help; I'm paying them good money to do so.*

'You finish your tea, Mum and I'll unpack my things. Then I'll 'phone Mary Cardew and arrange to see Jenny. You'd like to see Jenny, wouldn't you?'

Gladys nodded, her heart too full to speak. *If only I weren't so frightened of him. He is my flesh and blood; I carried him inside me and nursed him, when he nearly died. Yet I am terrified of upsetting him.* She looked at the calendar, in two weeks, he would be gone again. She would be alone until the next time. Would there be a next time? In many ways, she hoped not. She was caught like a fly, in a spider's web but the web was life and no matter how she struggled, she could not disentangle herself. She put the cup and saucer on the bedside table, pushed herself upright and pulled the lacy, hand knitted bed jacket around her. Looking at the delicate intricacy of pattern, she realised, that was where the idea of spider's webs had come from. What nonsense! Her much loved son was home, fancy thinking about death at such a time. How would he feel, what kind of homecoming was it? As though she had plucked strength from the air, Gladys took a deeper breath and felt the blood in her veins quicken a little. She would ask him about that girlfriend of his, when he came downstairs.

Jenny had settled quite well, into her new school. It did not worry her unduly that she was often on her own at playtime. She had developed her powers of observation and enjoyed what, in latter life she would call, people watching. Her teacher was a large elderly man who spent much of his time out of the classroom. He had elected the largest boy in the class to be his second-in-command and report on the misdemeanours of pupils, in his absence. The boy, Mark, sat next to Jenny. She did not like him but secretly admitted that he frightened her. So frightened was she, that when on duty for the absent teacher, Mark asked her who had spoken and she told him. To her horror, Mark then added her name to the list of pupils who had disobeyed the teacher's express order not to talk.

With barely disguised outraged indignation, Jenny walked to the teacher's desk to receive the customary three whacks of the ruler. She bit her lip and walked unsteadily back to her desk. She was determined that the repulsive and now smirking Mark would not have the satisfaction of seeing her cry. Quietly, she got on with her work, moving her throbbing and wealed left hand from desk to lap and finally tucking it under her thigh in an attempt to curb the pain.

'Stop fidgeting will you, you're jogging my arm.' Mark whispered.

Jenny turned and looked at him. Her eyes were blazing and made clear her contempt and disgust. For a moment he felt uneasy, then checked himself, how could he be frightened of a stupid girl, an ugly girl with glasses? But he was. Jenny vowed, to herself, that she would never speak to him again.

As she walked home, she decided she would not tell Grandmother. Her hand had stopped hurting and as she examined it, it was hard to see any marks. She had been surprised, when at break time several class mates had spoken to her. She had even joined in a skipping game. Perhaps Mark had done her a favour. Perhaps she would be accepted as one of them, instead of being the odd one out.

She skipped along the road, her bag bumping against her back. She called at the little sweet shop, on the corner and bought six pennyworth of her favourite coconut ice. It was utterly delicious and came in lumps and little crumbly bits. She licked her fingers and dipped them in the bag. It wasn't cheating to eat just the crumbs. She knew Grandmother did not like her to eat sweets before she came home for tea, a few luscious crumbs wouldn't hurt. She would save the rest for afterwards. Sarah would be home by now. She usually got home first. Her school seemed to have very short days. With considerable reluctance, Jenny closed the paper bag and firmly pushed it into her pocket.

Sarah was in her bedroom and said Jenny could not come in. She wouldn't say why. Jenny shrugged and went to the kitchen,

Grandmother seemed very preoccupied and not just with the meal. Jenny thought it might be to do with Mum.

Rachel had called quite regularly, on the last visit had talked about the new brother or sister which was due soon. Jenny had found it hard to respond to her mother's enthusiasm. Look what happened last time, she thought. She had wondered what started a baby growing. She had pondered even longer on how they got out. Looking at Grandmother's face, it seemed wiser not to ask such questions thus reminding her of the new baby of which, Jenny felt sure, Grandmother did not approve. So many questions but who to ask?

She wandered into her bedroom and sat on her bed. She could finish her geography or she could read her book. She was steadily working her way through the Dolittles. They were all right but she thought about the time Grandmother had taken her to Henry V, now that had been special. That in turn reminded her of the time Grandad and Grandma Warr had taken her to see 'A Matter of Life and Death'. She remembered the teardrop that had been shown, as evidence, to the judge and the amazing moving staircase, always moving, taking dead souls to heaven. She wondered if Grandad had climbed that long, long staircase when he died. She was sure he would have gone to heaven. She thought about Grandma Warr. She had not seen her for ages. Still, Dad would be home soon. She would draw and colour a picture for Grandma, she would like that.

'Dinner is ready, Jenny, wash your hands, please.' Jenny sat up and rubbed her eyes. She did not want anyone to know that thinking about Grandad had made her sad.

After the meal, Sarah disappeared into her room again. Jenny helped with the washing up, it was her turn. Then she got out her coloured pencils, they were her pride and joy. Lakeland pencils, in the prettiest box she had ever seen. She found some paper and put everything out on the kitchen table. She opened her pencil case and started drawing. Once she had finished, she opened the Lakeland box. Bits of coloured pencil fell out. She looked, in horror, every pencil point had been broken! She could not believe anyone would be so mean. She knew who had done it. Mark, getting his own back, because she had refused to speak to him all afternoon. She had been sent on an errand by Mr. Willis. That's when it had been done. Jenny put her head in her hands. Grandmother was in her sitting room, Sarah and Philip were in theirs, probably. She let the tears come. It was all so unfair. After a few moments, she felt better. Sarah's got a really good pencil sharpener. I'll borrow that. I will never let Mark know he has upset me, she thought. She went to the bathroom and washed her face.

What is Sarah up to, she wondered. She knocked on the bedroom door but there was no reply. She opened the door and there, on the bed, was Sarah's box of pencils. On the floor was yet another model village. Sarah supposed that was what all the secrecy was about. How silly. She went to the bed and picked up the pencil sharpener. At that moment, Sarah came in.

'What are you doing? I didn't tell you you could borrow that.'
Jenny knew that strictly speaking, Sarah was right but one way and another, it had been a horrid day and Jenny had had enough.

'You are just mean, you are. I was only borrowing it to sharpen my pencils. Some pig at school broke all mine.'

'You want to go to a proper school, like I do, instead of that dump down the road.'

'Well at least I learn things. I don't play all the time!'
Sarah stepped towards her, hand out stretched.

'Give me that.'
Jenny went to hand over the sharpener when she heard a crunching sound. Looking down, both girls saw the wreckage of a small house, made from card and match sticks. Jenny started to say,'I'm sorry......' but in a flash, Sarah was on her.

Nails scraped down her face and neck. Jenny desperately tried to defend herself but Sarah was like a thing possessed. Her breaths came in staccato grunts but in between, the voice whispered,'I hate you, everyone hates you! No-one wants you! Why don't you just go away?' The message echoed through Jenny's head, reverberating and pressing home its meaning. She had to stop Sarah, in desperation, she leaned forwards, shielding her head with her arms and fell against her adversary. Caught off balance, Sarah fell backwards, banging her head against the wall. With a shriek of pain. She ran out and Jenny heard the door of Philip's room open. Sarah would be telling her tale now. She was suddenly overtaken by weariness with it all. Her face was sore; when she gingerly touched it, there was blood left on her finger tips. What does it matter? What does anything matter? She walked very quietly to her room and closed the door behind her.

The sun shone brightly on this June evening. Jenny slipped her shoes off and stood on her bed. She gazed out at the cloudless sky, suffused with crimson and gold. Above the sky was the same colour as the walls of her room, her sanctuary. She opened the window and leaned out. The air was soft and seemed to sooth the fire of the scratches Sarah had left. Pigeons were flying home, so were other flocks of birds that Jenny did not recognise. She opened the window further and sitting on the window sill swung her legs round until they were dangling over the ledge. There was a ridge she could rest her feet on. The sounds from below were faint, unintrusive - an amiable buzz, like a swarm of friendly bees, going about their business.

Jenny took a deep breath and wished she were a bird. If I could just step off this ledge and soar through the air, I could leave all my troubles behind. She was still holding on tightly to the window sill with one hand while she gazed over the tree tops. The breeze ruffled her hair and caressed her burning cheeks. She loosened her grip and looked down. It was a very, very long way. She sat, she did not know how long for, but what did it matter? She had turned her back on everything. Looking skywards, watching the birds, she was free. She had only to step out, lift her arms and she would be borne heavenward. That would be best, wouldn't it?

She noticed the movement from the corner of her eye and looked across at the houses opposite. Someone was waving. She waved back. You must be nice, she thought, to wave to someone you don't know. I wish I could reach out far enough to touch you and say 'Hello'. She shivered, it was getting chilly now. Suddenly an arm grabbed her, dragging her backwards so that she fell on the bed. She looked up and saw Philip, who was panting slightly and Grandmother who looked angry. Sarah stood in the doorway, ashen-faced and tear-streaked.

'What in God's name are you doing, you stupid child?' Philip shouted. Jenny felt stunned and totally disorientated. One minute she was at peace, surrounded by beauty and now suddenly the rage and the shouting were all around her. She could not speak.

'Answer me!' Philip's face was scarlet and in a flash, Jenny realised that along with anger, was fear. Fear, surely not of her but perhaps of what he thought she was going to do. And what had she been going to do? She was not sure.

'Look at her face.' Grandmother spoke. Every word fell into the silence like a bomb. Sarah started to snivel but was silenced by a glance from Grandmother.

'Who has done this to you, child?'
Sarah looked despairingly at her father and started to cry. Mary and Philip exchanged glances.

Mary asked, gently, 'Did Sarah do this?' Jenny nodded.

'I think you had better have a serious talk with your daughter while I do something about this child's face.'

Mary sat on the bed and rested her hand on Jenny's. Jenny started to cry, silently at first as large tears welled in her eyes and scalded the raw patches on her face.

'Come here child, what troubles you?'

Jenny sat up and leaned against Mary. Half dragging, half lifting she got Jenny onto her lap. Tears flowed, unabated and great gulping sobs made the child's body heave and shake. Mary waited until the torrent of sorrow and pain had eased. Jenny told her everything that had happened that day. Mary wondered at the child's fortitude and speculated about what she had already coped with.

'I shall go to your school and discuss the whole thing with your Headteacher. I shall also be having a serious talk with Sarah. I will not tolerate such behaviour in my home. You should not have tried to borrow without asking but there is absolutely no excuse for what Sarah did.' Jenny listened and managed a watery smile. She looked at the wet patches down the front of Mary's dress and touched them, lightly with her finger. 'I'm sorry, Grandmother.'

'It really doesn't matter, my dear. Lets look forward to something nice. I have had a call from your father, he is coming to see you tomorrow. So we must try to do something to hide your war wounds. Promise me you will never sit out on the window sill again.'

'I wasn't going to do anything silly.'

'I should hope not indeed. That poor woman who saw you nearly had a fit. She and her husband worked out which house it was and he ran round to tell us where you were.' Mary looked stern. 'She was frightened you would fall before he got here.' The unspoken floated between them and both knew it was best left unsaid

Rachel stretched and then rubbed the small of her back. It ached, it ached all the time. She would have to walk round to school, to collect Stephen. The weather had turned surprisingly hot, for June. The air was dusty, even though they were so near to Hampstead Heath. She buckled on her sandals, wishing she could walk barefoot in the street, as well as at home. While it was so hot, it was as well to have some protection from the pulsating heat of the pavements. She felt restless and constrained. Alec was always at work. Stephen was at school. She felt isolated. Their lives were so full while she was just waiting for something to happen. The baby kicked hard and Rachel rested her hand on her taut stomach. Would it be a boy or a girl? Stephen wanted a brother. He would. What an aggressive little boy he was. He had too much energy for his own or anyone else's good. She sighed and thought about Jenny. Never could two children be so different in temperament. She hoped that one day, when they were older, they might be able to have some kind of loving relationship. It reminded her of Eleanor, the sensible older sister, so aloof, so determined to get on with life. They had never got on. They still didn't.

This new baby is bound to be like either Stephen or Jenny, at least two of my children should be friends. I'm tired of conflict, people arguing, I want some peace, she thought, as with a flat-footed lumber, she went downstairs to the street. She saw several other mothers walking towards the school, going to collect their children. She nodded to them, they returned the acknowledgement but contact never got further than that. Rachel was bored by housework, didn't much like talking about what she was giving her husband for his tea or what exploits little such a body had got up to.

Other young mothers were at a loss as to how to take Rachel; she could be very odd. Sometimes embarrassingly loud, she would draw attention to herself in a most unseemly way. At other times, she did not seem to be aware of anything at all. She was most unnerving. In addition, she was a very attractive woman who apparently did nothing to face or hair, yet attracted many a wolf-whistle from any nearby workmen. Such action always led to Rachel striding past with her nose in the air but a twinkle in her eye. All in all, the other mothers thought she was someone to whom they should give a wide berth.

Today, the sparkle had deserted her. She could sense the black cloak of despond settling inexorably on her shoulders. Worse would come, she knew. This was just the beginning. The glorious exaltation she had felt for months had been slipping away, day by day, like life blood oozing from a wound. As always, ever since the pattern of her moods had become familiar, she tried to fight the depression. As always, she knew she would fail. Of one thing she was certain, she would not go back for more E.C.T.

Stephen raced out of school to greet her. As usual, hurling himself into her arms. If only I could absorb some of his vitality at times like these, she thought. If only his energy would pass through his skin and be absorbed by mine. She took his hand which was hot,sweaty and distinctly grimy.

'I want to go to the park, Mummy. Let's go to the park!' He was hopping from foot to foot. Rachel knew she ought to take him, let him run about, he would sleep better and not come bouncing into their room at the crack of dawn. Somehow, it was all too, too much. Let Alec take him after tea.

'I'm too tired, Stephen, Daddy will take you after tea.' With a howl of frustration, he pulled his hand away and started stamping his feet and shouting. Rachel sat on the little wall in front of a neat house and garden. Her legs were throbbing, she was sure she had a varicose vein. She hoped the owner of the house would not come out and move her on. By now, Stephen's shouts had increased in volume as Rachel showed no signs of doing what he wanted. He threw himself onto the pavement and drummed his feet and fists. Suddenly, Rachel let out a piercing scream that startled Stephen into a tear-streaked silence. A group of young mothers walked past, carefully averting their gaze as they hurriedly discussed the weather. Rachel picked Stephen up and brushed him down. They walked home in a subdued silence.

Jenny decided that her face did not look too bad. You could still see the scratches but they were not sore now. She had decided that if Daddy asked, she would tell him exactly what Sarah had done. Grandmother had assured Jenny that she would explain to Dad and it would never happen again. She felt quite glad in a way. Sarah deserved to be in trouble for once.

Jenny wondered what to wear. Not the red dress, anyway it was much too warm. She picked out the white dress with the red spots that she had worn to the presentation. It was a good thing Grandma Warr had allowed for growth. It was a bit short but Jenny had not grown much in the last two years. She decided it would be all right. She wondered what Daddy would wear. He always seemed to have his uniform on. Surely he must have other clothes. She wondered where they would go. Dad usually arranged something exciting. Jenny had often wondered if it was best to have a dull dad who was there all the time or an exciting dad who rushed in and swept you up, and then sooner than you could blink, was gone again. She decided she was the lucky one, when her dad left the army and surely, he must one day; he would never be dull. She wandered through the flat not able to do anything but wait. She went past Sarah's room. The two girls had been polite to each other after their fight but had kept apart by mutual consent. She leant on the window sill in Grandmother's sitting room. Her nose pressed against the window pane, she looked down into the street. Dad should be here soon. He was never late, not like Mum. Jenny remembered Mum had been very quiet when she came last time, sad almost. Jenny could not understand why she felt sad. The new baby would be coming soon. It must be lovely to have a baby all to yourself.

She was reminded, most vividly, of baby Stephen with her on the bed. Mum and Dad were there. It was the last time I saw Mum and Dad together. She swallowed hard. Then taking a deep breath, walked firmly to the kitchen, to see what Grandmother was doing.

Gladys had been dressed for hours now, having decided she would not be in bed when Jenny came to visit. She reflected on the conversation she had had with Charles, that morning. She found, since Albert had died, that her dependence on Charles made her tentative in her dealings with him. He could be so fierce and angry if she did or said the wrong thing. She had thought about Charles' girl-friend and decided that she must ask or risk putting her foot in it. She was surprised by the dismissive way he talked about the young woman; his last letters had spoken of her so warmly. I'm glad I asked before Jenny arrived. As far as Gladys could make out, Jeanette had returned to England and Charles had not had much contact with her since. He would not, therefore, be mentioning the relationship to Jenny. Gladys could only speculate, on the reasons for the relationship faltering, since Charles was not going to tell her anything. Perhaps the woman did not fancy taking on someone else's child.

Gladys picked up her knitting. She only had Jenny to knit for since contact with Caroline and family was limited to cards at Christmas and birthdays with a very occasional visit. It seemed strange to be knitting cardigans and jumpers when it was so warm but at least it helped to pass the time. Now that Gladys had almost permanent breathing difficulties, it was impossible for her to go out shopping or even do much housework. This grieved her greatly. She hated being unoccupied so 'its knitting or nothing'. She glanced at the clock, Charles had said they would be back for tea. She itched to go into the kitchen and get things ready but Charles had given her strict instructions that she was to leave it to him.

Jenny saw her father's uniform as he strode up the street, buttons and buckles gleaming. Her heart leapt. She ran back to the kitchen, where she had been helping Mary to souse herrings.

'You are clever, Gran, how did you know he would be coming now?'

Jenny's cheeks were bright pink and the colour brought life and vitality to the child's face. Her bright green eyes twinkled behind the unflattering National Health spectacles. Mary looked at her with surprise. You may be an ugly duckling but they have a habit of turning into swans. Jenny ran down the hall and opened the front door, clattering downstairs to meet Charles as he walked up. Although the flat was so high up and there was a lift, Charles insisted on using the stairs. Using a lift is lazy, my girl, he had told Jenny on his last leave. Never be lazy, he had sternly admonished her. Now whenever Jenny and Mary went out, Jenny always insisted on using the stairs and often beat the ponderous, creaking lift that Mary invariably had to wait several minutes for.

Jenny launched herself into Charles' arms from halfway down the second flight and hung like a limpet around his neck. The buttons of his jacket and the buckles of his Sam Browne belt pressed into her chest and stomach but she didn't care. She breathed in deeply the aroma of St. Bruno's tobacco that would always be a reminder of her beloved Dad. He kissed her on the cheek and hugged her.

'My goodness, you do smell fishy, what have you been doing?'

'Helping Grandmother to souse herrings. They're lovely.' She took his hand and half dragged him up the stairs. 'Where are we going? Can I see Grandma? How long is your leave? Mummy's having a baby.' As soon as the words were out of her mouth, she knew she had made a mistake. Why am I such a fool, she thought. I should know by now that Dad gets cross if I mention Mum. Its not quite the same with Mum, she was always talking about Dad and saying how awful he was. I wish she wouldn't, it's wrong to tell lies. She glanced at Charles' face. It had that tight, hard look that Jenny had come to dread. Please, please don't let the afternoon be spoilt. 'I'm doing all right at school, Dad. I've been moved into a new class.'

'And is that because you are very clever, or because you are very naughty?'

She glanced at him quickly, was he teasing her? She decided that perhaps he was and protested. 'I'm not naughty, well not often.'

'I should hope not or I would have to slap your backside.' He tapped her lightly on the bottom as she ran ahead to announce his arrival. Mary met them in the hall, she was polite but cool.

'I'm sure you two will want to be off, at once. Do you know where you are going or has your father got a surprise for you?' Jenny shrugged her shoulders.

'We will go to South Kensington, to the Science Museum and then on to my mother's for tea. She's far from well. I had quite a shock when I got home.'

Mary nodded sympathetically.

'So I can expect you back tonight, can I?'

'At the moment, it is rather difficult to have Jenny staying overnight but I will see what I can do in the future.'

Mary bent down and kissed Jenny. 'Do have a good time. Your Daddy and I can have a talk when he brings you back.'

'No trouble, I hope.'

'Oh, no, I just thought you would like me to bring you up to date with her progress.'

Jenny walked quickly along the balcony to Grandma's flat. Charles had given her the key. She let herself in and rushed to give Gladys a kiss and hug. She too was shocked by Gladys' appearance. Always small in build as well as stature, Gladys seemed - to Jenny to have shrunk. The flesh seemed to have melted from her face and body, leaving a skeleton, thinly covered with skin. Jenny smiled tremulously. 'Are you all right, Gran? Its nice to see you.'

'It's lovely to see you too, my darling. Look what I've been knitting for you.'

She held up a bright red short sleeved jumper with different coloured bands which gave a rich glow to the garment.

'Oh! Gran, its lovely, thank you so much.'

Charles stood watching the only two women he could count on. He had been hurt by the lack of enthusiasm shown by Jeanette when he told her he was thinking of leaving the army. He knew she wanted to marry and have a family. He knew religion was a problem, but it wasn't his fault. He must contact her while he was home this time and see what she was playing at. Women were quite definitely a damn nuisance.

'I'll get tea while you two natter. We're having pilchards, tomatoes and bread and butter. You need building up, Mother. Better not give too much to Jenny though. She'll end up a real little porker.' He laughed at his joke and went into the kitchen. Jenny looked apprehensively at her Grandma.

'But, Gran...' Gladys put a finger to her lips

'Yes, but Gran,' Jenny whispered, 'you hate pilchards. What are you going to do?'

'Sssh, don't let your father hear.'

'But Gran, let me tell him, you could have a boiled egg.'

'No!' hissed Gladys, 'don't upset him.'

So Grandma was frightened of Dad. Jenny was amazed. How can anyone be frightened of their own child? There is no possibility that Dad would ever be frightened of me.

Tea was an uncomfortable meal, Gladys slowly ate her portion of fish, commenting several times on how good it was. Jenny thought that was a silly thing to say because surely it meant that Dad would dish them up for tea again. As soon as Charles had finished his, he bustled out to the kitchen to get the teapot and cake. Jenny held out her plate to Gladys who, without a word, passed what remained of her fish onto Jenny's plate. When Charles returned from the kitchen, he glanced at his mother's plate but made no comment. Jenny started talking about the visit to the Science Museum.

Mary sat in her sitting room playing patience. All was peaceful, everyone was out. She listened to the Third Programme which was presenting an excellent Mozart concert. She decided that she must have a family reunion. It was such a long time since she had had all three of her children under one roof. Eleanor had written to say she would be coming to London soon. I'll invite Malcolm and Joanne, Rachel and Alec and of course the indomitable Stephen, for a meal.

Suddenly her peace was shattered. The front door was banged open and then slammed shut. She could hear Sarah wailing and Philip shouting. I am never short of drama with those two! She walked to her sitting room door. The spectacle that met her eyes was truly amazing. Philip looked as though he was about to explode. Sarah stood, still wailing, totally unrecognisable. Her long glossy hair, deep tawny brown, the delight of her father, was gone. Her hair was cropped and not more than an inch, all over. Mary felt an insane desire to laugh. She could just imagine the grim delight with which Sarah's mother would have taken the child to the hairdressers. Mary could hear, in her head, the gloating satisfaction with which the words, 'Cut it all off.' would have been spoken.

'Have you ever seen anything like it. Mary?' Mary decided that silence was the best response. Let the storm blow itself out.

'The bloody woman's insane. How could she do this to her own child?'

'I tried to stop it, Dad, honestly I did. She wouldn't listen.' Sarah snivelled and anxiously smoothed her hand over her head.

'I'll bloody well take her to court over this. I won't have it. She won't see the girl again, that's it. I've had enough.'

'Be careful, Philip, I don't think you can stop Sarah seeing her mother.'

Mary's words, quietly spoken, had an electrifying effect on Philip. He stopped his tirade and stood, arms slack against his sides, his head drooping.

'Go and put the kettle on, Sarah. I think we could all do with a cup of tea.'

Sarah gave Mary a mutinous look but the glance Mary returned, left no doubt that she had better do as she was told. Mary took Philip's arm and led him to a chair in the sitting room.

'I just can't cope with her.'

Mary listened and wondered whether Philip was referring to Sarah or his ex-wife. Sarah rushed into the room, clearly enjoying the drama and frightened that she might miss something. 'I've done that, Aunt Mary.' She went to sit down.

'Now, my dear, I want to talk to your father. I am sure you are sensible enough to make a pot of tea. If you look in the cake tin in the pantry, you can choose what cake we will have with it.' Sarah, always reluctant to do anything around the house, looked at her father. The hoped for support was not forthcoming, so with ill-grace, she left the room. Mary hoped fervently that the child would not take her temper out on the crockery.

Philip looked crushed. Mary wondered how to start. After all, I am hardly an example of how to conduct a happy marriage. Someone famous had once said that ' Marriage was an institution and who wanted to live in an institution!' Was it Mae West or Groucho Marx? She could not remember, but institutions were for the insane. Does it drive us all mad in the end? She sat up decisively, from the kitchen came the sound of drawers being banged and crockery clattered. Doubtless, the child would return as soon as possible. Whatever I can say, may or may not help but I had better get on with it.

'Why do you think Sophia had Sarah's hair cut?'

'God alone knows, I just do not understand the woman. She always was a bitch this just proves it.'

Mary decided there was no point in asking why, knowing she was a bitch, he had married her in the first place.

'Who is going to be most upset by what she did?'

'Sarah, of course, what does the poor child look like?'

'No! Philip, you! She set out to get at you and she has succeeded, beyond her wildest dreams. Have no doubt, Sarah will tell her mother how upset you were.' Philip opened his mouth and closed it again.

'Has the haircut done any damage - permanent that is?' Philip shook his head.

'Will it grow again?' Philip nodded.

'I suspect Sarah quite probably wanted her hair shorter, particularly in this hot weather. But she could never have asked you, could she? You would never have agreed. All Sophia has done is to go much further than Sarah wanted. The best thing you can do, is play it down.

Next time you wash her hair, say how much easier it is to wash and dry. Don't give Sophia the satisfaction of knowing she can still hurt you. Aah! here comes tea. Well done, Sarah.'

Sarah pushed the trolley in and glancing from her father to Mary, realised that the atmosphere had calmed down and she had missed out.

Charles and Jenny sat on the top deck of the bus, in the front seat, Jenny's favourite. She breathed in the smell of Charles' pipe smoke. She could not get enough of the wonderful scent. It reminded her of the good times they had. She leaned against his shoulder and gazed out of the window, at the shops. It was on the tip of her tongue to tell Dad about Grandma hating pilchards but somehow, something stopped her. Such moments as these were too precious to risk spoiling.

'I wish I could stay at Gran's flat sometimes.'

'It's rather difficult while Grandma is so ill.'

'Is she going to get better?'

Charles paused for a moment. 'Not really well, no. I don't think she will. I just hope she will get a bit stronger so she can go out of the house a bit.'

'But who would take her out? You will be going away again soon.'

Charles glanced at Jenny, was that a criticism or just a statement of fact? He was not sure. One thing was certain, he was not having a child, not yet 10, telling him how to live his life. She had no idea what her mother had put him through.

'I think you can be sure, I will do what is best for your grandma as well as for you.' Jenny did not reply.

By the time they got back to the Kensington flat, Philip and Sarah had left Mary and gone to their own sitting room - in a much calmer state than when they arrived. As soon as Sarah heard the front door open, she realised it must be Jenny and her father. She came out of her sitting room and walked slowly to the bathroom. Jenny glanced at her, felt shock at the change in her appearance but decided to make no comment. Sarah looked strangely disappointed.

Charles sat, straight backed and attentive. Mary thought he looked as though he ought to be on the parade ground. She told him of the recent happenings, concerning Jenny. He raised his eyebrows but said nothing. Mary always made him feel at a disadvantage. It was like being interviewed by a prospective employer. It irritated him intensely that she could have this effect on him. After all it was her daughter who had behaved badly, not he.

Jenny came into the sitting room, washed and ready for bed.

'Have you had a nice day, dear?'

'Lovely, we went to this Museum and it was really good. You could turn handles and press buttons and things. Then we had tea with Grandma. She still isn't very well, is she Dad?' Charles nodded.

'Would it help if I took Jenny to see your Mother occasionally, while you are away?' Mary amazed herself as the words came, unbidden, to her lips. *I am definitely getting sentimental in my old age.*

Charles smiled and in that moment, Mary could see why Rachel had fallen for him. Although his looks were quite different from Malcolm's, both men had that same quality of magnetic charm.

'That would be very kind, you were quite concerned about Grandma, weren't you?' He put his arm around Jenny and pulled her to him.

'It's time you went to bed, young lady. School tomorrow.'

'When will I see you again?'

'I'll 'phone tomorrow night and tell you what I have planned.' He kissed her and tapped her bottom. 'Off you go, give your Grandmother a kiss. '

Mary smiled as she watched Charles re-establishing his parental role with the child.

Charles walked briskly down the road. He would 'phone Jeanette, it was ludicrous to let things drag on. He needed to see the woman, face to face, to find out exactly what the problem was. He would suggest a quiet drink at a local pub.

'Hello, may I speak to Jeanette, please?'

'Who's calling?'

'Charles Warr.' There was a pause for several minutes.

'Hello Charles, how are you?' She sounded warm and friendly. Perhaps he had been imagining things.

'I got home yesterday. I took Jenny out today and would like to take my other girl out tonight.'

'Oh! I'm in no state to go anywhere decent at such short notice.'

'What about the local pub in half an hour?'

'Where are you?'

'Kensington tube station. It won't take long to get to Earls Court. Where exactly is your house?'

'The easiest thing would be if we meet you at the station.'

Charles cursed silently, presumably the 'we' was Jeanette and the male who answered the 'phone. Tom, wasn't it, the son of some family friend.

'Fine,' Charles said, 'see you in half an hour.' He sat on the tube train, drumming his fingers on the arm rest. He wanted to see Jeanette on her own, not with some stranger tagging along. Still, let's re-establish contact and take it from there.

Jeanette and Tom stood at the top of the escalator steps. Charles was strangely consoled by his first sight of Tom. Insignificant was the only appropriate word. He wore spectacles, had a hearing aid and it looked as though he was going to lose his hair. Charles stepped smartly forward and strode towards them. He gave an extravagant bow, clasped Jeanette's hand and kissed it, clicking his heels as he did so. He smiled broadly at her. Then, turning, he bowed very slightly, took Tom's hand and shook it vigorously as he introduced himself. Jeanette's face was flushed with both confusion and delight. Whatever Charles did, it was always with a flourish.

'Now then, my dears, let me buy you a drink.' He shepherded them out of the station.

Once settled in the lounge of 'The Red Lion', Charles insisted on buying the first round. He ordered dry sherry for Jeanette, a pint for Tom, despite his protests that a half would be fine, and a pint for himself. Tom felt uncomfortable in the company of this larger than life military man; insignificant, incompetent and uninteresting. He could not swop stories of daring-do because he had none. He had been turned down for National Service because of his defective sight and hearing. He explained, apologetically, to Charles that his mother had had German Measles when she was expecting him. Charles listened but soon swung into another tale of the Middle East and the trials and tribulations of desert warfare against Rommel.

Tom had only drunk half his pint, when he realised that Charles' glass was empty. He excused himself and went to the bar, ordering one more pint and a sherry. Charles raised his eyebrows in surprise.

'Come now, my friend, where's yours?'

'I'm not really much of a drinker and actually, I do have a report I need to finish for next week. So if you don't mind, I'll be off as soon as I have finished this.'

He drank the remainder of his pint with determination rather than enjoyment, then left with a wave.

'Might see you for a coffee later. Good to meet you.'

Charles watched him go, no threat there. What a foolish thing to think, why should I be thinking about threats, threats to what? Do I really mean to marry the girl? He was not sure, being single had its advantages. You could flirt with as many as you liked but still go home alone. On the other hand, being single suggested that no-one wanted you - that was not the impression he wanted to give. He turned to

179

Jeanette who was sitting quietly, watching him. He smiled and took her hand.

'I've missed you.'

Jeanette smiled back, 'My dear Chas, with all those eager A.T.S. girls, I am sure you have not had time to give me a second thought.'

He gazed at her intently. 'I think you know that isn't true. I realise that I am not the ideal match; there's Jenny to think of. But, I want our relationship to continue and grow. I want it to be permanent.'

'Are you asking me to marry you?'

The answer to that was basically yes but the words seemed to stick in his throat.

'I know how Catholics feel about divorce. I realise how important your religion is to you so let's take one step at a time and see if there is a way round my previous marriage. Only then would I have the right to ask you to be my wife.'

Jeanette squeezed his hand. She thought of how she and her sister, as girls, had fantasised about the handsome young men who would propose on bended knee. This was not quite what she had dreamed of then, but sincerely said.

Maybe this was why Charles had been so reluctant to commit himself. Maybe he did not think he had the right. Perhaps the rather bluff exterior was a safety shield to protect his feelings.

'Come on,' she said, 'lets go for a stroll, then you can come back for a coffee.' The night was warm and still light, as they strolled arm in arm down the busy streets. There were many young people milling about, lots with Australian accents. Earls Court had become a warren of bed-sitters. The whole area had a lively atmosphere that lasted way into the night.

Charles felt very pleased, he was not going to rush into anything but the future looked less bleak. Jeanette was rather young but no matter, she would look up to him. Having been brought up in a military household, she was bound to share so many of his ideas about life. He gave her a hug.

'Now then, my dear, I had better not be too late. I don't want my mother to worry.'

He walked her home and after a quick coffee, with no sign of Tom, kissed her passionately and left to catch the last tube home.

Mary walked briskly down the road. She had made a lengthy shopping list for the luncheon party. She felt happy that all her children were coming to see her as well as her grandchildren. In deference to the children, she had decided on a traditional roast. She would make some of the potato soup that Jenny liked so much and apple crumble for pudding. Nursery food, as Nanny had always called it. No great subtlety of flavour but wholesome and nourishing.

She could rely on her local butcher to select a good piece of beef. The greengrocer was also obliging and normally delivered on request. Today, Mary felt light of heart, the weather was fine and there was something very satisfying about walking home with bags full of food for your family.

'Thank you, Jack, I'll take everything with me' She picked up her bags. Not too heavy, she walked out of the shop, humming under her breath. Jenny will be back from school soon, I had better hurry. She looked to the right, to see if the main road was clear. Both road and pavement were busy; there was no break in the traffic.

She did not see the young man, with the duffel bag, running up the road. He had seen his bus on the other side and was desperately trying to get far enough ahead to reach the next stop before the bus did. Mary and the young man were on a collision course. When Mary looked in his direction, she had enough time to see him but not enough to get out of the way. In that split second, he was upon her. His shoulder and the duffel bag crashed into her and knocked her off balance. With a shopping bag in each hand, she could not put out a hand to soften her fall. She hit the pavement awkwardly and heard a sickening crack. At first she felt nothing.

'Sorry, luv. Are you all right?' The young man bent down momentarily and was gone. The fall had winded her and all she could do was gasp. When she did not get up, people began to gather round. Willing hands tried to lift her. Then the pain started, searing down her leg which hung, useless. She screamed. The willing hands withdrew a little. An ambulance had been sent for.

'Don't move me, it's my leg. Oh! the pain.' She moaned and gritted her teeth. She disentangled her hands from the shopping bags. She lay on the hard pavement surrounded by the ingredients of a meal she would never cook.

Chapter 11

Stephen slammed out of the room and could be heard thumping his way up the hall. The noise reached a climax as he banged his bedroom door behind him. Alec sighed and looked at Rachel. She seemed singularly unperturbed by the outburst. But, then, she had finally got what she wanted. Jenny was going to live with them. The only dissenting voice was from Stephen. Alec wondered if instead of Rachel's constantly nagging voice asking why Jenny did not live with them, it would now be Stephen's asking why she did!

Alec knew that Rachel was depressed and had been for several weeks. It was not a subject they talked about and Alec hoped that the unexpected good news about Jenny might lift the black cloud. In any event, Alec hoped that Jenny would be an ally, helping him with Stephen when Rachel became immobilised by despair. He knew he should have talked realistically about Rachel's mental state, when decisions were made about Jenny's future. How could he? If anything would have been guaranteed to send Rachel completely haywire, it would have been his objecting to Jenny living with them. No matter how reasonable and rational his argument, Rachel would have taken it as an act of total betrayal and treachery. Alec had kept his mouth shut while Eleanor and Malcolm had made suggestions, not just for Jenny but also for Mary - presently in hospital with a broken hip.

Charles had also arrived and been reluctant to allow Rachel to have the child. He even suggested that Malcolm and Joanne should have her but Joanne was not enthusiastic. Alec supposed that Charles had finally run out of people with whom to place the child. He was determined to let everyone know that he was far from happy for Jenny to be with her irresponsible mother and wife stealing step-father! Alec smiled to himself, Charles had not once - during the family conference - spoken to him directly, referring to him only by surname. The pompous bugger cannot deny my existence so will only refer to me in a derogatory way. Mind you, it must make him want to choke me, knowing that the man who 'stole' his wife has now got his daughter living with him. He wants to come out of the army and take a more active part in the poor kid's life.

Jenny would be arriving later that day. Alec wanted to talk to Stephen, in an attempt to calm the boy down. Rachel was sitting quietly, too quietly. No matter how exhausting she was, it was better than this unnatural stillness.

'Go and have a lie down, love. You're looking tired.' He pulled her to her feet. It was difficult to get close to her. Her abdomen was huge with child and felt taut like a drum. She put her hand to the small of her back and stretched, arching backwards to ease the pressure.

'Not long now.' No, thought Alec, more problems. Another reason for welcoming Jenny. She could take Stephen to school. She would almost certainly help with the baby. After all, little girls liked babies, didn't they? Alec took Rachel's hand. 'Come on, you're having a rest.' He took her to the bedroom, got her settled and went to Stephen's bedroom. He was sitting on the floor, with his wooden bricks. Once piled up, he knocked them down. He did not speak or look up when Alec came in. He sat on the bed and waited. Stephen ignored him, carrying on with his construction/demolition work. After a while, Alec realised that he would have to make the first move.

'I know you are not very happy about Jenny coming here but what else can we do?' No reply.

'You know that your Mummy is Jenny's Mummy too.'

'No she isn't and you're not her Daddy so why has she got to come here?'

Alec gazed out of the window, the view over London was magnificent. On a clear day, you could see Big Ben. There seemed little point in arguing with a six year old or in trying to explain the complications of a shared mother and different father. A great weariness overtook Alec and he thought about the days he had spent with Gwen, a lifetime ago. Like it or not, Stephen would just have to get used to the idea of an older sister and, in a few weeks, a younger sister or brother too. I can see I will be in for a stormy time one way or another.

Eleanor went to the hospital with Malcolm and Joanne. Mary had shattered her hip, the femur had snapped, right at the top. She was in considerable pain and was distressed by the doctor's prognosis. She was in traction which was painful and left her almost totally immobilised. Mary hated the way doctors talked at you or over your head as though you were incapable of understanding the workings of your own body. She suspected, from what she had heard, that she would have to have a hip replacement. This was a comparatively new procedure and Mary felt uneasy about the whole thing. Although anything would be better than being stuck here, surrounded by the inane and the ga-ga.

She raised herself, painfully on her elbows, as soon as she saw Malcolm enter the ward. She managed a wave before she sank back on the pillows. She watched as the three young and handsome people walked towards her, two of them her own flesh and blood. She smiled and signalled Malcolm to sit beside her.

'How are you doing, Mother?'

'I feel like a trussed chicken and I can't get much sense out of the doctors.'

'I'll go and see what Sister has to say now.' With that Eleanor walked briskly up the ward. Joanne handed Mary some grapes murmuring words of comfort. Mary wondered why it was that, once in hospital, the real world seemed to disappear. It has made me totally egocentric, she thought. If I do not talk about myself and my hip, what else is there? I certainly do not want to indulge in idle chatter about my wardmates' medical condition. She asked Malcolm and Joanne about Jenny. She felt a sharp pang of regret on learning that Jenny was to go to her mother. It was a surprising but great sadness that any chance of Jenny coming back to live with her was minimal.

Eleanor strode purposefully back to her mother's bedside.

'Sister has shown me the X-rays. It seems unlikely that this fracture will heal unaided. Your bones are very thin and there is little to knit together. Although in time, the body can replace bone, it isn't a good idea for someone of your age to be confined to bed for too long.' Her pronouncement was met by silence. Joanne and Malcolm glanced at each other. Joanne felt uneasy. Was she going to be pushed into a situation she had not bargained for? Mary sighed and closed her eyes. Her hip was aching intolerably but she was loath to take too many painkillers.

'What about a hip replacement?'

'That seems to be the best option, but as I said, Mother, there is not much bone to attach it to.' The prospect of permanent disability opened before Mary like a black chasm. She was overwhelmed with feelings of bitterness. After all I have coped with, now this. She fought a great desire to weep and make a scene to say, 'it's not fair' but what would that achieve?

The rest of the visiting time was spent talking about Malcolm and Joanne's new home. It was a large detached house in Hendon, overlooking a park. Malcolm had borrowed the deposit from Mary. Joanne had been aghast to discover that Mary was charging interest on the loan. When she remonstrated with Malcolm, he shrugged his shoulders and changed the subject. Joanne could not comprehend how an obviously adoring mother could do that. She also felt stirrings of contempt for Malcolm's apparently spineless acceptance of what she regarded as Mary's dominance over her adult son. Joanne was a typical American, used to living in a matriarchal society, so she had no objection to female power per se, but to her way of thinking, in a marriage, it was the wife not the mother-in-law who called the shots.

Everything had been fine in the States, an English husband was cute - quite a catch - with his old world charm. She realised she did not fit into his world as well as he had appeared to fit into hers.

Perhaps things would be better once they had settled into the new house. If only she could get pregnant. She was feeling increasingly uneasy about the whole thing. O.K. so they had not been married for long but they had lived together for several years prior to marriage and she had never taken precautions - not once she had decided that Malcolm was her man. Time was not on her side. She watched Mary, deep in conversation with Malcolm and Eleanor. Why does that woman always make me feel like an outsider?

Jenny walked up the four flights of stairs and wrinkled her nose. There was a sharp, unpleasant smell, cat's pee most probably. The taxi driver was climbing the stairs behind her, muttering under his breath. Dad's leave had finished and he had left her with a feeling of guilt, that she could not explain. It was not her fault that she had to go to live with Mum and Alec, it was not her fault Grandmother had broken her hip. She felt nervous now; she had seen so little of Rachel over the last five years and even less of Alec and Stephen. She paused on the stairs aware, with a shock, of how much she wanted them to like her. I'm tired of moving around; tired of moving that horrid green tin-trunk from house to house. I'm like a snail except my shell isn't actually attached to my body. She was jolted out of her speculations by the taxi driver who had caught her up.

'Come on girl, for Gawd's sake, this thing weighs a bleeding ton!'

Jenny ran up the stairs, anxious now to get the dreaded moment over. She took a deep breath and banged on the front door of 25, Gainsborough Gardens. Her new home, would this one be for good? She heard footsteps coming along, what sounded like, an uncarpeted hall. The door was flung open and there stood her mother. With a cry Rachel clutched the child to her and sobbed and laughed and talked in such an outpouring of emotion that Jenny felt totally bemused and then embarrassed. She tried to pull away but this only seemed to make matters worse. Out of the corner of her eye, she could see Alec and Stephen watching the whole performance. The light in the hallway was not on so it was difficult to see how they were reacting. It was the taxi driver who came to her rescue. After a few moments, he cleared his throat noisily.

'That will be 15 shillings and ninepence, please Guv.'

Alec gave the man a pound note and told him to keep the change. The driver immediately offered to manoeuvre the trunk into the flat.

Rachel led Jenny into the kitchen, clutching on to the child, saying over and over how wonderful it was to have her here at last. Jenny had not known what sort of reception to expect but certainly not this. Stephen sat in the corner, glowering, not saying a word. Alec put the kettle on.

'I'm making us a cup of tea. Do you like tea, Jenny?' He smiled encouragingly. Jenny looked at him, unsure of how to respond. Dad had told her so much about this dreadful man, Davies, who was not to be trusted. He had taken her Mum away and most of Dad's furniture. If she was nice to this man, who had made her Dad so unhappy, what would Dad think of her? He would think she did not care, that she was disloyal. Alec waited. Jenny gave a tight little smile that moved no further than her lips. She nodded her head.

'Tea for three then, is it? What about you, Stephen?'

'I want tea too.' He looked defiantly at Rachel who usually insisted that he have juice or milk.

'Just this once, as it's a special day and your big sister is here at last.'

Stephen made no comment.

The kitchen was small and crowded, with a big table as well as the usual sink and cooker. There was a large dresser and next to it, in the corner, a comfortable and much used arm chair. In the fire-place, a black leaded stove threw out heat. Next to the stove, in the recess made for it, lay a cushion upon which was a black cat. Jenny leaned down and stroked the cat gently with one finger. She loved cats. The animal opened one amber eye, raised its head and yawned mightily, showing needle like teeth and a bright pink tongue. It stretched, extending the claws in its front paws so they dug into the fabric of the cushion. Giving a dismissive glance to the stranger who had interrupted his slumbers, he curled up and was immediately asleep. Jenny smiled and looked up at the others.

'He's my cat.' Stephen said.

Mary lay, listening intently to what the consultant surgeon was saying. At least they are talking to me and not just to each other, about me. She would be having the operation and if successful, she would have little or no disability. He made it sound very straight forward and for the first time since the accident, Mary felt that maybe things would not be so bad. She mentioned that she lived in a flat. The doctor thought that highly suitable until she explained that it was several floors up and the lift was temperamental.

'Ummm, well, Mrs. Cardew, we will just have to see. I assure you I will do my best, it just depends on how your femur behaves.' He smiled automatically and moved on to the next case. The moment of relief, from doubts about the future, disappeared as quickly as it had come. Mary picked up the book she had been reading but the words blurred into a tangle of meaningless squiggles. She lay back on her pillows and closed her eyes. She took a few deep breaths. I must not panic, think sensibly. I can sell the flat and buy something more suitable. Perhaps I could find a property nearer to Malcolm and Joanne. Then I would be able to employ a housekeeper who could live upstairs. If she were married, her husband could do any odd jobs. I would have live in help and it would be cheap if I offered accommodation free or at a nominal rent. It would be like having servants again.

'Having a little snooze are we, Mrs. Cardew?' Nurse Jones took Mary's wrist and checked her pulse. Mary opened her eyes and decided that she was really making a mountain out of a mole hill. It's being in this damned place, I'm losing touch with reality.

Jenny had settled into her latest school with few problems. It had happened too often for her to be upset. She enjoyed learning new things and next year she would sit her eleven plus. Already the cloud, this event generated, was present on the horizon. She knew Dad would expect her to pass and had, on several occasions, talked at length about the need for a good education. She was determined she would do well. Dad wanted her to go into the army. Why, she could not imagine. She thought only boys became soldiers and anyway the idea did not appeal. There was no point in saying anything, in any case that was years away.

She and Stephen had struck an uneasy truce. Reluctantly, he had to accept that she walked to school with him and that he had to stay with her. He refused to hold her hand. At home, there were frequent arguments between them which Rachel, in her final stages of pregnancy, allowed to rage around her. Although Stephen was half Jenny's age and physically smaller, he was a tough little boy. In any actual set to, they were evenly matched. While Jenny had been initially disadvantaged because she had not been in the habit of fighting she soon developed her own strategies. It had come as a considerable shock to be punched and kicked by her little brother. Self defence was going to be essential for survival. So if Jenny had bruises to show her mother, before long Stephen had a selection of scratches on face and arms as well as a sore head from vigorous hair pulling. Despite every entreaty by an increasingly exasperated Rachel and placatory Alec, the fights went on.

It was during one particularly fierce battle that the children heard their mother give a mighty scream. They both rushed to see what was the matter.

'Quick, Jenny 'phone for an ambulance. I think the baby is coming.' Stephen stood open mouthed. Jenny ran to the 'phone and, with trembling fingers, dialled 999.

Malcolm sat opposite Joanne, in the dining room of their new home. There were still many packing cases to sort out and the whole house needed redecorating. He picked at his food, uncertain of how to tell Joanne about the test results. She had harped on and on about having a family since they got married. It had surprised him since there had been no indication of maternal instinct earlier in their relationship. He could not hazard a guess as to how she would react to the news that, as a result of the V.D. contracted and treated before he even met her, he would never father a child.

Joanne looked at him speculatively, she had known from the moment he came in, something was wrong. Give him time, he'll tell me. Just carry on as though everything is fine.

'Have you any work this evening or shall we sort out some of these boxes?'

Malcolm put his fork down, leaned across to put his hand on hers. He seemed to have difficulty meeting her gaze. He cleared his throat but when he spoke, his voice was little more than a whisper.

'I have something very important to tell you which I fear will make you very angry with me.'

Joanne decided it must be something to do with Mary. He knew she found Mary tiresome. He wants her to come and live with us, that will be it. He can darn well think again. That woman may be able to make me feel an outsider in her home. She isn't going to do it to me, in mine.

Malcolm watched as emotions flickered across her face. She was a stunningly attractive woman but also a strong willed one. Will I be able to keep her, if I cannot give her the family she wants? A chill hand seemed to clutch at Malcolm's heart. A future without Joanne was unthinkable. He rushed into what he knew he had to say. Joanne sat, silent and stony faced as the sordid saga of a sailor's sex life was laid before her. Not just any old sailor, her husband. His seed was destroyed for ever as a result of a reckless lack of self-control and prudent self protection. Now it would be she who was the victim, deprived of her babies. O.K. she knew some women could not have children. That was sad but she would not have children through no fault of her own.

'Why didn't you tell me this before? You must have known there could be problems? If you had treatment for V.D.' She spat the words out as though their very utterance contaminated her mouth. She pulled her hand away from his, stood up so abruptly that her chair fell over. She strode to the door.

'I'm going out.'

It was a beautiful evening. She crossed the road to the park and with her hands thrust deeply into her slacks pockets, started to walk, she knew not where. Children and dogs were playing all around her. Everywhere she looked, there were families. Mums and Dads, pushing prams, toddlers staggering on splayed and unsteady legs. Fathers were running behind novice cyclists and over it all presided pregnant women walking arm in arm with protective, proud fathers –to -be, revelling in their role as the providers of the next generation. And here I am, Joanne thought, she sat down on an empty bench, a foreigner in this land of afternoon tea and polite conversation. I have an interfering mother in law, a spineless husband and an empty womb.

She had not realised how home sick she was until now. I want to be back with my folks. Her vision blurred and she was alarmed by her feeling of weakness. What am I going to do? It was difficult to concentrate with so much activity around her. She got to her feet and started to walk away from the play area. It would be quieter in the formal gardens, to her left. It would give her a chance to think. Do I want to stay married to Malcolm? We have had such good times together but seeing him in his own environment had shown her a previously unknown side of his personality. Do I want children more than I want Malcolm? She did not know for sure but she could not afford to let the question go unanswered for too long. What is the worst part of the whole situation? She stopped dead in her tracks, rage and hurt welled up inside her. He deceived me. That's what I cannot stand, that's what hurts. He deceived me, will I ever be able to trust him again?

Mary felt dreadfully sick. She slowly opened her eyes and saw the rest of the ward going about its business. She wasn't in pain but everything seemed to be moving slightly, as if she were being rocked in a cradle. She closed her eyes again, the sick feeling was still there.

'Are you awake, dear?' Mrs. Johnson, in the next bed, asked. Mary nodded, neither willing nor able to speak.

'Nurse, nurse, I think Mrs. Cardew is awake now.' Mary knew that Mrs. Johnson was only being kind but her voice seemed to reverberate in Mary's ears, setting off the waves of nausea again. She felt a cool hand grasp her wrist and gingerly opened her eyes. Sister was taking her pulse.

'Well, my dear, that's the worst bit over. It won't be long before we have you on your feet.' Mary managed a slight smile and then felt herself float and drift gently into a deep, dreamless sleep. Sister turned to Mrs. Johnson.

'She's asleep, I'll draw the curtains so she can have a bit of peace. Thanks for keeping an eye on her. Let me know if she wants anything.'

'Certainly, Sister, it's a pleasure.' Sister walked back to her office, smiling. God bless the Mrs. Johnson's of this world, where would we be without them?

She sat down and wrote up Mary's notes. The operation had gone according to plan. Now it would depend on how well her femur would cope with the strain of walking.

Jenny was frightened. Her mother was gasping and crying in between ear-piercing screams. Stephen had clamped his hands over his ears and run into his bedroom. The ambulance was taking ages. Jenny did not know what to do.

'Can I get you anything, Mum? Should I 'phone Alec? Perhaps it would be better if you were lying down.'

Rachel grabbed Jenny's hand. Sweat stood in fat beads on her forehead and along her upper lip.

'Yes, ' she gasped, 'phone Alec.'

Jenny ran to the 'phone, 'What's his number?'

'It's in the book.'

Suddenly, there was a loud knock at the door. Thank God, the ambulance men. They were big and burly in their serge uniforms. Jenny was so relieved, she wanted to cry. They quickly got Rachel into a chair stretcher, wrapped a blanket around her and started to carry her downstairs.

'I'll 'phone Alec, now.' Jenny called down the stairs.

He was out visiting clients, could not be contacted so Jenny left a message. She was not sure what to do now. He should be home soon. Perhaps she had better get some tea ready. She went to the larder and decided on spaghetti on toast. Stephen liked that, so did she. She felt very grown up making toast and stirring the spaghetti. She was not sure what they could have afterwards, there wasn't much in the larder. Mum had done little shopping recently. We can decide what to have later. She called Stephen and when he didn't answer, went to his bedroom. At first, she could not see him. Then she realised he was hunched up, in bed, under the covers, asleep. She shook his shoulder, 'Tea's ready.'

'Where's Mum?'

'She's gone to hospital, to have the baby.'

'Who's cooked tea?'

'I have.'

'Don't want any.'

'It's spaghetti, you like that.' He looked at her, wondering whether to give in or not. He did like spaghetti and he was hungry.

He got out of bed and walked, in socked feet, to the kitchen. It was the first meal the children ate on their own. They found some biscuits and shared an apple, it was only the question of washing up that spoilt the peace of the occasion. Jenny insisted that Stephen did the washing, which she disliked, while she did the drying. Responsibility was a heady experience and one she liked.

Stephen wanted to go out to play, after tea. Jenny thought they should both stay in until Alec came home. As Jenny bolted the front door, to stop Stephen from running out, there was little he could do but protest. The bolt was too high for him to reach. He went back to the bedroom. Jenny sat and watched Children's Hour on the television, waiting for the 'phone to ring. When it did, Stephen got there first. Jenny snatched the receiver and pushed him away.

'I'm in charge.'

He kicked her and ran back to his bedroom, banging the door.

'What on earth is going on?' Alec asked,.

'It's only Stephen being naughty, as usual.'

'I'm at the hospital. Your Mum has had the baby, it was very quick. You have a little sister.'

Jenny rubbed her shin.

'I'm glad, what does she look like?'

'I'll tell you all about her when I get home, I'll stay with your Mum a bit longer. Can you manage?'

'I think so, shall I try to get Stephen to bed?'

'No, better not. I'll do it when I get home.'

'See you later, Alec. Give Mum my love,' she paused, 'and Stephen's.'

191

At the other end of the 'phone, Alec smiled. The rivalry between those two was so tangible, you could cut it with a knife.

'Thanks for looking after things, Jenny. You're a good girl.'

Jenny beamed at herself in the mirror, by the 'phone.

'Bye, Alec.' She put the 'phone down. I'm a good girl, he said so.

Joanne walked slowly back through the park. The heat had long since gone out of the sun. All the smaller children had gone home, tired and ready for a warm bath, they would dream of more golden days in a childhood that would last for ever. Older boys were playing a noisy and enthusiastic game of football, occasionally hampered by the interference of stray dogs wishing to join in the fun. She did not know what she would say to Malcolm or, more importantly, what she would do. She had no job and no money of her own. She could cable her parents for advice and/or money but was reluctant to lose face. Although her parents had liked Malcolm, they had been concerned that to leave the U.S. of A. was too big a step. It had been Joanne who had insisted that she knew what she was doing. No, I got into this, I'll get myself out of it. I will tell the folks later.

Malcolm stood at the living room window. He had been watching Joanne for the last fifteen minutes as she slowly made her way back to this, their home. He knew, without a doubt, that he was in a most difficult and delicate situation. His whole future hung on a thread. The days of wine and rose were over. This was the grown up world, this was real and it hurt.

Joanne had not taken a key, she went around to the kitchen door. She noted that everything had been cleared away. Somehow that irritated her. Was Malcolm trying to be the good little boy, making amends for being naughty? Think positively, don't nit-pick, keep an open mind, she told herself. Malcolm walked towards her, his normally healthy, olive complexion had a yellow tinge and she could see fear in his eyes. Knowledge that he feared what she might say or do made her, for a split second, want to be cruel. In that blink of an eye, she wanted to hurt him, badly. Then she would tell him he was right to be afraid. Almost immediately she pushed the thought away. I loved you enough to leave my family, friends and my country. We must find a way out of this.

'Jo, I'm so sorry, I can't tell you how sorry I am. I never wanted it to be like this.' He held his arms out and, without hesitation, she walked towards him.

Alec stood, looking down, at the tiny bundle in the crib. The fragile looking head was thickly covered with damp black hair. The features were infinitely delicate. This baby was like a fine porcelain doll. Unmoving and silent, her grasp on life seemed uncertain. Alec gently stroked the black hair and felt the pulsating of the fontanelle. This was proof indeed of life. He tried to find some common characteristic between this new baby and Stephen, as he remembered him. Of course, he had not seen Stephen, when only hours old, he did not know how much babies changed in the first week. There was no similarity that he could see. Alec wondered if this had been how Charles had felt? Had it started with a slight feeling of unease that grew and, at last, could not be denied? Alec remembered Rachel's sudden and totally unexpected return from Paris. It was August now. The baby was small. He stopped. This will not do. Rachel's sanity is often in doubt, it needs one of us to be sensible. He decided, in that moment, that he could not and would not question the child's parentage. He would never know for sure but one thing he did know was that the baby needed a father. She also needed a name.

'What about adoption?' Malcolm asked. They were sitting on the settee, watching the sun go down over the trees. The football was over and only one or two solitary dog owners could be seen walking purposefully along the gravel paths. The rosy glow of the, fast disappearing, sun had bled into the still bright blue of the sky. There was just a hint of the moon, waiting to take over, when the sun finally disappeared. Joanne paused. She had never seriously considered adoption. She had never thought she would need to. One or two of her acquaintances, back home, had because they could not have children. She would have to pick her words very carefully. In her heart, she knew what she wanted. She wanted to know that she, personally, was creating a new life. She wanted to feel that unborn child kick and stretch inside her. She wanted to see her body swollen like a ripe fruit, announcing to the world, her fertility. She wanted to feel the urgency of pushing that new life into the world, of being able to say, I am truly a woman. I have risked death, to give life. Malcolm seemed to have been holding his breath for hours. He could hear the tick of the clock, a wedding present from Mary.

'Yes,' Joanne said quietly, 'we could consider adoption.'

'I'll make enquiries tomorrow.' Malcolm's voice was shaky and the sound of blood coursing around his body seemed to roar in his ears. He felt he might choke.

'Let's have a drink.' He got to his feet carefully, walked to the sideboard and poured two whiskies. Joanne smiled as she took her glass, not sure exactly what they were celebrating.

The 'phone rang, Malcolm answered it. Joanne only half listened, her mind was grappling with the idea of accepting a child of unknown parentage, to make their own. Was that truly possible? Any such child must come from a less than normal background, why else would it be offered for adoption? Maybe it would be the result of rape with who knew what potential for violence. Didn't Buddhists believe that personality was decided at the moment of conception. In which case, did parents - natural - or otherwise have any influence at all? It was all so confusing. She heard Malcolm replace the receiver, she looked up as he walked into the room. His expression seemed guarded.

'Who was it?'

'Alec, Rachel has had the baby. It's a girl.'

'How nice.' She could hear the mechanical and wholly artificial note in those two words which now seemed to echo in her head; how nice, how nice. She put her hands over her ears, in a vain attempt to shut out the mocking voice. Silently, Malcolm put his arm around her shoulders. He felt her muscles stiffen beneath his touch, shutting him out, excluding him from her sorrow.

Alec pushed the key into the lock and tried to open the door. It was bolted. He knocked. He heard the living room door being flung open. He could hear Stephen's voice. He really should have been in bed. With a sinking heart, Alec wondered where the boy got all his energy. Jenny unbolted the door and opened it.

'Hello, Dad,' Stephen launched himself at Alec, 'we've had tea and Jenny made me wash up.'

'Quite right too.' Alec smiled at Jenny, standing in the doorway. As he stood with Stephen, clinging to him like an octopus, Alec reflected that he had never actually touched Jenny. There was a separateness about the child, was it her natural inclination or was it because he was her step father? Heaven only knew what horror stories Charles would have told her about him.

'Thanks for looking after things, shall we have a cup of tea? Then you two must get to bed, school tomorrow.'

'What's the baby like?' Jenny asked as she filled the kettle, 'What's her name?'

'When's Mum coming home?' Stephen asked.

'I'm not sure, but soon.'

Later the two children lay in bed, reflecting on the events of the day. For Jenny there had been the satisfaction of having some control over events. She had decided what to do about tea and kept Stephen in. She would never again put up with being bossed about,all the time. She

194

was needed here, she wasn't a nuisance. She was a good girl, Alec had said so. She would be able to help Mum with the baby. She hoped she would like Ruth more than she liked Stephen. She had to admit that she didn't like him. He was noisy and rough and always wanted his own way. He always wanted to push her out of things. Well, she wasn't going to put up with that any more.

Stephen lay hunched up in bed. He felt miserable. It was bad enough having to put up with Jenny, now there was another one. He hugged his knees to his chest and smiled in the dark. Wait until tomorrow, when she would see what he had written on the wall, by her bed. I hate Jenny, over and over in big letters.

He had pressed so hard that he had broken two pencils but he didn't care. It had been worth it.

Mary sat in a chair by her bed. She was exhausted. The physiotherapist had made her walk halfway up the ward and back. The exercise had left her breathless and shaking. Her hip ached furiously but she felt pleased. Things could only get better. Malcolm and Joanne were coming to see her this evening. It would be nice to greet them from the chair instead of bed. She thought about her new grand daughter, Ruth, who she had not yet seen. She closed her eyes and said a silent prayer that all would be well with Rachel and her increasing family. I do wish I could think of her without this uneasy feeling in the pit of my stomach. It's like waiting for a volcano to erupt. Alec did seem to have a steadying influence, long may that continue.

Her mind moved to the question of her flat. Philip had brought Sarah to visit her and had seemed a little uncomfortable when she tried to discuss what would happen when she came out of hospital. The sharing of accommodation had only been partially successful and Mary could see that as Sarah reached adolescence, she was likely to be more rather than less precocious. Maybe now was a good time to reassess the situation. Perhaps Philip, too, was less than happy with the arrangement. She moved slightly in her chair, trying to ease the ache in her hip but determined to stay where she was.

She would discuss the matter with Malcolm, when he came. Much as she liked her flat, she could see it was a risk to have to rely on the lift. Without it, the strain of all those stairs could be dangerous. The idea of buying a house but only living on the ground floor, increasingly, seemed a good one. In warm weather, she would have a garden to sit in. She remembered, so many years age, her childhood, in the country. All her older brothers dead now, her baby half brother, so tragically killed in the First World War. So much pain, but physical pain could be controlled, emotional hurt had to be endured.

There was movement at the end of the ward, visitors were arriving. She had been day-dreaming for too long. Perhaps this is how old people fill their days, I shall do more than that. She watched and waited for Malcolm and Joanne, eager to tell them of her plan.

'Hello, Mother, how wonderful to see you up. How's the leg coping?' Malcolm bent to kiss her cheek while Joanne waited with the usual bunch of flowers and a polite smile.

'It's coping.' Mary smiled tenderly as she took her son's hand. 'I walked to the table and back. I feel quite proud of myself but it is amazing how quickly ones muscles weaken.' She patted the chair beside her, 'You sit here, my dear. Malcolm can perch on the bed. Now tell me how the house is coming on. It will be so good to see it for myself.'

Talking about the house was a suitably neutral subject but Joanne knew that Malcolm intended telling Mary about their decision to adopt. She also knew that Mary, like most women, was good at picking up undercurrents. She will be aware of my reservations. The longer we talk about the house the better. Joanne carefully described the rooms as they were and mentioned possible changes and colour schemes. Malcolm watched the two women, so different in background and attitude yet so unerringly the same. There was a common interest in home making. Malcolm let his mind drift as the question of curtains and pelmets was aired. He remembered how Mother had transformed her flat. He appreciated that if her recovery was only partial, she would have to move. It might help her then to fill her mind with practical matters.

Mary turned, to include him in the conversation.

'Don't you take an interest in your home?'

'Of course, but I leave the details to you women, you are so much better at it.'

'What are your neighbours like? If you have to live within shouting distance of other people, it is essential to have an understanding with them, don't you think?' She looked at Joanne, for agreement.

'I thought you English took a pride in keeping away from your neighbours.'

'Well, yes, but while you don't want them coming into your house, you don't want any antagonism either. After all neighbours are a bit like family, you can't choose them.'

'Umm, ' Joanne reflected, 'how true.'

196

'They seem pleasant enough,' volunteered Malcolm, ' young couple with er..is it two or three children?'

'That seems most suitable, particularly when you start your family..' Mary's voice trailed away as she noticed the look that passed between her visitors.

'What about the people on the other side?' There was a pause.

'It's empty at the moment but I believe there may be a buyer.' Joanne said firmly.

Malcolm cleared his throat, 'We have some news for you, Mother. It's about having a family.'

Mary glanced at them both and felt her heart leap.

'Are you pregnant, my dear, how wonderful.'

'No, mother, you know I had some problems in the past..'

Joanne looked at Malcolm. The English were not just good at being aloof to their neighbours; they were bloody good at understating the truth.

'...well Jo and I have decided to adopt.' There was a pause. Mary considered the fact that there would never now be a true son or daughter of Malcolm's. The only grandchildren she was likely to have were Rachel's with, who knew what, potential for mental problems. There seemed little likelihood that Eleanor would marry. So this was it. Adopt or nothing. She tried to read Joanne's expression but the younger woman would not meet her gaze. I sense trouble here. Mary knew Joanne had set her heart on a family. Would someone else's child fulfil that need? Only time would tell.

'How very sensible,' she said briskly, 'how long will it take to sort things out?'

'I don't know, Mother. I am making enquiries at the moment. We will keep you posted.'

The bell for the end of visiting hour clanged. Up and down the ward visitors hurriedly gathered their possessions and checked what they had to bring in next time. Affectionate goodbyes were said and within five minutes the ward was quiet; patients mulled over the news their relatives and friends had brought in. Mary had a great deal to think about. She had mixed feelings about adoption. You did not know the parentage of such children nor did you know the child's academic potential. Like many highly intelligent people, Mary was an intellectual snob; valuing intelligence above all else. She most definitely did not want Malcolm to be saddled with a dullard child.

The other piece of information that had given Mary considerable cause for thought was the empty house, next door to Malcolm's. If she made a full recovery, she would continue to lead a full and busy life and be no trouble to them. However, if things did not go so well, it would be easier for Malcolm to keep an eye on her if she were only next door. All in all, it seemed that fate was taking a hand and almost making the decision for her. Mary rang the bell, for a nurse.

'Will you help me into bed, please. I'm feeling tired now.'

The nurse linked one arm with Mary's and gently helped her to her feet. Without warning, Mary felt the most excruciating pain. She cried out and clung to the nurse, trying desperately not to put any weight on the injured leg. They stood clasped together as waves of agony swept through Mary. She gasped and closed her eyes. I'm going to faint. I cannot stand this pain.

'Sister, sister,' the nurse shouted.

The curtains were drawn round and, with infinite tenderness, Mary was eased into bed. She bit her lip so hard, she could taste the metallic saltiness of her own blood.

'I'll send for the doctor, my dear. It may be nothing worse than stiff muscles, after your exercise.' The Sister tried to look reassuring but the expression in her eyes, told Mary all she needed to know.

Chapter 12

Jeanette sat in the comfortable sitting room, she shared with Tom, reading the latest letter from Charles. He had applied to leave the army and hoped to return to England, permanently, in less than a year. This will give us time to sort out our relationship and the problem of Charles being a divorced man. Jeanette found it increasingly difficult to reconcile herself to that situation. She wanted to be married in church, in white, like her sister. She wanted the church's blessing. Also there was the problem of Jenny. They still had not met. No explanation had been given for Charles' reluctance. Was there something wrong with the girl? Charles rarely mentioned her or where she was. I wonder, if he feels a little guilty at not being more of a father to his only child? Jeanette was also well aware of the question of age. I'm scarcely old enough to be Jenny's mother She put the letter down and pondered the difficulties of life. She did not know what to do. When Charles was away, she missed him. However, life, in his absence, had a tranquillity that was soothing and comfortable. The minute she received a letter or he came home on leave, everything was turned upside down. Charles had a powerful magnetism, he somehow made life spark and crackle in a way that was both exhilaration and frightening. There was definitely a quality of danger about the man; she knew she would not like to cross him.

Jeanette had known Charles for four years. It had been her most serious relationship and the longest. Is it normal to feel a bit frightened of the one you love? Just because I have been his girlfriend for so long, is it no more than a habit?

If he is willing to leave the army which he loves so much, he must be serious. She thought about his last leave. Boating on the Serpentine, drives to Box Hill, tea in little tearooms. He did make a fuss of her but always, unseen and unheard lurked the spectre of Rachel. Jeanette had once made the mistake of asking about her. The effect had been dramatic. Colour had drained from his face and he had had the look of a haunted man. He, who was so utterly charming, became brusque, to the point of brutality. Jeanette had vowed she wouldn't make that mistake again.

However, a glimpse into the psyche, of this outwardly assured man, showed a deep well of bitterness that six years as a free man had done nothing to dry up. Maybe it is his apparent inability to forgive and forget that is so unsettling. I am used to the church's forgiveness. Surely Charles' inclination to judge and even condemn indicated a fair degree of arrogance that was less than endearing. Even though Rachel's behaviour must have devastated him, what might his reaction be if, in his eyes, I transgressed? There was no time to try to find an answer to that thorny question. The front door banged and Tom came up stairs. She checked to see if the teapot needed replenishing.

'I'm in here, Tom. Are you ready for a cup of tea?'

Tom came in, beaming, as usual. Such a comfortable person to have around. She smiled back at him. 'Good day?'

'O.K. but I'm always glad to be back home.'

'I sold a rather fine gate-legged table today.'

Jeanette had always been interested in antiques. It was with great enjoyment, that she now managed a shop in Kensington.

'Good commission?'

'Not bad.'

'You going to treat yourself with it?'

Jeanette paused, there was nothing much she wanted, just the answers to some of her doubts. Money was no good for that.

'Whose turn is it to cook?'

'Yours.'

'Oh, tell you what, I'll treat you to spaghetti at that Italian place, round the corner.'

'You lazy lump,' Jeanette laughed and stood up, 'anyway if I got the commission, shouldn't I be treating you?'

'You can pay next time.'

Jeanette fetched her bag and slipped a cardigan over her shoulders. It was still quite warm. We behave like an old married couple. Comfortable but no real excitement. I will just have to see what happens next time Charles comes home on leave. At least, for the time being, life is being very kind.

It was nearly six months since Mary's hip operation and the subsequent realisation that it was not going to work. It had been a very difficult situation for her to come to terms with. In fact, she did not think she would ever totally accept her physical frailty. She was now equipped with a calliper, elbow crutches and, horror of horrors, a wheelchair. There was nothing more the hospital could do. One thing was certain, she could not go back to the flat. She was going to convalesce for a few weeks, while decisions were made.

Philip and Sarah visited again and to everyone's relief it was decided to terminate the existing arrangement. It appeared that Philip had met a woman, of whom, he was becoming increasingly fond. He wanted his own home. Mary wished the poor woman joy, with the rebellious Sarah but was relieved she was not left feeling guilty. The house next to Malcolm's was in the process of being sold, as Joanne had predicted it would be. That had been a disappointment to Mary, but, by all accounts, the 'Sold' sign was up.

The thought of ploughing through estate agents handouts was too awful to contemplate. The only compensation for her physical handicap was that it would be impossible for her to trail around looking at the least disagreeable of the houses on the market. There was also the problem of selling her flat. Whilst she did have private means, they would not support a flat and a house. As Malcolm was working, there was a limit to how much she could ask him to do. She was loath to make demands of Joanne.

Mary was weary of living away from her own belongings. She always had to think ahead and list items of clothing and toiletries, that she would need to be fetched. She was determined that once she was established in her new home, where ever that might be, she would have every labour saving device on the market. She would retain as much independence as possible. The doctor had said there was no reason why she should not continue to drive. Public transport was out but with her own car, things looked much better.

Malcolm was coming to fetch her this afternoon, to drive her down to a convalescent home. There she would rest and receive physiotherapy. What a blessed relief to be out of hospital. This was the first important step to a new life.

Mary had decided to ask Malcolm to take her to his house before going to the home. She wanted to see where they lived. It was strange not being able to picture them in their own environment. She glanced at her watch, he would be here any minute. She checked her locker again, it was amazing how much clutter she had acquired during her stay. She had a tin of biscuits to leave for the staff then she would be off.

Getting from the ward to the car had been extremely tiring but it was like being let out of prison as she breathed in the fresh air. Malcolm gently lifted the callipered leg into the leg space while Mary swivelled around in the seat.

'I suppose I'll get better at this, with practice.'

'Of course you will, Mother. As it's your right leg, you will probably find it easier getting into the driver's seat, anyway. You'll just have to tuck the gammy leg in last.' He grinned at her. He would never intentionally show how much she had aged since the accident. Not facially, except for a few extra lines, caused by pain. She was an old woman now. He had never thought of his mother as old before, but of course, she was. He felt a great tenderness as he realised that their roles had been reversed. Although she had not physically looked after him much,when he was a child, she had always been there. A noble figure, serene, she had seemed all powerful. He wondered for a moment what life would have been like if his father had not killed himself. He had got on tolerably well with Edgar but there had not been contact since he left. Malcolm realised now how little love Edgar had shown them and yet Mother had adored him. Will I be able to show love to children that are not biologically mine? I couldn't do a worse job than Edgar. With which encouraging conclusion, he set off out of the car park with such verve, Mary had to clutch the door handle to stop herself falling against him.

'Do be careful, dear. I don't want to be back here too soon,' she laughed.

She glanced at him and again felt a pang of regret that he would never have children of his own. Best not to talk about it. She must not interfere, if they had decided to adopt, that was that.

'Before we go to Dorking, will you take me to see your house? I know you must still have a lot to do but I would so like to see it, well the ground floor, anyway.'

Malcolm looked at his watch. They had plenty of time, why not if it made Mother happy.

In less than ten minutes, they were parked outside 57, Hendon Way. Mary looked for several minutes and liked what she saw. Good solid houses, well proportioned, no garage but the road was wide and parking outside was no problem. She looked across the road, there was the park, how delightful.

'I'm sure you two will be very happy, dear.' She patted Malcolm's hand.

'Come along, help the old crock out.' She stood leaning against the car while she organised her crutches and handbag. I must get a bag with a long strap that will go over my head, like a child's satchel. I'm always going to need both hands free. She glanced at the house next door and noticed, with surprise, that there was no Sold sign up. It was still proclaimed to be For Sale.

'I thought that was sold.'

'Well, it was, as far as I knew. Perhaps the deal has fallen through.'

'Umm,' said Mary as she hoisted herself upright. Slowly and carefully she walked up the path to the front door. As long as I take my time, I'm all right.

Malcolm opened the door. 'Cooee, darling, I've brought Mother for a quick look round.' There was no reply. There had been no reason for Joanne to know he would be calling.

'She must be out, looking at wallpaper or some such, I expect. She'll be sorry to have missed you. ' They walked slowly from room to room. It was spacious and airy, high ceilings and big windows. Like houses ought to be, not one of those pokey little boxes that were springing up everywhere. Mary walked to the French windows, in the main reception room, at the back of the house. So convenient to be able to step out into the garden. She had loved her flat but it was not like having your own house. She turned to Malcolm. 'What's the estate agents number?'

'What estate agent?'

'The one selling the house next door'.

'I don't know, I'll look on the board.' He went out quickly, his mind in turmoil.

He knew that Joanne had reservations about his mother but once she had made up her mind neither Joanne nor anyone else would stop her. Obviously she had made up her mind, she wanted the house next door!

Mary dialled the number Malcolm gave her . It was quickly established that 55, Hendon Way was back on the market. It was vacant and yes, she could view it. Mary put her hand over the receiver.

' If they send someone over now, have we time to look today? You could go upstairs and check that it is in good order.' Malcolm nodded, what the hell!

Mary emphasised that time was precious and she expected someone to come over at once. Since, she explained, her son had the house next door, she was aware of the internal layout. Provided the price could be agreed, a sale could be made that afternoon, subject of course to surveyor's reports. All this was greeted by a stunned silence. A silence broken only when Mary added that if she was satisfied by prompt and efficient attention in this matter, the company would be given the job of selling Mary's flat for her. At this point, she was assured that someone, from the office, would arrive at 57, Hendon Way within the next ten minutes.

Mary looked at Malcolm with tenderness and relief.

'You have no idea how much I was dreading trying to find a house that was suitable. This will be the answer to all our prayers.'

Malcolm put his arm around her. 'Come on, old girl, take the weight off your feet for five minutes, you're looking tired.'

'Ten minutes.' Mary replied, looking at her watch.

'All right, ten minutes, are you timing them?'

Mary chuckled. She felt a lot happier all of a sudden. Malcolm went and stood by the window. All I have to do now, is tell Joanne.

Rachel walked down the road, pushing the big old fashioned pram. The two older children walked, one on each side. Jenny always felt embarrassed, being seen like this. Stephen was invariably being a nuisance and Ruth was often crying. It was difficult, under these circumstances, not to draw attention to yourself.

She much preferred to go shopping by herself, armed with a big shopping bag and a list. It meant taking the tram to Kentish Town, that was where the nearest Co-op was. Jenny took great pride in getting everything on the list and marking down the price. She always brought back the right change, Alec would then would give her something for going. This had to be done surreptitiously because on one occasion Stephen had found out and all hell had broken loose.

Increasingly, Alec found he could not stand the noise made by Ruth, Stephen, Rachel or any combination of the three. Although Jenny did not shout and scream like the others, Alec suspected that she was not above getting her own back on Stephen by other methods. All in all, he did not entirely blame her. So it was with a sigh of relief that he agreed to Rachel going on a shopping expedition with the three children. Ruth's birth had jolted Rachel out of her depression and if anything she was now moving towards her manic phase. He would need as much rest as possible before the going got really rough! He glanced at his watch and wondered if it was a little early to get the gin bottle out. After a moment's reflection, he decided it wasn't. A gin and tonic before lunch was quite normal, except I don't want any lunch. He sat, in the comfortable corner chair, in the kitchen. The cat yawned, stretched, got off his cushion and jumped delicately onto Alec's lap. As cats will, it moved in a tight circle until assured that it would be comfortable and then settled, asleep instantly. Alec stroked the silky fur and sipped his gin. It was worth while desperately wanting a drink - for a little while - in order to experience that euphoric moment when the alcohol started to work its magic.

The convoy reached Kentish Town without mishap, Ruth had fallen into a fitful sleep, she was teething. Stephen had been bribed with some sweets and Jenny felt mightily relieved that she had not seen anyone she knew. Rachel loved to sing and Jenny had to admit her mother had a lovely voice. However, it was deeply disconcerting to have your mother burst, spontaneously, into song in the street, to the surprise and amusement of passers by. At least, today, it was unlikely that such goings on would be general knowledge when she got to school on Monday.

'Where are we going?' Stephen wailed. He had finished his sweets and was feeling bored. 'Can we go to the toy shop?'

'No, Stephen, the only person you think of is yourself.' He started to wail again. Rachel stopped the pram and glared at him. 'Now just you behave yourself, we are going to the furniture shop. I want to choose some chairs and a settee.'

Jenny looked at her mother, in amazement. She knew, from what Alec had told her, that money was tight. What on Earth would he say? How would Mum pay for it? Jenny did not think Alec gave Mum money, not big sums, not after he sent her out to buy a winter coat and she came back with a guitar! Jenny started to say something but the look on Rachel's face was enough. It is not my problem.

The pram was now parked outside the store, it was very cold. Rachel lifted Ruth out of the pram, to take her inside with them. Had it not been such a miserable day, Jenny would have volunteered to stay outside and mind Ruth but it was dank and drear; as the lights in the shop window started to twinkle in the gloom, wisps of fog drifted ominously. It was warm and bright inside and Stephen soon found it was fun bouncing on the furniture. A short, dapper man bustled over, displaying a fixed smile while he watched Stephen's antics apprehensively.

'Careful now, sonny, we don't want you to have an accident, do we?'

'Oh, he's all right, ' Rachel said airily, handing Ruth to Jenny.

'I'm looking for a settee and some armchairs.'

'Oh, you mean a three piece suite.'

'Not necessarily, its so twee to have everything matching.'

The salesman bristled slightly. 'Well we can't break up suites, the manufacturers would never stand for it.'

'So they are more important than your customers, are they?' The salesman ignored this and walked over to a large settee in the back of the showroom.

'We do have this.' Rachel sat on it and called Stephen over. Jenny was walking up and down trying to stop Ruth from howling. The baby's cheeks were a flaming red and when Jenny tentatively rubbed her gums, they felt rock hard. She crooned, very quietly in Ruth's ear and rocked from one foot to the other. She just hoped Rachel would not ask for her opinion. She knew from past experience it was better not to be involved in any way with Mum's wilder extravagances. If she appeared to approve, Alec would hit the roof when they got home and if she disapproved, Mum would create a scene in public. She would take Ruth outside and wheel her up and down. When she glanced out of the window, she noticed, with alarm, that the fog was getting very thick. She thought about Grandma Warr and hoped she was all right. The fog always upset her chest. I'll write to her when I get home.

The salesman was writing something on his pad. She listened.

'And where do you live Mrs. Davis?'

'It's Mrs. Davies, with an 'e', 25, Gainsborough Gardens, Hampstead.'

'Right, ' He wrote some more. Jenny's heart sank, she was buying it.

'Now I want some chairs.'

'Wing back or ordinary?'

'I don't know until I've seen what you have.' The note of irritability in Rachel's voice was becoming more pronounced.

'It's Davies, with an 'e',,'

'Yes, madam.' The salesman was becoming increasingly obsequious as he sensed that here was an opportunity to get rid of some of his less saleable items. He moved around, almost bowing, pointing to this chair and that; suggesting that Rachel sat in each to check comfort. By now, Stephen was stretched full length on the settee that Rachel had decided to buy. The salesman rolled his eyes to an assistant, lurking amusedly, in the back of the shop.

Jenny was more and more alarmed by the weather but did not dare say anything. Rachel chose two chairs and watched as the salesman added them to the invoice.

'I've told you, it's Davies with an 'e'.' Rachel sounded thoroughly exasperated. The salesman, with an ingratiating smile, pushed the invoice towards her. 'Yes, madam, I know. I've put Mrs. E. Davis! Now when do you want them delivered? Will it be cash or H.P.?' Rachel seemed to swell before Jenny's eyes.

'You fool,' she shouted, 'Davies with an 'e' D.A.V.I.E.S. Come along children, I will not do business with idiots.' So saying she swept out of the shop. The salesman bundled Stephen off the settee, so suddenly back on the market.

'If your lad has damaged this settee, you're liable!' He shouted to Rachel's retreating back. He noticed, with satisfaction that it was only a matter of seconds before she and her entourage vanished in the thick yellow fog.

'Hope you bloody well get lost, you silly cow, wasting my time.'

Malcolm had left his mother looking settled and content, in her room. He had promised to chase up the estate agent and keep her informed of developments. As he drove back to London, he had a sense of foreboding. What would Joanne's reaction be when she heard that her mother-in-law was going to live next door! At least the adoption business seemed to be going ahead smoothly. Hopefully, they would soon have a baby to care for. That should keep Joanne busy, that and decorating the house.

When Malcolm pulled up outside number 57, it was in darkness. Joanne still was not back. Although usually at home when he returned from work, her absence this evening, gave him a chance to decide how to broach the subject of next door. He could also prepare a meal. All he wanted to do was please Jo and make her happy yet the very things she wanted were those he could not give her. He decided he was not going to make excuses or disguise his feelings. She would have to accept that he did have a feeling of responsibility for his mother and at least, if she were next door it would be easy to see her whenever the need arose.

It was 6.30 p.m. when Joanne finally appeared. She was flushed, breathless and extremely apologetic. Yes, she had been looking at things for the house, in town. She was so sorry it was so late, the fog had sent the traffic into chaos. She suggested a pre-dinner drink while the meal, Malcolm had prepared, was cooking.

Malcolm was heartened by her ebullient mood. Get the business of mother over quickly, then on to more acceptable topics, babies and decor.

'You missed Mother, today.'

'Oh?'

'She wanted to see the house before I took her to Dorking.'

'What did she think?'

'Very impressed,' he paused, 'so impressed, in fact, that she contacted next door's estate agent.'

'But it was sold.'

'Apparently the sale must have fallen through, the Sold sign had been taken down. It was Mother who noticed it.'

They stood looking at each other. Malcolm stepped forward and held her tight, he could feel her resisting him.

'Oh, listen, Jo, I know how you feel, but what can I do? I couldn't tell her we don't want her next door, could I?' He took Joanne's face in his hands and made her look at him. 'Could I?'

He was surprised to see Joanne's eyes full of tears. He had always thought she was quite tough, perhaps it was just a veneer.

'I'm sorry, I'm just being like this but your mother always makes me feel stupid and in the way. I always feel I should apologise for interfering between the relationship you two have. I just can't stand it. If she is next door, she will only have to click her fingers and you will go running.'

'Come on, Jo, you're just over-reacting. I know she's my mother but you are my wife and I promise she will not come between us. I love you too much. You will have to stand up to her. Let her know how you feel. She probably has no idea. The trouble is, she has had servants all her life, I think she sometimes forgets how to talk to people. Underneath that tough exterior, she's putty, believe me.'

Joanne said nothing, it was a fait accompli. She would just have to make the best of motherhood by proxy.

The walk back from Kentish Town had been arduous and in a strange way, exciting. The fog was so thick that trams moved at a snail's pace with a man walking in front with a flare. The light was eerie and the fog was the colour of sulphur. It clung to Jenny's face and clothes like dank seaweed. Breathing was difficult, as though the dense consistency of the fog clogged the tiny airways in the lungs, making the body cry out for oxygen. It was like being suffocated by a dense ocean of moisture and smoke that pressed in on her, leaving her face bedewed and her hair in lank rat's tails clinging to her face and neck. She put her scarf around her nose and mouth, trying vainly to filter out the choking fumes. Ruth wailed plaintively and Stephen kept up a steady and dis-spirited whining. Nobody spoke. They followed the lights of the tram and listened to the muffled sounds of people close by who, never the less, they could not see. Jenny wondered how they would manage once they had to turn off the main road. It was impossible to see any landmarks or to know which direction was which.

Alec woke with a start, the cat was scratching at the door, to go outside. It must be late, Alec looked at his watch, it was very late indeed. He looked out of the window and could see nothing. It was like looking at a solid yellow/grey wall. For Christ's sake, he thought, where has she got to? Those kids should not be out in this, particularly Ruth. He wondered if he should go out to look for them but what was the point? He would never find them in this; probably get lost himself. He put the immersion heater on. They will all need a hot bath and a hot drink. He put the kettle on a low light. I'll just have to wait.

He let the cat in and sat down again. What possessed her to stay out so long? Surely she must have noticed the fog coming down. Alec smiled to himself grimly, some hope. Rachel was the most infuriating, exasperating, unpredictable woman he had ever met. He had loved her to distraction, now he wasn't sure what it was that tied him to her. He sometimes felt she was like a leech, sucking the life out of him; just a husk of a man constitutionally incapable of breaking free.

He heard a commotion on the stairs, the familiar sounds of Ruth wailing and Stephen screaming. At least they are all alive and well, that is something to be thankful for. He got up slowly and went to open the door. The vision that greeted him was reminiscent of a Hogarth print of Bedlam. Stephen, tear streaked, dirty, was trying to inflict injury on Jenny who was grappling with him. Ruth was howling and had thick green ropes of mucus streaming from her nose. Her face had been smeared with it, she looked as though she had some frightful scaly skin complaint.

Her bare hands had that reddish blue colour, of freezing flesh. She was exhausted. Rachel looked dishevelled but exultant. Her duffel coat and her beret glistened with a fine dew. Her skin had a silky sheen and her brown eyes sparkled. She was as high as a kite. Of course she would not have noticed the fog. In her present state she would not notice a bomb going off!

'What an adventure we've had, haven't we children?'

Stephen started to sob. 'My legs hurt and Jenny kept pushing me and telling me if I didn't hurry, she would leave me behind.'

'Get inside, for heaven's sake. We can discuss this later. These children need a bath and something to eat.' Alec grabbed Stephen and hustled every one in. Rachel threw her arms around him with her embrace came the sulphurous whiff of hell fire and damnation.

'Were you worried about us?'

'Of course I was, but there was no point in coming out looking and getting lost myself. The water's hot, the kettle's on, lets get these kids sorted.'

'I'll bath Stephen,' Jenny said, 'and get in after him.'

'I don't want her to bath me, I hate her.' Jenny grabbed Stephen by the shoulder and marched him, protesting loudly, to the bathroom.

'Get in there, and shut up. I'm sick of you always trying to get me into trouble.' She roughly pulled his clothes off while the bath water

209

ran, filling the room with steam. She knew she wasn't being very nice but she couldn't help it. She checked the water and manhandled him in.

'I can wash myself.'

'No you can't, you're a dirty little tyke. I've seen the state of your neck. Come here.' She attacked him vigorously with flannel and soap.

'When Mum and Alec aren't around, I'm in charge. You do as I say.'

Stephen glared at her but decided it would be best to say nothing. After his bath Stephen walked into the kitchen, in his pyjamas. His skin was tingling, particularly his neck. He was cleaner than he had been for a long time. He was too tired to do more than eat his supper and go to bed. There was, though, mutiny in his heart towards Jenny, she wasn't going to boss him around, he'd show her.

Jenny stretched out in the bath, turning the hot tap on with her toes. A little more wouldn't hurt. Her legs looked red and raw, like corned beef, from the cold. As she soaked heat back into her body, she felt as though she were on fire. Being the eldest had its advantages, when it came to what time you went to bed. If you had someone like Stephen, to be responsible for, it was a nightmare. Still, it could be worse, if he were older than me, my life really would be a misery.

She soaped herself reflectively, she knew she wasn't nice to Stephen a lot of the time but he was never nice to her. She recognised that Stephen's jealousy was so great that they would never be friends. If she was left in charge, he would just have to do as she told him whether he liked it or not. With a new sense of purpose and confidence, she dried herself and went into the kitchen and had something to eat.

Alec and Rachel were having a cup of tea, while Ruth was fed. Rachel recounted the visit to the furniture shop. Jenny watched Alec's face out of the corner of his eye. As she had thought, the idea of another expenditure horrified him. Rachel tried to include Jenny in the conversation but she kept her eyes down and murmured non committally to everything Rachel said. After she had finished eating, Jenny went to her bedroom to read. Since Ruth had been born, Jenny had a room of her own. She treasured it. Stephen had always been messing about with her things, now he couldn't. She could lock her door and know that everything was safe.

She loved reading and long after her light was supposed to be out, would use a torch under the bedclothes. Often she would be awake late into the night. Sometimes, when everyone was supposed to be asleep, she would hear strange noises. Muffled cries, grunts and the noise of tossing and turning on the noisy bed in Alec and Mum's room, next door. She supposed one of them must be having bad dreams. She had asked Mum about it once but she had only laughed. She snuggled down with her book. She had moved on to the Horatio Hornblower series. She had often wished that she was a boy but she didn't think it had been much fun being a sailor in Nelson's day. Perhaps being a girl had its compensations.

She did not know how long she had been dozing. The book had fallen on the floor and Mum was sitting on the end of the bed.

'Sit up Jenny, it's time we had a talk.' Jenny wished Mum would let her sleep but there was no point in saying so, not with Mum in her present mood. She sat up.

'It's time I told you the Facts of Life.' Jenny looked blankly at her.

'You bathed Stephen tonight. Why do you think his body is different to yours?'

'Because he's a boy.'

'Yes, but why does he need to be different?' Jenny realised that she had never questioned why he had a willy and she didn't. She had just assumed that it was a bit like some people having brown hair and some having blonde.

'I don't know.'

'Where do you think babies come from?'

'Out of ladies tummies.'

'Yes, but how did they get in, in the first place?'

Jenny began to feel uneasy. I don't want to go on with this. I just want to go to sleep. She shrugged her shoulders.

'You will be going to secondary school in September. You need to know these things and I want you to be told properly, not have some old wives' tale.' At this point Rachel went out of the room, soon returning with paper and pencil. Jenny resigned herself to listening. Then perhaps Mum would go. Rachel started to draw complicated diagrams and Jenny watched, outwardly attentive.

'Now you see this is where the baby grows but the father had to put his seed inside the mother, before the baby starts to grow.' All this talk of seed, it must be like gardening, Jenny decided. They had grown some cress at school, from seed. She had often wondered about these things but had never felt able to ask whoever she was with at the time. Perhaps it was as well to get it sorted out, in case she were asked any awkward questions when she started at her new school.

'The father uses his willy to put his seed inside the mother.' Rachel busily drew a diagram of an erect penis, penetrating a vagina. Looking at the diagrams, in cross-section, Jenny found it hard to associate the diagram of a penis with Stephen's.

'But how does it get in and why is it so big? Stephen's is only little.' She thought about Stephen's body in the bath, this evening, pink and shining with a small, inoffensive willy like a tiny little finger. How could that plant seeds?

Rachel looked at her and said softly, 'But when the mother and father love each other, he wants to put his penis inside her special place and so it grows and gets hard, so it can be pushed in.'

Jenny gasped. She felt the colour drain from her face. The hair on the back of her neck prickled. She wanted a wee, she felt sick, she wanted to get as far away from Rachel as she could get; she scrambled backwards until she was pressing against the wall, at the head of the bed.

'Where is that special place?' she whispered.

'It's between your legs. ' Rachel smiled reassuringly.

Jenny felt dizzy, her mother's voice seemed to come in waves. She felt again the fetid breath of Uncle John on her cheek. She could hear so clearly his grunts and moans. Why had she never associated those noises she heard coming from the bedroom with what Uncle John had done? It all came back to her, after so many years, when she had pushed the horror and the pain of those walks in the private garden to the back of her mind. Now, here it was bursting open, like decaying fruit, spilling out its rotten stinking flesh, Flesh, his flesh clammy with sweat, rough with coarse hair, felt but never seen. Her hand made to grasp that great thrusting thing. What had she thought it was? A thick piece of wood pushing into her face, suffocating, crying out in anguish. Pushed against her body, between her legs, hurting her, making her sore. The pain from the past came flooding back and wrenched a cry of despair from her. Rachel stopped, surprised. She had not realised that Jenny had stopped listening to what she was saying.

'For Heaven's sake, what's the matter?'

Tears streamed down Jenny's face, she rested her head and arms on her knees. Her shoulders shook but she could not speak, tell of her past. Rachel tutted,

'There's nothing to be frightened of. Every woman has a period. Its Nature's way of keeping the special place for babies clean. You'll just have to get used to it.'

'No!' Jenny shouted between her sobs. 'No! No! No! it's disgusting. I don't want anything to do with it, it's horrible.' She put her hands over her ears.

'I won't listen to any more. It's hateful. I'll be a missionary, I'll go to Africa. I'll never marry! Never.'

Rachel felt alarmed. There must be something wrong with the child. Here she was, doing a proper job of telling her daughter, face to face, all about growing up and being a woman, and what thanks did she get? She thought back to when she was Jenny's age, well perhaps a few years older. Her mother had left a book in the library with some silly title like 'Boy into Man, Girl into Woman' The only instruction she had received was being told that the book was there and that she should read it! That was it. No questions, no discussion. She tried to put her arm round Jenny but there was no response.

'I thought you were a big girl now. That's why I decided to talk to you. It's no good getting upset. We all have to grow up. You will feel differently when you are older and meet a boy you like.'

Jenny made no reply but slid under the covers, pulling them over her head.

Rachel got up and put the drawings on the bedside cupboard. She bent to kiss Jenny, only the top of her head was showing.

'Funny child,' she said and put the light out as she left the room.

Jenny lay curled up, as small as she could get. She listened to the buzz of conversation, coming from the kitchen. Mum would be telling Alec everything. She couldn't stand it. They do all those disgusting things to each other. They would laugh at her. She realised that she was totally exhausted after the long walk in the fog. Gradually her body started to relax and she drifted into a fitful sleep.

Alec and Rachel sat in the kitchen. He listened while Rachel recounted Jenny's reactions.

'She's very tired, perhaps it was not a good time to tell her.'

'Nonsense, most children would have been fascinated, no matter how tired they were. Every child wants to know the Facts of Life. Stephen's started asking questions already.'

'Maybe, but she hasn't exactly had a conventional childhood. Maybe it's a bit much for her to cope with.'

'It wasn't my fault, I didn't want her to be taken away. That was thanks to her bloody father. God alone knows what he has said to her. He always was a prude and regarded sex as no more important than putting out the rubbish! Just another job that had to be done.'

Alec chuckled and grabbed hold of her as she walked past to the sink.

'Come here woman, for Christ's sake. You're like a cat on hot bricks. What you need is a good seeing to. I've better things to do than listen to you complaining about your ex-husband.'

Rachel's eyes sparkled and a flush came to her cheeks. She kissed him quickly. 'I'll just check Ruth and Stephen.'

Alec got to his feet, glad he had managed to sleep that afternoon. From the look in her eye, he was going to need all his energy.

Everything was red, bright blood red and in the far corner of her eye, Jenny could see a tiny worm, wriggling closer. It grew closer and wriggled more, great fat coils of segmented flesh writhing around her. She could not see much red now, everywhere was filled with more and more of the worm. It was swollen and pulsating. Threatening to engulf her, Jenny dared not scream, in case it tried to get into her mouth. She closed her eyes but she could still see it. Now there was no red left. Everything was a heaving and throbbing mass. She was surrounded, there was no escape! She was going to die. The worm would devour her. There would be nothing left. She whimpered and thrashed about. She could not bear to touch its slimy, sticky surface. It was pressing against her, leaving its slime on her hands and face. She tried to wipe it off but more appeared. It was squeezing her, its hot breath on her face. She could not stand it anymore. She lashed out with her arms and suddenly fell, with a heavy thud, out of bed.

She lay in the darkness, sweat was pouring off her. Her heart was pounding so hard, she feared it would burst from her chest. She tried to sit up but was shaking so much she could not move. She lay listening to the night sounds and her own heart beat as it gradually slowed. Carefully, after a few minutes, she felt strong enough to sit up. She leaned against her bed. In the light from the Moon, she could make out the paper with Mother's hateful diagrams on it. I don't want them in my room. They're disgusting. She picked up the paper and walked slowly to the window. The Moon bleached all colour from her view. It must be very late, no lights were on except the pale gleam from the lamp standards, stretching down the road. They gave a grey light like dingy pearls. Slowly she raised the sash window and leaned out. Unexpectedly, she heard a throaty chuckle, then the familiar sound of bodies moving. She tore the paper into tiny pieces and held out her hands in supplication to the heavens. A light breeze caught the squares of paper, they fluttered slowly to the ground, brilliant white when they caught the light of the Moon. As Jenny watched, she heard her mother cry out. Then silence.

214

Chapter 13

Jenny sat by the hospital bed, uncertain of what to do or say. Charles had left her with Gladys, to 'say her goodbyes'. Jenny looked at the slight, infinitely frail figure in the bed. She looked like one of the Egyptian mummies in the British Museum. It seemed awful to compare this poor old lady with a long dead stranger, from another time another place. She tentatively stretched out her hand, lightly touched the gnarled and fleshless one that lay, as still as death, on the counterpane. The wedding ring was so loose; it was held in place only by the grossly swollen arthritic knuckle. The skin felt dry and unyielding. Jenny assumed that, since there was so little flesh left on her grandmother, all she was feeling was bone, with a slack covering of skin.

Jenny glanced at the face behind the oxygen mask. There was no movement and no indication that Gladys knew anyone was with her. I should be feeling sad, even tearful. Why do I feel nothing? Just a great void. Of course it's sad to see someone so ill but I don't think Grandma wants to go on living any more. Not after all that has happened. She sat very still on the chair. Her hands were in her lap now, there seemed little point in holding Gran's hand. Besides, she had to admit, it felt horrible, as though it were already dead! The thought of death, brought memories of Grandad flooding back and she smiled, just for a moment. She quickly adopted a more solemn expression; she did not want people to think she did not care.

It hadn't been an easy year, there had been many times when Jenny had felt frightened. She thought Gran had felt frightened too, at times, of Dad. This was a mystery that Jenny had pondered over long and hard. There were times when she felt scared of what Dad would say, if she let him down. That was only to be expected. She still felt an overwhelming sense of relief that she had passed her 11+. Dad had bought her two dictionaries, one for Latin and one for French. It had made her feel very grown up and learned. A new bike would have been nice but, as Dad had said, she would outgrow a bike. She would have the dictionaries for the rest of her life. Her thoughts returned to Gran, for her to be frightened of her own son could not be right. Jenny had had little opportunity to speak to Gladys on her own, now it looked as though the unresolved situation would go, with the old woman, to the grave.

Jenny thought back to Charles' last leave. It was supposed to be a big celebration because he had told Gran that he was coming out of the army for good. Gran had been so pleased. She would not be on her own any more. Charles would share her flat with her and Jenny could come and stay at weekends. He had laughed when 'the two women in my life' had cried at the good news. The delight had not lasted long. Charles had prepared a special lunch, roast chicken, with all the trimmings. Like a second Christmas, Gran had said. So why had Dad been so cold and silent throughout the meal? Jenny knew. What she did not understand was why Dad did not say, 'Don't start yet Mum, wait until we are all served.' Grandmother Cardew had taught Jenny well so she had sat quietly with her meal in front of her while Dad served himself. Gran had started immediately and it was as though the temperature, in the room, had suddenly dropped to zero.

Jenny leaned towards the so still figure. She watched the flat, angular chest give a shallow, regular jerk; allowing enough oxygen in, to retain that slender hold on life. 'I didn't know what to do, Gran. I didn't want Dad to be cross with me, too. I'm sorry.' Now the sorrow did fill her heart and her vision became blurred with tears. 'I love Dad so much,' she whispered, 'but I didn't mean to let you down. You do understand, don't you.' She stroked the hand, still motionless, for a moment it seemed to be the hand she had so often held. The hand that had washed and dressed her, when she was little and soothed her when she was ill. Jenny wasn't frightened any more. She stood and leaned over the bed, lightly pressing a kiss on her grandmother's forehead.

'Goodbye, Gran, God bless, give my love to Grandad.' She walked slowly up the ward to the waiting room where Dad was having a cigarette. She did not look back.

Charles was pacing up and down, looking out of the window. He was beside himself with rage. It was two days since he had contacted Caroline and Jack, to tell them Mother was dying. Still they did not come. Well, as far as he was concerned, that was it. He would never speak to them again. If they were so callous that they could not even visit a dying woman, he had no further time for them. He knew Mother could not last much longer. She had fought long and hard, was so looking forward to his being home for good, it was not to be. Her heart was failing, the doctor had told him there was nothing more they could do. They would keep her comfortable and wait.

Jenny joined him in the waiting room. She had obviously been crying. At least she has some finer feeling, he thought.

'I'm going to go back for a bit, will you be all right here?' Jenny nodded.

'Keep an eye open for your Uncle and Aunt, though I doubt if they will turn up now.' Jenny blanched and opened her mouth to speak, but Charles had gone. The dutiful son, he strode up the ward, to keep watch at his dying mother's bedside.

Jenny sat down a little shakily. It would be fine, she didn't have to speak to him. They would be in a public place. She was safe. She looked out of the window, it was getting dark, even though it was only late afternoon. It would soon be Christmas. Jenny did not like Christmas. There were too many bad memories.

You should be with your family, Mums, Dads, Grans and Grandads, Aunts and Uncles, lots of children. Jenny realised, with a start, that she did not know what would happen this Christmas or where she would be. She had very carefully pushed it to the back of her mind. Dad was home on compassionate leave but she supposed that once Gran died and everything was sorted, he would go back to his posting in Singapore.

Grandmother Cardew had moved into the house next to Uncle Malcolm and Aunt Joanne. Jenny did not think she would be able to go there. That left Mum and Alec but Mum was in hospital and likely to be there for a long time. Jenny wondered if Alec was going to get Stephen and Ruth ready for bed or if Gwen, his friend, would come round to do it? It was a nice change not to have to put Stephen to bed. People would think me very strange, if they knew what I was thinking, she supposed. Fancy preferring to sit in hospital, waiting for your Grandma to die rather than put your half-brother to bed. I had better think of something else, but what? There was always Mum, that was dangerous, so fearfully painful that she recoiled from the thoughts. Like Pandora's box, once open, there was no going back. She tried to recall all of it , tried to make it make sense.

Rachel's euphoric state had evaporated rapidly after the incident in the furniture shop. She became quieter and quieter, relying ever more heavily on Jenny to shop, cook and care for Stephen and Ruth. Ruth had been a sickly, fretful infant, often having to be taken to the doctor with coughs and colds. Stephen, on the other hand, became tougher and more difficult all the time. Now he was nearly seven, he was able to go outside, to play in the street, with his gang of friends. The games were wild, rumbustious and noisy. At least he wasn't being a nuisance indoors. Jenny would leave him as long as possible - preferably until

Alec got back. Let him sort Stephen out, I can't and Mum is too depressed.

When Spring came, Alec decided that Rachel and the children should have a holiday.

'It might buck your mother up,' he told Jenny. A distant relative of Rachel's had a farm in the Cotswolds. She and the children could go for Easter. Alec could not have any time off, except for the Easter weekend. He would come down then. Jenny was sure he would look forward to a bit of peace and quiet. Jenny too would look forward to a visit to the country. She had not had many holidays. Grandma and Grandpa Warr had taken her to a boarding house, in Eastbourne, a couple of times but that was all.

Now sitting in the hospital waiting room, she remembered how excited she had been, sitting in the train, with Stephen, Ruth and Mum. She had asked about Cousins Alison and Bernard. What were they like? Did they have children? Did they have animals on the farm? Mum seemed vague, eventually admitting that it was many years since she had visited. They would just have to wait and see.

Jenny looked out of the window. Green fields had replaced the endless expanse of houses and gardens. There were cows and horses in the fields. Jenny wondered if there would be cows to milk. She wasn't sure she would want to milk a cow. She thought they were probably a lot bigger than you imagined. The clackity clack of the wheels had soothed Ruth to sleep, even Stephen was quiet. The sun was warm on Jenny's face, she too felt sleepy. Glancing at her mother, sitting opposite, she wished she understood more about what made Mum so sad. Looking at her now, who would guess that she was going on holiday. She looks as though she is going to a funeral. Jenny smiled encouragingly at Rachel but the poignant half-smile that was returned, filled Jenny with dread. Remembering it all now, she wondered if, at that moment, it had been in her hands to stop subsequent events.

When they arrived at the station, Cousin Bernard was there to meet them. He was a large quiet man who efficiently stowed their motley collection of bags and cases in his elderly Morris van. Rachel sat in the front with Ruth, still asleep, on her knee. Stephen and Jenny were told to get in the back with the luggage. There were no seats but they sprawled on the floor of the van, which smelled of hay. Soon after leaving the station, they were bouncing down country lanes. Both children giggled and fell about, happy to be out of the smell and dirt of London.

Cousin Alison greeted them somewhat austerely. She had the ruddy, raw boned complexion of a country woman, out in all weathers, with hands to match. She clearly was not someone who would stand any nonsense. The visitors were going to have two bedrooms in the large, plainly furnished farmhouse. Stephen and Jenny in one, Rachel and Ruth in the other.

After they unpacked, they went downstairs for something to eat. Richard and Andrew were introduced, they were Alison and Bernard's sons. Richard was two years older than Jenny but Andrew was exactly one year younger. Jenny hoped it was a good omen that this distant relative should share her birthday. It seemed a special link, Jenny hoped they would be good friends. While they were eating, Alison told them that this was a working farm so although they were on holiday, they would be expected to help out. Jenny thought it could be good fun. Stephen looked mutinous but said nothing. Alison had decided that Jenny would feed the geese and help to churn the butter. Stephen had to feed the chickens and help muck out the stables. Andrew would milk the cows, as usual; Richard would work with his father, digging and planting. Jenny noticed an expression of acute anxiety on Andrew's face. She looked inquiringly at Richard, who was sitting next to her, at the large scrubbed kitchen table.

'He's scared of cows,' Richard whispered. Jenny looked at Alison and decided it would not be a good idea to get on the wrong side of her.

They went out exploring, after they had helped with the washing up. It all looked so fresh and green, after London. There were still some Spring flowers, the fruit trees were smothered in drifts of fluffy white blossom, against the reddening sky of dusk. The air felt soft, roosting birds clouded the clear air before settling in a cackling cluster in every tree top. Jenny looked at the sky and could just see the faintest hint of a crescent Moon. I wonder if Dad can see it too. Tired but deeply content, she went with the others, back to the farmhouse. Tomorrow, the first job, before breakfast, was to feed the geese.

Jenny's only experience of geese had been in nursery rhymes and fairy stories where they seemed amiable enough. She was totally unprepared for what happened, that first morning. Alison had kitted her out with wellingtons and given her a large bucket filled with a rather disgusting kind of mush. She was then directed to the field. She was to let the geese out of the wooden hut that kept them safe from marauding foxes. It all seemed very easy. She set off humming to herself. Imagining she were a proper country girl, she climbed over the stile and trudged up the incline to the wooden hut. She could hear movement and strange noises, as though the inhabitants were restless and not too happy. She put down her bucket beside the large aluminium bowls that the mush was to go in. Poor things, she thought, fancy being shut up in there all night. I'll let them out first and them tip their breakfast into the bowls.

The door of the house slid upwards and was rather stiff. She had only managed to heave it up about a quarter of the way when she was mobbed by the most fearsome, hissing, squawking, pecking monsters. They surrounded her, pecking her legs and fingers, hissing in her face as she tried to get the door up higher. Crying in frustration and fear, she turned, they were all around her, jostling to get at her. She cried out for help but she was alone. She tried to get to the bucket. She must give them their food or Cousin Alison would be cross. Tears streamed down her face. Failed at her first job. Her legs were smarting from the repeated peckings. In desperation, she kicked out first at the birds, then at the bucket. It fell with a clatter. The noise made Jenny jump, it was the final straw, she ran, like the wind, leaving two large wellingtons behind her.

She arrived back at the farmhouse kitchen, dishevelled, tear streaked, with very muddy socks. When she told Alison, the only comment was,

'You will have to go back for the wellingtons and the bucket, you will need them for tomorrow.'

Jenny looked fearfully at Rachel, who was giving Ruth her breakfast. There was no reaction.

The rest of the day more than made up for the early disaster. After lunch, Richard and Andrew helped retrieve the bucket and boots. Later Alison introduced her to the delights of a dairy. Skimming cream from the top of milk was good fun. Even better was putting the cream into the wooden barrel where it was churned into butter. It was like magic. Alison let Jenny make little balls of butter using proper butter pats. Then she made the glistening, golden lumps into thick curls for supper that night. Jenny thought it was the best butter she had ever tasted.

Stephen had enjoyed himself, tearing round, ever more covered in mud and straw. The country air and physical exertion brought about a transformation. He was positively amiable. Jenny listened to his steady breathing, across the bedroom. As she lay in bed, warm, relaxed, she thought about those wretched geese. I'm not having that every morning. She decided that she would tip the food out first, then release the birds. She thought about the height of the house, it wasn't that tall.

Supposing I climb on the roof. If I lie flat, I can lean over and pull the door up. The geese will rush out and while they are busy with their food, I can creep away. She smiled to herself, in the dark. That should do it. Her plan, next morning, worked perfectly.

That first week of the holiday was such bliss. The children were outside most of the time. Jenny could not help feeling worried about Mum but what could she do? Rachel spent most of her time in the kitchen with Ruth. At least Alison was there. If anyone could keep an eye on Mum, Alison could. Alec would be coming down, the day after tomorrow, as well. Jenny pushed the worries aside and still in her morning wellingtons which with a second pair of socks, had become a permanent fixture, rushed down to the stream with the others. They were looking for frog's spawn.

On Maundy Thursday, the sun was hot. Alison suggested that they go up to the bluebell woods that afternoon. It was not warm enough for a proper picnic but they could take some sandwiches and a bottle of cordial. Bernard said he was going to put his feet up and would keep an eye on Ruth if Rachel wanted to go too. She opened her mouth to say she was too tired but before she could speak, Alison said, 'Of course you will come, Rachel. It will do you a world of good. You have hardly set foot outside since you arrived. What will your poor husband say when he sees you, still with your city pallor?' She held her hand up imperiously, Rachel's protest died in her throat.

The walk was made fascinating by all the things they saw on the way. Richard and Andrew, truly country bred, pointed out rabbit holes, nests in hedge rows, delicate wild flowers. They showed Stephen and Jenny how to make coarse grass into a reed and use it to make a piercing sound. Jenny wondered how she would ever be able to leave it all behind. Only one more week. Perhaps I'm really a country girl, perhaps Mum was given the wrong baby. Perhaps my real Mum and Dad are living on a farm somewhere with a girl who yearns for the city. She would still be luckier than me, she would have her Mum and Dad together.

The woods were beautiful, a haze of blue carpeted the whole area. Sunlight filtered through the trees, dappling the flowers and grass with molten gold. Jenny remembered the magical day in Kew Gardens, this was even better. She knelt down and looked closely at the tiny bells, so delicate and such a vibrant colour.

'Don't pick them will you. They only wilt. They're best left where everyone can see them.' Jenny looked up, her eyes shining and nodded at Alison, in agreement. It was only then that she realised that her Mum was crying.

'What's the matter, Mum?'

'Nothing, nothing at all. It's just so beautiful.'

Jenny looked, in bewilderment at Alison.

'Off you go, dear, I'll look after your mother.'

Jenny walked off slowly, trying not to crush the flowers. She looked back apprehensively, but Alison had taken Mum by the arm and they were walking away, back down the track, to the farm house. For a moment Jenny felt quite panicky. Something awful is going to happen, I just know it. It felt as though the sun had gone in, she shivered. She could hear the shouts of the others, deep in the woods, thoughtfully, she went to join them.

As dusk approached, Stephen announced that he was starving. The others agreed and they all trouped down the track. Jenny walked the slowest, she did not want to confront her mother's problems but knew she must. Richard waited for her.

'You're very quiet, are you O.K.?' She nodded, he was really nice, he doesn't ask awkward questions. He just accepts. I wish Stephen were more like him. She heard the soft hoot of owls in the darkening gloom and saw the quick dart of bats. It was too early in the season for them to find much insect life. She was still a bit afraid that one might get caught in her hair. Richard had not laughed but convinced her that that was an old wives' tale. She would miss all this terribly. Here is one place I would like to come back to but I don't suppose I ever shall. No matter what, I will always have my memories.

The kitchen was warm and welcoming. Alison had made a huge pan of stew. The children hurriedly washed hands and faces, settled down like a swarm of locusts, to demolish the lot. Rachel was not there, neither was Ruth.

'Where's Mum?'

'She has a headache, so I helped her to put Ruth to bed; now she's having a lie down. She will be fine tomorrow.' Alison smiled at Jenny.

'Alec's coming tomorrow, isn't he?'

'Umm, on the 2 o/clock train.'

After they had eaten to bursting point, the older children played Monopoly while Alison read Stephen a story. He was so sleepy that Bernard carried him up to bed. He and the boys then went to check the livestock before locking up for the night.

Alison and Jenny sat in front of the range.

'I don't know what to do, when Mum's so miserable.'

222

'I don't think there is much you can do, really. Just do what you can and see the little ones are all right.'

'But why is she like it?'

Alison paused, 'I don't know a lot about it but sometimes people's brains don't work quite as they should. We all feel sad sometimes and happy at others but with your Mum, it is so extreme, she can't cope.'

'Will she always be like it?'

'That depends, doctors and scientists are working on new medicines and treatments all the time. Maybe they will find something to make her better, lets hope so.'

Jenny thought for a moment, yes, lets hope so. She stood up.

'I think I'll go up to bed now. I can read my book for a bit.'

Alison smiled, 'Sleep well, see you in the morning.' Jenny walked very quietly up the stairs, trying to avoid the steps that creaked. At the top of the stairs, she stopped, undecided. Then she slowly pushed the door to Rachel and Ruth's room open. Mum might be awake, then I can say good night. Rachel was lying, sprawled out on top of the bed. Ruth had kicked her covers off. Slowly and carefully she tucked her baby sister back in. She saw, by the light on the landing, a crocheted blanket on the end of Rachel's bed. She opened it and spread it over her mother. Rachel stirred, Jenny bent to kiss her.

'Good night, Mum,' she whispered.

Back in her own room, she quickly undressed, checked Stephen was covered than hopped into bed. Alec had lent her 'The Cruel Sea' by Nicholas Monserrat. It was a book that both fascinated and frightened her. She did not understand all those rough, tough men said and did but she felt very grown up to be reading it. She was sleepy after so much fresh air and put the book down.

It was impossible to read when the words were a blur because your eyes were too tired to focus. She took her glasses off and soon felt herself begin to float. This was the best bit about going to bed. Alec would be down tomorrow. He didn't like much exercise so he could stay with Mum. I shall feed the geese, have breakfast, then who knows what, but it will be good. She smiled as she drifted further and further into sleep. Slight murmurings, from the kitchen, combined with the steady sound of Stephen's breathing, rose and fell in her consciousness, soothing her to sleep.

She woke with a start. It was light but only just. It must be early. She was surprised to see Rachel sitting beside her. Jenny looked, with sleep bleared eyes, at her mother's face. She looked strange. After the

223

tears and the silences, there was a glint of determination that Jenny had not seen for a while.

'What's the matter, Mum? It's very early.'

Rachel bent and kissed first Jenny and then Stephen, who still slept.

'I've come to say goodbye.'

'Where are you going, Can I come?'

'No, I'm going for a walk.'

'Will you be long?'

'No I won't be long.' She kissed Jenny again, got up and walked out. Jenny heard her footsteps going down the stairs, there was a click of the front door, as it was opened. She hopped quickly out of bed. Standing at the window, she watched her mother walk across the yard. Her hair blew in the wind but she had not put a coat on. She was just wearing her polo-necked sweater, with the tartan skirt. Jenny wondered if she should run down, call her back, tell her to take a coat.

Jenny realised that Rachel was walking too quickly to be caught easily. If she shouted, she might wake the others up. Alison, Bernard and the boys would be up soon but Stephen and Ruth should sleep on a bit. By now, Rachel was almost out of sight. She was certainly walking with great determination, perhaps that was a good sign, perhaps she was feeling better.

Jenny scuttled back into bed, her feet were freezing. It wasn't quite light enough to read, she didn't want to put the light on in case it disturbed Stephen. He was a pain if he was woken up. She lay curled up, rubbing her toes, slowly feeling the warmth come back. Birds were beginning to twitter, she could hear noises from the cow shed. In the distance, she heard the sharp whistle of the local steam train. These were the sounds she would take back to London with her, when the holiday was over. Only a week left.

Suddenly Jenny was aware that Charles was talking to her. For a moment, she had no idea where she was. The images of the country were much more vivid than the reality of this dingy, hospital waiting room.

'It's over, child. Did you hear me?'

Jenny shook herself, he's saved me from the awful bit.

'Sorry, Dad, I was thinking.'

'She's dead, dear. Your Grandmother is dead.'

Jenny blinked, she could not speak. She walked towards her father. He put his arm around her. 'She had a hard life but she's at peace now.' Together, arm in arm, they walked out of the hospital. This is the end of a special part of my life. Gran was the last link. In her head, the sound of a door banging shut seemed to reverberate through her memories. They walked, in silence, to the Tube Station. Charles would take her back to Alec.

The tube was crowded, they had to stand. Jenny felt herself sway, as she hung on to the metal pole by the doors. She rested her forehead against the cool metal. I must not faint. Once off the train, Charles suggested they walk to Gainsborough Gardens. He thought the fresh air would do her good. She wanted to talk to Charles, to tell him how awful it had been when Mum had thrown herself under the train. There was no point, he would not understand.

Jenny realised she would have to relive that dreadful day again and the days that followed. Once on that line of thought, it was like being in the cinema, she could not stop it. She sighed. Charles looked at her. Clearly, she had been deeply affected by the death of her grandmother. He gave her hand a squeeze. She looked at him and knew she would never be able to talk to him about how she felt when she thought her mother was dead. She would have to deal with it alone.

When they got to the flat, Charles hurriedly kissed her and said he would ring in a few days when he had got everything sorted. He wanted her to come over the following weekend, there were things to discuss. Alec answered the door, Charles, in a pinched, staccato voice, said that his mother had died, turned and walked briskly down the stairs without a backward glance. Gwen was in the kitchen, she quickly poured Jenny a cup of tea.

'Go and sit in the front room. You need a bit peace and quiet.' Jenny felt too tired to argue that the last thing she wanted was to be alone with her thoughts. She sat, knowing with absolute certainty that the 'cinema screen' had already started rolling. She sat back and closed her eyes.

She lay in bed, listening to the sounds of Alison in the kitchen. The boys were clumping about and Bernard was whistling in the yard. Then she heard the sound of a car. That was unusual, at any time, but this early was exceptional. The post van didn't come until much later. She got out of bed, Stephen was stirring. She went to the window and was surprised to see a police van. A policeman was talking to Bernard. The word 'accident' spread its toxic message like a cloud of poisonous gas. Jenny felt sick, she ran downstairs, she must know.

'Alison, has there been an accident, is it my Mum?' Seeing the expression on Bernard and Alison's faces was enough.

'She came in ever so early, I thought it was strange. She said goodbye.' The adults looked at each other, without comment.

225

'I watched her, she was walking so quickly. It was cold and she didn't have a coat. I hoped she was feeling better.' The last words came out in a choked gasp, a great sob of despair shook her from head to foot.

'Is she dead? Tell me.' Alison put her arms around Jenny and held her very tightly. 'No, she isn't dead, but she is badly injured.'

'Can I go to see her? It's my fault, I should have stopped her. It's my fault.'

Bernard patted her back awkwardly.

'Now, that's silly, how could it be your fault?'

'I should have stopped her, I knew something was wrong.' Her voice had risen to a shrill note, tears cascaded down her cheeks.

'Now, that's enough.' Alison said briskly. 'You're only a child, of course it isn't your fault. Go and wash your face and hands, comb your hair while I make you some breakfast.' The brisk authoritative manner was as effective as a slap on the face. Jenny gave a gulp and wiped her eyes with the back of her hand.

'Go upstairs, don't say a word to Stephen. We don't want him upset too. I will 'phone Alec, he can go straight to the hospital. You will be able to see your Mum as soon as she is feeling a bit better.' Obediently Jenny went upstairs.

The breakfast was a meal never to be forgotten. She sat with a boiled egg and bread and butter in front of her. All she wanted, was to sit with her head in her hands and howl. Her throat seemed to be in a vice, every morsel of food like a boulder. She was exhausted by the effort needed to swallow anything. Stephen babbled on while he ate his meal, after a perfunctory enquiry as to his Mum's whereabouts. He was quite happy to accept the information that he would see her later. Once he had finished eating, he rushed outside to do his jobs and play. Jenny sat, mute with shock. Alison, without a word, removed the uneaten breakfast.

'You know, there is nothing we can do at the moment. It would be best if you kept busy. Alec will give us more news, when he comes. Why don't you go and feed the geese? Richard will go with you. Then you can come and help me in the dairy.' The kind tone of Alison's voice, was more than Jenny could bear. It was so much easier to deal with sorrow, when no-one understood. You just had to shut it up inside. All the pain of the past welled up until it threatened to tear her apart. Such pain in her heart, she felt she would faint. Then the tears started. Her grief, sorrow and fears for the future flowed from her in burning streams that scalded her cheeks and dripped unchecked from her jaw. Alison sat down beside her, gave her a handkerchief but said nothing until the storm of weeping had subsided a little.

'You will have to be very grown up now, your Mum needs you and so does Alec.' Jenny looked at her. This is the woman who I thought was unkind and bossy.

' I wish you were my Mum,' she whispered. Alison stood up, quickly looking embarrassed.

'Nonsense child. Now come along, those geese must be starving.'

Jenny opened her eyes, realised she had let her tea go cold. What an interminable day it had been, only eight months ago. She remembered how Alec had looked when he eventually arrived. To Jenny, he had looked like an old, old man. His shoulders had become stooped and his face was grey. He has never really lost that look, Jenny thought. Of course, that was the end of the holiday. On Easter Saturday, they took the train back to London. Stephen clung to Alec as though he were frightened that his father too would disappear. The children had not been allowed to see Rachel. She was too badly hurt. Her head had been cut in numerous places, a great gouge of flesh had been ripped from one thigh and she had a multitude of other cuts and bruises. The young and deeply shocked train driver had been praised for having the premonition that the woman by the track was going to 'do something silly'. He had already started to slow the train some distance up the track. Nevertheless, it was generally agreed that Rachel was lucky to be alive. Her injuries could have been a lot worse.

She had been transferred to a London hospital as soon as she was well enough to travel. That meant the children could visit. Although Alec had warned them, neither was prepared for how she would look. Her head had been shaved and was crisscrossed with wounds, all stitched. Her face was covered in bruises, so were her arms. Looking at her mother's battered body, Jenny got a vivid and terrifying picture of how that body must have looked on the railway line. There would have been so much blood, perhaps the train driver thought she was dead. Poor man, how dreadful, it wasn't his fault. Perhaps it wasn't my fault, either.

The image of her mother, on the day of the accident, was confirmed by the contents of the parcel Alec was given at the hospital. Such an innocuous looking brown paper parcel. Jenny unwrapped it slowly. Alec said it contained her mother's things. Even eight months later, the shock of seeing the tattered clothes could move her. There lay the bright green polo necked sweater. It was stiff with blood, her mother's blood, and black with oil from the train engine. Jenny fingered the material that was frayed, where it had been cut from her mother's body. Perhaps it had been the brilliance of the colour that had attracted the driver's eye. Jenny wondered why the hospital had returned it. It was no good any more. It felt stiff, unyielding with a sickly smell. It bore no relationship to the garment Jenny had always liked. This was contaminated, defiled and merely reminded Jenny of what she wanted to forget. She pushed it away, underneath was the tartan skirt, that too was cut but there was a great ragged tear down one side. The blood and oil had embossed the edges so they crackled as Jenny touched them. She quickly rolled the garments back into the brown paper.

'Lets throw these away.' Alec had watched her, wordlessly. He nodded, then topped up his glass with gin. Jenny noticed that his hands were shaking.

Alec had informed Charles, by telegram, of Rachel's accident. Charles had immediately contacted Mary Cardew. He was not prepared for Jenny to stay in Alec's flat when Rachel was not there. Mary read the letter with dismay. What on earth had he in mind for the girl now? Since Mary's accident and Jenny's move to Rachel's, the two had seen little of each other. It would be impossible for Jenny to come back again. She would discuss the matter with Malcolm, when he came home. He had got into the habit of popping in after work, every evening, for a cup of tea and a chat. It was the best part of Mary's day. Maybe Jenny could stay with Malcolm and Joanne. Joanne was not working. The more Mary thought about it, the more logical it seemed.

Mary was surprised by Malcolm's reluctance, Jenny was no trouble. He could hardly explain that his relationship with Jo was less than good. It would only upset his mother. Jo deeply resented Malcolm's nightly visit to his mother, before - as she so forcefully explained - you even come to say hello to your own wife! Having started the routine, Malcolm could see no way to get out of it without hurting a lonely old lady. Besides, he still owed her money. He kissed her on the cheek.

'I'll put it to Jo and let you know what we decide.' Mary nodded, she never saw Joanne now unless they both came over or she was invited to their house. It was impossible to ignore the unspoken antipathy.

'Hi Jo, I'm back.' Malcolm walked into the kitchen where Jo was noisily preparing a meal. This is not going to be easy, Malcolm thought. He walked over to where she stood at the stove, with her back towards him. He put his arm around her waist and rested his chin on her shoulder.

'How's my lovely wife?'

228

'O.K.'

'Did you 'phone the adoption agency, like they asked?'

'Yes.'

'What did they want?'

'They want to interview us again.' She placed heavy emphasis on the last word.

'Surely, that's good news, it means they are just doing a final check.' Joanne turned and looked at him. 'You do realise that even after all this, they could still turn us down.'

'They won't, don't worry.' He started setting the table.

'Mother's had a letter from Charles, you know, Ray's ex. Apparently he won't let Jenny stay with Alec, on his own. Stupid sod, don't know why he can't leave things alone. Still, that's not the point. Problem is, there is nowhere for the kid to go. I suppose he has run out of people to palm her off on to.'

'What are you suggesting?'

'Well it's not for me, it's Mother. She wonders if we can have Jenny, just for a little while, until something can be sorted out.'

Joanne looked at him with disbelief. 'What about the adoption business?'

'What difference will having Jenny make?'

'Oh, I don't know, but it might.'

'Don't be silly, it will show we are good with kids.'

'So I'm silly, am I. Well you had better do what you and your Mummy have decided, hadn't you! First in your life is your bloody Mother, second we've now got your bloody niece. Just where do I fit into all this? Eh! Well sod you, Malcolm. Sod you.'

She strode out of the kitchen, ripping her apron off as she went. He heard the front door close behind her. Malcolm went into the living room and poured himself a drink.

Jenny had been pleased to see Grandmother Cardew again. She had changed a lot though. Now, so immobilised that any walking was difficult, painful and slow. They could still play patience, do crosswords and embroider. School was a problem. It was not considered wise to move her from the excellent grammar school where she had started only months before. Sometimes Malcolm gave her a lift but she always had to use tube and bus to get home.

Joanne never showed active dislike of Jenny but the atmosphere suggested that she was not entirely welcome. She tried, therefore, to keep out of her aunt's way, as much as possible. There were several occasions when Jenny saw a man leaving the house as she returned from school. Joanne told her it was the insurance man. She and Malcolm were updating their cover. Like Malcolm, Jenny often called on Mary when she got back from school. They had an arrangement, Jenny would go round to the back of the house, to the conservatory. Mary could open the door, without getting up. Jenny would make a cup of tea and put biscuits on a plate. Mary was always interested in what Jenny was doing at school and helped with homework.

Mary now had a married couple, with two young children living upstairs. It was not ideal as Mrs. Williams was fully occupied with her two children but she would help out in an emergency. After interviewing countless applicants, the Williams seemed the best option. The couples without children had either been too old or the wife had had a full time job. The present arrangement was an acceptable compromise. It was, however, particularly pleasant to have her young afternoon visitor without having to call on her tenant.

Unfortunately, the arrangement did not last long. One afternoon, two months after Jenny had moved in, she arrived back to an empty house. This hadn't happened before. Jenny assumed that Joanne had gone shopping and been delayed. She noticed that there was a sealed envelope on the kitchen table with Malcolm's name on it. She decided to go next door to see Grandmother. She might know where Joanne was. They had their usual afternoon tea. Mary had no idea what had happened. At six o/clock, Jenny went back to 57; still empty. Malcolm should be home soon. She went back to her Grandmother, together they prepared a meal. They were sitting eating, when Malcolm arrived. He was as surprised as they by Joanne's absence. He went to get the letter. It was a while before he returned. He looked like a man in a trance.

'She's left me!'

Jenny stood up and stretched. She had been sitting with her memories for hours. She could hear Gwen and Alec in the kitchen. She walked through. I've gone through the nightmares again, I've only the dreams now. I will sleep tonight. I wonder what Dad wants to discuss with me.

Chapter 14

Charles paced up and down; he felt extremely nervous. It is stupid to feel nervous about talking to my own daughter. He had talked to Jeanette about Jenny, the previous evening; there was another problem. He could not quite put his finger on what was wrong but something was. It was all most frustrating, he was only trying to do his best. Like he had with his mother.

He had sorted out her affairs and been amazed by the welter of rubbish she had left behind. He found, now unlabelled, tins that he had sent home, after the war. Typical, I did my best to make rationing easier, by sending food, which she just hoarded. The next shock had come when he opened the Welsh dresser; it had been a part of his parent's home all of his life. It was crammed with medicines; patent medicines, half used courses of pills and capsules, half filled bottles jostled to fall out as he opened the doors. Dear God, he had thought, there's enough stuff here to set up a pharmacy. He wondered whether to take it all back to a chemist. Looking at the labels, the medicines would be out of date anyway. He filled carrier bags and took them all down to the bins, in the yard.

Next were her clothes. Suddenly saddened as he fingered the pathetic pile of black and grey garments, she never came out of mourning for Dad. Will I ever feel like that about someone. Thoughts of Rachel slid insidiously into his consciousness. It would have been like that for me too. You, Rachel, with your treachery, have deprived me of a happy marriage and a contented life. What you stole from me is irreplaceable. He sat down on his mother's bed and put his head in his hands. Eight years since he knew she had been unfaithful. Would the pain never stop? I've tried to shut it out but it always comes back, the knife in the gut, twisting whenever I try to relax and be happy.

His thoughts moved to Jeanette, was he being unfair? She was very nice; comfortable to be with, the ideal girl-friend. He knew he did not love her, did he want to love anyone again? It hurt. Surely it would be better to have someone who loved you but keep your own feelings out of it. He would be a good husband, he wanted another child, to be precise, he wanted a son. Why should Rachel have a son, when he did not?

Last night, he told Jeanette that he was going to request release from his final term in the army in order to look after Jenny. If she wanted to live with him, he would have a very good case. The army life had suited him well for years but now he wanted to be at home in England. He wanted to be a family man. Recently, he had felt increasingly aggrieved that he, the innocent party, had been made an exile. His hysterical ex-wife got all the sympathy of course. This train episode was just another indication of her refusal to face up to her culpability in the whole business. The more he thought about it, the more certain he was that all this mental illness nonsense was just that, nonsense. She is just using it as an excuse for her promiscuity. She behaved like an alley cat and got caught; I have been suffering ever since. It won't do. She is no more mentally ill than I am. Of one thing he was determined, his daughter would not follow in her mother's footsteps. It had come as a shock to realise she would be twelve, next birthday. If he were not careful, she would be grown up before he knew it and he would have had practically no influence upon her.

He had tried to explain how he felt to Jeanette. They had sat comfortably on the settee in her sitting room. Fortunately Tom had been out. Charles had always found it hard to show his feelings, always fearful that he might appear weak or vulnerable. It took several whiskies for him to start. She had listened attentively.

He had felt that her sympathies were not entirely with him. The only comment she had made was that throwing yourself under a train was a very dramatic way of escaping your responsibilities, if you were not mentally unbalanced. He had looked at her in amazement.

'You don't think she really expected to be hurt, do you?'

'She must have known she was taking a terrible risk; if anything dreadful happened, she would leave three children behind.' The words fell like stones from her lips, for a while they sat, silent, deep in their own thoughts. Jeanette looked at Charles and wondered if she could live with the bitterness. The handsome profile, in repose, seemed cold and forbidding. Will my overwhelming desire for children be enough? Charles sipped his whisky and cleared his throat.

'I'm going to talk to Jenny tomorrow, tell her that I want her to live with me.'

'I'm sure she will be delighted, she must have missed you dreadfully.'

Did he detect a note of sarcasm? 'You know, I never wanted it like this.'

Jeanette squeezed his hand.

'I want you to meet her soon, I'm sure you'll like her.'

'What's more to the point, will she like me?'

'Why shouldn't she?'

Jeanette shrugged her shoulders.

'I want her to like you for our sakes.' He put his arm around her and kissed her gently. She sighed, this was the Charles she could love and spend her life with. Why was this side of him so often hidden? He could be so hard and implacable, so lacking in compassion. Which was the real Charles? She could not be sure. Did he really believe that Rachel was feigning mental illness? Surely not, the idea was too bizarre.

He stood up and looked at his watch.

'I'd better be going, I've a lot to do before tomorrow.'

She stood and put her arms around him, 'Take care dear, I hope it all goes well tomorrow. Remember she doesn't know you very well.'

He felt strangely irritated by the remark. It suggested that she knew more about his daughter than he did himself. She, who had not had children, was giving advice. I must stop this, he thought, I'm becoming more and more touchy. It's because I'm frightened, frightened that what Jeanette says is true. Frightened that Jenny doesn't know me well enough to want to live with me. Frightened that I might lose her too.

He put his coat on and walked to the station. By the time he got home, he was sure that he had nothing to worry about. Here he was, not yet middle-aged, intelligent, good looking. He had been a good husband, he knew. He had been a good father, albeit from a distance. He had done his duty. He had got on well enough with Jenny when he came home on leave. Of course she would want to live with him.

Jenny did not sleep well that night. She kept dreaming that she had lost something but did not know what it was or where to find it. When she woke up, her bed clothes were in a heap. She could hear Stephen and Ruth yelling and banging about, in the nursery. She wondered if Alec was awake yet. He was sober when she got back from the hospital but that didn't mean much. Today was   Saturday, it was more than likely he had spent the evening - after she went to bed - drinking. Jenny wondered if Gwen would come round. She sometimes did at weekends. Since Alec's drinking had increased, her visits had got less. On occasions, Jenny had heard heated conversations, when they thought she was asleep. Gwen must be as concerned by Alec's drinking as she was. More than once, Jenny had had to help an incapable Alec to undress and get into bed.

I'll have to get up and see what's happening. Dad is expecting me at 12 o/clock. What will I do if Alec doesn't get up? I suppose I could

233

'phone Gwen. She wandered into the kitchen and put the kettle on. The cat wrapped himself around her legs, miaowing piteously.

'Go outside and have a wee, Puss. I'll get you some milk.'

Stephen came clattering into the room. 'When's breakfast?'

'Just wait, or get it yourself. Go and see if your Dad wants a cup of tea.'

He pulled a face; Jenny grabbed his hair and pushed him out of the door. He banged up the hall, muttering. Jenny could hear Ruth, wailing, now she was on her own. Stephen did not come back. He really is a pig, she thought, as she went to Alec's room herself.

'Do you want a cup of tea?'

The still mound, in the double bed, did not move. He looks like a beached whale, Jenny grinned. 'Alec, do you want a cup of tea?'

There was a grunt, the covers moved and were still.

'I'm going to my Dad's this weekend, you haven't forgotten, have you?'

No response.

'I've got to go soon, shall I ring Gwen?'

Slowly, Alec sat up, he looked dreadful.

'Christ, my head!'

Silently, Jenny went for some tea. She handed it to him and awaited instructions.

Stephen bounced in and landed on the bed, practically knocking the mug from Alec's hands. 'Get that little sod out of here.'

Jenny hustled him out but he stood outside the door, rattling the door knob.

'What do you want me to do?' From experience, Jenny knew that when Alec was like this, you just had to be persistent.

'Don't ring Gwen I'll get up.'

'Right, I'll get some breakfast, do you want any?'

Alec rolled his eyes, Jenny laughed. She wasn't sure she wanted anything herself. The collywobbles must be because Dad wanted to discuss things with her. What things? Now Grandma is dead, he is on his own. I wonder if that is what it is all about.

Jenny walked briskly down the road. She swung her suitcase. It was only small, almost like a toy one. Grandma had given it to her. It was very old fashioned with a leather strap as one of the catches was temperamental. The sun was shining and Jenny felt happy. Mum was making progress; thank goodness her hair was beginning to grow. It made Jenny shudder when she remembered how carefully she had had to bathe the stitches and wounds all over Mum's head. That was after the train accident. Now of course she was recovering from her brain operation. Alec had said it was to stop her killing herself. A lobotomy, it was something to do with cutting the front part of the brain. Jenny had wondered how the surgeons got to those bits. She had thought Alec was being silly when he said they would take Mum's eyes out to do it and put them back afterwards. Apparently that was just what they did! Even in the bright winter sunshine, Jenny shivered. Alec said she wasn't to worry, Mum was definitely getting better. She had spoken to her on the 'phone, Mum had sounded so cheerful. If she gets really better, Jenny thought, she can look after Stephen and Ruth and I can see Dad more. That would be great.

Charles had spent the morning shopping, going from shop to shop. He sought out every bargain. It made such an expedition a long winded affair but he had the satisfaction of knowing he made his money work hard. He had a limited repertoire of meals, all of the basic meat and two veg variety but none the worse for that, he knew. No need for all that fancy foreign muck. He believed in routine. After years of army cooking, when you knew what day it was by what was on the menu, he intended to do the same.

He had realised, with a sense of shock that he knew little of Jenny's likes and dislikes. He knew she liked a Sunday roast, pilchards of course but after that, he was not sure. She was not going to be fussy, he would not sanction that. Today must be happy, though. He had lashed out and bought a piece of beef, as a special treat. As always, he had timed everything to the minute. They would eat at 12.30.p.m. sharp. The table was set, he put out two wine glasses. Just a little wine with her meal would do no harm. After all French kids were weaned on the stuff. He checked the oven, meat and potatoes were browning nicely. He had the sprouts and carrots ready to go on. He glanced at his watch, 11.45 a.m. he would walk up to meet Jenny's bus.

Jenny stood on the bus platform, waiting for the bus to slow down, as it got to her stop. Her heart gave a lurch. He was waiting for her, Dad had come to meet her, how lovely. She gave him a big grin as she leapt off the bus. He gave her a quick hug and took her case. He offered his arm.

'You're too old for holding hands, aren't you?' She linked her arm through his. She looked at him, almost shyly, overwhelmed by his presence. There's just the two of us now, but one day I'll marry someone like you. They strode down the road, Dad had always walked fast. She remembered that when she was smaller, she could never keep up. She heard in her head, her much younger voice.

'Slow down, Daddy, my legs hurt.' She would never say that again, no matter how fast he walked. She would match him, stride for stride. They did not say much as they walked; Charles was preoccupied with his thoughts and Jenny was out of breath.

It was the first time she had been to the flat since Grandma died. Her bed had gone from the living room, upstairs presumably. The place looked subtly different. The furniture was the same but rearranged. Perhaps it was the smell; the clinging smell of illness and old age that had gone. Now the aroma of roast meat and potatoes was all pervading and Jenny realised how hungry she was. Charles went into the kitchen, there was the sound of clattering crockery and pans. She felt slightly at a loss. He had set the table, the meal was cooking. She would normally have sat and talked to Gran, now there was no-one.

She went to the kitchen door and watched as Charles carved meat and strained vegetables. 'Don't you come interfering in my kitchen.' Although he smiled as he said it, she picked up a note of warning, so remained in the doorway.

'It looks very nice, Dad. I'm really hungry.'

He handed her a plate, piled high and steaming.

'You'll feel better after that, my girl.' He poured her some wine.

'Just sip it.'

She raised the glass to her lips. The taste was strange but not unpleasant. Wait until I tell my friends at school that Dad gives me wine for my lunch.

Charles asked her about school, was she doing all her homework? She suspected that this was an oblique way of checking if her duties, caring for Stephen and Ruth, were impinging on her education. She realised that Dad would never refer to Mum directly. He behaves as though she does not exist. She could not decide whether that was less painful than Mum's habit of constantly running him down. With an insight, beyond her years, she realised it would never change, she would just have to make the best of it.

After the pudding, shop bought apple pie and custard, Charles let her help with the clearing up. He put the kettle on, telling her to sit down. When he joined her, he sat and then patted his knees. Jenny did not understand what he meant.

'Come and sit on my knee, dear.' Jenny was amazed, it was a considerable time since she had sat on anyone's knee. Echoes of Uncle Jack made her feel stiff and awkward. It was with embarrassment that she perched uncomfortably on his lap, pulling her skirt well down over her knees.

'I want to have a serious talk with you.'

She nodded, encouragement for him to continue.

'You do, of course, realise that years ago, when you were only small, your mother did a terrible thing.'

Jenny felt her body stiffen, her mouth went dry. *I don't want this. I don't want to hear it from you, Dad.* She said nothing nor did she look at him, in case he could read her thoughts.

'Because of what your Mother did, I was forced to stay in the army, away from you.' He paused, waiting for a response.

Jenny's mind was racing. *Why should what Mum did keep Dad in the army? That's silly, in any case it wasn't my fault, why was I the one to be punished?* She wanted to say that she knew he loved it in the army. If he had really wanted to be with her, he would have managed it somehow. For a moment, she felt angry with him. He was making excuses for doing what he had wanted to do. She said nothing.

'Now that your Grandma had died, I feel the time has come for me to leave the army as soon as possible.'

She looked at him and the anger evaporated. He was coming home, she knew he had intended to do that anyway because he had told her and Gran, on his last leave. At the time she had not quite believed it. She had longed to have him with her for so long that the wish had taken on a dream like quality that could never be real. Now it would be.

He watched her face and felt reassured. Her lack of response, up to this point had unnerved him. *Did she care, or was she as disloyal as her mother?* He continued.

'I shall live here, I've cleared that with the council. I've arranged to see my old boss in the G.P.O. tomorrow. He may be willing to give me a job. If he does,' he paused and took a deep breath, 'I want you to come to live with me.'

Jenny felt quite faint, she slumped against him. She wanted to cry for her lost years, bounced around from pillar to post. *It is going to end at last, a proper, permanent home.* Charles tightened his arm around her, realising that he had been holding his breath. *I am behaving like a love sick suitor, waiting for my lady's yea or nay. How silly, this is a child, my child; I have custody, I don't have to ask. I can just tell her.* He knew he wanted Jenny to show her love, her gratitude and most of all, her need for him. After all, he was her father, he had done everything for her.

Jenny sat up straight and smiled at him. He wanted her with him but he wouldn't want her to be irresponsible or selfish. *I must act like a* grown up because that is what he would expect. 'Of course I want to live with you, Dad. Now that Gran's dead, you don't have anyone. Mum's got Alec, Stephen and Ruth so she's all right, but you've only got me.'

Charles felt his limbs go heavy, like lead. He could not believe what she had said. He leaned back in his chair and closed his eyes. A great weariness swept over him. She felt sorry for him! She, a mere child, would be so kind as to grant him her presence because, in her view, he had no-one else. And why do I have no-one else, whose fault is that? The same old tune, on the same old record, played in his head. Rachel, always Rachel, a ghost haunting him. Even now this child/woman sat still, with her hands folded in her lap, as Rachel had always done.

Jenny, increasingly uncomfortable, felt cramp in her thighs as she tried to keep her full weight off his lap. She watched him, something was wrong, she must have said the wrong thing. She remembered the awful atmosphere when Gran had done the wrong thing during the celebration meal.

'Are you all right, Dad?'

Charles opened his eyes and shifted in his seat.

'You'd better get down, dear, you're very heavy.'

'Will I have to change schools?'

'Not if you don't want to. I'll discuss it with your Headmistress.'

In the silence that followed, Jenny listened to the ticking of Grandma's clock.

She checked with her watch to see if it was still half an hour slow, as it had been after Grandad died. That had been to help Gran get through each day; it was always later than it seemed, another day closer to being over. Jenny wondered if she would ever be so unhappy that she would rush with eagerness towards death. She hoped not. She remembered the evening when she had sat on Grandmother Cardew's window sill, so high up, yearning to fly like a bird, away from everything. Had she really wanted to fly? Or was it that she wanted to fall, like a stone into nothingness. She could not be sure. Still, that was in the past. If she moved in with Dad, she might be able to visit Grandmother. She would be able to see Mum and the others because they lived so close to school. How would Alec manage if she left? Mum had been in hospital a long time, no-one had said anything about her coming home yet. Who would get Stephen to school and Ruth to the nursery? Or collect them at night? Gwen was nice, she helped out but she worked full time.

Jenny did not suppose Mum would be too pleased if Gwen spent more time with Alec. She didn't think Mum liked Gwen much.

'Would it be all right, if I stayed with Alec until Mum comes home?' She wanted to explain but the look on Charles' face left her fumbling for what to say. Everything is going wrong, I'm making him cross and I don't mean to. Surely he doesn't want me to just walk out and leave them in the lurch. Alec has always been kind to me but instinct told her to say no more.

'I will discuss the matter with the school. Let your teachers decide the best time for you to move, so it does not disrupt your education.' His lips felt stiff with the effort of not shouting at her. He wondered if she were doing it on purpose. Was she trying to hurt him? Did she not realise what sacrifices he had made? He stood up and walked silently into the kitchen. While he waited for the tea to brew, he stared out of the window. He gripped the edge of the sink until his fingers ached. It was all going wrong. Instead of her coming to live with him, he felt like telling her to sod off back to her bloody mother's fancy man, but then Rachel would have won. It's because she's seen so little of me that she's like this. When we have lived together, for a while, things will be different. He poured out tea for them both and as he carried it in said, 'Drink this then we will go for a walk, if you don't get some exercise after all you've eaten, you'll get fat.'

Sitting on the bus, going home to Gainsborough Gardens, Jenny thought about how she would tell Alec. Dad wanted her to move in before Christmas. That didn't leave much time for Mum to get better. She felt torn between what she wanted to do and what she felt she ought to do. If she did what Dad wanted, how would Alec manage and Mum would be upset. If she did what Mum would want, Dad would be upset. It wasn't fair, she shouldn't have to sort this out. It's not my fault Mum and Dad hate each other, I didn't ask to be born. She looked out of the bus window, watching the people hurrying by. Everywhere it seemed to be Mums and Dads with their children. Of course it couldn't really be so. There must be others like me, except, I don't know them. Perhaps I should get to know that girl, Sheila, at school, her parents are divorced. She realised that the bus was approaching her stop, she rushed to ring the bell and be ready to get off.

Everyone sounded very cheerful when Jenny let herself in. Stephen rushed up to her in the hall. 'Mum might be home for Christmas!' Jenny smiled, maybe there was a God or a good fairy or something. She walked into the kitchen.

'Hello Jen, he's told you then.' Alec was looking so pleased and relaxed, Jenny knew that it was happiness, not drink.

'Yes, when did you find out?'

'Went to the hospital today, saw the doctor. They want to get her home for Christmas. We'll make it the best Christmas ever.'

Jenny sat warming her hands on the mug of tea. She sipped thoughtfully. Clearly Dad was going to expect her to spend Christmas with him. As she had told him that afternoon, he had no-one else. She would have to miss the homecoming here.

'Did you have a nice weekend?'

'Yes, Dad had a talk with me, he wants me to live with him. He's coming out of the army.'

'Oh, what do you think about that?'

'I do want to go but I want to go on seeing everyone here.'

Alec looked at her fondly, she might not be his but she was a good kid and he could not have managed without her.

'When does he want you to move in?'

'Christmas, if he gets out of the army in time.'

'Ummm, you know we will miss you.' She pulled a face, 'Stephen won't.'

'He may not show it, but I bet he does.'

Jenny finished her tea. 'I think I'll have an early night.'

'Don't you want any supper?' Remembering what Dad had said about getting fat, she shook her head.

Tom was cooking a meal for the three of them, spaghetti bolognaise with lashings of garlic and crusty French bread. Charles smiled grimly, what's wrong with English food? Jeanette did not seem to object. At least while Tom was in the kitchen, they had a little time to themselves. Jeanette was eager to know how the weekend with Jenny had gone. Charles had thought long and hard about how much to tell her. He had decided just to say that the child had agreed to move in. No, not agreed, that sounded like a business deal; she wanted to move in. That was better. He could talk more about his job. He had been to see old man Walker, his ex-boss. Very grey and long in the tooth, he looked now. Not far off retirement, he had confided. Charles had wondered if there was a hint about his future prospects. Yes, he could talk a lot about that. If they were going to marry one day, he could not expect her to live in a council flat. He would need a good income, to provide a home she would find acceptable.

Mary Cardew gazed out of the conservatory window. The garden, that would have given her so much pleasure, seemed empty of colour.

Just an untidy patch of ground, with an ever increasing number of weeds. The arrangement with her tenants had proved to be less than satisfactory. Mrs. Williams did her best but she had a young family to care for. Her husband could charm the birds off the trees but seemed reluctant to do anything more strenuous in the garden, even though that had been part of the deal. Life had such a nasty habit of presenting you with the unexpected, just when you thought you had sorted things out. The decision to buy this house, had seemed the perfect solution to her problems. Now here she was, dependent on a couple who either could not or would not give her the level of service she should reasonably be able to expect. The world had moved on. I am like a dinosaur; still alive, after my time. She remembered the ever diminishing band of friends. Friends she had made during her time at Cambridge. We were in the vanguard of Women's Suffrage, such heady days; the world had been our oyster. Now my world is no more than the ground floor of this house, even getting around this is not easy. Old age can be very cruel. She thought again of her oldest and dearest friend, Hetty. It had come as a shock to read her obituary, in the Times that morning. That is probably why I feel so depressed. She wondered if this black gloom was the kind Rachel experienced, during her darkest days. Poor girl, I didn't realise.

It was some time since she had seen Rachel but Alec had kept her up-to-date with progress. She prayed, with all her heart that Alec would never give up on her wayward daughter. With him she had some hope. Not like Eleanor, who did she need? So independent, self-assured, she breezes in and out of my life. Mary felt more and more certain that Eleanor would never marry. Bearing in mind her experience of marriage within her immediate family, who could blame her. It was with heavy heart that Mary contemplated Malcolm's problems. Joanne would not be coming back. Initially, Malcolm had hoped they would be able to resolve their problems. After yesterday's letter that was out of the question.

He had called after work, having collected mail en route. She had watched as he fumbled to open the letter.

'It's from Jo.' She had hoped it would be good news. He had looked so ill recently, lost weight and probably was drinking too much. She had held her breath but slowly released it as she watched his face. Without a word, he had passed the letter to her. She had skimmed over the flowing script; its message, a dagger in the heart. She was pregnant and wanted a divorce so she could marry the father of her child. So that was that. She had got her own way. Mary carefully folded the letter and put it into her pocket. She wondered who the father was, Jenny had said something about the insurance man often being there, but surely not. Still, it didn't matter, only Malcolm mattered now.

'I think we could both do with a drink, dear.' She watched him pour a generous measure of whisky. 'I'll have a sherry.'
They sat silently, lost in their own thoughts. Mary thought about the stupidity of maintaining two houses, should she suggest that Malcolm sold up and moved in with her? That would be the logical thing to do, now was not the time to suggest it. Malcolm knocked back his drinks in two gulps and rose to get another.

'I can't stay in that house, Mother. You do realise that, I will never be able to make a new start, not there.'

Once again embryonic hope withered and was still born. She could understand his feelings. She had left her matrimonial home quickly enough, once Edgar left her. Even though she had had no choice in the matter, she suspected she would not have chosen to remain. Moving next door, would not be the answer. It was now up to her to set him free from any feeling of obligation or responsibility.

'Shall we have a meal together tonight? You must eat, you know.'

'Thanks, Mother, I do appreciate it but I think I would be better on my own. 'He came across to her chair, bent down and kissed her. To the casual eye, he looked tired but Mary noticed the slight tremor and the exaggerated care he took in his movements. Drinking on an empty stomach was never wise. So it was that he had left her yesterday evening. Each lost in misery, in their own homes.

Mary looked at her watch, he would be back soon. She got awkwardly to her feet, once balanced on her crutches, she pushed the trolley that went everywhere with her, in front of her to the kitchen. She rehearsed what she was going to tell him. It was the only way. He had the rest of his life, he was still young enough to get over a broken heart. She poured the boiling water into the pot and laboriously trundled herself and the trolley back to the conservatory.

Malcolm's face had a grey tinge, there were dark shadows under his eyes. He smiled but inner tension make it more like a grimace. Mary longed to smooth away the lines, to heal the hurt. You could only do that with a child and even then only sometimes.

'You look tired, my dear. Come and sit down.' She poured his tea. He slumped into one of the cane chairs and loosened his tie.

'I am so sorry Joanne has done this to you, I only wish I could make things easier.' She rested her hand lightly on his.

'I just can't believe it, but I'm going to have to. If I'm honest, Mother, I want to get as far away from here as possible.' She nodded her understanding, conscious of the pang of misery that made her own heart heavy.

'I know, I do understand and I too have to get away.' He looked at her in surprise.

'But you've only just moved in.'

'I know, but I realise now that I am not going to get any more mobile. The arrangement with the Williamses has not been an unqualified success.'

'But what will you do?'

'I'm going into a residential home.' She felt proud that the statement had come out without a quaver. 'I do not want to be a burden to anyone, least of all you. I shall start looking now and hopefully by the time the tenants' lease has expired, I will have found somewhere that suits me. All I ask of you, is that you ferry me about a bit. I should like to see where I am going to live for myself, rather than rely on brochures. I expect they are on a par with estate agents' handouts!' She smiled brightly at him but was unable to maintain the veneer of cheerful acceptance when he sank on his knees and buried his head in her lap. As she listened to his outpouring of grief, tears flowed, unchecked, down her cheeks, for Edgar, then Rachel, the loss of Jenny and now Malcolm.

Leaving Gainsborough Gardens had been dreadful. Rachel had been allowed home, for the weekend before Christmas, to see how she coped. Alec had decided that, for Jenny's sake, they would have a small celebration, with presents, Christmas tree and chicken. He knew it was a risk. Rachel might react very badly when she knew Jenny was moving out. The alternative seemed even worse. For Rachel, coming home for Christmas, to find Jenny already gone would have spoilt the homecoming for everyone. He was still not sure if he had done the right thing; there were many tears shed by both mother and daughter. More like a wake than a celebration, it was done now. He had helped to get Jenny's tin trunk downstairs and watched, with very mixed feelings, as the taxi drove away.

Rachel was still upstairs, crying. He had to get her into a more settled frame of mind. If he took her back to the hospital like this, they might decide she was not ready to come home next week. He walked slowly up the stairs. He would give anything for a large drink but he would have to wait until much later. He had had to ask Gwen to come round to look after Ruth and Stephen while he took Rachel back to

Friern Barnet. Rachel had raised objections but what could he do? Already, Jenny's absence was making itself felt.

Jenny sat in the back of the taxi, resting her feet on the trunk. Please, please let this be the last time I have to drag this thing around. She was glad to have a little time to get her feelings in order. It would not do to arrive at Dad's looking upset. The knight in shining armour who had swept into her life, bearing exotic gifts from far flung places, was becoming a man. Jenny knew that her feelings for him had undergone a change. She was getting better at picking up the signals that indicated his mood.

In a matter of days, it would be Christmas. It would be the first Christmas she could remember spending with just one other person. It was bound to be very quiet. She wondered if Dad had many friends. Perhaps they were still in the army, he would miss them. She would have to make it up to him somehow.

When the taxi arrived, at Peabody Buildings, Jenny ran upstairs to get Dad. Together he and the driver hauled the trunk up to the flat and into her bedroom. It was cold. It had an old gas fire, set in to the wall, Jenny decided she did not like the look of it and didn't risk trying to light it. She unpacked and found a place for everything. The furniture was large and dark. It had been a wedding present for her grandparents. She ran her hands down the smooth polished wood and wondered if Grandad and Grandma would be glad she was going to live there. The large dressing table stood in front of the window. She tipped the mirror so she could see her reflection. A serious face, with dark rimmed spectacles stared back at her. Her short dark hair, as always, didn't hang right. She pull a face and opened one of the little drawers that had fascinated her years ago. The three white cards with the black borders were still there. The commemoration cards to mark her infant uncles deaths. They would have been Dad's brothers. Poor Gran, no wonder she was sad.

Jenny walked down the hall of her new home, new yet so familiar. Charles was in the kitchen, making tea. She smiled when she saw what it was. Good old pilchards and tomatoes. It's just as well that I like them. She helped carry everything in. She could relax after tea, no-one to put to bed. She might watch a bit of television. Dad had bought the set for Gran when she was first ill. Jenny did not know many people with televisions. It would be a treat.

'Have you got something special to wear?' Charles asked.

'Why, where are we going?'

'Nowhere tonight, but I'm taking you to the Palace Theatre tomorrow, to see the Christmas Show.'

Jenny was delighted, she had not been to a real theatre before. She thought about the contents of her wardrobe, she didn't think there was anything suitable for a trip to a theatre.

'Do you want to have a look and see what you think?' She suggested.

'Ummm, after tea.'

He opened the wardrobe door and flicked through skirts and blouses. There were a few dresses; he noticed the red one Rachel had brought from France. Why on Earth had the child kept that? Not only was it gaudy, it must be too small.

'I think we will just have to go shopping tomorrow.' It was almost too much to cope with, new clothes and the theatre. Whatever next? Charles decided that Marks and Spencer would be the place to go. You could rely on their quality. Jenny will start growing soon. We'll get something she can grow into.

Jenny gravitated towards the party frocks, jewel coloured velvets with lace collars, vibrant taffetas that rustled as you walked past. It was like Aladdin's cave. Charles had other ideas. He grasped her elbow and steered her firmly towards the tweed skirts and twin sets. He called an assistant over.

'I want a sensible skirt and jumper for my daughter, will you help me?'

The middle aged assistant smiled encouragingly at Jenny but she felt numb with disappointment. After a great deal of discussion, in which Jenny took no part, the garments were selected. The twin set, which the assistant had assured Charles was a better buy, was pale grey. The skirt was gored in dark grey with an emerald thread running through it. Jenny dutifully held the carrier bag while Dad paid then they walked to the bus stop.

'That will look very nice. You will get plenty of wear out of them.' He felt pleased with himself, having a daughter to care for was not so daunting.

'Thanks, Dad.' Perhaps they would look better on. Anyway, we've got the theatre tonight. I shall feel very grown up and make Dad feel proud of me.

Once home Jenny went to her bedroom to try on the new clothes. They did look rather dull, not a bit special. She got undressed and tried them on. She looked at herself in the mirror. She had to admit, grudgingly, they did not look too bad. She definitely looked older, even grown up. I wish I had a necklace or something to make it look a bit more fancy. She walked into the living room, where Charles was reading the paper.

'Very nice, dear. Very nice indeed, the waist isn't too tight is it?' He put a finger into the waist band, to check.

'Do you think it looks special enough for the theatre?' she asked very quietly, 'I wish I had a necklace or something.' Charles looked up, from his paper.

'I'm glad you said that, I've got the very thing.' He got up and went to his mother's bureau. He took a battered box from the top drawer.

'These were your Grandma's.' He held out a string of seed pearls.

'Would you like to wear them?'

'Oh! yes please, I'll be very careful with them.' He put them around her neck and fastened the clasp. She looked at herself in the mirror, over the fireplace. That was better.

'Now sit down, I want to talk to you.' Jenny sat in Grandma's favourite chair.

'We're meeting a friend of mine, at the theatre.'

'Oh, is he one of your army friends?'

'It isn't a man, it's a woman, called Jeanette.'

'Oh.' There didn't seem much else to say. Jenny wondered why she had never thought of Dad having a woman friend. It was silly really, why shouldn't he have.

'Does she know about me?'

'Of course, I've told her a lot about you.'

But I don't know anything about her. Suddenly she felt quite sick with jealousy. She never really had anyone to herself. Even Dad wanted her to share him. Again she thought of Stephen, she understood better why he had been such a pain.

'Have you known her long?'

'Yes, she was in Singapore with me. Her father was my commanding officer.'

Jenny tried to imagine what the daughter of such an important man would be like. She gave up. How could she possibly know?

'What is she like?'

'She's not much taller than you. She has dark hair, she's pretty and I'm sure you will like her. She's very easy to get on with.'

Jenny wasn't convinced. 'Why didn't you tell me about her before?'

'I didn't know whether she would be coming to England or not so there didn't seem much point.' Jenny said nothing, she was not sure she wanted to go to the theatre to meet this woman. She wanted time to be on her own with her dad. She knew she would feel awkward and probably say something stupid. Charles watched her, she would just have to accept it.

Jeanette felt as nervous as a kitten. It didn't seem fair to meet Jenny like this. Not when she was so unsure of her feelings for Charles. He had insisted. She picked a dress from her wardrobe, nothing too fancy. It was only the local variety theatre. Tom had said he would drive her over to meet Charles, since he did not have a car. Tom was a dear, good man. She glanced at her watch. They would have to leave soon. She checked her makeup and put plain gold hoops in her ears. Tom was waiting downstairs.

'How does it feel to be under the scrutiny of your fella's off spring?' Tom grinned at her and gave her a hug. 'I think you look stunning.' Jeanette laughed and immediately felt a release from the tension that had been building up all day.

'Come on Cinderella, your coach awaits.'

Charles and Jenny walked up the road. It was a cold evening and Jenny was glad of her school raincoat, with the thick tartan lining. Dad had cleaned her shoes, even the instep. He said all soldiers did that. She had clean white knee length socks, to keep her legs warm. It was a pity the coat wasn't quite as long as the new skirt but Dad had said she could carry her coat as soon as they got to the theatre.

She had thought a lot since Dad had told her about Jeanette, she must not be unfair. Mum had Alec, why shouldn't Dad have someone too? She just wished she did not have this sick feeling in her stomach. Even though it was cold, her hands were sweating with nerves. Would she have to shake hands? What would Jeanette think? It was all going to be awful. She knew it.

The front of the theatre was ablaze with lights. Jenny smiled, in spite of herself. People were streaming through the doors and there was a buzz of conversation. They walked into the foyer. Charles craned his neck to see if Jeanette had already arrived. With so many people, it was difficult to see. Jenny tugged his sleeve. 'Dad, I want to go to the toilet.' He pointed to the Ladies and continued his search. Eventually, he saw Jeanette and beckoned her over. He had better stay where he was, in case Jenny couldn't find him. Jenny was just coming out of the toilet as the couple embraced. Jenny wanted to go back into the toilet and lock herself in. She felt tears prickle her eyelashes. She swallowed hard and watched them, standing so close. Why can't I have him to myself, just for a little while? I'll have to go over or he will send her in to look for me, that would be even worse. She took a deep breath and wiped her eyes on the cuff of her new grey cardigan. She put her raincoat over her right arm, so she wouldn't be able to shake hands. She stood very still for a few moments. He is my Dad, no-one can take that away from me. She put her shoulders back and stood very straight, arranged her smile and walked towards them.

Jeanette was aware of movement, out of the corner of her eye. Many people had gone to their seats and the foyer was clearer now. Such an old-fashioned little soul, she thought. Whoever had chosen the clothes, had not been catering for a child. Charles put his hand out. He knew the child; she was his child!

'Jeanette, I want you to meet Jenny.' They smiled at each other politely.

Charles delved into the pockets of his trench coat and like a magician, produced two identical boxes of chocolates.

'For my two girls,' he said, presenting one to each of them.

'I'm very pleased to meet you, Jenny, I've heard so much about you.'

Jenny smiled but could think of nothing to say. She could hardly say what she felt. Her rival was so beautifully dressed, she looked so elegant, I just look stupid and dowdy. She thought again of the beautiful velvet dresses and longed to be wearing one of those. She clutched the box of chocolates to her chest. We both got the same, he must love her as much as he loves me. I want him to love me more. She looked down, embarrassed, frightened that the jealousy would show on her face. Jeanette watched her, I hope she will accept me as a friend, she looks as though she needs one. If there is to be any hope for Charles and me, I must make sure she does.

Charles took them each by the arm. This is my family, in the making. A new beginning, Rachel might as well never have existed. He realised that Jenny was smiling at him at the very moment he had been thinking of Rachel. He gave a little laugh - false only to his own ears.

'Come on my girls, it will be starting soon.' They stood, linked, together in body; their minds intent on their individual hopes and dreams for a happy ending. Smiling brightly, they moved, as one, into the stalls. They had just settled into the seats, as the curtain went up.